FOREST MOON RISING

A Tess Noncoiré Adventure #4
By Irene Radford
Writing as P.R. Frost

Book View Café
304 S. Jones Blvd. Ste #2906
Las Vegas, Nevada 89107

Table of Contents

More Books by P. R. Frost

Tess Noncoiré Novels:
HOUNDING THE MOON
MOON IN THE MIRROR
FAERY MOON
FOREST MOON RISING

Copyrights & Credits

Book View Café
304 S. Jones Blvd. Ste #2906
Las Vegas, Nevada 89107

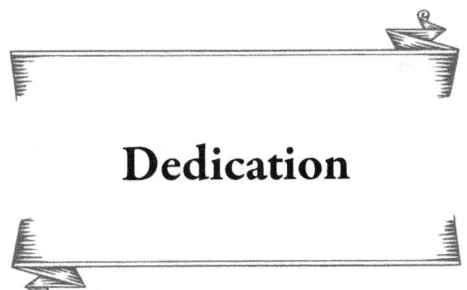

Dedication

This book is dedicated to the armies of volunteers and professional foresters who work very hard at maintaining the treasure of green spaces in urban areas everywhere.

Acknowledgments

A lot of a writer's time is spent in isolation: our minds engaged in a fictional world, our thoughts shaped by the imaginary characters, and the impossible demands we put upon them. But no book is totally created in solitude. We need to come up for air upon occasion and take inspiration from reality (no matter how you define it), and from the people around us who graciously allow us time alone, the right to be cranky when the plot ties itself in knots, and rejoice with us when all the puzzle pieces fall into place.

So, I must give hearty thanks to Tim Karr, my beloved husband of fifty+ years. Without you I couldn't do any of this or be a complete person. My brainstorm crew of Deborah Dixon, Lea Day, Sara Mueller, Jessica Groeller, Lizzy Shannon, Bob Brown, and Big Brother Ed deserve more thanks than just a mention here. These are also my first readers. They help lever my wandering prose into a story that is actually readable.

The lovely filk song "Heart's Path" by Chris Dickenson is printed here with her kind permission. A recording is available on the "Harmony Heifers" CD produced by Mystic Fig Studios, available at www.mysticfig.com[1] or CD Baby.

Many years ago, ElizaBeth Gilligan and I sat in a filk circle at Orycon and crooned "Where Are All The Aliens." I thank her for the loan of the lyrics we compiled together.

And I can't forget Sheila Gilbert, editor extraordinaire, the best in the business.

---

1.   http://www.mysticfig.com/

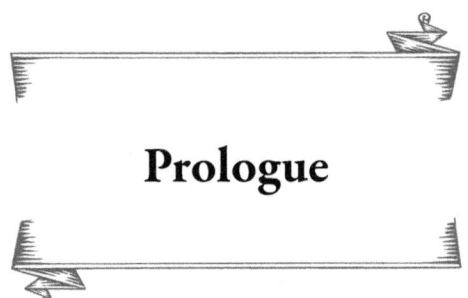

Prologue

In the Chinook Jargon, Devil's Lake was called me-sah-chie-chuck which means evil water. There are many stories about malign spirits and creatures inhabiting the lake's clear turquoise waters.

"Tess Noncoiré, Warrior of the Celestial Blade, you really don't want to do this," Scrap whispered in my ear. A strange way for him to communicate. Usually his thoughts came into the back of my mind. Everything was different here.

In the chat room—that big, white, blank space between the dimensions with portals to all of them—my interdimensional imp had substance and size. He no longer fit on my shoulder or on top of my head. So, he stood beside me. His potbelly looked thinner than usual and his bandy legs stronger—we'd been working too hard. A lovely scattering of warts decorated his chest and his bum. His tattered wings stretched from above his head to his heels. They fluttered in agitation.

His normally gray-green skin flashed between yellow and pink. He was scared and we were in danger.

I knew that. I was as scared as he. Maybe more so.

My scar, which ran from right temple to jaw, pulsed and burned, a clear warning that I needed to either fight my way clear or flee. Rapidly.

I couldn't accept either option.

"If this is such a bad idea, why'd you bring me this far?" I asked, trying to keep my teeth from chattering.

"I brought you here to scare you into going home." Scrap's actual voice came through deeper than his normal telepathic communications.

I caught sight of the demons on guard duty in the distance. Their bright blue, stacked-tire bodies with pink feather ruffs at neck, wrists, and ankles loomed larger with each giant stride toward us. Think the Michelin man decked out for an Easter parade.

"B'Cartlins," Scrap whispered. "Their stupidity makes them more dangerous than their size. They need everything repeated six times before they understand."

"I think I want to hide." No shadows presented themselves in the limitless white. The B'Cartlins grew by the heartbeat as they approached. Without a thought, either of them could squash us to unidentified road pizza.

"No trespassing in the chat room," one of them boomed. Demons took seriously their duty to keep everyone in their home dimension.

I covered my ears against the cannon roar of sound.

"Imps go anywhere, anywhen," Scrap announced to them with authority and dignity.

"No imps outside Imp Haven. Those are the rules," they both repeated by rote.

Full blood, or Midori, demons aren't terribly bright.

"If we stay very quiet, maybe they'll forget we're here," I said quietly.

If we needed to remain quiet, why were we talking? It was either that or run away and leave this essential errand unfinished.

"I have to do this, Scrap."

"I know. This is going to cost me some warts. I worked hard to earn these!" He heaved a sigh that might provoke a hurricane. "You couldn't wait for backup?" He produced a black cherry cheroot out of nowhere and lit it from a flamelet atop his thumb.

"I don't have backup anymore."

"What about more information?"

"I dismissed my archivist." I would not think about Guilford Van der Hoyden-Smythe, PhD. I would not. I had to cut Gollum out of my life and my heart.

I did not like where this conversation was leading. So I took a couple of steps toward where I thought the proper portal should be.

Scrap grabbed my arm and steered me in the opposite direction. My frail human flesh began bruising beneath his solid, unrelenting grip.

"Are you sure this is the right way?" I asked, trying to peel his talons off my forearm.

"Unfortunately, I am." He led me at a ninety-degree angle to the guardian demons.

The burning along my scar flared higher. The B'Cartlins were the least of my problems.

In the blink of an eye, an elegant brass door with stained glass panels to either side loomed before us. It just showed up to block our way. No dark spot in the distance that grew larger as we approached. One minute nothing but white stretching on forever, misting to more white to hide corners and angles where floor or ceiling met wall. The next heartbeat the door became a solid barrier.

Or a chance at salvation.

A blob of mottled bile green and sulfurous yellow flesh pooled across the entrance, sort of growing out of the white on white.

"You know there's a reason Donovan told you that few beings who faced the Powers That Be have survived the encounter, and never a human," Scrap grumbled, eyeing the blob between the door and us.

"I can't trust anything the former gargoyle says. He betrayed his calling and his creation. For that he doesn't deserve to raise his daughter Lilly. He lies as easily as he breathes."

And I couldn't allow him access to the neutral ground where he could open a rogue portal that by-passed the chat room.

"He didn't lie about this."

"Then we'll just have to make sure we get what we want before they execute us."

"Today is a good day to die."

"As good as any," I replied, not sure I believed my own lies.

The blob stirred, raised a bulbous head with two intelligent eyes and a parrot beak. At least eight legs stretched outward, flicking their tips.

I recoiled before it could strangle me. Another eight or more legs kept it anchored to the suddenly shifting ground.

Or were those my knees shaking hard enough to upset my balance?

"Mind if we pay a visit?" I asked.

The beak snapped once, hard enough to break my body in two if it chose.

I accepted that as a yes and stepped around the beast—I didn't want to chance it changing its mind and grabbing me with one or more of those tentacles. With one deep breath for false courage, I grabbed the lion's head door knocker and let it drop. I wished I had some scotch to help with the courage thing. It didn't have to be single malt. A cheap blend would do better; I could drink more of it faster.

A loud bong resounded around the chat room, bouncing off walls that shouldn't exist, compounding with each repeat of sound. Tsunamis of noise built and echoed. The bong grew louder yet, more insistent.

I had to grab my ears. Then I collapsed to my knees and shrank within myself.

Still, the knocker flapped and boomed and let the entire Universe know that someone had the audacity to approach the Powers That Be without an invitation.

That's me, Tess Noncoiré, Warrior of the Celestial Blade, who bounds in where no one else dares, and bullies my way through.

Chapter 1

F *orest Park in Portland, Oregon, was established in 1898, has 5156 acres,*
a hundred types of birds, sixty (known) species of animals, seventy miles
of trails, and is the largest naturally forested area within the city limits of any
municipality in the US. It is the third largest city park in the country.

Eighteen Months Later

Stinky, stinky. I smell demon-inky.

Demon and baby poop.

If demons are breeding I need to follow my cute little nose and find them so
my dahling Tess can wipe them out. After I find some bleach to clean up after
them.

Screaming draws my attention along my line of smell. This is sounding
ominous. My spine shivers and stretches. I need to transform into the Celestial
Blade. Where is Tess when I need her?

Off to a fencing tournament so she can avoid work.

I'll gather information before I summon her to my side. Then the two
of us can lash and lunge, slice and stab. Such a wonderful way to end the
domination of a demon.

My nose leads me to a strange room within a hospital. Locked doors that
need codes to get in or out. Triple locks on the drug stashes that are carefully
disguised behind normal cupboard doors. Casually clad nurses dash about,
converging on a gurney where a hysterical woman thrashes about, trying to
push away the newborn baby on her tummy. But her hands are lashed to the
sides of the portable bed with thick layers of bandage so she can't reject her
child.

The child looks human. But it stinks of demon, demon laced with
astringent pinesap.

A bit of scaly bark clings to the baby's feet. His (oh, yes, he is male) fingers look a bit like twigs, too long and skinny for such a tiny morsel of life.

Even as I watch, the abnormalities fade along with the demon stink. Just an afterthought of pine cleaner, that might be part and parcel of a hospital, clings to him.

The woman still screams. A doctor in blue surgical scrubs approaches with a big syringe hidden behind his back. "Hold her arm, Nurse," he commands in that all too calm and soothing voice of one who has dealt with this before.

"Third case this year," the squarely built nurse with disastrous blunt cut hair mutters. She too wears blue scrubs. "This is looking like a new postpartum syndrome."

"Strange one. I wonder what triggers it," the doctor says as he stabs the patient with the syringe and depresses the plunger. "I think I need to research a new paper."

I've found our next mission. Tess isn't gonna like this. She has a thing about babies. She'll want to give the infant a chance to grow up normal and human, not letting me take it down until after its demon half inflicts unnamable horrors on humanity.

PORTLAND, OREGON'S Forest Park is a wonderful natural treasure. Most of the time.

Five thousand plus acres and over seventy miles of hiking and biking trails. One nasty little dark elf had lots of places to hide. Lots of places to ambush weary hikers, joggers, and mountain bikers. Too many victims had fallen into his traps lately. He probably ate the homeless pets that got dumped here too.

So why had he avoided me for over a year?

"Where are you little Nörglein?" I asked sweetly as I jogged slowly along the well-beaten path. "Tonight the moon will show a waxing quarter. That's the time of a demon's greatest power. You should be out trolling for victims."

Tonight was the time a goddess showed her face in the skies, the sickle moon defining her cheek like the scar on mine. The starscape behind the moon revealed her face and the Milky Way became her hair blowing in a celestial wind.

I'd seen the goddess a couple of times and felt her power infuse me with the strength to fight demon hordes.

Not tonight. Even a goddess can't break through the thick clouds and rain the weather service predicted.

"Scrap, do you smell anything that doesn't belong here?" I called to my otherworldly imp companion.

It's a forest, he shot back at me. *I smell green—trees, shrubs, and moss. That's what forest denizens smell like.*

"How do you know that?"

I'm an imp. I know these things.

"If you say so."

I do say so! Scrap landed on my shoulder with more clumsiness than usual. I barely felt his weight, just a bit of dandelion fluff. That's because he lives only partway in this dimension and is invisible to everyone but me or another Warrior of the Celestial Blade.

"He won't come near me if you are this close," I complained. Only another mile to the trailhead. Another day wasted searching for our quarry.

This trail is too popular. A blind rat could find his way home.

I passed a couple hiking uphill with daypacks and water bottles slung on their belts. They wore sensible low cut boots, matching black shorts, and bright red Tees that complemented their chocolate and *café au lait* skin nicely. They also had black sweatshirts slung over their shoulders. The sunny Saturday morning in mid-September had warmed up, but this late in the year, the weather could turn wet and/or chilly with only a moment's notice. The equinox didn't have a lot to do with determining the actual season change in Portland. Next week could be bright and beautiful and ninety degrees.

Don't like the weather here? Wait a minute.

Don't like the forecast? Change the channel.

This is the Pacific North *Wet*, after all. Great coffee, wonderful microbrews, and frequent rains sweeping in from the Pacific Ocean.

The couple hurried a little faster than normal hikers out for a Saturday morning walk.

I sweated heavily from my five mile run—mostly uphill—in my loose shorts and tank. My sweatshirt was tied around my waist and my light running shoes felt every imperfection in the dirt trail.

I felt naked without my mother's pearls around my neck. The strand was too short to hide beneath the tank top. Pearls while jogging? Even I knew that was a fashion disaster. They'd come to Mom and then to me through a long and unbroken chain of women. I wished Mom was still alive to wear them. I'd never seen her *not* wearing them.

The hikers and I nodded in mute acknowledgment of fellow travelers in the wilderness. Never know when you might need help. Or if one of us turned up missing, we'd remember seeing each other and the basic location when searches began.

Too often in the last year solitary hikers got "lost," then walked out the next morning, dazed and mumbling about the ugly little guy who sheltered them overnight.

That shelter and directions came with a price.

The Nörglein had a bad reputation in the Italian and Swiss Alps. His reputation in the western hemisphere was nastier.

I looked to either side of the trail into the thick ferns, underbrush, and moss-covered fallen tree trunks crowding around tall Douglas Firs. A million shades of green melded into each other, shifting with each breeze whispering through. Ripples and mounds showed just how uneven and precarious I'd find the footing off the beaten path.

I saw faces in the whorls of bark and moss. Images of the Green Man so popular in forest lore popped into my head. I shook myself to get rid of a fear that every plant and tree embodied a malicious creature peering out at me.

"High noon and not a lot of sunlight penetrating." I slowed to a walk. Time for a cool down.

Perfect for a dark elf.

Put the emphasis on dark in that description of the Nörglein. Nothing tall and elegant or beautiful in this critter. Nothing honorable or enchanting either. This was the real thing, not High Fantasy fiction.

Take that little game trail on your left.

"That's not a game trail, that's a runoff channel." It meandered down a really, really steep hill. Portland has built up from the river plain across numerous cinder cones and volcanic ridges. It was the only city I'd ever visited that you had to climb uphill both directions of any trip. Nothing was ever downhill for very long unless it was really steep and scary.

A light wind that smelled of salt and damp riffled the ferns to my right. A single frond continued to wave at me several seconds after the air had paused for breath. The scar on my face grew warm.

I veered off the trail onto a slight separation in the underbrush barely as wide as one of my size six shoes.

Scrap took himself off into the top of a Douglas fir two hundred feet up. His gray-green skin blended perfectly with the short evergreen needles. Even I couldn't see him. And we were so closely bonded I could find him anywhere. He could find me anywhen, across five dimensions.

He waggled his butt at me, showing off his seven warts. Imps won those—er—beauty marks in battle.

A tiny hint of pink on his wing tips told me that something less than nice lurked close by. My scar was a less accurate alarm system. Maybe he'd earn another wart today after all.

The sparse sunlight disappeared beneath a cloud. Uh oh. Maybe the weather critters on TV got it right for a change, predicting afternoon showers and a twenty-degree drop in temperature.

Autumn in the Pacific Northwest is rarely predictable. About the only certainty is the presence of good coffee on every other corner and a decent brew pub on the corners in between.

I could do with a drink of either about now. I gulped a long swig of water from my sports bottle hanging on my belt pack and took three more cautious steps.

Ten paces away a fern beckoned. Scrap turned hot pink in the tree directly above me, the same color as his favorite feather boa.

"I think we're on to something, buddy."

You got that right, babe.

"What's he look like?"

Woody skin and green beard, what do you expect a forest denizen to look like?

Okay, not easy to spot.

Buff-colored knickers and linen shirt, a dark green short jacket, and three-cornered hat are so last century, dahling. More like two centuries out of date.

That about summed it up.

With my eyes on the slowly advancing movement through the underbrush, I stepped forward and ...

Snagged my foot on a blackberry vine stretched taut across my path. The spiked tendril came alive, coiling around my ankle and tugging.

My face met the dirt. I came to my knees spitting out crushed fern fronds and gagging on something sluglike.

Then the vine tugged again and I flailed forward.

A ragged, moss-covered stump caught me across the middle, taking my breath away.

I heard evil chuckles off to my left.

I yanked my left foot free of the entanglement and threw myself further off-balance.

Was that an alien hand pushing against my back?

Bracken and sword ferns crumbled beneath me as I rolled and tumbled downhill. I tried desperately to grab hold of something. Momentum pushed me faster and faster.

Sticks dug into me. Reaching shrubs scratched my face.

And still I rolled. The world twisted and spun. My eyes couldn't focus. Dizziness robbed me of any sense of direction.

Then with a back-numbing thump, I fetched up against the base of a tree.

Every inch of my body ached inside and out.

Each desperate attempt to draw breath met with knife sharp pain.

"MISS, MISS!" A MALE voice inserted itself into my hearing.

"Hhuh," I mumbled, not yet comfortable with consciousness.

You can wake up now, babe. Bad guys have gone bye-bye, Scrap sneered at me.

I couldn't ignore my imp's mental jab. It felt somewhere between a migraine and a shrill whistle. Or maybe both at the same time.

With a wince and a groan, I opened my eyes and tried to raise myself to my elbows.

Wrong move.

Fire demons raced around and around my chest, pressing tighter and tighter.

"Lay still, miss. You might have broken ribs." That intrusive male voice again.

Nah, you're not broken, just bruised and sprained. Had the breath knocked out of you. Scrap landed on top of the jagged stump. He conjured a black cherry cheroot from the ether, lit it with a flame on his fingertip, and blew a smoke ring in my face.

I had to cough. I couldn't cough. Each breath hurt worse than the last.

The man I heard but couldn't see dribbled some water across my face. The urge to cough the smoke back at Scrap eased.

The impudent imp waggled his eyebrows at me. *See. If you'd broken something you wouldn't have coughed at all.*

Thanks a lot. I thought you were my friend.

"Easy now. I'm a paramedic. Let me see if we need to get a crew up here or if you'll be able to walk out." The man must have been crouched at my head, uphill and out of my line of sight.

He pressed gently on my ribs and neck with dark hands. Nothing hurt any worse.

"She's not walking on that ankle," a female said from behind him.

The man sucked in a whistling breath. He moved around to my side. I recognized him then as the African American who'd passed me going uphill a little while ago. Another shrill breath through a gap in his front teeth. "That needs an X-ray, miss."

"Scrap?"

No answer from my buddy.

"It's crap all right," the woman said. "Raquel Jones." She sort of offered me a hand to shake, then realized I'd have to sit up to reach it, or she'd have to move downhill onto uncertain footing. So she looked at her hand as if at an alien being, then stuffed it into the pocket of her shorts.

"I'm Jordan Jones," the man said, putting his hands to better use assessing the damage to my left ankle. "JJ to most people."

"Tess Noncoiré," I said on a sharp inhale as he touched the rapidly swelling and bruising ankle. My lightweight shoes felt six sizes too small.

Raquel gasped. "Tess Noncoiré the writer? I've read all your books. What are you doing in Portland? Research?"

"I live here now," I ground out. What a horrible, ignominious way to meet a fan! I tried brushing twigs out of my short sandy blonde curls to fix *some* of the damage. "I bought a condo in John's Landing last year."

"I'm so proud to meet you. Oh." She put a hand over her mouth. "Sorry it has to be under these circumstances. I'm just glad JJ and I can help."

"It won't be comfortable with those bruised ribs, but I think I can carry you over my shoulder to the trailhead," JJ said, oblivious to his wife's gushing, fan girl chatter. "We'll drive you to the emergency room. It's only a few miles across the river." Middle height and wiry, he didn't look big enough to carry me two steps, let alone one hundred yards to the parking lot.

I'd fallen far enough downhill to almost meet the snaking path again. Could I crawl that far?

Not with those ribs, dahling. Scrap informed me.

Obviously, Raquel and JJ had no idea he was there.

"If you can just get me to my car, I'll drive myself," I replied to JJ. If Scrap said I hadn't broken anything, I believed him.

"Not a good idea, Tess." Raquel shook her head emphatically. "I'm a nurse and I can guarantee you'll feel dizzy and maybe nauseous from the pain. Then there's shock, which will set in as soon as the adrenaline wears off. How about if I follow you and JJ to the ER in your car? That way it'll be available when you can *safely* drive home." She efficiently relieved JJ of his daypack, placed it and her own on the path, then returned to help get me upright.

"You've had the breath knocked out of you," JJ said as he shoved one of his hands beneath my shoulders to heave, while Raquel grabbed my hands with her own to haul. "It's gonna hurt, but I promise you, things will look better once we get you back to the cars."

That was not fun. Nope. No way in hell.

About halfway up, balancing on my right foot, I passed out. As a tidal wave of blackness washed over me, I heard a demonic chuckle in the far distance.

Round one to the Nörglein.

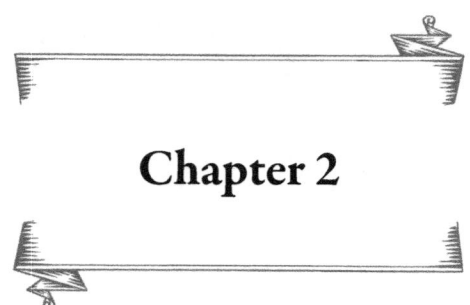

Chapter 2

I n February 2007 Fit Pregnancy Magazine named Portland the fourth best city to have a child.

"Are you going to behave yourself and stay off that ankle for a few weeks, Tess?" Dr. Sean Connolly asked me. He looked maybe thirty, a year or two younger than me. Dark circles ringed his eyes like a raccoon and his white coat needed a good washing and pressing.

"You've been on duty too long, Sean," I replied. I banked on his longing for a shower and eight hours of sound sleep before his next shift. "Of course, I'll take it easy," I lied.

"Good one, Tess. I don't want you in here again for at least two months. We've got to stop meeting like this."

I grumbled something. So I'd taken a few falls and fencing accidents this past year. It's not like I was stalking him.

"You'll have better luck putting her in a body cast and drugging her insensible for forty-eight hours," a familiar voice said from the doorway. "If you want to know why she winds up in the ER so often, read her books. She takes her research seriously."

"Steve!" I called to my brother. He was a taller copy of me with sandy hair that curled too tightly and a lanky build. But unlike me, he stood six feet tall, topping me by a good ten inches.

Not the voice I truly wanted to hear, (I'd probably never hear again from the man my heart called to) but welcome nonetheless. "Aren't you supposed to be in Chicago?"

"Can't I come visit my baby sister?" He bent to kiss my cheek. "I have some good news to tell you and wanted to do it in person."

"You didn't call first. How do you know I'm not on deadline and therefore cranky and dedicated to solitude?" I scooched to sit a little higher on the hospital bed and winced at the pressure on my ribs and ankle.

"You're always on deadline," Allie Engstrom, my best friend since kindergarten, said coming around the corner. "Don't worry, Steve and I won't intrude on your precious privacy." She too kissed my cheek. When she straightened and caught Steve's gaze across the bed—they stood nearly eye to eye in height—something strange and wonderful clicked in my head.

"You two, together? You came all this way just to tell me you got together." I pointed first to Allie then to Steve. "When and how did that happen?"

"Long story short, you decamped from Cape Cod after your mom's funeral, leaving the family at loose ends. I picked up one of them," Allie said with a quirky grin that was half remorseful at Mom's tragic murder eighteen months ago and half full of the joy of new love.

My own heart sank. I'd never get that kind of happiness. The only man I loved and truly wanted had married another woman. I knew his heart belonged to me, but his loyalty and honor were legally tied to the woman his family had selected for him to marry when they were infants.

"More than just together. We're engaged," Steve added.

"Since it looks like you'll have family to look after you for a couple of days," Dr. Sean Connolly said, "I'll see about releasing you. After we put a cast on that ankle. I doubt an air cast or boot will be enough to keep you down. There's a lot of soft tissue damage that might never heal properly if you don't *stay off it*." The doctor left, taking his tablet with the digital x-rays with him.

"Anything broken?" Steve asked with a frown.

"No. Bruised ribs. The ankle's badly sprained, and he's afraid I'll walk on it too soon and permanently damage things." I dismissed the diagnosis. Part of being a Warrior of the Celestial Blade was the ability to heal fast and clean.

"Even you will have to take a few days' rest," Allie said, as if she'd read my mind. She knew my role in keeping a balance in this world between the humans who belonged here and the demons that didn't.

That nasty little Euro trash Nörglein from the Italian or Swiss Alps (they used to have a big range until tourists and industry civilized most of their habitat) didn't belong here. He didn't belong anywhere in my world.

I needed to get back out there and take care of the little bugger, not sit on my rear end nursing a sprained ankle.

"So how did you find me?" I finally asked.

"I pinged your cell phone's GPS," Allie said, still gazing fondly at my brother.

My eyes went to my fanny pack that rested on a corner chair along with my shoes. The phone pouch sagged emptily.

"It was in your car, Li'l Bit," Steve said on a chuckle. "If your car is in the ER parking lot, then you must be in the ER."

"And you have three missed calls from your sister-in-law, Doreen Cooper." Allie pulled the phone out of her pocket, checked the screen, and tucked it into my fanny pack.

"Doreen can wait." I'd put off meeting her for weeks. "How ...? Not just anyone can ping a cell phone."

"I'm a cop, Tess," Allie replied. "I have access to those sort of things."

"An off duty cop out of your jurisdiction. Way out, by three thousand miles." I have to admit I pouted a bit, envying these two their happiness in each other.

"Well, that's another long story." Allie dropped her gaze to her hands and fidgeted with the tasteful diamond on her left ring finger. A new diamond in a modern setting, not much more than a half carat. Quite a bit less gaudy than the three-carat antique I'd turned down in Vegas last year. Donovan Estevez had offered it, not the man I wanted to marry. I wanted the ring, not him.

No regret there. The ring had gone back to Faery where it belonged.

A nurse bustled in with a wheelchair and my chart.

"See if there's a way to put rebar in the cast so she can't saw it off," Steve stage-whispered to the nurse.

NASTY DRUGS THEY KEEP pumping into my Tess. Everything they give her they might as well shoot into me. We are tied by bonds of love and loyalty, blood and magic. What happens to her happens to me.

I'm too sleepy to keep up with the complex ins and outs of her family.

I trust Allie to take care of my babe. She's one of the good gals. Maybe if I scoot through the chat room and back to Cape Cod for a bit I can purge the drugs from my system.

Some people call the chat room limbo. To others it's purgatory.

Not just anyone can slip through the chat room from here to there or now to then. But I'm an imp. A special imp because I'm bonded to a Warrior of the Celestial Blade. I know ways around the guards the dumb beasts never thought of.

If the adrenaline rush of a quick trip through the chat room doesn't help cure me of the numb sleepies, then maybe I can take a bit of a nap with Ginkgo, my life mate. He and his warrior, Gayla, run the Citadel where Tess took her training.

Hmm, just a little nap with my lover to watch over me. Then I'll listen in on the gossip in Cape Cod. I promise.

"WE HAVE TO ASK HER!" I heard Raquel's voice from a long way off as I swam up through layers of drug-induced sleep. Pain meds, my cotton ball stuffed mind sort of remembered. Just a little something to take the edge off while they twisted and folded my ankle before slapping a cast on it.

That "just a little something" became three increasingly strong doses as my body rejected the first one and most of the second. I have weird reactions to drugs.

"What can she do? She can't even stand on her own two feet," JJ snorted with disgust.

"There are rumors in the SciFi community that her books are based on a real-life Sisterhood of Warriors," Raquel whispered. "They fight demons all the time."

"We're not dealing with a demon. We're fighting a dark elf."

How did they know? Unless they'd had a child stolen.

"Same difference," I muttered. Oops. Not supposed to let on to civilians about that sort of stuff. Curse those drugs. But the sleep felt so good. I wanted to drift away on worriless clouds.

I heard Scrap giggling in the background. He loved it when I stuck my foot in my mouth (figuratively of course) or fell flat on my face.

"See," Raquel said excitedly. She dragged her husband over to my bedside, back in the curtained cubicle in the ER after a stint in the X-Ray room and then the cast room.

I thought Steve and Allie were over at registration filling out reams of paperwork to spring me from the hospital. Takes longer to complete the forms than it does to treat the emergency.

I noted with some despair that my incredibly heavy left leg was propped up on a wedge shaped pillow. It was also decorated in pink and lavender swirls. Nothing discreet about that fiberglass cast. Dr. Sean meant business in keeping me off my foot. Allie must have picked out the colors.

Or Scrap. Did I mention his penchant for pink feather boas along with his black cherry cheroots? He's normally more tasteful in picking out my clothes and accessories.

Where was the brat anyway? He shouldn't be able to get very far from me when I'm hurt or sick or wounded.

"Can you help us?" Raquel asked desperately. As she leaned over me, I caught a hint of a tummy bulge I wouldn't expect in a thirty-something woman as fit as she seemed to be.

Inspiration hit me like a two by four between the eyes. The Nörglein had victimized her, probably four or five months ago. So how come she *remembered?*

"I don't know if I can help, until I know the problem," I hedged. "I also seem to be in less than fighting shape at the moment." I tried lifting the leg with the cast but that was beyond my strength at this point. So I waved at it weakly.

"We didn't say we needed you to fight anything," JJ said sourly. He stood very upright on the other side of me.

More foot-in-the-mouth-itis.

"You were hunting that awful dark elf in Forest Park this morning, weren't you?" Raquel insisted.

"This isn't a Tolkien novel," I hedged.

"I've done some research," JJ said. He pulled a battered trade-sized paperback book from the inside pocket of his black windbreaker.

I recognized the book. Guilford Van der Hoyden-Smythe (Gollum to his friends), my once-upon-a-time archivist, short-time lover, and missing friend, kept one just like it in the glove box of his battered van. I had my own newer copy of the *"Field Guide to Gnomes, Trolls, and Ogres."* In fact, some of the green sticky note tabs on this book looked remarkably like the ones Gollum used.

And that illegible scrawl...

"Where did you get that?" I grabbed the book from JJ. Sure enough, it fell open to the page describing the Nörglein, complete with a drawing that looked like a copy of an antique woodcut. The black and white rendition showed the moss-covered Tyrolean jacket and three-cornered hat, fat bare feet covered in frondlike fur, full beard of more fern fronds beneath a long hooked nose, and strong body. It didn't show the deep red eyes or rows and rows of razor sharp teeth.

I was more interested in the notes scribbled in margins and on those sticky squares.

"I spoke with a folklorist at McLoughlin College. He loaned me the book." JJ snatched it back as if it were his most treasured possession.

My temper roiled up from the ache in my foot to the crick in my knee to my very empty stomach.

Calm down, babe. JJ and Raquel are victims, not the source, Scrap reminded me on a deep yawn. He sounded far away.

"Did Dr. Van der Hoyden-Smythe tell you to look me up?" I ground out.

And why was the love of my life hiding from me just a few miles up river from my new home? He was supposed to be in Boston with his *wife*.

"No, he didn't. Say, how do you know..."

"I knew him a long time ago." A lifetime of memories crammed into two days and one night of loving each other. "Don't suppose you've got his phone number?" I'd deleted his cell phone from my speed dial. I didn't need the temptation to call him, just to hear his voice mail message.

"I have the number at home. I can call you later to give it to you," Raquel offered.

"Do that. I'm in the book."

"Does this mean you'll help us?"

"Not today." I waved at the cast again. "First tell me how you know about the Nörglein?"

"I—um—" Raquel blushed.

"We went hiking last spring. A thunderstorm blew in suddenly. An unpredicted storm. We took shelter beneath a rocky overhang. Next thing we know, I'm tied up with blackberry vines, and this ugly guy is raping my wife," JJ spat out.

"Crime of opportunity. No time for seduction or spells or whatever he uses to block memory," I mused.

"That about says it all," JJ said. "I called the police and they just looked at me blankly when I described the guy. They said I was delusional from the shock of spending a night in the cold."

Or they'd been blackmailed, coerced, bespelled, or bribed to consider reports of the Nörglein delusions.

"I want to kill the monster!" Raquel cried. "I just don't know how. I should have aborted the baby. But I couldn't kill it. I just couldn't."

"I promise you, I will end that little monster's reign of terror before you deliver your baby."

That didn't give me a lot of time, considering I'd be out of action for six weeks if Dr. Connoly had his way.

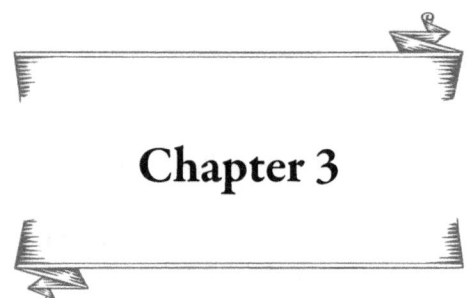

Chapter 3

A climate survey in the 1890s revealed Portland's rainfall near equal to New York and Philadelphia. But more days of rain spread over six months, and more cloudy days, give the impression of perpetual precipitation.

"Who are you and why did you kidnap my friend?" Allie asked just inside the doorway of my third story condo on the Willamette River.

"I'm too tired to play head games with you, Allie," I muttered as I heaved myself up the last step on crutches, being careful not to let the cast on my left foot touch down. I had to stop five steps short of my doorway. My lungs felt on fire and the wide elastic bandage around my ribs couldn't contain the bruises. I had to stop and breathe, carefully, shallowly, letting my heart rate calm.

And I was damp from the last onslaught of rain that blew down the river into my face the moment I lurched out of Steve's rental car. Copious sweat from the exertion of getting up the stairs didn't help.

Call you Miss Cranky Pants, Scrap taunted.

"Don't push, Steve," I pleaded as he applied gentle pressure to my lower back. "I can't go any farther yet."

"Want me to carry you this last little bit?"

"No. You're a computer geek, not a super hero. You'd drop me and then Allie would have to take us both back to the ER."

I hadn't experienced this kind of fatigue since I'd become a Warrior of the Celestial Blade, dropped fifty pounds, and taken up running and fencing as hobbies. Speaking of which, I needed to call my coach and explain why I wouldn't be in class tonight.

"This place is *clean!*" Allie protested. She stood in the open doorway, hands on hips, a scowl marring her strong face. "Not a single piece of dirty laundry or moldy coffee cup littering the place. No research books strewn across every flat surface. No piles of unanswered mail. I mean, Tess, this can't possibly be your home."

Not home. Just a temporary lodging. I didn't know where home was anymore.

My hand went to my throat. No pearls. My talisman, my last connection to my mom wasn't there.

"What did you do with all your furniture?" Steve asked as he peered inside at the same time he prodded me forward.

"I sold most of my stuff along with the house to Dad and Bill. They needed furnishings to open a Bed and Breakfast." The mahogany dining table and twelve chairs had come with the house when Dill, my deceased husband, and I bought the two-hundred-seventy-five-year-old monstrosity. The earnest money agreement included the dining set, appliances, the curtains, and the ghosts. I made sure Dad and his life partner bought them too.

Taking a deep breath, I muscled my wobbling way inside. Then I stopped again, more because I saw my condo as my brother and best friend did than because I couldn't take another step without rest.

"I guess it is kind of minimalistic," I half apologized.

"Not minimalistic. Stark," Steve clarified.

"Try stark naked," Allie added in disgust. She took the bag of groceries she carried toward the galley kitchen.

I usually ate at the countertop with barstools that separated the kitchen from the dining area and sunken living room. That eliminated the need for a table and chairs. The empty space spread wider than I remembered. The parquet floor was as new and unscuffed as the day I bought the place. A simple banister of Craftsman-style pale wood protected the upper level from the drop-off. Two steps near the entry hall and another two steps in the corner from the dining area were covered in the same textured carpet in mottled cream, seafoam green, and stone blue as the main floor.

A wall of windows overlooking the river and marina dominated the spacious living room, almost half the square footage of the apartment. A white stone chimney with a raised hearth and a gas log filled the adjacent wall. My one piece of good furniture, a comfortable sofa with foldout footrests, sat before a big screen HD TV with surround sound.

The kitchen at least got used more than the rest of the house. Even then a single sparkling wine glass occupied the hanging rack over the counter in a space for two dozen.

"You never watched TV much," Allie said cautiously. "Only two sets in your old house, the entire rambling house designed to house three generations." She rummaged around the kitchen, opening and closing every cupboard and drawer. She only paused when she stuck her head into the fridge. "And you never cooked much either. You've got all the makings for a dozen gourmet meals stockpiled."

"I have more time now that I'm not maintaining a colonial era house that sprawled in uneven levels and up three stories," I grunted. "Dad and Bill seem to be making a go of their B&B in the place though." I flopped onto the sofa and did some sprawling myself.

Allie creased her forehead and looked at me strangely. But she kept her mouth shut.

"What's going on here, Tess? This isn't like you." Steve crouched beside the sofa at my eye level.

I turned my head away.

"You have a right to be upset over Mom's death. My God, you were there when she was murdered. She died in your arms. I understand you wanting to get away from the house she shared with you. But you've always been the strong one in the family, Tess. The one we could rely on. Now you're falling apart."

"Not to mention you've pared down your skinny frame to a bony husk," Allie muttered. She carried a few pounds more than she wanted, but on her tall, long-limbed body you couldn't tell. "I'm heating up some of your homemade soup and making sandwiches. You need to eat in order to heal."

Listen to her, babe. Scrap sounded more alert now but still far away. I knew he'd maintain a connection.

"You two can have my bedroom. I'll sleep here." I rolled over so I wouldn't have to look Steve in the eye.

Over my head Allie and Steve exchanged "The Look." You know, that weird silent communication two people have when they are thinking the same thing.

"Where's your cell phone, Tess?" Allie asked, all smart and businesslike.

"Why?"

"I'm calling Gollum."

"No, you aren't. I deleted his number right after he went back to his *wife.*" I sneered the last word. Not that Julia had been much of a wife to him over the past fifteen years. She'd been locked in an insane asylum for most of their marriage.

"Don't you remember the number?" she asked.

Of course I did.

Instead of answering I pulled a pillow over my head and pretended to sleep.

"That does it. If I can't get hold of Gollum, I'm calling your other boyfriend, Donovan Estevez."

"Not on your life!" I bolted up to prevent her from doing anything so drastic. Dumb me forgot about the pounds of fiberglass on my lower leg. Sharp pains shot, wiggled, and zigzagged in all directions.

With a muffled scream I lost my balance and fell back where I'd been. Panting through the pain, I couldn't prevent Allie from fishing my phone out of the fanny pack strapped around my waist.

"Donovan, this is Allie. Tess is hurt. We need you now!" she said and hung up. I presumed she spoke to his voice mail.

I wondered why the sexiest man alive, sort of my stepbrother, champion of demon rights, and one-time suitor wasn't glued to his business number like his life and fortune depended on the next call. They usually did.

DAWN FOUND ME ON MY balcony cuddling a lidded travel cup of coffee with both hands, bracing myself on the crutches. I'd almost spilled the precious brew of life twice, even with the lid, when I'd stumbled out to watch the moon set and the sun rise.

But I had my pearls back on. I felt dressed even in my pajamas and robe.

I faced east, looking across the river as light gradually revealed lines of hills marching up to the base of Mt. Hood. The snowcapped peak towered majestically above the city. For about two seconds the low light sparkled against new snow. Then scudding low clouds raced across the lowlands and piled up against the mountain, blocking my view.

The Ross Island Bridge half a mile north had clogged with early morning Sunday traffic. People rushing to get out of town and enjoy the last of the mild weather. Cars on the Marquam Bridge, the double-decker freeway bridge next in line, still flowed freely. The mist obscured the other bridges that gave Portland one of its nicknames: Bridgetown.

Scrap perched precariously on the railing. Today his transparent body took on a shade of green content and he almost glowed. At least he'd gotten lucky recently. He faced south, upriver toward the Sellwood Bridge, in the direction of McLoughlin College, the small, exclusive, incredibly expensive institution of learning that was almost as old as the state.

"Did you know he was there?" I asked Scrap. We both knew I'd only speak of one "*he*."

I knew he was close. I didn't look to see how close.

"Why didn't you tell me?"

You didn't want to know.

"You're right."

What are you going to do about it?

"I don't know." Why had Gollum come to Oregon when his insane wife was locked up in an asylum outside of Boston? Surely if he were free of her, he'd look me up.

He'd said he would remain my friend, help me when I needed an archivist, just before the door closed on his retreating back.

"I don't need him."

If you truly believe that, I've got some Alpine cottages in Kansas I'll sell you, Scrap offered with a toothy grin.

The moisture-laden air carried an autumnal edge of chill. It smelled sharp and musky, of fallen leaves and ripening fruit. I caught a whiff of pumpkin spice from the bakery down the street. My mouth watered. My stomach growled with a hunger I hadn't felt since Gollum had left me, and Mom had died at the hands of a rogue Warrior.

Those spiced muffins would make a perfect breakfast.

Maybe my soul was coming alive again after the deep grief. Maybe I could write again. My dwindling bank account sure would like me to finish the book that was more than a year overdue.

But I couldn't just dash out and grab a muffin to go with my excellent coffee while I pounded away at the keyboard. I was stuck in this apartment, chained to the crutches and the heavy cast.

"Tess, I'm fixing omelets," Allie called on a yawn.

I might not be able to dash out, but my brother could. "Send Steve to the bakery for pumpkin spice muffins!" I closed the lid on my cup and stuffed it in the pocket of my robe. Then I made the awkward turn on the crutches to go back inside. That wind seemed colder and wetter than it had a minute ago. Fat raindrops splattered on the edge of the balcony. I made it through the French doors half a breath ahead of the onslaught of the next shower.

Uh oh, Scrap said. He rose up from the railing on his stubby wings, large bat-wing ears flicking forward. His contented green flashed back and forth between angry orange and hot pink. Not complimentary colors.

Instantly on my guard, I balanced on my right crutch and foot, prepared to swing the left.

"What?" I whispered so that only he could hear.

Tall, dark, and toxic has entered the building! Scrap landed on my right shoulder, cocking his head, trying to figure a way for me to hold him while he stretched and solidified into the Celestial Blade.

"Donovan Estevez," I sighed.

Scrap really doesn't like Donovan. For the first year of our acquaintance, remnants of Donovan's gargoyle aura repelled Scrap completely. The only time the two could get within ten yards of each other was when the presence of a demon or tremendous evil overrode the repulsion.

Donovan spent about eight hundred years as a gargoyle, keeping demons and evil away from whatever structure he protected. Some of that apotropaic nature remained after his fall. He claims that he was inexperienced (gargoyles don't learn and grow after they are assigned a statue). Smarmy persuasion and vast numbers of demons overwhelmed him about fifty years ago. Whatever the cause, he was kicked out of the gargoyle business. A half-blood or Kajiri demon rescued him from his fall. I'd only recently learned the rescuer had been my deceased husband. That knowledge still ate at my gut.

I had a hard time convincing myself that a few family photos I'd accidentally tucked into a box of Dill's stuff I had sent his family were worth bringing back painful memories. His sister Doreen wanted to return them. I didn't want to have to think about all the people I'd lost in the last few years. Mom, my best friend Bob, Dill...

Those were just the ones who'd died.

After Donovan's fall, Dill had sheltered and nurtured him for a time before The Powers That Be passed sentence—condemned him to be fostered by Darren Estevez, a Kajiri of the Damiri tribe and nowhere near as nice and nurturing as my Dill.

Donovan claimed he hadn't been involved in Dill's murder at Darren's hand. I didn't believe him.

You see, Donovan developed sympathy for those he'd been charged to keep out of sacred space and now served as their human champion. Scrap had a darkness in his soul that made him and Donovan mutually repulsive, sort of like magnetic fields. Scrap overcame his problem. I'm not privy to the details of his time of trial.

Now the two can face each other and snarl.

I didn't like Donovan or approve of his mission to create a homeland for half-breed demons in human space—for that reason I had helped my aunt MoonFeather gain custody of Donovan's daughter, Lilly. The baby's mother certainly couldn't care for her in an asylum for the criminally insane.

But I trusted Donovan with my life. Several times we'd fought side by side and triumphed over some truly nasty Midori (full-blood) demons.

"What about Donovan?" Steve asked, emerging from the bedroom, blond hair scraggly—longer than he usually wore it and in need of a good cut—jeans zipped but not snapped, T-shirt half tucked in, feet stuffed into loafers, sans socks.

"He's approaching the front door," I said and flopped onto the sofa amidst the tangle of pillows and blankets that had made my bed. My hand automatically went to the strand of pearls.

"How?"

"Don't ask. Call me psychic like MoonFeather." Our father's sister was an avowed witch. We'd learned long ago not to question her powers of observation, intuition, and healing calmness. Who's to say I hadn't inherited her talents?

Allie, of course, knew about Scrap. She'd been deeply involved in one of our little escapades a while back. I hoped she'd kept that information secret.

Scrap flitted to the door, growling and gnashing his teeth, glowing an angry dark pink.

If he'd truly meant it, he'd turn deep red and stick himself to my right hand. If Scrap thought for an instant that Donovan threatened me in any way he'd have stretched and curved halfway through transformation into the Celestial Blade without my command.

A loud knock on the door and a simultaneous peal of the bell demanded attention.

"A bit impatient, isn't he?" Steve shuffled to the entry, peered through the spy hole, then unlatched the dead bolt and security chain. The door thrust open, nearly knocking him into the wall. He harrumphed and departed, presumably for the bakery and my requested pumpkin spice muffins.

"Good morning, Donovan. Have you visited your daughter lately? You look like you drove all night," I said, gluing my gaze to the weather report on the big screen TV. I didn't want to take in his lean, muscular frame, the high cheekbones and copper tone to his skin. His long black braid touched with silver at his temples could send me into paroxysms of joy when he tickled me with its silky ends.

Nope, not going to think about that, not one little bit.

"I'm flying out next week to testify on my custody appeal for Lilly. What's wrong with you?" He stalked over to stand between me and the map of the region with predicted high temperatures plastered over it. "Did a demon invade your dad's place and open a new portal? I can't believe you actually sold that very vulnerable piece of land to someone you love."

A memory flashed behind my eyes. My head reeled and my present location and condition reverted to an earlier time.

I lived again the gnawing fear that drove me to the most dangerous portal of all in the chat room. Once more I stood before the tall elegant door with stained glass panels to the sides. I heard again the deep reverberations throughout the Universe when I dropped the knocker. Felt the vibrations as my pearls picked up the harmonics. I shuddered anew with the bone deep, burning cold of the doorknob when I finally screwed up my courage to open the damn door to the Powers That Be.

Seven beings from seven different dimensions sat in judgment of the entire Universe. Seven beings hidden and shadowed by long cloaks and deep hoods. I had no way of knowing who they were or where they came from. If any of them were human or had human sympathies they didn't betray them.

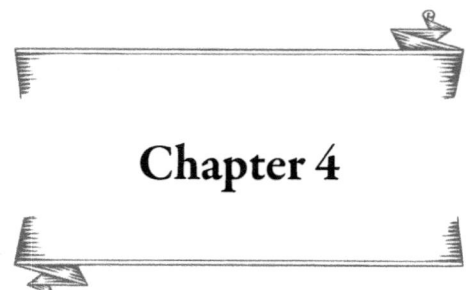

Chapter 4

Portland is sometimes called Bridgetown. Nine bridges cross the Willamette River that bisects the city: Sellwood, Ross Island, Hawthorne, Morrison, Burnside, Broadway, St. Johns, and the two double-decker freeway bridges, Marquam and Freemont.

Then the vision was gone as fast as it came.

Back in reality, I pointed to my pastel-swirled cast sticking out below my pajama bottoms. "I tangled with a Nörglein. Actually, I tangled with a blackberry vine trip wire he strung across my path."

"L'Akita," he said gently, sitting beside me and taking my hand. His thumb stroked my palm sensuously.

Part of me tried to melt into a puddle of desire. Been there. Done that. Didn't like the consequences. But, wow, did we have fun in the middle of it.

"You should have called me. I'd have helped you hunt the monster. What kind of demon is he?" His gaze met mine full on, without shying away. A sure sign he knew more than he implied. This man could lie more convincingly than most people told the truth.

I knew him too well to fall under his spell.

I jerked my hand away from him. "Nörglein are forest elves. Dark elves without conscience or a molecule of sympathy for others. They blur and change the paths before solitary travelers until they are thoroughly lost. Then they offer to show the way out in return for favors."

Donovan had the grace to look away.

"Sexual favors from women hikers, the demand of a night with the wives of males. Any children born of the liaison belong to the Nörglein after weaning." I coldly recited the *modus operandi* of the beasts, like reading a police blotter.

"I can't allow you to endanger yourself with this guy, Tess. I've heard about him before." Donovan took my hand again, lacing his fingers with mine.

Somehow I found the strength of will to reclaim my hand and my heart. There was a time when he could dissolve all my fears and reservations. Not anymore. I loved someone else. I'd broken his power over me.

That was one of my problems with Donovan. I never knew if that intense desire and willingness to share my mind and body with him was true attraction or part of his magical glamour.

"How does the Nörglein get the wives of his male victims to cooperate?" Allie asked. She brought me a plate piled high with a veggie and cheese omelet and chunks of fried potatoes. The food smelled heavenly and I dug in without reservation.

For the past year and a half, I'd looked at food as fuel and picked at it only when necessary. Everything tasted like straw. I'd taken up exotic cooking in an attempt to find something, anything that appealed to me. I took more joy in the preparation process than the eating. My neighbors loved me for my leftovers.

Now it seemed the challenge of a demon quest had awakened my appetite as well as my mind.

Or maybe I'd finally worked through the seven stages of grief and could live again. About time.

"As near as I can tell, from hints in old legends and letters, the elf binds the lost man and then shape-changes into his form. He walks out of the forest and has a joyous reunion with his wife. During the night he slips away and releases his prisoner at the trailhead," I related between bites. "When a baby is born nine months later, the woman remembers who fathered it. Not unusual for her to have a complete nervous breakdown. Two years later, the husband takes their baby and turns it loose at a designated spot in the woods. That was in medieval times. Modern women aren't so obedient. If they fight giving their baby away, the Nörglein kidnaps it."

Donovan snarled angrily.

"Ew, does he eat the kids?" Allie looked as if she was about to gag on her own omelet.

"Unknown. If he dines on toddlers, you'd think he'd just prowl the city kidnapping them at will. No, he seems most particular in claiming children with his own DNA."

But Raquel remembered. The pattern was breaking down. Something had changed. I needed to know what in order to exploit his weakness.

"What's the plan, Tess? This guy needs to be taken out. Fast." Allie moved to the middle of the room, hands on hips, balance forward, outrage written on her grim face and aggressive posture. She pulled up the belt of her jeans as if hitching her utility belt full of weapons. Her fingers twitched, eager for the grip of a weapon.

"The plan is to watch and wait until I'm out of this friggin' cast and can fight again." I almost threw the now empty plate at her.

"If the Nörglein tripped you, then he probably spotted Scrap and knows who you are and the resources at your command," Donovan mused. Somehow my hand was back in his again. His gentle thumb caressing my palm and up my wrist was more an extension of his thought process than seduction.

"So I'll go in as bait. You two can follow at a discreet distance. Scrap can keep an eye on me and guide you to the lair. Easy." Allie looked as if she wanted to draw her gun. Once a cop, always a cop.

"Don't you have to go back to work?" I asked.

Allie looked away. "Steve should be back with your muffins by now." She marched to the door and opened it, leaning out into the open stairwell. "Couldn't you buy a condo with an elevator and interior corridor?"

"Limited access for bad guys following me. Corner unit with limited access to vulnerable neighbors. Metal stairs so I can hear anyone who approaches," I mumbled. "Allie, what's wrong with you and work?"

Steve appeared in the doorway. He kissed Allie and squeezed her shoulder. "She shot a man in the middle of a domestic dispute. She's on administrative leave until state authorities complete an investigation."

"I'm sure you'll be exonerated," I murmured. "You'll be called back soon."

"I'm not sure I want to go back to work." Allie kept looking at her feet.

"You love being a cop," I protested. "That's all you ever wanted to be from the first day we met in kindergarten."

"I hate dealing with men who beat their wives to death and then rape their thirteen-year-old daughters. I had to shoot him to keep him from coming after me with a baseball bat. I'm glad he died. Monsters like that shouldn't be allowed to live," she claimed righteously. Then her face fell and sadness clouded her eyes.

"I'd rather fight demons than my own kind who behave worse than demons." She looked up and glared at me defiantly.

"Huh?" Steve said. His mouth hung open and he held the bakery sack loosely.

"Okay, there's only one thing we can do." I struggled to my feet—or rather one foot and the crutches.

Donovan leaped up and offered to pull me. Or carry me. I batted him away.

"What can we do, Tess?" Allie asked. Wisely, she stayed out of the way and let me manage on my own.

"What I should have done when I first moved here."

"Find Gollum?" Allie offered hopefully.

"No."

Silence all around as they looked at me speculatively.

"Go buy some furniture from my sister-in-law."

Chapter 5

Portland has more microbreweries and brew pubs per capita than any other US city.

"This is a really bad idea, Tess," Donovan says as he drives his pretty cream-colored Mercedes across the top level of the Marquam Bridge. The rain-swollen Willamette River passes beneath us, muddy swirls catching on the bridge supports.

"If it's such a bad idea, why are you driving me out to Cooper's Furniture Emporium?" Tess asks from the backseat. She sits with her cast in Allie's lap. Steve is riding shotgun.

And I'm perched on the window ledge behind Tess. It's a pretty drive on a late Sunday morning. I don't have enough calm to add to the acid mixture upsetting my tummy to appreciate the scenery. Showers and broken sunlight offer different perspectives on lovely vistas at every turn.

"For once in your life, I think you should listen to him," I whisper to Tess. I've tried tugging her hair to make her pay attention to me.

She's ignoring both Donovan and me.

"I'm driving you so you don't go off on your own and get into more trouble." Donovan scowls. He does that beautifully. Too bad he's not gay. I could really go for him. But no, he's in love with Tess in his own twisted, selfish way. "You should meet Doreen on neutral territory, tell her what you need and have it delivered."

"How much trouble can the Coopers cause?" Tess asks. "We're customers. And they are Damiri. They like money almost as much as they like blood."

"Um . . . what's a Damiri?" Steve asks. He looks car sick. But I think it's the conversation.

"It's a tribe of demons," Allie supplies him the information. *"The Coopers are half-breeds, otherwise they couldn't shape-change to human form in this dimension."*

"Um . . ."

"Get used to it, Steve. Your baby sister has gotten involved with some really bizarre lifestyle groups," Tess tells him.

I almost laugh. But that would mean she's winning this argument. I can't have that. I need her to go home and nurse her hurts and spend some quality time with her brother and his lovely fiancée.

"More bizarre than the kids at science fiction conventions who dress up as demons?" Steve asks hopefully.

"Modern day demons hang out at those cons and win hall costume prizes, but they aren't really costumes," Tess says. *"I found that out the hard way."*

"Tess, is it legal to tell Steve the truth?" Allie asks. *"I mean ... didn't you take an oath of secrecy?"*

"Too late now." Tess flashes them a grimace of a grin. *"I'm out of the broom closet."*

Oh, boy. We're all in trouble now. When she gets that determined look on her face, nothing can dissuade her.

What if I got sick? Imps don't vomit like humans do. We reject toxic food in other ways. If I blow enough flammable gas in her face she'll just open a window and throw me out.

What to do? What to do?

"THE COOPERS WILL RECOGNIZE you, Tess. You married their son. Hell, they *know* me!" Donovan protested.

I rolled my eyes. I'd only met the Coopers twice. Right after I married Dill, then again at their son's funeral three months later. They'd avoided me through the entire painful procedure, barely recognizing my short time with Dill as a real marriage.

We'd reached a compromise on Dill's estate only after I threatened to take them to court with an ironclad will. They got his trust fund—or what was left of it after he liquidated it as a down payment on our house in Cape

Cod, the one I sold to my father and his partner last year—and the income from his share in the mysterious furniture store on a back country road out in the middle of nowhere. I got the house and his life insurance—double indemnity for murder or accident.

Only Doreen seemed intent upon contacting me again, to return a few family photos of mine that got mixed up in Dill's stuff I couldn't bear to look at again. In the last month she'd become even more persistent in trying to arrange a meeting.

I'd driven by Cooper's dozens of times in the last year and never had the courage to stop. They didn't seem to keep normal business hours or to have any customers. The open sign never changed to closed, even at two in the morning.

"I think I'll start with a dining table and chairs. Something simple, Craftsman design to match the railing. Lots of plain wood, light colored, to accent the parquet floor and kitchen cabinets," I replied. "And maybe some end tables and lamps." That is, if the Coopers had in stock anything but heavy, dark, gothic stuff for their fellow half-breed demons.

"She's serious, Donovan," Steve said. "I wish someone would fill me in. I'm a computer engineer, not a superhero." He flashed me a wry grin, parroting back my own protests.

So, I told Steve all about the year I went missing after I buried Dillwyn Bailey Cooper.

"Only you, Tess, would find a Citadel hidden in a dry canyon in Central Washington that houses a Sisterhood of dedicated demon fighters. I thought you made that up for your books." Steve shook his head and frowned in disapproval. "Part of me dismisses this as illogical, the stupid wanderings of your imagination. But it explains a lot. And Allie believes you. She's hinted... I just thought her reading material had latched onto her mind a little too tightly."

"Where do you think I got the idea, Steve? I may be a bit crazy but I'm not delusional. You know me. I changed the situation in my books to a post-apocalyptic world to protect the guilty from witch-hunts. Last time that happened a lot of innocent women died horribly," I said nonchalantly, as if everyone should know about my secret life.

"So, where's the imp?" he asked.

"You *have* read the books!"

"Only the ones you've had published, not the one that's a year overdue," he replied.

That was hitting below the belt. I had my reasons for not writing a word since Mom died and Gollum deserted me. I had this mental block. Every time I sat down to write, the words evaporated. Nothing. Nada. And I was running out of money.

What would I do if I never wrote again? I felt like only half a person without stories and characters running rampant through my brain demanding I give them life through words.

My checking account was also growling like an empty stomach.

I was tapping the money Mom left me for furniture. But that was blood money and I hated using it. I didn't feel like I had a right to it. Everything else Dad had tied up in investments.

The rain evaporated and the clouds thinned. A bit of bright sunshine peeked through the tattered remnants of mist.

Donovan wove deftly through traffic headed east toward the mountain. Most of the cars turned off into the farm country, probably looking for corn mazes and harvest festivals. And don't forget the wineries and microbreweries.

Not once did Donovan ask for directions. He drove like he really knew his way around, getting into the proper lane on the freeway well before interchanges and exits.

"Did you drive all night from Half Moon Lake?" I asked when the conversation wound down, and he turned uphill from the freeway toward the Mount Hood Parkway and took the quick left turn onto Elsewhere Avenue. This was the back way into Cooper's, not the simpler, but longer route offered by the road signs.

He'd been here before.

"I was in town already," he growled. "I have business and friends in this town other than you. I even have a new girlfriend. But I'll dump her in a minute if you take me back." He flashed me an almost sincere grin in the rearview mirror.

A hay wagon pulled out in front of him and crawled at twenty-five miles an hour in a forty-five zone. It shed bits of straw like a long-haired cat snoozing before the fire. Donovan backed off to avoid soiling his lovely car.

"Who is she? I want to give her my blessing or warn her about you. I'll have to meet her before I decide which," I riposted brightly. I didn't dare settle back in the luxurious seats. I might get too comfortable and let someone else make decisions for me.

Me, a control freak? You bet your sweet patootie I am. For a good reason.

"You'll meet when I decide you deserve to meet her. Mostly, I'm here on business." He clamped his mouth shut, a clear sign that he didn't want to talk about it.

"Halfling Computer Games business, family business, or Cooper's business?" I never know when to shut up.

"You work for Halfling Computer Games?" Steve asked in awe. "I love their games."

Donovan might legally be described as our stepbrother. His adopted father married our mother then got himself murdered thirty-six hours later. I don't think Steve and Donovan had met any time other than Mom's funeral. Steve normally lives in Chicago, far enough away that our wacky family couldn't just drop in on him but close enough to get home in an emergency. Donovan only showed up to Mom's funeral because he was executor of the massive fortune Mom had inherited from his adopted father. Most of that money was supposed to come to me now.

I couldn't bring myself to touch one filthy dollar.

"I own Halfling," Donovan said proudly.

"Wow, if you ever need a beta tester, let me know," Steve replied eagerly. The two men rolled off into geek speak about various role-playing games and the logic puzzles of programming them.

I sighed. No more information coming from Donovan.

I let the luxury car cradle me and turned my attention to the autumnal colors beginning to show on the trees, mostly golden cottonwood and brown alder in the foothills, with just enough splashes of red vine maple to delight the eye. With the sunshine breaking through the broken cloud cover, those crimson leaves nearly glowed from within. They looked like something a faery would paint.

The last time Gollum and I had been together we'd helped some lost faeries get home.

Don't go there. Don't even think about those few magical days with Gollum.

"The place looks closed," Donovan said almost happily as he pulled into the gravel parking area in front of the single story building. Blinds covered the multitude of windows beneath the flat roof. A big sign nearly filled one corner. CLOSED. No hours of operation. The brick house behind the store had plywood nailed to all the windows and doorframes. The door of the barn/garage sagged, showing three empty bays.

"If I didn't know better, I'd say this place had been deserted a long time," I said. "But I drove by two weeks ago. It was open and well kept."

Maybe it's not deserted, Scrap whispered to me. *I smell demon glamour. Like they knew you were coming and disguised the place. Like someone tipped them off.*

Someone like Donovan? I whispered back to him.

Someone like the Nörglein.

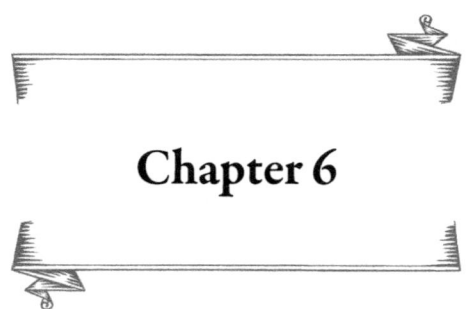

Chapter 6

*E*ighty-four waterfalls plunge off Mt. Hood along seventy-five miles of the Columbia River Gorge. The highest concentration of waterfalls in the world are in the fifteen miles between Ainsworth and Crown Point State Parks, including Multnomah, the highest double falls in the US, Wahkeena, Bridal Veil, Horsetail, Shepperds Dell, and Latourell Falls.

"Stop the car, Donovan!"

"No." Gravel spewed out from his tires as he peeled out onto the road between a twenty-year-old tank of a sedan and a tail-gating oversized pickup.

"Scrap smells the Nörglein. He's here. We have to stop." I leaned forward between the seats reaching for the steering wheel. Too far. I needed to put both feet down and push my body halfway through the gap.

"The man said no." Allie grabbed the back of my sweatshirt and yanked backward.

At the same time, Steve put his arm across the divide.

"But he's here! The Nörglein is here. He's disguised the place to keep me from finding him."

"What can you do about it, Tess?" Donovan asked calmly. He let the pickup pass with a flash of lights and a blaring horn. "This elf is tricky. He's smart. He's mean. And he's a shape-changer. For all we know he could be that big leaf maple tree ready to drop a thousand pound dead branch on us."

"I agree. We can come back when we have more information and you are fit again." Allie refastened my seat belt and planted my cast back in her lap.

"You are in no condition to fight," Donovan continued. "I can't take this guy down with mundane weapons. And we have two humans on board who won't survive a confrontation with a dark elf. Especially one as nasty as this one."

"I beg your pardon. I know exactly how to fight a dark elf," Steve interjected. "I've made it through all six hundred sixty-six levels of *Halfling*. I know how to wield every weapon in the game arsenal."

Donovan and I both snorted in derision.

"It's not the same, Steve. Believe me," Donovan replied.

"Scrap . . ."

"Doesn't like me. And I don't like him. I can't and won't use him as my weapon." Donovan clamped his mouth shut and sped around the ambling old Dodge.

"You're going the wrong way." I couldn't let him get the last word.

"No, I'm not. We're going to drive until you calm down. Besides, you need to show Steve and Allie the sights, like a good hostess. How about a late lunch at Timberline Lodge, then we continue around the mountain and take in the waterfalls of the Columbia River Gorge? Maybe dinner at Multnomah Falls Lodge. I've got a digital SLR camera in the glove box. We have our phones. Lots of fun pictures we can email to your father." He set his course.

"Tess," Allie said hesitantly once Donovan had turned onto the major highway again. "Maybe we should call Gollum. He'll know what to do."

"I hate to admit it, but I think she's right," Donovan agreed. He didn't look any happier than I did at the prospect. "Where is your boyfriend anyway?"

"He's not my boyfriend." But, oh, how I wished I had the right to claim him as mine.

Donovan raised his eyebrows at that and peered at me through the rearview mirror. "He was your boyfriend in Las Vegas last year."

Allie squeezed my knee in sympathy. She knew the whole story. Steve studied the autumnal colors, carefully avoiding eye contact with anyone. He must have learned about Gollum's loyalty to his crazy, fragile, dependent wife from Allie.

"Where is he, Tess?" Donovan demanded.

"I don't know."

"Yes, you do. I know you. You wouldn't let him disappear completely."

But I had. Until yesterday.

"Leave her alone, Donovan. Gollum gave me an emergency number before he left Cape Cod," Allie said. She whipped out her cell phone and pressed the first name on her speed dial. "Damn, no signal up here."

Scrap laughed. *Not yet, Allie. Not yet. I'll let you call later. But not yet.*

What was *he* up to?

Protecting your heart as well as your ass. With that, he winked out in a puff of black cherry smoke.

"LOOK, DAHLING, DO YOU really want Allie, or worse, Donovan, to be the first one to call your Gollum?" Oh, the things I found out while Tess and clan were touring the grand sights. I got caught up in watching and forgot to go home until almost midnight.

Normally, I'd love to tag along on sight-seeing trips. There's something exhilarating about playing with the water gushing off our mountain and then tumbling over steep cliffs, spraying droplets hither, thither, and yon, moistening neon lichens or carving rivulets in rock. Then there are the ones that careen down broken inclines, twisting and turning through channels gouged over aeons. Always the same, ever changing. A philosophy of life. Sacred since time began.

Water droplets forming rainbows in the sunshine are perfect hiding places for imps. Gives me practice in changing colors at will to match the arcing prisms.

Sigh. Another time I'll wax poetic about waterfalls and bright leaves.

"What do you mean, Scrap?" Tess roused from her computer. Sunday night and she'd only written three new pages. But that's three more than she's written in ages and ages. This from a best-selling author who churned out a fat, fat, fat book every nine months or so until the dark side of life caught up with her.

I shouldn't interrupt her, but this is important too. I'm hoping that once she's talked to Mr. tall, lean, scholarly, and absent, she'll feel better. At least maybe that huge gaping hole in her soul will shrink a bit.

How can I find true and utter happiness with my Ginkgo when my warrior is so sad and empty?

How am I going to find the time to spend with my beloved if Tess isn't occupied with her writing? Her lack of a love life is putting a strain on mine.

"Letting Allie call him is the coward's way out." *I feel like whispering because I know Steve and Allie are asleep in the next room. No sense waking them to share in this very private conversation.*

"Calling him at all is the coward's way out." *Tess plants her face in front of the computer screen and pretends to type.*

I insert my cute little body behind the screen and peer out at her making funny faces.

She jerks away with a gasp. "Warn me next time you do that," *she snarls.*

"If I warn you, you wouldn't pay attention," *I pout with just a perfect bit of jutting lower lip that Ginkgo finds irresistible. Then I waggle the tip of my black and silver boa in her face. Pink is fine for daytime wear and my favorite. For evening calls the black and silver is proper attire.*

"I can't do it, Scrap. I can't call him out of the blue. I don't know what he's doing, how he's coping, where he's living."

"What if I could show you?" *I slip through the computer screen—these new flat pieces are more porous to my kind and it's easy.*

"It's after midnight. He's probably sleeping. And I don't want to see who he's sleeping with."

"Not to worry. He's awake. I promise you we'll just take a quick peek from the chat room. If things get embarrassing, we'll dart back home so quick you won't have time to blush." *I let the barbed tip of my tail glow a little, green with lust. I'd love to see what goes on in that household. If Tess knew what a voyeur I'd become she'd spank my bottom good and hard.*

Oooooh, if only Ginkgo would do that!

"I hate the chat room. I'm in no condition to fight whoever is guarding it today ..."

"So stop with the excuses. I've got a few tricks up my sleeve, dahling. I would never endanger you. I just wish I could lick that wound and make it better." *I pout again. Imp spit works wonders on demon tags and infections. We have a natural antibiotic attuned to our warriors. Sprains, strains, and breaks are beyond our healing ability though.*

Only the person who broke a heart can repair that kind of wound.

"Okay." *She gives in reluctantly after a long silent pondering.*

I bounce to her shoulder and whisk us through the dimensional portal and into the white nothingness of the chat room before she can change our mind. I spot a few doors here and there, some on the edges in neat rows, some randomly placed above, below, and in the middle. There are glass doors, brass doors, leather curtains, and painted screens. Little ones, human size ones, bigger ones, and giant openings with no visible cover at all. Pick a dimension, any dimension; the chat room opens to all of them, anywhere, anywhen.

Tess stands unsteadily on one foot blinking rapidly. Her cast has paled to a translucent echo of the real thing. Reality twists and fades in the chat room. It also grows big and fast and slams you in the face. You never know.

"Don't think about the cast, babe. In here you can put your foot down without danger. I can see the bruises and torn muscles. They are healing clean but slowly."

"It's the dragon growing from butterfly size to nearly fill the room I'm scared of." *She points needlessly to the bright blue and yellow scaled beastie.*

"Oh, yeah, the J'appel dragons. That skinny Larper quaking on top of his closed portal must have stumbled on the guardian's real name."

For the uninitiated, Larper stands for Live Action Roll Playing gamer. They stumble into the chat room all the time without knowing how they got here. Most of them have enough sense to back out by the door they came in by. A few don't realize they are beyond reality and keep plowing forward, hoping to find Impland—the freeze-dried garbage dump of the Universe. Lots of magical artifacts end up there and are highly prized by critters more dangerous than the J'appel dragons. I've given a couple of those artifacts to Tess.

Tess stomps over to the Larper who's hunkered down with his hands over his head. "What did you say to him?" *she demands.*

"I ... I ... said ... hello."

"Crap. That's what the dragon changed his name to about a minute before you came through. Call his real name and he grows to dragon size until he decides to change his name again. Now get out of here." *She pulls him off the splintery wooden door with chipped white paint and tarnished metal fittings, opens it, then shoves the poor mite back where he came from.*

"Um . . . Tess," *I call as I flit over to her shoulder.* "I think we need to get out of here. We've attracted some unwanted attention."

"No kidding. Do we have to fight?" *She takes up a stance en garde.*

"Not here, babe. Just follow me." I lead the way around the perimeter of the room without true dimension. I'm an imp. I know how to use the chat room. I've learned a few tricks over the decades. I may be small but I'm tricky.

The dragon lowers his head, swinging it in a wide arc, sniffing. He's nearsighted. Great. Those are the most dangerous kind. He can smell Tess and me but he can't see us. So he's going to flame us just in case we don't belong here.

At the last possible second I drag Tess into a side corridor I discovered while doing research on that magical diamond Donovan tried to give her as an engagement ring. It's back in Faery now where it belongs, but, oh, it was a gorgeous ring. Both Tess and I lusted after it.

Dragon flames lick my hind end. "Stop that." I slap the beast's nose with my tail. His snout helps me beat the flames down to embers.

He backs off, looking hurt and confused, as if his mother had just reprimanded him for overcooking his dinner.

I'll have to remember that next time.

"Oh, my!" Tess covers her heart. A tear trickles down her cheek. She's looking through a little window into Gollum's home office. He's staring at his computer. An image of the Nörglein and a lot of text in Italian fill the twenty-four-inch screen. I think that's the language, though it looks a bit like German. He speaks and reads both—modern and medieval.

Tess half reaches out as if to caress his face or run her fingers through his fine silver gilt hair.

Her hand lingers, fingers frozen half reaching for him. She forgets to breathe. The single tear gains sisters.

Her other hand clings to her pearls as if to a lifeline.

"I'd forgotten how tall he is," she whispers. "He needs to fix those glasses. They keep sliding down his nose."

His hand reaches for the phone.

I grab Tess and drop her back in her own office just as the first chirp comes from her landline.

She stares at the phone as if it's an alien being singing the "Halleluiah Chorus."

It might be.

Chapter 7

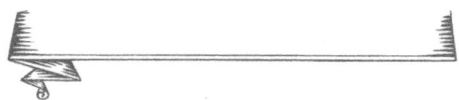

G old Hill, Oregon, where balls roll uphill and people appear to stand sideways, is known as the Oregon Vortex.

The caller ID showed "private name" and a number with a local area code and exchange.

It rang a second time.

I hesitated.

Pick up the damn phone, Scrap yelled into the middle of my mind.

Okay. I could do this.

A deep breath for courage.

A third ring.

One more and it would go to voice mail. I could return the call.

He might not leave a message.

I'd not hear his clipped tenor voice with hints of upstate New York mellowed by the dozen languages he spoke and read.

Desperate, I grabbed the phone in the middle of the fourth ring. "Hello." I tried to keep my voice from sounding breathless with anticipation. My heart raced and my teeth nearly chattered.

A long moment of dead air.

"Hello?" I tried again.

"Tess," he breathed.

"Who is this?" As if I didn't know.

"It's me, Guilford ... um, Gollum." I could almost see him blushing.

"Good morning Dr. Van der Hoyden-Smythe. A little late to be calling."

"Tess, please. We need to talk. I've found some new information about your ... um ... problem." He rushed through that, as if afraid I might hang up on him.

I thought about it.

"What kind of information?"

"Not over an open line. We need to talk. In private. Before it gets any worse."

"How could it be worse? Seven women in less than a year."

"The problem is escalating. Please. Where can I meet you?"

"How did you get this number?" I'd changed it right after leaving Cape Cod.

"JJ and Raquel gave it to me. They said you're in the book."

Damn.

Yeah!

What did I really feel?

Anger certainly. Fear. Deep and abiding longing to keep this conversation going forever.

"Tess, where can I meet you? Neutral territory if you like."

"Do you know Bill's Café on Bancroft, right off Macadam?" Two blocks away. Surely I could manage to hobble two blocks on my crutches. No way I could drive my car with a stick shift. Maybe I could hotwire Steve's rental ... No, he was leaving at zero dark thirty and returning the car. Allie was staying with me. I wouldn't ask her to drive.

"I'll find it. Eight-thirty tomorrow ... this morning?"

"Why not earlier?" He'd always been an early riser, even after a late night of deep conversation and a bottle of single malt between us.

"I can't get away until eight when Julia's nurse is available. Then I have to be back at the college for a ten o'clock class."

"Back up. Julia? Your wife is with you and not locked up in an insane asylum?" I started shaking with chills that began in my gut and spread outward. My hands grew so cold I almost dropped the phone.

"She's had a remarkable breakthrough but I'm not comfortable leaving her alone ..."

I dropped the phone back in its cradle, cutting him off.

The phone rang again.

I turned it off without answering.

Too angry to cry, too filled with loneliness to think, eyes too full of tears to see the computer screen, I hauled myself off to my sofa, hugging a pillow so tight I burst the seams. It spewed down feathers, like a snowstorm had vomited all over my living room.

I watched tiny specks of white flutter to the floor at the same speed as the tears dripping off my cheeks.

As dawn crept around the edges of the blinds, I turned on the gas log in the fireplace and cleaned up the mess. I had to use a hand broom and dustpan while crawling. Scrap didn't help much, fluttering around, scattering clumps of feathers to the far corners.

I kept at my silent sweeping. No sense in letting Steve and Allie know how much I hurt.

Or Donovan.

AT EIGHT-THIRTY ON the dot I swung up to the front door of Bill's Café, sweating and limp with fatigue. Manipulating crutches is hard work. I had to stop and breathe deeply before figuring out the awkward process of getting through the heavy swinging door.

A long arm reached from behind and above me to hold the door open.

I knew that hand. Long fingers, hairless knuckles, ink stains on the middle finger.

"Thank you, Gollum." I had to close my eyes and force air into my lungs.

"I wasn't sure you'd show up," he said softly.

I couldn't not show up.

He looked damp and a bit rumpled. His usual polo shirt and khakis had lost their crispness. I hoped I looked less battered by life than he.

Fat chance.

Bill, the café owner, bustled up and swung the door open further. Balding, middle-aged, once heavy but slimming down nicely from all the hard work of owning, managing, and cooking in his own place, Bill and

I had struck up a friendship right after I moved into the neighborhood, a week after he opened.

"Tess, what happened?" He ushered me to a center table and pulled an extra chair over for me to prop my foot on.

"I tripped while jogging." I followed him very slowly.

"Tsk, tsk. You must be more careful. You're my best customer. I might have to close down if you stopped coming."

Fat chance of that. People filled the line of booths under the windows on two walls. The five tables in the middle of the long narrow room were mostly occupied as well.

Big windows offered a glimpse of the river between tall office buildings across the highway, and a good look at the state of the rain. I'd learned that in the Pacific Northwest people depend upon a lot of big windows to let as much light in as possible. We consider the sun a UFO.

Maybe that's why we have such excellent coffee, to brighten our moods when the sun can't do it.

"Nothing's broken. You won't get rid of me so easily," I quipped back.

"The regular, Tess?" he asked, helping me settle.

"Yeah, the regular. Black coffee and whole wheat toast with strawberry jam."

Gollum quirked a questioning eyebrow at me. Then he handed his menu back to Bill without looking at it or sitting. "Pancake sandwich. Eggs over medium, patty sausage. Blackberry syrup if you have it. Coffee with cream and sugar."

At least one of us hadn't changed appetites. And he hadn't tried to change my order to something more substantial. Donovan would have, in the name of taking care of me.

As I dropped into a seat ungracefully, Gollum gently raised my injured foot to rest upon the extra chair. "That should be more comfortable for you."

"You've talked to JJ and Raquel so you know what happened." I fingered the pearls nervously, wondering if I'd have had better luck in the forest if I'd worn them.

"Yes."

We stared at each other in uncomfortable silence.

"Do you still have Gandalf?" I asked about the long-haired white lump of a cat Gollum took everywhere.

"Of course. He's quite the elderly gentleman now. Spends more time sitting on the windowsill looking out than anything else. But he has become quite attached to Julia. She needs him."

"Oh." His wife again.

"What are you teaching this term?" I finally asked just to break the silence.

Bill brought us big eggplant-colored pottery mugs and an emerald thermal carafe of coffee—freshly ground beans, dark roast, the house specialty. A ceramic cream pitcher in Bill's colors and a clear sugar dispenser were already on the table along with cutlery wrapped in printed, paper napkins also in the same deep colors.

We fussed with the details of pouring and accessorizing our drinks.

"Oh, Tess, I almost forgot." Bill came back with a second pitcher, this one in beige plastic. "I laid in a supply of soy coffee creamer. You aren't my only lactose intolerant customer. Try it. If you don't like it, I'll get you a fresh cup. Your orders will be up in just a minute."

He left us alone again, too busy to chat. Although with the six booths and three tables nearly full we weren't really alone. Not the best place to carry on a private conversation about otherworldly critters I needed to fight with the Celestial Blade.

Gollum took a sip of his coffee, smiled and nodded at the excellent brew, then answered my question. "McLoughlin College hired me to teach all levels of anthropology, including a class on the persistence of old folklore into modern urban myths."

"Your area of expertise."

He nodded, falling back into silence.

"Why McLoughlin? With your credentials you could go anywhere."

"When I knew for sure I'd have Julia with me, I needed more than adjunct work, a term here, a year there. I applied to fifty different colleges. McLoughlin was the only one to offer a tenure track position. And it's three thousand miles away from Julia's mother. And mine."

"So, tell me about your wife's breakthrough." I had to know just how well she'd recovered after fifteen years of institutionalization. Maybe if I knew she was fully functioning in modern society I'd finally accept that Gollum was lost to me.

But if she were fully functional, why did she have a nurse? Why couldn't he leave her alone for more than a few minutes?

A small niggle of hope burned in my heart.

I squashed it.

"Julia's caregivers noticed years ago that on Wednesdays she was bright, cheerful, and coherent. Then on Thursdays her mother visited—blew in and took over. Within the hour, Julia reverted to mute wandering, and refusing to acknowledge her surroundings, or other people. By the following Wednesday she was on the road to recovery again."

"Until her mother descended and convinced her she was useless, a hypochondriac, and a drain on her resources," I finished the thought.

My own relationship with my mother had been weird, but at the end we'd found rapport. Mostly I'd given up running my life in a futile attempt to win her approval. She'd never acknowledge that I could do anything right until ... until after Donovan's foster father died. But she depended on me to take care of her, no matter what guise she put on her actions.

"How'd you get her mother to stop exerting control over Julia, keeping her dependent and useless?"

"Bridget found a new charity. She's turning vacant lots into mini parks, planting trees and community gardens, and commissioning murals on ugly walls. She doesn't have time to run up to Boston every week." He flashed a half smile. Just a brief glimpse of the warped sense of humor we shared.

"Are you well? Other than the bunged up ankle that is?" he asked before I could pursue the topic of his wife.

"Mostly."

We fell back into silence that lasted until Bill brought our plates. He fussed about for a moment, refilling coffee mugs, grabbing extra butter, and satisfying himself that we wouldn't starve in the next few moments if he left us to tend other patrons.

"I found a psychiatric nurse who works swing shift at the local hospital," Gollum blurted out between bites. "I give her room and board. She gives Julia companionship when I'm tied up at the college."

"Precautionary or necessary?" No polite way to ask that.

"Necessary. Julia had a couple of relapses early on, short-lived, but scary when they happen. Nothing serious for nearly three months now." He stared at his half finished meal.

I wanted to ditch my toast. Bill had put too much butter on it.

We both found solace in coffee.

"I'm not sharing her bed," Gollum finally said. He kept his mug close to his mouth, muffling his words.

My heart skipped a beat and my breath caught in my throat. I don't know why. I was the one who ended our affair. I couldn't carry on with a married man and I couldn't ask him to divorce the woman who always asked for him first during her moments of coherence.

"I'm sorry, Gollum, I can't do this. I need all of you or nothing." I knew that he was safe if not happy.

More than I could say for myself with the Nörglein preying on women in the hills above Portland.

I fumbled for my crutches and ended up losing my balance, banging my cast on the floor and nearly falling off my chair.

Gollum was right there helping me with a strong hand. He settled me on my feet and escorted me to the door after flinging money on the table. More than enough to cover the bill and a generous tip.

"Take this file, Tess. I printed out something that might help you. Call me if there's anything else. But please, I beg you, don't go deeper into this until you heal." He handed me a manila file folder from the folds of his leather jacket.

"I'm going to High Desert Con in three weeks. I should be mostly healed by then," I mentioned the science fiction convention in Pasco, Washington where we'd first gotten to know each other and begun our adventure with rebellious teen Sasquatch and hellhounds out of Indian legends. "I won't do anything about the Nörglein until after that."

"I'll hold you to that." He kissed my cheek and ran off into the rain, disappearing into the mist rising from the river. As substantial as a dream.

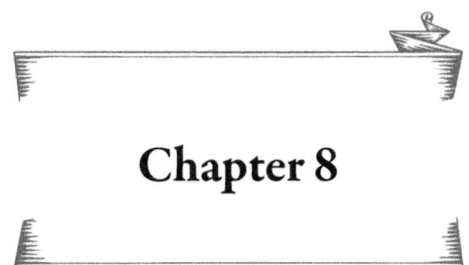

Chapter 8

*D*epression *from too much rain and too many cloudy days in a row in western Oregon led to a diagnosis of SAD—Seasonal Affected Disorder or light deprivation depression—in 1872 by historian Frances Fuller Victor.*

"I'm in a holding pattern," I told myself. "Just waiting. I can't do anything about the Nörglein until I'm fit and cast-free again." I repeated the mantra later that week at dawn as I watched from my balcony the sunrise behind Mt. Hood. This morning I watched a lessening of the dark more than an increase in light.

Winter approached.

Maybe if I said the phrase often enough, I'd feel less frustrated and channel all my energy into writing. Two pages yesterday. That's all I managed.

But that's two more pages than you're used to doing, Scrap reminded me.

I cradled my hot cup of coffee in my hands and repeated my words.

"If I have to stay cooped up in this apartment, I'll go crazy."

Crazier, Scrap commented from his perch on the railing.

"I need to do something, *anything.* What do you think about contacting Doreen Cooper to get those photos?"

You aren't going to Cooper's by yourself.

"No. I know I can't confront that nest of Damiri demons on my own. What about neutral territory? I'll meet her for coffee at Bill's." I hadn't been back to my favorite café since meeting Gollum there. What better image to banish his association with the place than my wicked sister-in-law?

Scrap just shrugged. He shifted to straddle the railing and stare at the depths of the river. It ran swift and dark today, swollen by recent rain. He reminded me of a curious cat.

"See anything interesting out there?"

Not today. But soon. Something important is connected to that river. I just don't know what yet.

The cell phone in my pocket droned a phrase from "Dance Macabre." I'd changed it back to the *Star Wars* theme, but somehow, no matter what phone I had, the ring tone changed daily to the weird and weirder.

"Speak of the demon." I recognized Doreen's private number on the screen. The ring tone fit. It always did.

"Why are you putting me off, Tess?" she asked without preamble.

"I'm not anymore." I gave her directions to Bill's.

"I'm in the area. I'll buy you breakfast. Twenty minutes."

"Make it thirty." The thought of the long trek on crutches didn't appeal to me in the least. Next week I'd get a boot over the cast or something so I could actually walk. Today, I was still handicapped.

You're building upper body strength, Scrap reminded me cheerfully as I dressed in navy blue sweats—the only slacks I could pull over the cast. *When you're fit again you'll be swinging the Celestial Blade around like a toy.*

I snorted something impolite.

One half minute before the appointed time I wrestled with the swinging door at my favorite café.

Donovan of all people jumped to help me.

"You? Why are you here?"

He shrugged and motioned me toward a booth in the back corner.

"How long before I can expect my favorite customer to manage the door on her own?" Bill asked from behind the prep counter.

"Soon. I miss this place. And you." I gave him a genuine smile.

"That's my girl. Coffee, of course. Something more substantial?"

"Don't know yet."

"Someone is waiting for you," Donovan reminded me.

"She commandeered the back corner booth like she owned the place," Bill whispered as I stumped past him. "He seems to be taking orders from her."

Totally unlike the Donovan I knew. My hackles rose. "Careful or they might leverage you out," I replied sotto voce.

"Is that worse than 'careful or I'll put you in my novel'?"

"About equal." This time I wasn't joking. More than one Kajiri demon had been embarrassed by a thinly disguised, not very flattering, version of themselves in one of my books. A few normals, too. Nothing I could get sued over though.

"I'll leave you two to talk. Call me when you're ready to leave, Doreen," Donovan said. He leaned over and gave her a gentle kiss on the top of her head.

Huh?

Doreen lifted her gaze from the depths of her coffee cup, black, no sugar or cream to add extra calories, and with a jerk of her head granted me permission to sit.

I did. Awkwardly. But I had a better vantage point to study her.

Her espresso-brown eyes tracked Donovan to the door and along the window line to his car in the back of the lot.

That was why I hadn't seen the distinctive vehicle before I entered the building. That, and being preoccupied with the cumbersome crutches.

Dill's sister had twisted her thick mane of black hair into an intricate knot on her nape. A white streak from each temple drew dramatic lines up and away from her full cheeks, making her face look thinner than it was.

Her elegantly cut black slacks and blazer over a pale pink blouse disguised her robust curves, bordering on Junoesque. Two-inch heels on her sensible pumps would add to her above normal height, furthering the illusion of slenderness.

She looked Damiri through and through.

Except for the pearls, so fine and translucent, they picked up hints of pink from her skin and her blouse. Her strand appeared to be a duplicate of my own. I touched mine through my sweatshirt just to make sure Doreen hadn't stolen them.

The hair on my nape rose and my Warrior scar throbbed.

"Oh," she said flatly as I scooted and shifted to find a comfortable position with the leg elevated. Her gaze remained fixed on my cheek. She could see the scar. That confirmed her demon ancestry.

Not all half-breed demons are menaces to normals. A lot of them want to blend in more than they want to highlight their otherness.

Scrap remained transparent. No hint of pink or red to warn of danger.

"Just, oh? No hello? No, 'how've you been for the last four years'? Just, oh?"

So much for family reunions. I noted that she no longer wore a wedding set on her left hand and wondered what had happened to the husband she clung to at Dill's funeral. I couldn't even remember his name or what he looked like. Just a vague shadow. But then I'd been so filled with grief, and the beginning of a raging fever, I barely remembered my own name at the time.

"I ... I expected ... I don't know. Maybe this was a mistake." She rose as if to leave.

"Not yet, Doreen." I blocked her exit from the booth with a crutch.

She settled back with her coffee.

Scrap took a seat on the back of Doreen's bench. He stuck his tongue out at her, then reclined, crooked his arm to support his head, and settled in to listen intently.

He faded so transparent and remained so still I had trouble seeing him. Clear evidence that I could forget his presence and we'd compare notes later.

Doreen offered me no threat.

Bill came over with my coffee and soy creamer. He helped me twist and leverage the cast onto the seat beside me. I thanked him and took a sip of his excellent brew.

"Can I get you ladies some biscotti or pie? Maybe a late breakfast?" Bill hovered a little longer than necessary. A friend showing caution around an unknown.

"Nothing for me," Doreen said. She didn't have to look at her full hips. All Damiri developed weight problems in middle age. Only the most rigorous diet and exercise kept the pounds off.

When I'd known Dill, he'd still been young and active, maintaining a slender and well-muscled body. A lovely body. And a keen mind.

I ached with missing him for a very long time. Now I ached for a different absent man.

"I'll have the huckleberry pie." I loaded another spoonful of sugar into my coffee.

"You have pursued me, almost to the point of stalking for several months, Doreen. Why?"

"Donovan says I need to give you these." She handed me a large manila envelope. "I'm not your enemy, Tess, no matter what impression my parents have given you."

"They haven't done anything hostile, just ignored me, pretended my marriage to Dill never happened."

"I loved Dill. We were very close. Circumstances... I'm sorry we didn't get a chance to know each other when he was alive."

I accepted her apology with a nod. Then I peeked inside the envelope. Sure enough there were a couple of faded photos of me and Steve and our sister Cecilia from our teen years. As usual Cecilia managed to give the illusion she stood separate from Steve and me.

But there was also a picture of me and Dill, arms draped around each other, staring lovingly into each other's eyes. The rough, violently sculpted terrain behind us belonged in the high desert of central Washington State. I pulled it out and looked closer. Of our three months together, only one week had been spent rock hounding on the Columbia Basin Plateau. I wore my hair longer then, pulled back into a tight ponytail. A few unruly curls always escaped, framing my face in corkscrew tendrils. I hadn't Doreen's grace to disguise the fifty extra pounds I'd carried then.

Delicately I traced the line of Dill's jaw with my fingertip. Almost reverently I brushed the same finger over the few white hairs at his temples.

Then I closed my eyes against tears I thought I'd forgotten how to shed.

I recognized Dill's plaid shirt with the sleeves rolled up over tanned and muscular forearms.

My breath caught in my throat.

"You okay?" Doreen asked. She looked almost concerned.

I handed the photo back to her. "Where did you get this?"

"It was in the stack with the others."

"No, it wasn't. I've never seen this photo before. It was taken the day before Dill died. I don't remember posing for it. I don't remember anyone being around to snap it five miles from nowhere in a deep arroyo between gouged cliffs."

"Shit! That's why Donovan said you needed to see it."

"Shit is right. Who took this photo and why do you have it?"

"I don't know who took it. My guess ... only a guess but based on other information ... it was Darren Estevez. Probably through a high-powered telephoto lens."

"Donovan's foster father."

"Your stepfather."

I snorted at that. "Darren's marriage to my mother only lasted two and a half days before he was murdered. Now my mother is dead too. Donovan and I have no more connections. How'd the photo get mixed up with the others?"

"Planted among Dill's books and academic papers along with the legitimate photos. Darren needed us to know he was the one who set the fire."

"He had an accomplice."

"How ...?"

"I was there." Actually, I didn't find that out until I went back. Imps can time travel if they have to. Scrap didn't want to do it, but he'd taken me back to that fateful night so I could see who had murdered my husband. I'd seen Darren clearly. His helper remained in the shadows behind him.

"I have no idea who worked with Darren then. Oh." She paused and put her hand over her mouth.

"What?"

"My guess about that time isn't as well-educated."

"Donovan comes to mind."

"No," she said emphatically. "More like his assistant, Quentin. His loyalty has always gone to the highest bidder. Darren could buy and sell Donovan twenty times over."

I spread the full contents of the envelope on the table. Two printouts from a Web site followed the photos. Duplicates of the information Gollum had given me about the Nörglein, including the critter's full name.

Names have power. Knowing it could be an advantage. If I chose to use it.

"Want to explain that?" We both knew this was why she'd pursued me so relentlessly. The photos were just an excuse, or a diversion.

"No. I suspect it's information you need. Donovan prepared the envelope."

I met her gaze with silence.

"Okay, he said you needed that information when I saw him using my computer and printer. He had the information on a flash drive. Is he," she tapped the printouts of the Nörglein with a long fingernail painted pale pink to match her blouse, "the reason you're on crutches?"

"Yes."

"Then, I'm sorry. You can't help me. I need a Warrior capable of standing on her own two feet." She stood up and threw a ten dollar bill on the table. "Enjoy your pie. It's on me. I won't bother you again."

As she strode gracefully toward the door, I detected a trace of moisture in the corner of her eye.

"Bother me. How and why are you connected to ... this person?" I held up the printout.

"Not today." She exited with less grace than I'd expect from her. Donovan pulled into the parking lot after circling the block a couple of times. He got out and helped her into the passenger seat, fastening the seat belt for her.

"What do you make of this, Scrap?"

She's hurting. He's worried about her.

"Obvious."

Eat your pie. You've strength to regain before you clump back home again. I have a feeling life is going to get messy. Again.

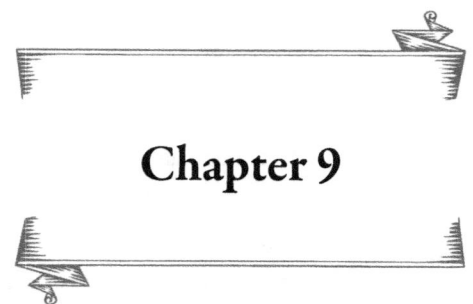

Chapter 9

A 1978 survey in "The Oregonian" reported that most denizens of Oregon welcome the return of rain each autumn.

When I finally got home again, damp and exhausted, I flopped onto the sofa, foot propped up on three pillows. Allie brought me soup and crackers at about noon.

Days passed. I wrote a little. The manuscript grew slowly. Too slowly for my liking. When the words refused to budge out of my brain I retreated to the balcony. I had things to think about. Doreen left me more puzzled than informed. She needed help. From a Warrior of the Celestial Blade.

Why?

Her demon blood should make us natural enemies.

Only another interdimensional creature could threaten her. The Nörglein came to mind. Why else would she bring me information on how to banish the bastard?

I knew the dark elf had some kind of connection to Cooper's Furniture Emporium. What had he done that Doreen needed help getting rid of him?

The rain faded to a thick mist and the wind died down. A tug hauling three long barges headed north, toward the ports on the Columbia River. I followed it with my gaze as it disappeared into the thick air beyond the bridge.

Things lurked in the mist and shadows. Things more dangerous than gravel barges on the river.

I heard a car door slam. Nothing between me and the river but a public paved path and access to a marina. All the cars were parked on the other side of the building. Whoever disturbed the midday, mid-week quiet had packed some anger into the closing of the car for me to hear it so clearly.

Serious footsteps clanged on the exterior staircase; I felt the vibrations in the railing.

Knowing my neighbors and their routine visitors, I suspected I was the target of all that energy. With a sigh, I pivoted clumsily and wrestled with the French door that wanted to close too quickly in the increasing breeze at my back.

I had no idea if Allie had retreated to the bedroom or gone out to avoid my moody silence or not.

"Who is it, Scrap?"

Hrmf t hmmm grblt.

Since I was out of action Scrap spent more time with Ginkgo than he did with me.

Jealous? Scrap came through clearer.

"Get your ass back here. We've company of the unpleasant kind."

I hobbled over to the door, opening it at the first trace of a knock, before the visitor could pound it to smithereens.

"Why, Donovan, how good to see you. Would you like a cup of coffee?" I hadn't seen him since he'd dropped off and picked up Doreen from the café two weeks ago.

"How'd you do it, Tess?" he snarled. His fists clenched at his sides and his face darkened with suffused blood. The copper highlights in his skin grew dominant. His chocolate-colored eyes became deep holes of blackness.

The force of his emotions pushed me backward, almost physically. I raised my hand to the talisman of my pearls. They didn't help. This must have been what Scrap felt whenever he and Donovan were in the same room before Scrap overcame the darkness in his soul, the repellant force field of an active gargoyle.

He's human now, I reminded myself. *He's no longer a gargoyle.*

I turned away and fussed with the coffeemaker in the kitchen rather than face him. "How'd I do what?" I returned.

"I've just come from my appeal on the custody hearing for my daughter."

"I gather that it did not go well. MoonFeather retains custody." My aunt hadn't called in tears to tell me she'd lost the baby. Therefore, she hadn't been forced to turn Lilly over to Donovan.

I added soy creamer and sugar to my cup along with fresh coffee. Donovan's cup of black brew remained untouched on the counter.

"Your aunt has no right to my daughter. I'm Lilly's father." He moved closer, looming over me with barely controlled anger.

I had the crutches to fend him off if necessary.

"King Scazzy, prison warden of the Universe, ordered MoonFeather to raise WindScribe's child," I replied mildly.

"That has no bearing in mundane courts. Lilly is *my* daughter."

"So, what did I do to push the courts to honor MoonFeather's commitment to the baby? She is darling. Only nine months old and trying to walk already." My aunt emailed me pictures every week.

"My DNA test. How'd you get it altered? According to the lab my genes aren't even close to Lilly's." He wrapped his hand around the coffee mug like he wished it was my neck and he could strangle me.

"I did nothing. Perhaps Lilly isn't your daughter. Perhaps WindScribe slept with someone else." I shrugged and moved past him into the living room. If I had to defend myself I wanted space. "Rumor has it she seduced the king of Faery just before she killed him."

Scrap, I think I need you.

Coming. He popped into view behind Donovan's head, his wings beating wildly enough to create a draft. He bared his multiple rows of dagger-shaped teeth and made ugly faces. Then he turned his hind end toward our guest and farted so loud and noxiously I was sure Donovan could hear and smell it.

If Donovan did, he didn't let it divert him from stalking me.

Scrap landed on my shoulder, glowing pink. He prepared to turn into the blade and defend us. But he stayed pink, not vermilion. Donovan wanted to scare me, not hurt me.

"You and I both know that Lilly is mine."

"WindScribe did not name you as the father. She did sign a paper requesting MoonFeather, her mentor and friend, adopt her child. The courts agreed."

"I am Lilly's father. How'd you alter my DNA test showing differently?"

"I didn't."

"You must have. No one else ..."

"King Scazzamurieddu has more reason than I to keep you away from the baby."

"He wouldn't dare."

"Why not? What are you going to do, tattle on him to the Powers That Be?" My insides quaked in memory of my one and only interview with the board of seven beings, each from a different dimension, each with a different agenda, each shadowed deep within a robe's cowl, and unidentifiable.

"Why have you dared breach our portal?" I heard again the deep booming voice. A ten-foot tentacle stretched across the tall judicial bench toward my throat. "What are you prepared to offer in return for your audacity?"

Forcibly, I yanked myself away from that memory.

"Oh, God, they're still punishing me," Donovan gasped, dropping onto the sofa. He set the cup down and buried his face in his hands.

Scrap faded back to his normal grey-green. *Time for a snack, babe. We going out or eating in?*

I didn't answer him.

In. He popped out, probably to the laundry room in the basement where mold grew thick and deep behind the washing machines.

"Maybe they are ensuring Lilly is loved and cared for by the best person for her to learn about life, from both sides of the chat room. Maybe they need you to settle down and live a normal life with a wife and no more plans to create a homeland for half-breed demons before entrusting you with a precious child," I said soothingly.

"Marry me. Help me prove that I'm the best person to raise my daughter." He looked up, catching my gaze and holding it.

"Sorry. Wrong formula again." His third proposal and he still didn't get it that he needed to ask me because he wanted me, just me, to be the love of his life. He always put his agenda ahead of that, not realizing that if he loved me, and me him, then I'd gladly help him with anything he needed. "Why don't you discuss it with your girlfriend? I believe you are seeing Doreen."

"Doreen can't compare to you and what you and I have together, what we can do for each other. What's it going to take to convince you that we belong together? The other women are just diversions to distract me from you." He rose up to his full six feet of height, shoulders hunching upward in anger again.

"Figure out what I need and we might have something. Until then, I'm sorry you can't have Lilly. Maybe you should move to Cape Cod. Then you could at least visit her more often."

"If you're trying to get rid of me, I don't have to move three thousand miles away. Good-bye."

The doorframe shook for long seconds after he slammed it in his wake.

ALLIE HUMMED SOFTLY as she thumbed off her phone.

"So, when's the wedding?" I asked casually. Since I'd discarded the crutches in favor of an ugly strap-on boot over the cast—Dr. Sean still refused the lighter air cast, wanting to keep me as immobile as possible—I'd retaken control of my kitchen. In a few minutes we'd have fish baked in a gentle lime and mango chutney sauce, brown rice pilaf, and a salad with a variety of fresh local produce from the farmers market.

At least I had an appetite again. My brain had only partially awakened along with my stomach. I'd added three chapters to my manuscript, enough to send to my editor as proof of my progress. That should buy another extension on the due date.

Unfortunately, I couldn't squeeze any more money out of them until I finished the book. Maybe my royalty statement next month could breathe some life into my checking account.

"We have to decide some things before we set a date," Allie said. Her dreamy-eyed gaze and humming halted abruptly. She began twisting her ring round and round her finger.

Until that moment, she'd looked happier and more relaxed than I'd seen her in a long time.

Uh oh, trouble in Lovesville, Scrap chomped down on his cigar. *Don't want to hear it. Don't want to deal with it.* He flew from his perch on the wine glass rack, which now held two glasses, through the closed French doors onto the patio.

"Decide what?" I hadn't asked why she lingered in my apartment a week after she'd been cleared of wrongdoing on her job, two weeks after Steve returned to his house and job in Illinois.

"If I want to go back to being a cop. Do we want to live in Chicago," she mumbled almost inaudibly. "Can I stand living in Cape Cod if I'm not a cop? Can Steve tolerate going home again? Can we find jobs out here?"

A long moment of silence. What did I say to that?

"Tess, I've wanted to leave home for a long time. But I didn't dare get too far away from The House without you there to guard it. How could you leave that vulnerable plot of neutral ground containing the right energies to open a rogue portal to a demon dimension? How could you leave your father and his husband alone with no protection?"

"Your cop partner can guard it," I mumbled.

"Mike went back to Miami."

"Say again?" I'd heard her. I needed confirmation.

"Mike, the part water demon, went back to Miami now that Darren Estevez no longer holds his family hostage. The House is wide open to attack."

"Would you believe I took out some insurance before I left?"

"What kind of insurance?"

The scar on my face grew hot and knife fresh. I was surprised Allie couldn't see it glowing. "Insurance that cost me a lot."

I set my chin in an expression she had to know meant I would say no more.

I couldn't say more.

My hand shook as badly as it had when I held a very special onyx fountain pen. I felt it between my fingers, watched myself dip the nib in a pool of my own blood and sign my name. My full name that only my mother used: Teresa Louise Noncoiré. With each stroke my veins and arteries filled with searing warmth, a precursor to the flames that would consume the document and myself from within if I ever violated that contract of silence or returned to The House for more than five days at a stretch.

The House stood on neutral ground. It had to remain in neutral hands. As a Warrior of the Celestial Blade I was decidedly not neutral. My dad and his partner were.

Donovan had signed a similar oath about his past as a gargoyle after he fell. I'd had to figure out his "Big Secret" on my own.

Allie set her chin in a similar stubbornness to mine. "Tomorrow morning I'm going to make some calls, start looking for a new career." She pocketed her phone decisively and rose from her curled position on the end of the sofa.

"Doing what?"

She shrugged and began setting places for us on the bar.

"Allie, this isn't like you. You don't know how to not be a cop. I remember you breaking up a fistfight between two bullies when we were ten. You read them their rights!" I paused in scooping rice onto our plates. "I've driven patrol with you, helped close down bar fights. Being a cop is who you are."

"I know." Her eyes moistened. "Police work made me feel useful. I could protect ordinary people, make the streets a tad safer, bring a sense of order and balance into our chaotic world."

"But then life showed an ugly side you want to run away from." *Been there, done that. Just now crawling out from under my rock.*

"Yeah. I can't be a good cop if I'm looking at every teen as a potential drug addict, every poorly dressed female with a passel of children she can't afford to feed as a potential thief." She gulped and closed her eyes. "Every adult male as a potential child abuser and rapist." She bowed her head and turned her back on me.

Welcome to my world. Only I look for demons, not criminals. Same thing, I guess. There's a reason Earth has no demon ghetto. We are our own demons.

I gave her a couple of moments to master her emotions.

"So what will you do?"

"Steve's not really happy in Chicago. So he's pursuing some leads in the job market in the Portland area."

"What about you?"

She shrugged again.

"Allie. You can hide from yourself, but you can't hide from me." Just like I'd tried a number of times to hide from myself, only to have her ferret out the truth.

"I got my masters in criminal justice while you were off getting yours in demon fighting. I'm looking into teaching at the Police Academy, maybe one of the community colleges." She finally looked me in the eye. "Gollum gave me some leads."

So that's what she'd been hiding. Not the change in career, but the source of her contacts.

Gollum was keeping tabs on me through my best friend.

"You're welcome to stay with me for a while," I said quietly. "I have really enjoyed having you here, appreciated your help while I recover. I still need you to drive me."

"Thanks, Tess. I'll repay you, someday, somehow."

"You'll earn your keep next week driving two hundred miles each way to High Desert Con."

"That's where you met Dill. Where your friend from college got killed."

"Yeah, I've got a lot of memories tied up with that Science Fiction convention. Time I stopped running away from them." And myself.

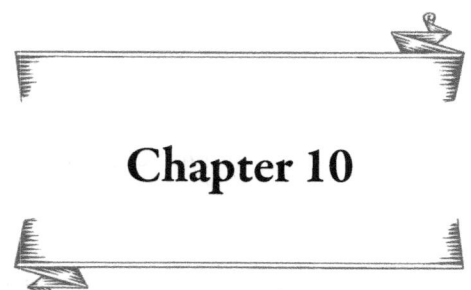

Chapter 10

E nglish Ivy was imported to Portland by early settlers to remind them of home. It escaped and now threatens to strangle entire forests of native trees.

"Tess!" a female alto voice that bordered on a tenor called from across the hotel lobby.

I looked up from signing a registration form for Allie and me. Allie had driven me the two hundred miles east of Portland to Pasco, Washington, home of the High Desert Con.

"Squishy!" I called back, beckoning the squarely built, forty something woman with board straight hair dyed an impossible blonde. I knew no other name for her than the handle she used on-line and for con badges.

"I need to talk to you," my acquaintance said on an urgent whisper.

"Go have a cup of coffee. And put your foot up. I'll take the luggage to our room." Allie urged me toward the garden café in the middle of the hotel ground floor. She hoisted her overnight bag and dragged my wheeled suitcase toward one of the sprawling wings. The desk clerk had taken one look at my booted cast and walking staff and changed our room from the quiet third floor at the far end of the most inaccessible wing to a close handicap room on the ground floor.

I'd have to remember that trick next year. Might save me about three miles of walking each day.

Scrap turned bright yellow and popped out of my vision. He loved exploring conventions, sniffing out who wore a costume and who used costumes as an excuse to shape-change into demon form. Most of the attending demons were relatively benign, just trying to fit into modern society. A con gave them the chance to let their hair down, so to speak, and be themselves.

Donovan claimed that these were the Kajiri demons he worked to find a homeland for, the ones who were too human to live as a demon and too much a demon to truly live as human all of the time. They needed to shape-change at least once a month and take an occasional sip of blood.

Gave new meaning to "That time of the month."

I suspected from oblique conversations that Donovan really dealt with those Kajiri who used their human facade to prey upon the innocent. The closer to their demon roots they remained, the more they needed hot fresh blood to survive.

Lady Lucia Continelli actually lived as a vampire in Las Vegas, finding it a more socially acceptable way to drink blood than admitting her very dilute demon heritage. In fact, Lady Lucia hadn't craved blood until she tasted some as part of her facade. She worked hard at maintaining her image as the vampire crime boss of Sin City.

"What's up, Squishy?" I asked, stumping toward the café.

"Something weird I need advice on. But more important, what happened to you?" She claimed a booth just inside the arched entrance to the eating area.

Artificial shrubs and a chest-high brick wall gave the illusion of separating patrons from the mass of convention goers. Illusion only. We could check out and be checked out by all those who wandered around in search of old friends.

"I tripped over a blackberry vine while jogging," I muttered as I plopped into my seat and scooted toward the wall so I could stretch my leg sideways along the bench.

"You know that I'm a nurse. Anything I can do to help?"

"I guessed you were a healthcare professional from the detailed answers you give to research questions on our email list." I shifted and squirmed to get more comfortable. The four-hour drive in a small car had been a nightmare. Now my foot had swelled because I hadn't been able elevate it.

"What did you break?" She peered at the redness of my exposed toes.

"Soft tissue damage. The doctor put the cast on to keep me off it and slow me down. He didn't trust me with an air cast. If I could figure a way to saw it off I would. At least I'm not still on crutches."

"Don't." She glared at me sternly. "And get some ice on your toes, soon."

Our coffee came and I dumped sugar into it, thought about indulging in the savory richness of real cream, and settled for packets of dry whitener I carried with me. I'd had one bout of lactose intolerance—inherited from my tight bond with Scrap—and studiously avoided all dairy products ever after.

"It hurts. I may have to do a bar con this year," I muttered.

"I've never known you to sit still long enough to let the con come to you in the bar or the café," she laughed, more of a snort.

"So, what's so weird it couldn't wait?" I kept half an eye on the increasing crowd wandering the open area in and around the café. The con didn't officially start until noon the next day, but early arrivals were beginning the party already.

"First off, I brought a ... er ... friend to the con. It's her first. Her husband reads a lot of SF and attends the occasional con. She wants to understand the attraction and I'm trying..."

"You want to protect her from the weirdest of the weird."

"Yeah. She'll probably spend most of the con in the room reading or with costumers. But ... um..."

"My word of honor I won't mention this conversation to you again except in deepest privacy. Now, what is so weird you have to talk to me about it?"

"Back to being a nurse: I've worked most every department at one time or another. So, even though I'm now in a specialty ward, when other departments get busy I fill in. Last month I did a stint in the ER. On the night of the full moon, a Tuesday I believe, I assisted in an emergency C-section. We didn't have time to get the mother to surgery. Didn't even have time to get an OB GYN resident out of bed... except they were all busy in their ward with deliveries." Her ruddy complexion paled a bit and stress lines around her eyes and mouth deepened. That experience must not have been pretty.

"I hear that happens fairly frequently on the night of the full moon."

"It does. But not like this one."

"I'm a fantasy writer. Why do you need to talk to me about a medical problem?"

"The whole thing felt like something from one of your books." She studied her milky tea as if it held the answers to all universal mysteries. "Or one of my horror short stories. Not sure where to draw the line between horror and dark fantasy these days."

I'd never read her fiction. Maybe I should search it out.

"Describe the baby." I sat straighter, instantly alert. Scrap had told me about the scaly skin and wood scent of newborns with hysterical mothers. "You know that reality is often more horrific than fiction," I hedged. "Describe the baby."

Squishy dropped her gaze back into the depths of her tea. "When he first came out, breech, the skin looked dark. Mom is Caucasian. I hadn't met the father, but mixed couples aren't unusual anymore, so I didn't question it. As more and more of him presented, the skin looked mottled, scaly, like bark. And he had one tuft of green hair that looked like moss. His cries were weak—he was about five weeks premature—sounded like tree limbs sawing together in the wind. But his eyes... red and very aware."

My gut sank. "What ... what did you do?"

"The attending and I sort of stared at each other. I could tell he was thinking the same thing I was, some kind of terrible birth defect. We wondered if it would be kinder to everyone involved if we just sort of.... We'd never do it, but sometimes we think it might solve a lot of problems." She shook her head as if rousing from a nightmare.

I wondered if in the same situation I'd have the courage to go through with a mercy killing of a horribly deformed baby.

"Then, before we could decide to do anything about it, the baby took a deep breath and squalled like a normal infant, and he just sort of morphed into a regular pink baby with a shock of dark brown hair on his head. The bark scales sloughed off. I saved them in a baggie but I haven't figured out how to get a DNA test and keep it anonymous."

"You're trying to tell yourself it was a trick of the light, but the image won't go away," I finished for her.

"Yeah."

"And the mom started screaming as if living a nightmare."

She nodded. "In the psych ward I'd seen another mother with the same reaction. The attending is researching to see if we have a new form of postpartum hysteria. I don't think it's from imbalanced hormones. I think there is something in the babies."

"So why talk to me about it? It was a trick of light. Mom had a stressful birth and was in a lot of pain."

"But..."

"Convince yourself it was a trick of the light. You'll be safer both physically and mentally. Burn the scales."

"The hysteria?"

"Uneducated women, or unemployed families subsisting on welfare, who barely know how to care for themselves let alone an infant."

"You're probably right."

"I am right. So why tell me about your nightmares? We're Internet and con acquaintances, not best friends."

"Word gets around. You have a reputation for stumbling into trouble and the explanations are a bit contrived. In this community, people believe in the stuff we write. Some other weird things have happened too. And I found that ER attending looking on the Internet for other 'woody' babies. I've begun to wonder just how blurred the boundaries between realities have become."

"Ground yourself in mundane details and you'll forget about it before long," I promised her. Actually I lied. I knew she'd never forget. I hadn't.

But then I had Scrap to remind me of my responsibilities to maintain a balance between dimensions.

Speaking of the brat, where had he gone?

Right here, babe. He flitted to my shoulder, an almost weight. He'd returned to his normal translucent gray-green. *Squishy's the nurse I saw in the psych ward with the first baby I noticed. You're safe with her.* He yawned.

Then, within another heartbeat he began to glow bright red.

Huh? Why the color of danger if I was safe with Squishy?

"There's another thing, Tess," Squishy set her chin and fixed my gaze. "There's a gang of kids here for the con."

"Three boys, two girls. Their costumes look an awful lot like that baby. They look too real to be latex. Woody skin, mossy hair, and red contact lenses." I described the phalanx of Nörglein flowing out from the glass corridor that led to the party wing. "Their jeans and T-shirts are brand new, fresh out of the package, never been washed. Since when do teens at cons look like store models?"

Yeah, that's what I was going to tell you.

A HUSH FALLS OVER THE hotel lobby. Time seems to jerk into a new flow. The humans are moving slowly, like treading water. All light concentrates on the forest children and my Tess.

I smell rotting vegetables and putrid water. My body needs to stretch and sharpen.

Tess sits, wounded and inert. She cannot fight. We cannot fight here in a public place.

The compulsion to transform into the twin, half moon blades makes my every bone and muscle ache. My ears elongate and meld together above my head. My tail stretches and curves, flattens into half a scimitar.

Not yet.

I cannot go beyond this until Tess commands me. And yet the need is so powerful I wonder that I continue to live half in one state, half in another.

"Um ... Tess, what's that red glob on your shoulder?" Squishy asks, pointing directly at me.

Apparently, the forest teens see me too. They stop short in their march around the central lobby. The youngest boy hesitates and half turns as if ready to retreat back up one of the arms of the hotel.

The girl next to him grabs his arm. "Don't even think about it!" she chides him. I hear a bit of German—or maybe it's old Italian—in her accent.

Yep, these kids were raised by a Nörglein.

I don't believe in coincidence. Our Nörglein sent them to deal with my Tess.

My body feels as if every joint will twist into a huge knot if Tess doesn't command my transformation this very instant.

The kids turn to their right and head toward the conference center where the gamers are setting up in one of the divided ballrooms.

They stop just shy of the double doors they seek. Donovan, dressed all in black, as usual, stands in their way. They exchange quiet words and the kids slink out into the parking lot. He starts to follow them, thinks better of it, and heads to the registration desk.

He has no luggage. We've never seen him carry any. But he always has clean, freshly pressed clothes.

Doreen joins him at the desk. She's pulling a full-sized rolling suitcase. And she looks angry. She and Donovan exchange a few words. Then he smiles that all too charming smile, kisses her cheek, and saunters off. Doreen clenches her teeth and leaves finger impressions in the handle of her rolling suitcase. She's pissed. Really pissed. At Donovan?

I don't know if Tess sees her or not. Her focus remains on the double doors that block her view of the forest children.

The grinding heat inside me tamps down to glowing embers. I fade to dark pink.

Tess relaxes, or is that collapses, against the banquette of her booth. Her grip on her walking staff loosens and her knuckles turn from frigid snow to warming spring pink.

Squishy shakes her head and mutters something. She sits back as if she only imagined me.

When I see Allie circle around the café looking for us, I know my dahling Tess will be safe for a few moments.

"See ya, babe. I need a smoke." And I flit off in the opposite direction in dire need of some mold to soothe my frazzled nerves and upset tummy.

The high desert of the Columbia River Basin is notoriously dry and mold free. But I know a few air conditioners that need cleaning.

Chapter 11

Dandelion seeds first crossed the Rocky Mountain in the 1830s, brought by fur trappers for garden sass at spring green up. The plant escaped to become a nuisance. Now, the rich saw-toothed leaves are highly prized by restaurants for Oregon Field Green salads and the flowers for dandelion wine.

One forty-five a.m. on Saturday I held down a sofa on the outer reaches of the bar, waiting. Small knots of people littered the coffee shop and the hallways, talking quietly. On the ground floor of wing two, parties continued at high volume. The gamers played on in their enclosed ballroom, oblivious to the passage of the sun.

The bartender polished the bar one last time. All his paying customers had left. He eyed me suspiciously.

Reluctantly, I made a move toward heaving myself out of the soft cushiness of the sofa.

My prey strolled past, head swinging right and left as he searched for someone. Not me.

I flipped the end of my staff in front of his knees.

He spotted it just before he fell flat on his face.

"Want to help me up, Donovan?" I tried to look pitiful.

He scowled. One of his more attractive expressions. Actually, I don't think he had an ugly one. Too bad I'd grown immune to his beauty and his charm.

"No."

"Will you help me up? This cast is more than a bit awkward, even with the boot."

He stuck out an arm. We clasped elbows and he heaved. I almost flew past him into the lobby.

Without apology he tried to push past me.

I blocked his way with the staff again, but this time I held the knobby end decorated in turquoise and knotted leather level with his groin. "Why are you here, Donovan?"

"This is a public gathering. I have every right to be here."

"But why did you come?"

"This is my home con. I live about an hour north of here. Why shouldn't I come?"

"Because you don't read science fiction or fantasy. You live it. So does your girlfriend. I saw her check in but not since."

He shrugged as if disinterested. "It's none of your business."

"I'm making it my business."

"You threw me out. It's none of your business why I'm here or who I'm with. Jealous?" He flashed me a cocky grin.

"This con is my turf too. I intend to protect the normals that love this con and only came for a good time so they don't get mauled and maimed by your pet Kajiri. Like the ones who killed my friend, Bob."

"You're wasting your time and mine. I always come to this con to promote Halfling Games. You should have gone to bed hours ago. Do you need help getting to your room?"

"I'll take her," Squishy said from deep inside the bar.

I hadn't known she was there. Or why.

"Tess, you need ice on that foot again." Squishy wrapped an arm around my waist and propelled me in the direction of my wing. "I'm sticking close to you until I know more about those tree kids and what they're up to."

Donovan didn't follow us.

When I looked back he remained where we'd left him, a puzzled frown on his face.

"Is he one of the bad guys?" Squishy whispered when we were out of earshot.

"That changes from day to day, hour to hour," I replied.

"One of those," she snorted.

"What's that supposed to mean?"

"Read some of the gaming manuals from Halfling. Shape shifters and tricksters. Sometimes they are your best ally, sometimes, your worst enemy.

A roll of the dice says which. In real life we don't get a roll of the dice to tell us ahead of time which side they're on."

"I FEEL LIKE A STALKER," Allie whispered to me Saturday afternoon as we elbowed our way through the crowd in the wake of the only teens wearing store-fresh, stiff jeans and tees.

"We are stalking prey," I replied. My ankle ached. I'd been on my feet all day. When my foot was swollen, the cast fit snugly. After icing and elevation, every time I stood up, the cast slid down, banging on the injured tissue. Each time felt like Scrap was playing tic-tac-toe on my foot with one of his lit black cherry cheroots. Today it had swollen up again. No more banging, but now the cast was too tight, threatening to cut off circulation to my toes.

"You should sit down. Better yet, go back to the room and take a nap. You look like a zombie. I know how to follow suspects discreetly," Allie continued.

As much as possible, we'd followed the Nörglein teens. I still hadn't fathomed why they'd come to the con since they spent the majority of their time in role-playing games, the tabletop variety, not the live action.

I wished I dared take Allie's advice and sit. Truth be told, this was the first time in a year and a half I felt a stirring of my old self. I'd grown into the science fiction/fantasy community through conventions. My first professional sales had been short stories to editors I met at cons. I loved playing with colors and textures to create my own costumes. I was at home among these seriously weird folk.

"If I look like a zombie then I should fit right in with the other costumes. I wonder why the kids haven't gone into dark elf mode. Not just the people competing in the Masquerade tonight are dressing up," I said.

To prove my point, a Green Man—he looked benign like the fanciful plaques and medallions for sale in the vendors' room rather than evil, like the faces I'd seen in Forest Park—clothed in swaths of fake oak leaves and acorns, strode past us toward the grand ballroom where the costume competition gathered. A hefty woman with dozens of black braids, wearing a bikini made of chain mail and rabbit fur that didn't cover near enough of her, scurried behind the Green Man. A troop of preschool girls in wispy pink and fairy wings added to the festive mood.

"Maybe the elves are behaving themselves because they have Donovan calling the shots," Allie said. From her perspective over the top of most of the crowd, she had a better view of the grand picture. At five foot two and hampered by the cast, I saw mostly the backs or chests of the increasing crowd.

Scrap was useless. He swung from chandeliers, nearly drunk on excitement and gorged on mold. I suspected he'd taken a side trip to the Citadel with his lover only a hundred miles north of here.

"Donovan's still here?" I craned my neck seeking a glimpse of the familiar black braid with silver slashes in the shape of wings at his temples. "Usually, he sticks to me as if he owns me. I haven't seen him at all since Friday night." More like Saturday morning. "But then he's got his girlfriend, Doreen, stashed in a room somewhere."

"I've seen him all over the con, usually not too far from the forest children." Allie angled our path to the right toward the gaming rooms instead of the masquerade in ballroom.

And there he was, standing tall and grim at the head of a long library table filled with cards, miniature figures, oddly shaped dice, and other arcane equipment important to the players. I'd never indulged in gaming so I didn't know how to use those bits of junk. I knew more about my aunt's herbs and elemental symbols for ceremonial magic than this stuff.

Donovan kept his hands locked behind his back and his chin high, supervising initiates. As if he knew I watched, he turned and flashed me that magnificent smile that turned my bones to pudding and my will to thistledown blowing in the wind.

The elf children scurried into the room bearing nachos and pizza for a large group. They settled in with another group of teens. I wanted to back away from the thick odor of day old pizza, unwashed teen bodies, and spilled soft drinks.

"L'Akita, you should be resting before you jump into charades." Donovan flowed to my side and took my arm. Gently, he steered me away from his charges.

"You know my schedule better than I do," I replied, digging in my staff to balance against him. That cast wasn't moving until I willed it, which was my decision, not his.

"You are my priority here, Tess." A complete reversal of his previous attitude. Another reason not to trust him.

"I thought controlling the junior Nörglein was your prime purpose for being here. No, wait, you said you needed to promote Halfling Games. What is it you truly want, Donovan?"

He frowned. "Not so loud. They might hear you." He jerked his head toward the five forest children.

I couldn't tell if the greenish cast to their skin was natural or an aspect of the flickering fluorescent lights.

"So you did follow me here to supervise them."

"I don't need excuses to come to my local con."

Liar! Scrap proclaimed from the crystals dangling from the light fixture. *You'd only been to one con before meeting my babe—and that was dressed as a bat surrounded by cousins and nieces and nephews. You haven't been to a con since we battled the hellhound and lost a dear friend to a knife wielded by one of your Kajiri bat children.*

I kept my face bland, pretending to believe Donovan.

"Are you going to challenge those children to a duel?" Donovan looked at my cast and staff with stern disapproval.

"If I have to. Or I may call for help." I forced myself to look away from his beautiful face and body and watch the five teens. This was the first time I'd been close enough to really study them. Three boys and two girls ranging in age from about twelve to fifteen. But being otherworldly in nature, they could have lived a hundred years to reach this level of maturity. I knew for certain that Donovan had "fallen" fifty years ago and gone to live with his foster family with the appearance of a teen. He could pass for late thirties, maybe forty now, even with the silver hair at his temples.

All of the junior elves had brown hair that tended to stick out in tufts, in shades ranging from cedar to oak bark. Their skin, minus typical teenage acne, was uniformly two shades lighter than the hair with just a hint of green. The girls had the appearance of short and slender saplings or sturdy vines. Their faces had angles and hollows, brown eyes tilted slightly up. The boys had more muscle mass similar to fast growing trees. Their noses and jaws were blunter and their heavy-lidded eyes barely opened.

"Tess." Allie dragged my attention away from the Nörglettes' quick and furtive glances as they wrapped their hands around their paper plates, protecting nachos and pizza from thieves. "Do you see how they're eating?"

"They are shoveling greasy junk food into their maws like they haven't eaten in a week and are afraid someone will take the food away before they get their fill."

"Yeah, I know a lot of teens have the manners of a troll. But these kids are really enjoying that food, as if they've never tasted anything like it. And they're smiling and talking to the other gamers."

"Your point would be?"

"They are redeemable. I deal with gang refugees all the time. These children need education and socialization, but there is hope for them." Allie sounded truly excited. Her face took on an expression of crusading glee.

I'd seen her in the same mode when she tried rehabilitating an aggressive pit bull rescued from a dog-fighting ring. Amazingly, she'd succeeded and found a home for the beast guarding chickens from coyotes on a farm. Rumor had it the dog babysat the children with loyal and gentle protectiveness.

I had little hope of convincing my friend of the inherent evil in the minions of the Nörglein until she watched them kill or rape. Even then she'd order therapy for them before going into battle.

"Donovan, the filk circle begins at nine in the executive meeting room. Bring them." I turned to retreat to the cooler and fresher smelling lobby.

"They won't want to come."

"You can make them listen to you. Do it. For me. I have a theory that might save them from their upbringing."

Chapter 12

Teasel thistle seeds were brought to western Oregon by Methodist missionaries to card wool in their mission mills. It escaped to become a prolific nuisance and impenetrable barrier in ditches.

The Nörglettes have barely been back to their room for two and a half days. While my babe entertains friends and fans on a panel discussion of etiquette for first contact with aliens, the forest children obsess over the gaming table. I'm going to check out their digs.

There's hair in the shower drain and on the bar of soap, so I guess they know about basic hygiene. The cute little triangle folded at the end of the TP roll by the maids has been mangled and the seat is up, so they know what a toilet is for. The two queen beds have not been slept in. Dirty underwear spreads across the floor in distinctive patterns. I'm reminded of a dog peeing to mark his territory. The guys are doing it with their discarded clothes. The girls too. Boxers in three of the piles, white cotton panties for the girls—high waisted and low legged preferred by older women, not the scanty and silky stuff of modern teen girls. No bras. Didn't notice if the two girl trees are well enough stacked to need them.

Fresh, unopened packages of underwear lay neatly in the dresser drawers. Five sets. I count two in each of the five piles on the floor. The kids are wearing a set. They plan on staying one more day. They'll leave the con when Tess does Sunday evening.

They haven't changed their jeans and Tees. The ones they are wearing begin to crumple enough to look normal.

Where'd they get the money for clothes and transportation, lodging and food? Someone in this family has a job or a trust fund. That could be the link to Cooper's Furniture Store.

Hmmm, if all these clothes are brand spankin' new, I wonder what they wear in the woods? Anything more than skin? Or do they live in bark?

I CLOSED MY EYES AND let the words and music of a song flow from my heart.

> *There is no such thing as requited love*
> *I have seen it enough to believe*
> *It is not enough that I open my heart*
> *A heart in love must receive.*

I sat on a straight chair with my cast propped on a matching seat. Beside me a young man with a guitar strummed the chords of the song based upon a love triangle in a popular SciFi TV series. I wondered if I could manage to choke out the entire piece before breaking down. The semi-tragic fate of the two men and one woman mirrored my own situation with Gollum and Julia too well.

But I had to get the sentiment out of my system. My mother had used music as a catharsis. This wasn't a bar in Las Vegas with a karaoke machine. For me, it was better. It was a familiar venue among true friends.

And I had my mother's pearls to help me imitate her sultry command of the music.

> *I have watched you go; I have seen the change*
> *Though my pledge to your side I will keep.*
> *It is not enough to be who I am*
> *And to savor your smiles in my sleep*
> *He will tell you now that three is a crowd,*
> *And you know that I leave with my heart*
> *It is not enough to just take what is left.*
> *So I'll love you and serve you apart*
> *Follow your heart's path, in Valen's name.*
> *Now it leads me away to defend*
> *I will fight, I will die, I will be what you wish.*

And my love for you will never end.

I bit my lip at the end, lost and alone, believing that Gollum heard my thoughts two hundred miles away. When I looked up again, Allie and several others scrubbed at their eyes, some openly, some surreptitiously.

Donovan stood against the far wall, the forest children in a line beside him. His chin quivered a bit. He brought a folding chair and set it beside me. I caught a glimpse of Doreen's back hastening down the corridor away from here.

"You don't sing that song for me, Tess," he said sadly.

I looked away from him, unable to answer. He'd used my name, not his pet endearment. I still don't know the true meaning of L'Akita, or its linguistic evolution. I might have solved the mystery of Donovan's origins, but he had depths and secrets I didn't quite dare compare to mine.

Paul strummed the opening chord of a brighter and livelier tune. The crowd of about fifteen joined in on the chorus of a saga about never being able to leave the dealer's floor of a con.

"Life might be less complicated if I could love you, Donovan. But I don't. I can't order my heart."

"Do you have to love only one? I'll settle for being second best, if only you'd settle with me." He took my hand and kissed it with hope in his eyes.

"Not yet. My wounds are still too raw. You've found someone else who suits you better."

He dropped my hand like a burning ember. "What did you hope to accomplish with my charges?" He shifted his gaze to the five teens propping up the wall.

"The devil does not stay where music is."

"I don't know that quote."

"Martin Luther. If you stood guard over a cathedral..."

"Lutherans didn't attend my cathedral."

"Perhaps you are more familiar with Milton: Music doth soothe the savage breast."

"If you say so. It all sounds the same to me," he growled.

But the Nörglettes were tapping their feet. The two youngest, a boy and a girl joined a clapping game on the next round of nonsense songs based upon a goblin character from the gaming community.

"Maybe they are redeemable," I whispered, oblivious to Donovan's latest sensuous assault on my palm.

Then they started whooping and dancing—more like stomping and banging themselves against the wall.

I spoke too soon.

Squishy appeared out of nowhere. Deftly she grabbed the hands of the tallest of the Nörglettes and danced him out the door. The others followed, imitating her nimble hopping and sliding.

Scrap jigged above their heads, nearly drunk on their enthusiasm.

"I didn't know she could be so graceful," I whispered.

"Size and grace are not mutually exclusive," Allie snorted. She sidled after them. "You should be in bed. We'll keep an eye on the guests. I think they'll enjoy the dance and rock music more than this quiet interlude of song."

"She's right. May I escort you to your room?" Donovan stood up too. He offered me a hand.

He was back to being nice and charming, his usual seesaw between angry resentment toward me and trying to woo me into compliance.

I resisted, not trusting his charm any more than his anger.

"I can manage," I returned. Instead of taking the assistance I sorely needed, I grabbed my staff and leaned heavily on it as I levered myself upright. I'm perverse that way.

My staff seemed to have a mind of its own. The rubber tip slid along the vinyl flooring, nearly taking me with it.

Donovan moved with demon quickness to grab my elbow and slide his foot in front on my own skidding one.

I flailed wildly, trying desperately to right myself on my own.

"One of these days you will learn that you can't do everything by yourself," he growled.

"Pratfall practice is three doors down," the guy with the guitar called.

A general laugh went around the room.

Then he strummed "Old MacDonald Had A Farm" and sang:

Good ol' Tessie had a cane
Ei eye ei eye ouch
Without the cane she is quite lame
Ei eye ei eye ouch
With a yowl yowl here and a
Yowl yowl there
Here a fall, there a fall
Everywhere a pratfall
Good ol' Tessie had a cane
Someone throw her on the couch!

Somewhat steadier on my feet, half supported by Donovan, I sketched an awkward bow and stumped out to a round of wicked applause. My face burned with embarrassment.

Donovan's lips twitched with a half-suppressed smile.

"Don't start."

"Start what?" He opened his eyes in feigned innocence.

And then I lost it. Gales of laughter poured from the tips of my toes to the depth of my gut. I laughed at the ridiculousness of my grim approach to life these last eighteen months.

I laughed for the joy Mom had found in singing the last few days of her life.

I laughed for the freedom Julia had found away from her mother and her locked hospital room—were they symbolic of the same thing? Oh, my, I had a story in there somewhere.

I laughed at the idea of trying to tame five elven children.

And then I laughed at the wrong turn my depression had taken my book into and I knew how to write the next chapter properly.

"What's so funny?" Donovan asked. He looked bewildered.

"You. Me. Squishy dancing with the Nörglettes. Allie and my brother, Steve, engaged. I'm laughing at life. Come on, Scrap. I've got a book to write." I limped down the hallway, spine straighter and lighter than I'd felt in a long, long time.

"Let me help you." Donovan was at my side again, his hand under my elbow.

For half an instant I considered letting him take me back to my room to enjoy a few minutes of privacy...

Nah, we'd done that before and I always ended up distrusting him and hating him for his lies while thoroughly enjoying his sexy body. Even now I envisioned his sleek muscles sliding beneath his smooth skin, his braid draped over one shoulder caressing my breasts.

Gulp.

And then I remembered Doreen.

And I remembered the sweetness of Gollum's kiss.

Suddenly, Donovan wasn't so attractive. Or maybe I just didn't need him in the same way I needed Gollum.

How to get out of this gracefully?

A whiff of smoke drifted past my nose. I looked up to see if Scrap had broken the no smoking rule inside the hotel.

No sign of him or his cigar.

I sniffed cautiously. More than a bit of burning leaves outside. Only sharper, more acrid.

Trouble, babe. Scrap landed on my shoulder, glowing bright pink.

Donovan slammed his fist into the nearest fire alarm, grabbed me around the waist, and threw me over his shoulder as he ran for the nearest exit.

ISN'T IT AMAZING WHAT runs through our minds when being rescued by a hunky male!

Tess keeps batting at her denim skirt so that it doesn't fly up and reveal her dark blue panties. I picked out this skirt for her ages ago, but she never wore it much because she lives in jeans, unless she's dressing up. She wears tailored slacks with a silk blouse and blazer when she needs to look professional. For parties and awards banquets—too few of either since Mom died—she lets me choose glitzy dresses with sparkles and drapes and interesting necklines.

But this skirt has proved perfect for her incarceration in the cast. Jeans don't slide over the bulky thing. This skirt hangs just below her calf and closes up the front with brass buttons. The eight inches of slit below the last button gives interesting peeks at her legs. It's casual enough for a con, but dressy enough to remind people that she is a professional writer.

Much more stylish than plain sweats.

"Why did you hit the alarm?" she yells at Mr. Toxic.

"Because there's a fire. Can't you smell it? It's the responsible thing to do." He continues carrying her across the courtyard, beyond the pool and hot tub.

I can tell by his pheromones that he's thinking about how sensuous a hot tub can be. Then he remembers my babe can't get the cast wet and his scent turns from lushly sweet to icky sour.

"Not at a con!" She slams her fists into his back. "Kids pull the fire alarms as pranks all the time. No one heeds them. Call 911. The kids will come out to see what the sirens are about. They won't even notice the alarm."

"Oh."

Well, duh. More proof that he doesn't hang out at cons like he claims.

"Hey, babe, my nose tells me that the fire is small. So far. But it's in some shrubbery near the back door to the vendors' room. No, not shrubbery. On the sidewalk. A planned fire, built of presto logs and newspapers."

I can't fly away from Tess. My instincts to stay with her override my need to know who started the fire and why.

I should not be able to smell moss and damp wood in the middle of the high desert. Even in October when rain does fall here, moss is not an option.

My instincts are always right. The who and the why have something to do with Donovan taking her as far away from the fire danger as possible. Right into more danger. Demon danger.

Heat builds inside of me, fueling my transformation into the Celestial Blade. This time I cannot, I will not wait for Tess' command. I stretch and stretch and sharpen. She grabs the shaft of my body with both hands. This is our destiny. This is why imps were created.

Tess is still draped over Donovan's back.

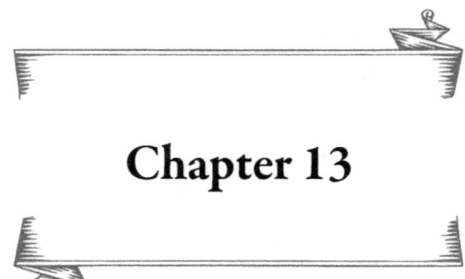

Chapter 13

The Tillamook Burn, in the Oregon Coast Range 1933, began in a logging camp. 400,000 acres of old growth forest burned in two days; ten days later, 250,000 acres still burned. Smoke rose eight miles high. Ash fell on ships 500 miles at sea.

"Ouch! That hurts, Tess. What are you doing swinging your blade around?" Donovan squirmed and shifted, but he didn't put me down.

"Why in the hell is the blade out anyway?" he continued.

"Put me down and find out," I snarled. A dim shape that might have been a tree, but was too stout and massive to be native to the high desert, moved toward us from the archway between two wings. Nothing but an abbreviated parking lot over there that abutted a dry and deserted lot devoid of anything bigger than a tumbleweed.

"Thank you for bringing me this woman," a deep voice echoed around the courtyard and swimming pool. I caught a whiff of pine. "I know she is attracted to you. I will need a moment to assume your shape. You will take possession of the item we discussed yesterday while I take care of this business."

The cool lights beneath the water only heightened the shadows and obscured details. Other than two arms, two legs, a head, and a stout body the size of a young black bear, I couldn't tell who or what addressed us. Then two red eyes opened and glowed with menace.

"Your reward, Donovan Estevez, is free passage back to where you came from. You have succeeded where my children have not. You have proved yourself a friend."

"You're a little out of your element here, Nörglein!" I yelled. I circled the Celestial Blade from my awkward position. "You have no power here, no trees to hide within, no paths to blur and confuse."

"Ouch!" Donovan yelped and jumped a little as the twin half moon blades with tines extruding from the outside curve brushed his calves.

"Put me down if you value your body parts, Donovan Estevez."

"If I put you down, will you try not to take off my head with that thing?"

"No guarantees."

"Look, I'm trying to save you. I had no idea he set the fire and waited for you to run out the opposite door. You can't fight in your condition."

"Wanna make a bet? How about the Mercedes if I turn him into firewood." I ignored, for now, the idea that Donovan knew of the plan.

Now, dahling. I need to taste demon blood now! Scrap reminded me that my blade was alive and hungry.

Donovan bent his knees and ducked beneath me. "Not bloody likely," he sneered.

I came up swinging.

The right hand blade met resistance, then flew free.

Yuck! He tastes like tree sap. And he's not a sugar maple.

Scrap doesn't usually have the energy to converse while in blade form.

Adrenaline is a marvelous drug. I forgot my fatigue, the aches and pains, my depression. Nothing existed but me, my blade, and the enemy. I spun in a slow circle, using my casted leg as an anchor and pivot, weaving my weapon up and down, back and forth.

The obscure form sulked behind the signpost that announced, "NO LIFEGUARD ON DUTY."

"Want another taste, Scrap?" I edged toward the elf in a kind of sliding lunge, right foot forward, slightly dragging the left.

"Estevez, you are to blame for this. I told you to deliver her subdued and rational. She is not like other women."

"You bet your gnarly ass I'm not like other women. I kill demons. I don't lie down and submit to rape by them." I stumbled on an imperfection in the dry grass. I needed a moment to center myself again. I lost track of my quarry. I sought movement in the shadows.

My blood still ran hot.

"All you have to do is say my name, Warrior," the Nörglein said sweetly from my right, the other side of the pool. "Say my name and I will disappear from your domain forever." He slid away from the metal pole.

"I know that. I even know your name, thanks to my friend, Gollum." That's what was in the file he gave me, as well as some details about cycles. The Nörglettes were nearly ready to go out on their own, find their own patches of forest to terrorize. That's why the attacks had increased in the last year. He needed a new batch of young to rear to his evil ways.

"But if I speak your name out loud so that you can hear it, you will disappear from my proximity but not this dimension. You'll just find another patch of forest and continue your sexual predation upon innocent women." I flashed the blade and he ran around the hot tub.

With my weapon in my hands, I felt stronger, more confident, and less clumsy with the cast. I followed him, moving onto the cement walkway that encircled the expanses of water.

"No woman is innocent," Donovan snorted behind me. Wisely, he stayed out of my reach, or I just might have taken him out too for that remark. I'd been tempted before when I discovered his lies and treachery. But in a serious fight, I trusted him to protect my back better than anyone else. He'd saved me from Sasquatch, Windago, and mutant black faeries.

The big question remained: Would he protect me from demons he found useful?

Ask me again why I couldn't marry him.

"Modern women are no longer true women," the Nörglein whined.

"You mean because we think for ourselves and defend ourselves against monsters like you? You mean we are no longer property to be traded back and forth as favors by men?" My temper pushed me closer and closer to my prey.

Another few steps and I'd have him.

Most demons attack. This guy looked for a way to run. "Coward. Sneak. Pervert!" I yelled at him.

Maybe he just looked for a way to trip me up like he had a few weeks ago in Forest Park.

No blackberry vines here to twine across my path at his command.

"Precisely. I have to use all my strength changing into the form of the man she will accept. My children are born weak because of that."

"If your kind is so weak that they can only propagate by rape, then maybe they need to consider extinction." I lunged, all my weight on my stable right leg, the cast anchoring my back foot. Scrap tasted blood again. Just a little from a scrape across his potbelly though.

The demon ducked and ran. "Who will defend and nurture the forest if there are no Nörglein to protect it?" he called over his shoulder.

He ran back toward the hotel, growing taller and more humanlike with each step. His height, his gait, and the swinging braid down his back, looked exactly like Donovan.

If I hadn't known where Donovan stood, I couldn't have told the difference. Could the Donovan Doreen argued with at registration have been the Nörglein in disguise?

I was beginning to suspect as much.

They smell different, Scrap reminded me. *I know who is who. Now. Thursday's sighting is undecided.*

The demon favored his left arm. The one I'd cut with the Celestial Blade.

Donovan moved into my path, preventing me from following.

I ignored him and shifted my grip, bringing the shaft of the weapon to my shoulder for a javelin throw.

"I'm not part of this. I never agreed to help him. Just because he orders, doesn't mean I do his bidding. I would never harm you," Donovan pleaded. "You have to believe me on this, Tess. I'm not lying."

"Fool me once, shame on you. Fool me twice, shame on me. I'm not going to fall for that line of Blarney on your say so." I adjusted my grip.

"Father, what's going on? Everyone is leaving the games and the clanging noises hurt our ears." A teen voice cracked up and down two octaves.

Suddenly, all five of the Nörglettes surrounded their sire and helped him into the sanctuary of the hotel. Dozens of people spilled out the doors—finally—in reaction to the fire alarm and the sirens in the distance. I couldn't follow my prey. I couldn't pursue this fight to the end.

My vows to the Sisterhood of the Celestial Blade demanded discretion in public. Protecting the innocent sometimes required keeping them ignorant of the nastier things that have invaded our dimension.

I slumped with exhaustion, hunger, and defeat. No more adrenaline to fuel me.

Scrap shrank back to his normal gray-green self.

"You okay, buddy?"

Yeah, babe. I tasted blood. We didn't win this fight, but we didn't lose it either. We've got the enemy on the run. I'll earn a wart for this. Now I need mold. And some sleep.

"Me, too."

I TOOK MY MOLD IN THE form of a B&B salad in the garden café. That's blue cheese and thin slices of rare roast beef on a bed of greens. Soft cheeses are not the best choice for lactose intolerance. Hard cheeses are better. But close to midnight after a frustrating confrontation with the Nörglein, I needed something special.

I'd pay for it in the wee small hours of the morning though. I didn't care while my tongue savored the creamy sweet and tart of the blue cheese.

"Nice to see your appetite has returned," Allie said, flopping onto the bench seat opposite me. She looked tired but in a happy sort of way. She'd enjoyed her first con. "We'll have you up to snuff in no time." She grabbed a hunk of beef slathered in blue cheese crumbles from my plate.

"What happened with the fire alarm?" I asked, then stuffed enough garlic toast into my mouth so I couldn't speak for a few moments and also to keep her from stealing it. I was as bad as the Nörglettes.

"The Fire Marshal threatened everyone at the dance with jail time if he didn't get a confession from someone about who built the little campfire on the arse side of the building." She grabbed my second piece of toast.

I almost slapped her hand away. On second thought, I knew I was having trouble finishing my fourth meal. My appetite had returned but not full force. My stomach must have shrunk during my months of gloom and doom.

"Did anyone confess?"

"Two girls in our quintet of forest elves." She signaled the waitress for decaf coffee. She took hers black and strong enough to get up and walk off by itself. I think that's how all cops drink coffee.

"Decaf?"

"I want to sleep tonight. In case you don't remember, I'm driving two hundred miles tomorrow evening."

I shrugged and speared more lettuce and cheese into my mouth.

"What did the local boys in blue do with the girls?"

"A stern lecture and release to Donovan, who claimed to be their father."

"Was he favoring his left arm?"

"Yeah." She suddenly sounded very interested and wary.

"That was the dark elf. Who happens to be their genetic father. I left Donovan unharmed. Reluctantly."

"Let me guess, he's playing both sides against the middle."

I nodded, chasing the last crumb of blue cheese around the plate.

"Miss, may I speak with you?" The middle brother in height of the Nörglettes stood beside my table, twisting his hands together. I think I'd placed him eldest in the lineup.

"Since you asked politely, pull up a chair."

As he dragged a chair from a nearby table to the end of my booth, I laid the staff with the knobby end encased in blue leather with dangling bits of turquoise on knotted leather thongs along the table, within easy grasp.

Not a Celestial Blade but still a weapon in trained hands.

The kid sat silently staring off into a distance I couldn't fathom.

"Speak up, umm ... What is your name?"

"Oak," he replied automatically, still only half here.

"That makes sense. You have the coloring of an oak tree. You're broad in the shoulder. Deep roots anchoring you to life, too, I bet."

He roused a bit. "My brothers are Fir and Cedar. Taller, less stable, shallow root balls that spread wide but don't hold up in a fierce wind. My sisters are Blackberry and Salal."

"I'm surprised one isn't named Fern or Bracken."

He shrugged. "The next batch maybe."

"So what do you need to talk about, Oak?" I fiddled with the leather wrappings on my staff.

Allie shifted uneasily, as if she missed her utility belt with gun, taser, flashlight, and handcuffs.

"Our father is sorely injured. We must take him home tonight, before the gaming ends. He cannot heal in this dry land. Our home is the deep, damp forest on the other side of the mountain. He needs moss and lichen and mushrooms to bind the wound. We will miss the end of the gaming. We will never know who wins. I will never know what fascinates my father in the dealers' room."

I nodded. The sooner the dark elf left the better. I needed about another week off before I healed completely and could defeat him.

The Celestial Blade is one of the few substances in this dimension that can penetrate demon hide. I hoped he'd need longer to heal than I.

"We do not understand why you hurt him so dire." He looked up from studying his hands to capture my gaze.

I saw true perplexity there. This child was as much an innocent of my world as humans were of his.

"Do you understand how much he hurts his victims?"

"Victims?"

"The women he rapes to get more children."

"I do not know this word rape."

"It's the most heinous crime I know of." Allie leaned forward so that her face was only inches from his. "It's a violation of a woman's soul as well as her body and her dignity."

"I do not understand. Trees must spread their pollen."

"But trees allow their pollen to be carried by the wind or by insects. The fertilized seed lands where it may, grows without the helping hand of a parent. Our children must be reared carefully, with love, from the moment of conception," I tried to explain.

"Women have the choice to decide if they will accept a man's seed within their wombs. A woman has the right to choose the man who will plant a child within her body," Allie took up the litany.

Something in what we said landed on fertile ground within his brain. I saw a light of understanding. Maybe not complete comprehension, but something for him to think about.

"I chose not to accept your father as the sire of a child," I pressed him. "For him to force himself upon me is rape. If he tries it again, I will kill him. Our laws will treat me lightly and not call his death much of a crime."

"Self-defense. Most courts wouldn't even order your arrest if you killed him during the act," Allie confirmed.

"Soon you will go out and find your own patch of forest to nurture. You must ask yourself if you will choose to force women to bear you children or if you will woo them and gain their consent first."

"But my father changes into the form of the man these women love."

"But he is not the man she loves. He will not stay with her and help her raise the child to adulthood."

That caught his attention. "Do you mean that your children have both a mother and a father past the time of weaning?"

"Got it in one."

"I cannot believe this. My father says that all creatures have only one parent. Look at the deer and bear. He would not lie to us." Oak pushed his chair back, preparing to leave.

"Look to the wolves. The entire pack raises the cubs. Deer fawns stay with their mother, but she has the help of her sisters and older daughters. They form a herd. We call them families. Your brothers and sisters are part of your family. But where are your mothers? Do the women who bore you not grieve for the loss of you?" I found my language growing more formal, settling into a similar cadence to his.

Maybe he'd appreciate the words better in a familiar form.

"My father does not lie." This time he shoved his chair so fiercely it tipped over.

"Oak, take my card. If you or your siblings ever need to talk again, you can find me." I fished a business card out of my belt pack and stuffed it in his jeans pocket.

He grunted and fled, leaving the chair on the floor.

"That went well," Allie said sarcastically.

"We planted a seed. That's all we can hope for at this stage."

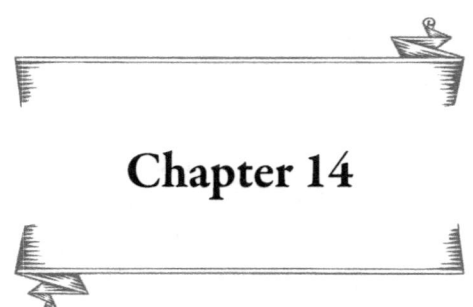

Chapter 14

*T*he Oregon State rock is the thunderegg, actually a geode. It looks like an
unassuming lump until you break it open to reveal marvelous agate or
crystal cores.

Sunday morning I sat on two writer-oriented panels with fair
attendance for the last day of a con. If the topic of discussion had been
fan based, like "Are virgins the natural prey of dragons?" no one would
have been awake. Unpublished and under-published writers are a different
breed, even if they come out of fandom. I looked out on eager faces primed
with notebooks or lap-tops, willing to drink deeply of my well of
knowledge.

My brain wanted to follow the Nörglein home. Fortunately, three other
published writers sat with me and carried much of the discussion.

"Tess, did the injury interrupt your career badly? How do you cope
with personal problems that rob you of writing time?" About the only
question I felt qualified to answer.

"Actually, the bad fall woke me out of a long depression. I'm happy to
say I'm writing again, even if I am overdue on my deadline. I didn't cope
with personal problems. I let them consume me. And my career suffered.
So now I'm playing catch up."

Scrap had told me time and again I needed to get back to work. I didn't
listen. I wallowed instead.

We went on to discuss ways to make time for writing around busy
schedules, how to channel anger and frustration into characters, how to
recognize the symptoms of clinical depression and when to seek help. Just
as the audience members began comparing antidepressant prescriptions,
Allie came to collect me.

"Is the car packed?" I asked, my mind already on strategies for removing the Nörglein from my neighborhood. How I'd deal with his children, I had no idea.

"Yeah, all packed up and checked out. I'd like to take one last cruise through the dealers' room first," Allie said. She adjusted her gait to match mine.

"What are you looking for?"

"A corset." She blushed. "It's white brocade with a lily-of-the-valley pattern. I was thinking of my wedding night."

I swallowed my smile. "Okay. There's a rapier I'd like to fondle again. My collection is in mini storage and I'd like something trusty but inexpensive to keep in the house. I feel half naked without a backup weapon."

"Me, too," Allie said quietly. "Tomorrow morning, first thing, I'm going to buy a gun and get a carry permit. I feel so vulnerable without one. Last night..."

"A gun wouldn't have worked on demon hide, or bark, or whatever."

"But it will make humans stop and think twice about snatching your purse because you're in a cast and can't move fast." She slapped the hand of a grubby teenager (couldn't tell if it was male of female in generic jeans and a black Tee, with short hair gelled into hornlike spikes) away from my belt pack.

The kid slunk away grumbling about life not being fair.

"It's not just here. Most of the con community is well behaved. Out in the real world we are both in greater danger. I'll feel safer with a gun. I'm trained when to use one and when not to." Allie veered off to the costume racks of capes and corsets, hats and feathers.

Oooooh, Tessie, look at this! Scrap popped into view directly in front of me and led the way to a different table in the crowded room. Two dozen dealers with twice as many tables or racks lined the walls of the large ballroom. Another dozen filled in squares in the middle. Scrap zoomed in on a display of crystals in the back corner. Hanging sun catcher crystals, crystals in jewelry, candlestick dangles. And a crystal ball.

From twenty feet away I felt the power pulsating from it. A real crystal ball made of beryllium or goshenite, not blown glass or rock crystal. Three inches in diameter, it would fit nicely in the palm of my hand. Mineral traces made it a bit milky. As I approached, the imperfections seemed to swirl and coil, giving peeks at something beyond the here and now.

At least I now knew what fascinated the Nörglein père in the dealers' room. If the kids had broken away from the gaming long enough to look, they'd know too.

My pearls grew warm and my scar throbbed.

"What is it?" I asked Scrap out of the side of my mouth as he landed on my shoulder. He turned bright green with lust.

The real thing. If I didn't know better, I'd say it came from Mum's garbage dump—you know where I found your magic comb, the dragon skull gargoyle, and the Goddess brooch.

Imp Haven is cold. Nearly freeze-dry cold. Magical artifacts tend to get dumped there. No one other than imps and the occasional gamer goes there by choice. The cold preserves the magic but makes it inert. Otherwise, the power within would broadcast their location across every dimension. So they remain jumbled up with the rest of the Universe's garbage until someone like Scrap finds them and brings them out.

I understand Scrap lands in the middle of the dump frequently when his Mum swats him out of the house for being inadequate, a runt, or too smart for her to understand. He's lost more than one of his hard-earned warts to his mum's broom.

The merchant peeked out from behind her display boards filled with earrings and pendants.

"Starshine," I called to the familiar figure.

Like most dealers, she made the circuit of cons, Renaissance Faires, harvest festivals, small town celebrations, Highland Games, and pagan gatherings. We ran into each other frequently. Today she wore her usual uniform of long, gathered black skirt, pink peasant blouse, and laced gray bodice. She contained her springy black hair with a pink scarf worn Gypsy style. A few tendrils escaped showing traces of silver. She also displayed samples of her jewelry on her wrists, at her ears, around her neck, and dangling from the scarf. She sparkled in the artificial light. In full sunshine she'd near blind the unwary.

"Tess," she said brightly, immediately moving a tray of unset crystals toward me. In years past I'd made some of my own jewelry from her wares.

Much as I tried to find something interesting in the tray of aquamarine and morganite—colored forms of the goshenite—my eyes kept wandering toward the little ball anchoring a stack of silk handkerchiefs in a basket.

Starshine laid a possessive hand atop the polished crystal, covering it from view.

The power within it still vibrated on my own personal frequency. I think I could locate that ball anywhere in the Universe now.

I picked up a pair of drop earrings with rough heliodor beads. That's the greenish-yellow variety of beryl. Not my favorite color, but a useful distraction. Now if she had emeralds, the rarest and most precious of beryllium colors, I'd jump on the beads in a minute.

"Where are these from?" I asked.

"You know I can't tell you that. My rock hounds would skin me alive if I revealed their secrets." Her deep whiskey sour voice almost chanted. She bustled back behind her table.

Hmm, the ball no longer sat in the basket, and the top silk square—a red one—had gone with it. The silk dampened the crystal's aura but didn't entirely mask it.

I put down the beads. "Actually, I'm looking for something larger."

"Oh?" That almost tenor voice rose to an alto. She opened her eyes wide, feigning innocence. "I have some crystals still in the rock matrix in the back. I didn't know you collected them."

"I don't. What about the crystal ball?"

"The what?"

"The crystal ball you had in the hankie basket."

"Oh, that old thing. You don't want that."

"I think I do. It speaks to me."

She froze in place, blinked several times, remembered to breathe again. "Do you hear it?"

"In my own way." Yeah, it was sort of like a distant chime calling me to Mass or reminding me of a banquet waiting.

Only the banquet wasn't of food. With that crystal ball I could eat and drink of spiritual journeys and quests. I could fill the empty places in my soul left by my mother's death and Gollum's desertion.

I needed that hunk of beryllium more than I needed food.

"It's not for sale."

"Everything is for sale." I mentally calculated the balance left on my credit card.

"Not for one thousand dollars."

I gulped and did some fast math in my head. I'd have to tap some of Mom's inheritance to cover it. "What about two?"

"Um."

Could I survive on salad and peanut butter until I conned Donovan into cutting me a check? "Two-five will cover all your table rentals and percentages for the next six months. Everything you sell will be gravy."

"Make it three."

I gulped.

Do it, babe. We'll find a way to pay for it later.

I hesitated, fingering the card in my belt pack.

With that ball, we can bypass the chat room.

"I can't. I just can't. That's too expensive." My credit card would bounce faster than Scrap caromed in and out of his mum's dump.

As I turned away from the table, I hesitated. Starshine looked a bit stunned. "Here's my card in case you change your mind." I handed her the one I reserve for business contacts with landline and cell phone numbers as well as private email and Web site addresses, the same card I gave to Oak.

"YOU SHOULD HAVE BOUGHT the rock," I tell my babe for the umpteenth time. She doesn't even look up from her computer screen.

So I slide inside and peer out at her, making faces until she acknowledges me.

Actually, she hit the delete key and that kicks me out of the system as fast as Mum's broom.

"*Starshine wants too much for the crystal ball,*" *she mutters and types another short paragraph.*

"*We'd have found a way to pay for it,*" *I insist.*

"*I won't go crawling to Donovan for money.*"

"*What about Gollum? He's got that mega trust fund for Warrior expenses while on quest.*"

"*That crystal ball is not part of the current quest. Besides, I'd almost rather take money from Donovan than Gollum. And I won't call either one of them.*"

"*But ... but ...*"

"*No buts about it. I can't afford a crystal ball. No matter how much you want it.*"

"*But we need it!*"

"*How can you tell?*"

"*I just can. I'm an imp. With that ball we can spy on the forest elf and his band of juvenile delinquents.*"

"*We can?*"

"*Yeah, and we can keep an eye on Donovan and Gollum.*"

"*No!*" *she screams at the top of her lungs.* "*Go do imp things and leave me alone. If I finish this book before the end of the year I just might be able to salvage my career and my credit balance.*"

"*If you hadn't let Dad tie up so much of your money in retirement accounts...*"

"*Out!*"

So out I go. Allie's no fun. She's making phone calls and pretending to read bride magazines, in between petting the matt-black revolver cradled in her lap. Now if she'd let me design her gown we could put together the wedding of the year on a budget. But no. She can't see or hear me, and Tess won't interpret for me. I settle for marking a page in a magazine on the bottom of the pile and move it to the top.

What's this? Allie's talking to the community college. They've got an opening for an instructor in the Criminal Justice Department. Woo Hoo! She and Steve are gonna move here. Tess needs that. She misses her family, though she won't admit it. She's been lonely for too long.

I can't help Allie write up her resume. But I can do something about the crystal ball. I know my babe needs that artifact of power. The Universe or the Powers That Be wouldn't have put it in her path if she didn't.

So I pop out to the chat room.

What? I can't see any demons on guard. Usually, they are visible as the only spots of color in the vast expanse of nothing.

(I'll tell you a secret. You know that white light people talk about when they have near death experiences? That's really just the chat room. Imps aren't allowed to know what happens after death. For us there is nothing. The end is the end. But some races and tribes get to start over again. To do that they have to wander through the chat room from one dimension to the next, or one life to the next. Whatever.)

Eeeeeek! It's the Politbutts. Big as trees, shaggy with a fur made of lies. See, a Politbutt can't tell the truth if you paid them to do it. And every time they tell a lie, it shows up as a long tendril of fur, some white, some black, some mixes of colors. The white guys are the worst. They make their lies sound so very believable.

This guy is white, barely discernible against the white-on-white room. It lumbers toward me. I scoot to the right, the opposite direction from where I need to go.

Politbutt anticipates me and snakes out an arm the size of a sewer pipe. It slams into me; I can't move fast enough to avoid something that big.

The breath whooshes out of me. My mouth tastes metallic—like copper. I hope it's not blood.

The blow shoots me straight across an acre or two of empty space, down a long corridor with windows into the past. I scream past glimpses of the crystal ball's origin and history.

I came here with the resonance of that ball in my mind. The windows show me what I'm looking for. But I have no control over my flight. I can't breathe. I can barely look at the scenes in the life of the Crystal.

I catch pieces of its discovery by a druid in Scotland. The ball changes hands dozens of times, from grandmother to grandson, to distant cousin. A clan of Romany takes it in trade for healing magic. The clan sells it in desperation during the Holocaust where they are hunted down with the same zeal as if they were Jewish. And then ... and then ... our Starshine finds it in a pile of junk at a flea market. She pays a pittance for it. I see another buyer, can't tell who it is, but she (?) finds it too late. Starshine doesn't know what it is; she just knows it is valuable. And powerful. She lusts after it with greed, not with understanding.

My Tess understands it. I can show her how to use it.

Then I smack into a solid door. My wings crumple. Pain lances like fire along the full length of every bone and cartilage. I sink down to the floor that suddenly goes squishy and starts to absorb me.

Revelation. Imps don't truly die or pass into nothingness. We, with our special powers that allow us to travel through the dimensions anywhere, anywhen, become the chat room. We don't need fixed portals, we make our own. My ancestors have become the walls of this transition place. We live forever, continuing our duty to the Universe in a new way.

Peace and warmth flood me with this knowledge. I can pass into this new existence with ease. It won't hurt.

Much.

Lingering stabs of fire remind me of who I am and what I am.

I've got to find some life deep within me to cling to.

If I die, Tess dies. It's not her time. She still has so much good she can do.

If she'd just bought the damn crystal ball I wouldn't have had to chase it through the chat room. I might live to become the Celestial Blade once more.

If I die, she dies.

The white envelops me....

Chapter 15

*T*he Beaver coin in $5 and $10 denominations was legal tender in the Oregon Country for one year before Territorial status was granted by the US in 1849. Beaver coins were melted down and reminted as the gold content was worth more than coin denominations. The few coins left command collectible prices ten to twenty times their face value.

The computer screen blurred. I blinked my eyes several times to regain my focus. How long had I been at work?

My vision cleared enough to check the time at the bottom of the screen. Six twenty-three. Was it morning or evening? Hints of dull, rain-washed light paled the sky. In late October, that could mean either sunrise or sunset.

Static filled my eyes. White static. I tried to shake my head to clear it of the fuzzy vision and scattered thoughts. My head was too heavy. So were my arms.

I needed to put my head down. The desktop seemed a league away and retreating.

Sleep. If only I could sleep a little.

I flopped back against the high back of my office chair, letting my head loll to the side. I closed my eyes.

Just for a couple of minutes. Allie would be calling me to dinner soon. I'd be okay with just a short nap.

"TESS, WAKE UP. TESS?" Allie shook my shoulder vigorously.

I swam up through layers and layers of white mist, trying desperately to speak, hearing only a gargled croak.

"Tess, what's wrong?" Allie crouched before my chair. Her long fingers encircled my wrist, testing my pulse. She shook her head and moved her touch to my throat.

I think I breathed.

"You're alive. For a while there I wasn't sure." She stood up and glowered down at me from her superb height.

"Huh?"

"You scared me. What happened?"

"Wh ..." I licked my dry lips and swallowed deeply. Then I tried again. "What happened?"

"That's what I asked you?" She ran the back of her hand across my brow the same way Mom used to check for fever.

"Time?" I blinked a couple of times, trying to focus my eyes. The room kept trying to spin away from me. After a couple of tries I found a scratch on my desk to focus on. Gradually, things stopped sliding away from me.

"It's after nine. Have you eaten anything? Have you even been to bed?"

"Nine in the morning!" More than just lamplight filtered into the room. Dull and gray outside, but still brighter than when I'd succumbed to sleep.

Or was it more than sleep?

"Scrap. Where's Scrap?" I shoved my chair back in panic. I had to find him. Something was wrong. Terribly, awfully wrong.

The room lurched right then left. I fell heavily against Allie.

"Easy, Tess. Take it easy. Let's get you to the kitchen and pour some coffee and food into you. I'm calling Gollum."

"No."

"Yes. Either him or Dr. Sean. You know he'll put you in the hospital and run a thousand expensive tests that will show nothing. You need help. So swallow your pride along with your coffee. We're calling Gollum." She slipped her arm around my waist and braced us both for the trip across the hall to the tall counter between the kitchen and living room.

I eyed the swivel barstool warily. I knew that if I tried climbing onto it, it would twist and fling me away.

Allie solved that problem with a heave and a push.

"I feel as helpless as a child."

"You are. Drink this and think about letting someone help *you* for a change. You don't have to do everything alone."

"Tell that to Scrap. He's alone somewhere and hurting. I need to find him."

"You need to regain some strength so he can. You two are bound so tight with magic and love and blood you're almost the same person."

I sat listlessly staring into the black depths of my coffee. Black and strong like a hungry black hole in space, bitter enough to etch the sugar spoon I stirred.

The whirlpools within the cup drew me deeper and deeper. If only I could see through the murkiness, I was sure I could find Scrap. I knew I had to find him before this terrible listlessness would dissolve.

I DO NOT KNOW THIS door that pushes so insistently at my back. I should know every door in the chat room, all six hundred sixty-six of them. This is one that has never revealed itself to me before. It wants me to rise up and push it open.

But I know if I do that, it will swallow me whole and I will leave my beloved Tess to drift into nothingness, neither alive, nor dead.

This is worse than the time the Guardians of the Valley of Fire trapped me within the Goblin Rock. They at least asked questions. They demanded I look deep within myself and find the source of the darkness in my soul. Only when I brought forth my guilt for allowing my bloodlust to extend beyond those who sought to kill me to the onlookers who cheered them on did I find a sliver of light within the darkness. Only when I admitted that I didn't need to kill them did I loosen the hold that guilt had upon me.

Only then could I stand within the same room as Donovan Estevez, the former gargoyle who still repelled those who would taint the sanctuary he had guarded for eight hundred years.

This solid and unmoving door reminded me of all that. Inspiration born of instinct tells me to get away from that door. Behind it lies a dimension from which I can never return.

Slowly I roll to my dimpled knees. The door tries to follow me, pressing against my bum like a lover.

Death stalks me like a lonely lover.

I crawl back the way I came. I cannot return Death's affection.

My wings sag over my shoulders. Tiny movements rock them with pins and needles of fire. I do not think them broken. Just sprained, like Tess' ankle.

The windows I passed on my way down the corridor of curiosity have closed. One shot. That's all you get on a search. One lousy look. The window decides how long you can peer through, taking note of details that might prove useful later. Then it slams closed, never to open to you again. I don't know if it will open to another searcher. I hope not. Otherwise, our enemies will know what we know.

Tess might come here and learn that the magic ring she gave back to the faeries connects her by blood to Lady Lucia, a demon masquerading as a vampire. But that's another story I'm not going to tell her.

Without landmarks I have no sense of time or distance. But with each painful slide forward the pressure from the door lessens and the floor becomes more solid. If I can just find the main room I'll be able to pop back to Tess. We can heal together.

While I languish in this half state of living so will she.

I WOKE UP ABRUPTLY to the sounds of blue jays squabbling over a morsel of stolen food—blue jays always steal food and they always squabble—and the smell of stale coffee and burned toast. My own rather ripe and unwashed body added to the pungent mix.

"A hospital would smell better." I must have mumbled out loud. The sound of my own voice startled me. My throat felt as if I'd torn each word from a fixed position inside it.

"You're alive!" Gollum whispered. His hands encased one of my own, and his head rested on the side of my bed within the cradle of his arms. He looked up, blinking blearily at me without his glasses. For once I could truly see his emotions through the mild blue irises. He smiled a bit. "You're alive," he said somewhat louder.

I reached over and caressed his fair hair as if I had the right to touch him so intimately and lovingly.

"Did you say something?" Allie peeked in. She wore a maroon suit, complete with flared skirt, matching blazer, and a pink blouse.

"You look like me at a publisher's lunch," I said, somewhat surprised.

"Job interview. Welcome back to the land of the living. I've got to run, Gollum. You okay alone with her?"

"Of course." He removed one of his big hands from atop mine and fumbled for his glasses.

I found them next to my pillow and handed them back, though I'd miss the honesty of his expression without the disguising lenses.

"You shouldn't be here," I said, when he was safely hiding behind his glasses once more.

"Yes, I should." He raised my hand and kissed my fingertips.

"What about ... Julia?" I couldn't bring myself to call her his wife.

"Pat is with her."

"The nurse?"

He nodded as he checked my brow for fever with the inside of his wrist.

"But Pat works nights and you've been here all night."

"Don't worry about me and mine. I need to know what happened to you. You've been in a kind of coma."

"I don't know. I think Scrap is hurt. My back aches like it's been hit with a two by four."

"How?"

"I don't know. I told him to leave me alone and let me work. So he left. Sometime later I couldn't keep my eyes open." I tried to recall those lost hours. "I think I dreamed about some Gypsies and a crystal ball."

"Why?"

"I ..." After gulping and organizing my thoughts a bit I told him about the ball of beryllium.

He didn't question why I had refused the price.

"Try calling Scrap with your mind. He might respond to a direct order to return to your side."

"If he can."

Gollum raised his eyebrows in mute question.

"I think I also dreamed of death. Something about a big heavy door that leads to a dimension from which there is no return."

"Try calling him. You are alive and awake, therefore, he must be also."

Scrap, get your ass back here!

Yeah, yeah, I'm coming. Hold your horses. A perfect donut ring of cigar smoke preceded him. He poked his head through a crack in reality, wearing the ring like a lei.

"You can stop playing games now. I was worried about you."

You were worried? I was worried, he snarled sarcastically. *Catch me!* He popped through, landing on my belly with a whoosh.

My breath expelled explosively.

"You're heavy," I complained when I could breathe again. "You're heavy? You don't weigh anything in this dimension. How could you knock the breath out of me?" I reached to hug him.

Relief at his reappearance outweighed my discomfort.

He mumbled and grumbled and waddled around until his back was to me.

"Nice wart on your spine," I complimented him.

He humphed and grumphed.

"Oh, your wings are ... a bit droopy." The cartilage on the up-sweep had lost stiffness and the barbed joints looked a bit dull and twisted.

Droopy! Droopy? Is that all?

"Tell me about it," I soothed him. I ran a gentle hand along the outside of the wings, amazed that I could feel the suede-like texture.

"Good to see you in the flesh, buddy," Gollum said, peering at my usually invisible imp. "You've grown a bit since I last saw you. Got a few new warts too. What can I do to make you feel better?"

Mold. And lots of it. Scrap thought a minute. *And some beer and OJ. And could I please have my favorite pink boa?*

"You got it. Coffee for you, Tess?"

I nodded. "Hey, how come you can see *and* hear him?"

"Ask him while I get some fortification for both of you." He exited with his usual long stride.

"Talk, Scrap."

Don't wanna.

"Nothing to eat until you tell me why we both almost died."

I guess. He sounded like a recalcitrant teenager caught playing hooky or with a stash of marijuana.

"Talk. I won't judge you."

More mumbles and grumbles. And then the story of his time in the chat room with the Politbutts came out in one long burst with hardly a breath.

Gollum came back in with a tray of treats and drinks about the time Scrap speculated how the bodies and souls of dead imps made up the chat room. Professor Van der Hoyden-Smythe nodded sagely and reached for his everything in one cell phone to take notes. His glasses started slipping down his long nose.

The geek I fell in love with was back in true form.

"You going to get an academic paper out of this?" I asked.

Scrap finished his tale with his long slow crawl back home. Before the last word dribbled from his mouth, he scooped up a glob of mold—from the balcony baseboards judging by the color and texture—plucked out a tiny spider and swallowed it in one gulp. Then he chased his tidbit with a long slurp of beer mixed half and half with orange juice.

His skin turned bright orange and began to fade.

"Is he still here?" Gollum asked, staring right at Scrap. Or maybe staring through him.

"Of course. He must be feeling better to go transparent. I wonder why he was so visible when he was hurt."

"Probably an instinct thing. So you could care for him."

Hey, I'm still here. I can hear every word you say.

"We know that, Scrap. Why don't you take a nap. Your eyes look very heavy."

Stay with me. He waddled up to the spare pillow and curled up in a ball with his wings spread out over him. In seconds he began snoring.

"He's sleeping," I whispered. "I didn't know he did sleep."

"All creatures need sleep to heal." Gollum knelt beside the bed and captured my hand again. "I am very relieved that you are both safe now."

"Thank you for keeping vigil. I can't think of anyone I'd rather have beside me if I died." My throat started to close. I had to look away, knowing what I had to do, no matter how much it hurt.

"I had to be here."

"And now that we are healing, you need to go."

"Tess, you can't keep on doing this by yourself. You've gotten hurt too many times this last year. You need backup. You need help."

"I do what I have to do, the way I have to do it." A stubborn wall of hurt pride rose up around me.

"Tess, I ..."

"Go. Please, go now, while I can still release you to your obligations."

"We may not be able to be together as a couple, Tess. Not the way we want to. But I am your archivist. You are as much my responsibility as Julia. You need help. I am always available."

"But not to love. Just go. Before I make a fool of myself and both of us sorry you came at all." I turned my head to the wall so I wouldn't have to watch him leave. Again.

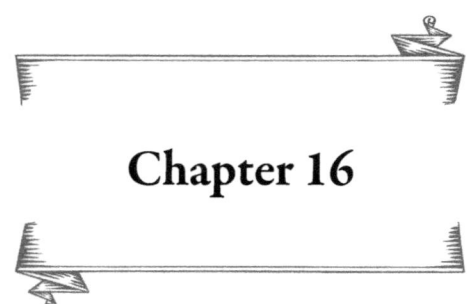

Chapter 16

O *regon's 1848 Territorial motto was* Alis Volat Propriis—*"She Flies with her own wings." It remained when statehood came in 1857. In 1957 patriotic citizens changed it to "The Union" to commemorate the upcoming centennial of the Civil War. In 1987 the legislature reverted to the original.*

Three more days I lingered, half awake, aching all over, gorging on any food Allie fixed or left in the fridge while she went about her business.

I noticed new smells with every turn of my head. Was my own sense increasingly sensitive? More likely, my bond with Scrap deepened as he glued himself to my shoulder. His thoughts became my thoughts. His hunger my hunger. His keen nose spilled over into my own.

During the day I wrote, reverting to older habits. When the going gets tough the tough keep writing. I'd been someone else in my depression, letting my frantic lack of accomplishment rule and push me into a self-defeating loop.

I stared out the windows toward the river a lot, absorbing the life and routine of passing barges, and the venturesome few who took out sailboats or tried water skiing this late in the year. The honking of migrating geese invaded my soul with a restlessness my body couldn't keep up with.

The damp grass and falling leaves smelled of sleep and quiet.

My thoughts wandered back over the events of my life. What could I have changed? Did I make the right decisions? Where did I go from here?

Gollum's absence gnawed at me like a sore tooth.

A car backfired on Macadam Avenue. I jumped and crouched with my hands over my head.

Once more I was back in the chat room, reliving the reverberating door knocker on the portal that led to the Powers That Be.

"You ask a lot," a reedy voice intoned as I stood before the high judicial bench. I thought the voice came from the huge creature hovering behind the panel. It alone did not sit in a thronelike chair. Maybe it was just too big for the available furniture. An occasional questing tentacle reminded me of the Cthulu demon on guard outside.

Scrap kept a very low profile close to the door. He looked like he wanted to flee, but as long as I remained, he had to remain as well.

His nose twitched constantly, seeking a whiff of danger.

"I ask for no more than what you want," I told the court, forcing my fears down into a tight knot behind my heart. The same place where I bottled up my grief over my mother's murder. "My home on Cape Cod is on neutral ground. Sacred in its neutrality. It has always been neutral since before the coming of humans to that land. You want it to remain neutral."

"You are decidedly not neutral, Warrior of the Celestial Blade," the booming bass voice flowed out of the deep hood on my left.

"I propose a compromise."

Seven cowled heads turned toward each other, bent in some silent communication.

"Explain," said a new voice, definitely female, with musical undertones and an accent that might have originated in Faery. This being sat dead center, more senior than the others. Her vote weighed more than all the others as well.

I addressed her directly.

"My father and his partner wish to buy the house from me and turn it into a Bed and Breakfast, a kind of an inn. They are neutral. Neither Warrior nor demon. They are normal, without power or interest in rogue portals."

The faery nodded in agreement. The others remained silent in their grim mysterious secrecy.

"But the energies around the house make it vulnerable to the opening of a rogue portal. It's a kind of vortex that attracts ghosts, faeries, and demons. I have no fear of the ghosts or faeries. I do fear the demons."

"Rightly so," boomed the one on the end.

"I want protection for my father and his partner. I want your guarantee that no one will use the land to open a new portal. That no other beings will try to take over the land. It must remain neutral."

"And what will you give in return? If we agree to this."

At that moment I knew why Scrap's nose twitched so incessantly. Danger didn't lurk here. Nothing lurked here. It was absolutely sterile. No dust, no mold, no growing things. Not even cleaning fluid invaded this chamber. No smell at all.

To my world filled with tiny odors and bad smells underlying the sweet scents of trees and grass and flowers and animal musk, this place smelled more dangerous than a charging black bear.

Or a lurking Nörglein.

Abruptly, I fell back into the present. I made the right choice going to the Powers That Be. I'd never had any doubts about that. Especially since I'd sent Gollum away and refused Donovan's proposal.

Things change, Tess. A year from now that might not be the right choice. Think about the victims of the Nörglein. Think of the upheaval in their lives. Think of the choices they don't have, Scrap reminded me.

"I think about that every day. No woman should have to give her child to a monster. Not me, and not the victims of that horrible dark elf."

I turned away from the churning, rain-swollen river that rushed toward the sea in its endless change that remained much the same.

"I've made the right choices. Now it's time to get on with my life. I need to call Raquel Jones and the other victims I know about. I wish I knew how to contact Squishy. She should know about other victims. They need to talk to each other, make plans and preparations. But first I need to get rid of this cast."

I'll find an email address for Squishy. You make an appointment with Dr. Sean. Scrap dove into the computer as if it were the familiar chat room.

"DOES THIS HURT?" DR. Sean asked as he gently rotated my left ankle.

After being in a cast so long my leg looked shrunken, wrinkled, and hairy.

"It's stiff but not painful," I replied. Yeah, there were a couple of twinges at the extreme end of each manipulation. Not enough to complain about and risk having the cast put back on.

As if he read my lie, the good doctor smiled and began massaging the weak muscles. He winked at me as if he shared the secret. "If you don't injure it again, you should be fine now. Ribs okay?"

"Never were much of a problem. Bruises heal faster than sprains and breaks," I replied. But the huge bruise on my spine that I shared with Scrap was taking longer to fade.

I needed to give the right answers to Dr. Sean so I could put on socks and shoes and *walk* out of the clinic. If the physician would just let go and stop that heavenly massage of my foot.

I could get used to this.

"You'll need physical therapy," the physician said. He paused his massage long enough to make a note on his order forms. "If you promise to follow up with that and do your exercises, I think we're done here." He placed my foot back on the exam table almost reluctantly. "I'll just sign off on your treatment and you cease to be my patient. Until the next time you do something self-destructive." He half grimaced as he applied pen to paper.

"Do you think I'm self-destructive?" I asked, suddenly alarmed.

"I think you've been depressed and not as careful as you should be. But I see improvement in the sparkle in your eye. It started the moment your brother and his fiancée walked into the ER."

Gollum's words came back to me. I couldn't do it all alone. I didn't have to. Was that part of the problem, just plain loneliness?

Dr. Sean cocked his head and looked at me with an appraising eye. "You do look a little pale though. Is your family feeding you right?" He ran a gentle finger down my cheek.

Anyone else and I'd have said he just wanted to feel the texture of my skin. My rational explanation was that he tested for fever and clamminess.

"I had a touch of … of a tummy bug earlier this week. It's gone now. I'm eating better." Easier to explain my near coma and Scrap's languish in the chat room as an illness rather than spill the very complicated truth.

"In fact, I'm eating better than I have for a year and a half." I smiled brilliantly knowing that I still was not eating as well, or as much as I should. As Scrap healed, his appetite ruled mine less and less.

"Good. Wouldn't hurt you to continue taking it easy for a few more weeks, rebuild the strength in that leg gradually. Use a cane if it helps. And do your exercises. Start with this one until you see the PT. Do it with both pointed toes and flexed foot." He rotated the ankle in a full circle left and right. Then he handed me some paperwork. "You are officially dismissed and no longer my patient."

That was the second time he'd used that phrase.

"Right." I took the papers and read them carefully. Lots of strange codes indicating what he'd done today—mostly removed the cast, took new X-rays, and examined them. There was an order for his receptionist to make an appointment for me with physical therapy. No mention of massaging my ankle.

"Right. Then how about we do something about your eating and go to dinner tomorrow night?" He quirked a full smile.

My heart panicked. He wasn't Gollum.

But I'd probably never see Gollum again. I needed to get out and ... and ...

Too soon.

"Okay." I overrode my own arguments.

"Pick you up at six?" He handed me the spare shoe and sock I'd brought with me.

"Fine." I pulled on the foot gear and lowered my pant leg to hide the ugly, shrunken, *hairy* leg. "My address and phone number are in your file."

"I memorized them a year ago."

What could I say to that? Instead of putting my foot in my mouth I let him help me down from the table and escort me all the way to the outside door of the clinic with his hand warming my elbow. "My receptionist will call you with the PT appointment. Don't let that slide, Tess. You'll be less likely to re-injure yourself if you work at strengthening and limbering those joints and muscles."

And the glass door swung shut between us.

Now what have you gotten yourself into? Scrap demanded.

"I accepted a date with a handsome, intelligent man," I replied blithely.

He's mundane. He's got no part in your world of fighting demons.

I spotted Allie in the parked car. She'd been on her cell phone the whole time I'd been inside, talking to Steve and other people she wouldn't tell me about.

"True, Scrap. Maybe I need a strong dose of reality now and then. Especially after I host a meeting with Raquel and three others in my living room tonight. We need to stop at a bakery for desert for them."

He's not Gollum, Scrap pouted, waving his cigar stub at me.

"No, he's not. And I think that's the point." I slid into the car next to Allie, not nearly as happy as I should be.

"So, what's new with you and Steve?" I asked my friend, putting as much brightness into my voice as I could. Maybe if I pretended my heart wasn't breaking, I'd eventually convince myself it wasn't, and I could move on.

"Steve got a job offer in Hillsboro. I got a job offer at the community college not far from there. We're getting married at Christmas! We both start work right after the holidays." She whooped and threw her arms around me.

"I'm very happy for you. Do I get to be a bridesmaid?"

"Of course. I just wish you could find the right guy." She paused. "One who's unattached."

"We'll see. I have a date with a cute doctor tomorrow night."

"Way to go, Sister." She high-fived me.

"In two months, you really will be my sister as well as my best friend," I said somewhat awed.

"So, let's go shopping for your matron of honor dress. Something lovely that you can wear again and again."

"Then we'd better let Scrap pick it out." Maybe that would brighten his mood. "Why aren't you torturing me with the ugliest gown ever designed that costs way too much? That's part of the ritual, sort of a test of how much I love you."

"I'm buying you something lovely because I want you to love me after the wedding."

Tomorrow I'd test that love to the limits by going off on my own, exercising my newfound freedom from the cast and do some investigative shopping.

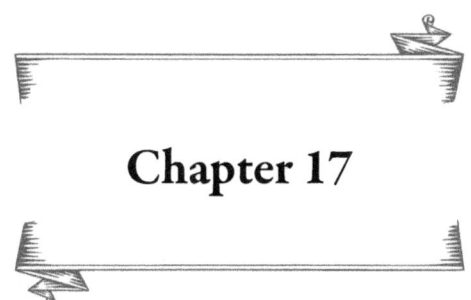

Chapter 17

The International Rose Test Gardens in Portland were created in 1917 to preserve European hybrid roses that might be wiped out due to World War I devastation.

"Nice to see you out of the cast," Raquel Jones said upon entering my condo. She held a plate of cookies in one hand and half hugged me with the other.

"I'll be fit again very soon," I told her. "I have physical therapy tomorrow morning. You're the first here. Did you have any trouble convincing JJ to stay home?"

"He's downstairs walking the river path. Patrolling is more like it."

"This will be easier if we keep it girl talk. Less embarrassing that way. My friend Allie is hiding in my office. She's an ex-cop if we need her to talk about self-defense."

The clang of footsteps on the metal stairs alerted me to the arrival of more guests. Four more, all I could find in a hurry for this impromptu meeting of a potential support group. Two of the other women, like Raquel, were pregnant. The other two carried tiny infants, no more than two months old. Squishy had sent them.

Scrap flitted about cooing and making funny faces at the babies. Both of them reached tiny hands up to touch him. No one else could see him. Interesting. Did the dark elf blood in the children allow them to see the imp or just their innocence?

Raquel took charge when we were all seated in the living room with coffee (decaf in consideration of the pregnancies and nursing babies) and small pieces of rich chocolate cake, homemade chocolate chip cookies, and trail mix with chocolate nuggets. Hard topics always go down easier with chocolate.

"I don't want my baby stolen," Michelle whispered a little later, clutching her tiny boy against her shoulder where he drowsed, wrapped in the cocoon of a brightly colored blanket. She barely looked old enough or large enough to have given birth. Her perky short hair and rounded cheeks gave her a cherubic look. She was the mother who'd delivered in the ER with Squishy assisting.

"None of us wants the Nörglein to steal any more babies," I affirmed. I passed around photocopies of the dark elf from the field guide.

Michelle and Annie, the two mothers, took one look at the woodcut picture and shuddered. Both dropped their papers, as if touching them was like touching the monster himself.

"I can't believe I actually let him make love to me," Annie said, burying her face in her daughter's blanket.

"I knew he wasn't my husband the moment he walked in the door," Caroline said. At six months along, she and Raquel must have been victimized about the same time.

"How?" I asked.

"It was like my husband rode on top of a new core body. I can't explain it any other way. He looked, talked and moved just like Jeff. But, I don't know, something was off. Then he sort of solidified and I forgot what I saw." She shook her head.

Ask her what the guy smelled like, Scrap said, hovering in front of the athletic woman in her mid-thirties with stunning blonde hair and bright blue eyes.

I did.

"Smell ... I never thought about that. But come to think on it, he smelled of pine. Jeff doesn't use that aftershave anymore. Not since I turned up allergic to evergreens. We can't have a real Christmas tree anymore because of it." She paused to gulp back tears. "My baby will never have a Christmas tree."

"But the Nörglein made you forget your allergies, made you forget that something was wrong," I said. "He made you all forget that abortion is still a legal option for you."

"You make it sound like magic," Donna said. Clearly, she didn't believe in magic. Dark hair, trendy dark-framed glasses, her designer maternity jeans and turtleneck proclaimed her professional social situation. Raquel said she was an accountant.

I needed her to believe in magic before the evening was over.

"It was magic," Raquel butted in. "I know our science oriented society, our churches, our *logic* tell us that magic and dark elves don't exist. We all have proof it does." She cupped her swollen belly for emphasis.

"I can't believe our doctors didn't put two and two together," Donna continued.

"Did any of you have the same doctor?" I asked.

They compared notes and shook their heads. Only two of them had even been in the same hospital. Squishy encountered one in the ER and the other in the psych ward. No connections except a bit of skin that sloughed off bark-like scales. Allie was even now trying to track down the other postpartum hysteria patients.

"What can we do?" Michelle asked. "How do we fight magic?"

"You don't. I do," I replied.

Four sets of puzzled eyes riveted on me.

"Believe her," Raquel said. "She knows what to do."

I wish I did. "Michelle and Annie, are you in a position to uproot and move out of town? As far away as you can get."

"I can," Annie said. "I telecommute. I can work anywhere."

"What about your husband?" Caroline asked.

"I'm not married. I'll take a loss on my house if I sell now, but I can move. You think that will keep my baby safe?"

"I'm not certain. But I think so. The Nörglein seems desperate. That means he'll make a mistake. If he has to chase you halfway across the country, he's vulnerable. But he only takes the children after their second birthday. You've got a little time."

"My husband just lost his job. I suppose we could make an excuse to go live with my mom in LA," Michelle said.

"I'm not going anywhere. I intend to fight this guy," Raquel said. She sat straight, chin jutting in determination. "I've already started self-defense classes. As soon as I deliver, I'm taking up martial arts. JJ is too. We're going after him every chance we get."

"Let's back up a moment." I needed to get away from the idea of these women aggressively hunting the monster. Danger lay on that course, for them, not the Nörglein. "Annie, you said you weren't married. How did the Nörglein trap you if he didn't impersonate a husband?"

"I was hiking, alone. I had a backpack with essentials, so I didn't panic when the paths just disappeared. I dug out my compass and headed downhill. But it rapidly became uphill and the damn compass started swinging round and round, never settling on a direction."

"Then you blacked out and didn't remember anything until you walked out at the trailhead the next morning," I prompted her.

"I thought I just slept in the lee of a hollow log. When I woke up, the path was back in place, straight and clear."

"What did you think when you turned up pregnant?" From the quivering chins and rapidly blinking eyes I knew I ventured into territory these women didn't want to remember. "I need to know, Annie. The Nörglein varied from his usual MO by taking an unmarried woman. He's from a different era and culture. He feels that what he does is okay because he has the enchanted cooperation of a husband."

"I... have a couple of boyfriends. I figured that when I got a little tipsy one night not long after my night in the woods I'd been indiscreet enough to overlook an essential condom." Annie flushed with embarrassment. "When I went looking for the one I thought I remembered, I discovered he'd left town two months before the ... um ... incident."

"Something is wrong for the dark elf to go out of pattern twice. Once with you and once with Raquel," I mused. "I need to do more research."

"And we need to arrange our next support group meeting. With the men in our lives. And we need to find the other victims. I'm certain we aren't the only ones." Raquel said.

They set about arranging it.

I decamped to the balcony to think. No moon peeking through the clouds tonight to suggest a silver river that marked an ending and a beginning.

Why had the dark elf varied his pattern? A pattern that had worked well for centuries.

What had changed beyond women thinking for themselves and refusing to be treated as tradable property?

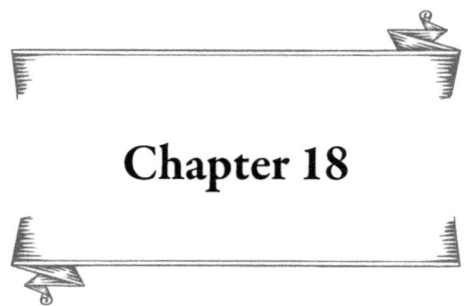

Chapter 18

In 1841 Ewing Young died without heirs or a will. The dilemma of how to handle his estate led to formation of the Provisional Government in 1843. An acorn planted over his grave is now a Heritage Oak Tree.

First thing the next morning after my PT session, Allie went off to meet a Realtor and look at houses closer to her new job.

"Alone at last," I sighed, sitting back on the reclining sofa with a cup of coffee and soft new age music on the satellite. I looped a huge rubber band around my foot and pushed against it until my leg straightened. I had to pause at ten and take a sip of coffee, then again at fifteen. Building up to fifty stretches was going to take some time.

"Good thing I am alone. I'd hate to have Allie see me sweating and panting after so little exertion."

You're never alone, dahling, Scrap reminded me. He perched on top of the flat screen, dangling his pink boa in front of it.

"You're leaking feathers, Scrap. Shall we go shopping for some new accessories?" I knew I needed to bribe him.

Only if you look for a necklace to go with the matron of honor dress. His skin brightened to pale green. He lusted after something at the mall.

I considered the route to my destination and picked a convenient shopping center for the ride home.

He fluttered up and down, exercising his still recovering wings. His skin took on an emerald green hue.

All the better. Whatever he wanted was really important to him. Almost as important as my true errand.

Engaging the clutch in my car was a little awkward at first. I jerked and stalled my way out of the condo parking lot until I found the right pressure with my weakened left foot. By the time I hit the freeway entrance half a mile up the road my muscle memory took over and I shifted smoothly.

But I did keep my speed down to the limit.

Hey! Why'd you turn off onto I84? Scrap bounced to the rear window, staring at I5 retreating in the distance. *You can't get to the mall from here.*

"On the way back," I reassured him.

Back from where?

"You'll see."

No, Tessie. Absolutely not. We can't go there alone. Scrap planted himself on the steering wheel, between me and the window. I could see the road perfectly well through him.

"You reminded me, not too long ago, that I'm never alone. I have you. You are my backup, the eyes in the back of my head, and my weapon of choice."

He sulked into an even more invisible white. He looked like the chat room walls.

"Are you okay? That color scares me!"

And well it should. This is more dangerous than you know. You aren't healed yet. Your leg is weak and your balance is off.

"So? What else is new? This can't be any worse than entering Lady Lucia's lair when I had a groin pull. She was serving smoothie Marys that night. I hope Mary recovered after donating the blood for the drinks."

Half an hour later, I pulled into the graveled parking lot of Cooper's Furniture. The open sign was in the window, the blinds were up, and the house behind the store looked well maintained and occupied.

"They aren't expecting us," I whispered.

You wounded the Nörglein. Let's hope he's not back to work yet.

"You think he works here?"

Makes sense.

Scrap clung to my shoulder as we moved from the car to the shop. A cowbell the size of a ten gallon barrel bonged loudly when I opened the door. The clapper sounded again when I closed it behind me. No echoes or reverberations. The heavily padded sofas and recliners artfully arranged in conversation groups absorbed the sound.

I felt like I'd walked into an elite salon. Graceful lamps and silk flowers accented the expensive furniture. Highly polished woods reflected the light, making the interior of the building look much brighter than the gloomy exterior suggested.

The light made the sales floor appear three or four times as large as it should be.

Maybe it was.

A tall, dark-haired woman looking near my own age glided out of an office area, separated from the floor by walls of glass. She hesitated only half a heartbeat when she saw me, then continued forward. Doreen Cooper, my former sister-in-law. I guessed that naming girls in the Damiri tribe held true as for boys. Doreen, Dillwyn, Darren, Donovan, all started with D and ended with N.

Made for a lot of confusion when they all jokingly referred to each other as D.

The Coopers also held true within their family by giving all the children B middle initials. Which one of them was the infamous D.B. Cooper, the first to hijack a plane demanding ransom money? Back in the early '70s he became a kind of folk hero in the Pacific Northwest. Not really a Robin Hood, but he put the screws to a major corporation, exploiter of the masses, and got away with it. At least that was the feeling when it happened.

Distinctive white streaks at Doreen's temples, running the full length of her magnificent mane of hair down to her waist, stood out like beacons in the darkness.

She looked thinner, more drawn in the face than she had a few weeks ago.

Her tasteful red suit hung loosely. She'd lost weight recently. Not as much as she'd probably like, but her figure had more definition today, less flab.

Stress had aged her a bit. She looked forty instead of thirty. She'd undoubtedly lived several decades (or centuries) longer than I had.

Scrap had seen her at High Desert Con, arguing with Donovan. I hadn't noticed her, so I couldn't tell if the changes in her had taken place before or after that.

I still wondered if she'd actually argued with Donovan, or if the Nörglein had worn that form as a disguise.

"Doreen, just the person I need to see about some new furniture." I strode forward, hand outstretched in greeting, with more confidence than I truly felt.

"Oh?" she said with a superior sniff. "I see you're finally out of that hideous cast. Still weak though, Teresa?" She didn't offer to shake my hand. Her gaze lingered a little too long on my slight limp.

"Tess. Only my mother called me Teresa, and then only when she was really angry."

"Yes." A long, pregnant pause. "So, what does a Warrior of the Celestial Blade want with a known demon establishment? Come to murder us in broad daylight, like you did Dill?"

"Huh?" I'd held her brother in my arms as he gasped his last breath with fire riddled lungs. The fire started in the middle of the night while we slept. "Dill was murdered by one of your own. Darren Estevez had a heavy hand in that. You acknowledged that when we met a couple of weeks ago."

A pattern of selective memory loss, similar to what the Nörglein's victims suffered.

Her sharp inhale caught in her throat as color infused her face. She coughed, turning discreetly to the side. "So you killed Darren in revenge."

She clung to the implanted memories. I had to break through that barrier. For her sake as well as my own.

"No, I did not murder Darren Estevez. Donovan's girlfriend did that."

"Aren't you ...?"

"Nope. He sleeps with a lot of women. Including Lady Lucia, the vampire crime boss of Las Vegas. You too?"

She had the grace to blush. "I hadn't seen him in quite a while. Then he turned up again a few weeks ago. We fell into dating."

"WindScribe did the dirty deed against Darren. Then Donovan knocked her up. She's incarcerated in a heavy security insane asylum. My aunt is raising their daughter."

"Oh." Her mouth formed the word, but no sound emerged. Then she coughed again. "We were told differently." Understanding began to brighten her eyes.

I bet you were, sweetie. These guys embroider the truth with lots of twists and curlicues, Scrap added.

I noted he hadn't bothered to light his cigar.

"I've decided to refurnish my condo and thought of looking here first. Keep it in the family, so to speak." I broke eye contact with her and scanned the delicate Louis XVI style dining set.

Doreen's gaze shifted to my left shoulder where Scrap sat. He wrapped his tail around my throat tightly, only partly for balance. I sensed new heat coming from him as his skin pinked.

Oh, yeah, this woman was a demon but, so far, not a threat to us.

"What exactly are you looking for?" she asked.

Double angled question

"This looks nice," I said, wandering over to an early American styled dining set in honey maple. Round table polished to a mellow gloss, four captain's chairs in the same wood. The price made me blanch.

Then I had a quick flashback to the kitchen nook furniture Dill and I had picked out for the house on Cape Cod. The extra leaves in the table allowed us to seat eight. We'd planned on having breakfast there with a whole passel of children. Mom and I had made seat pads, café curtains, and matching place mats in a delicate blue and brown calico.

Gone now. All gone. First Dill died in a fire. Then I'd burned the table and chairs and calico after being contaminated with Orculli troll blood. Then Mom had been murdered.

A wave of grief and loneliness nearly drowned me.

I must have staggered as I clutched a chair back. Doreen grabbed my elbow to steady me. "Dill selected that line of furniture for the store. It's one of our most popular," she said flatly. She fought as much emotion as I did. Dill was her brother. The humanity in their bloodline dominated when it came to family.

"Maybe something more Craftsman for my new place. I don't need reminders of what I lost every time I sit down to eat." Looking everywhere but at the table, I saw a basket of glass balls on a lamp table beside a more suitable sofa, loveseat, and wingback chairs that would complement my parquet floors and simple wood railing.

Not just any glass balls. At least one of them had the milky swirls of true beryllium.

Power radiated from it. I'd tasted that power before.

Without thinking my feet marched over to the basket. I reached for the crystal ball, anxious to truly hold it, caress it, bond with it, make it my tool and my companion.

Scrap added a layer of green lust to his pastel pink. Not a good combination.

Doreen moved to intercept me. "Those are not for sale," she whispered. She kept a wary eye on my imp.

Who was she hiding that information from?

"Not for sale? Or not for sale to me?" My feet adjusted to *en garde* without thinking. I had to shift my weight forward into a half lunge, taking pressure off the newly freed and still weak left ankle. I caught a glimpse of my profile in a mirror on the far wall. The pose made me look more aggressive than I felt.

Doreen backed off, the crystal ball in her hand. The other bits of blown glass in the basket remained inert.

"You really, really don't want to push this, Tess," she hissed, still keeping her words quiet and private.

Ask her if she knows the history of the ball, Scrap ordered. He'd lost his cigar and poised on his hind legs, ready to jump to my hand and transform if I commanded.

Something crashed in the back room followed by a series of smaller thuds. It sounded like a bookcase turned over, spewing books to the far corners.

Then the angry stomp of heavy feet. Multiple heavy feet, like four or five sets of them.

"Doreen!" a shrill female voice screamed. "Get back here now."

Doreen paused, staring at the prized crystal. Her gaze rose to meet mine.

"A woman came in yesterday. She said she'd been threatened and needed to turn this over to them. They trashed her storeroom looking for it, broke a lot of stuff. She had a black eye, favored her ribs, and limped when she came in," Doreen explained, just as quietly as before.

"Starshine?"

"Maybe. I bought it from her for a fraction of its worth. One thousand. Mom doesn't know I spent that much. It was my own money."

"Doreen, where the hell are you? I need your help," the other woman screamed. "Get out, weed-ridden, tattooed vermin. Get out of my shop and my home."

Uh oh. I only knew of one tribe that fit that description and had the audacity to invade another demon's territory.

"Scrap!" I held out my right hand, ready to charge in and fight the Nörglettes.

"Take it!" Doreen thrust the treasure into my hand. "I freely gift it to you. Take it and get out. Never come back. Especially with the imp. This is not your fight. It's mine! I don't want or need your help." She dashed for the back room.

I gimped toward the opposite exit as fast as I could and still retain my balance.

That went well, Scrap mused, peering closely at the ball.

"Time to hit the mall and get you a new boa," I groused as I put the car in reverse and fled. The ball nestled safely in my jacket pocket, absorbing the warmth of my body and reflecting it back.

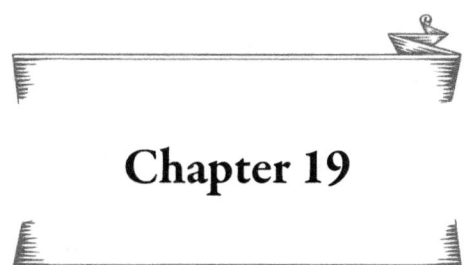

Chapter 19

In 1805 William Clark of Lewis and Clark named the bottomland on the South bank of the Columbia River for his sister: Fanny's Bottom.

A few blocks away from Cooper's the sun broke through the thinning clouds. Heavy showers nestled up against the foothills, but for a short time, I had light and a remembrance of warmth.

"We're stopping at the park," I told Scrap. He crouched in the back window watching for signs of pursuit.

Is that wise? he asked. *We don't want to get caught in a deserted spot of green when the Nörglein comes looking for you. They can manipulate green, if you remember the blackberry vine that tripped you.*

"We'll be safe enough at Lewis and Clark State Park. It's a block from the freeway. The guys fishing the Sandy River always fill the parking lot with their pickups."

Fishermen in this weather? Scrap flitted to the dashboard. He waggled his thinning boa at me.

"Fishermen fish in any weather, any day of the week."

He harrumphed and grumbled. *Don't forget you promised me a trip to the mall.*

"I won't." I pulled into a narrow space between a giant SUV and a rusting pickup that had seen better days about thirty years ago. My little hybrid looked out of place here, but it wasn't readily visible to the casual glance either.

We sat in the car in silence for many long moments. The crystal ball almost burned, begging me to take it in my hands, gaze in wonder at the miracles it could reveal. "You ready for this, Scrap?"

As ready as I'll ever be. He crawled to my shoulder and wrapped his tail around my neck in a choke hold worthy of a professional cage fighter on steroids.

I cupped my hands around the ball. But I watched a drop of rain caught on a sword fern reflect a rainbow in a tentative beam of light. I hoped its invitation proved stronger than the clouds threatening to fill in the pockets of blue sky.

Look at it, Tess. We'll never know for sure what it is, what it can do, if we don't look. Scrap leaned forward, nearly falling off his perch, eyes glued to the crystal sphere. He was totally entranced.

"Okay." I drew in a deep breath and shifted my gaze to the milky swirls. I traced them, learned them, followed them in, deep, deep, deeper.

I caught a tendril of floating minerals and rode the trail with the power of a celestial wind in our light sail.

LIGHT SQUEEZES AGAINST me. I twist and slide, dragging Tess in my wake.

The strange mineral deposits inside the ball twine around us and drag us around and around. My head spins faster than my senses can keep up.

I need to close my eyes. The real estate inside the ball passes by so fast I'm getting dizzy.

But If I don't watch and memorize it, I may not be able to get us home.

"Where are we?" I ask Tess as we slide around and around.

"I'm not sure. In a way it smells a bit like the mutant faeries. A bit of rot overlaying something that used to be sweet and pure.

"Yeah, it does smell like that."

Strange that her nose is more sensitive than mine in here.

We come to a stop with a thump that jars my neck and gives me a headache. At least we have solid ground beneath our feet.

We turn around and around taking in the landscape. I recognize the winding creek as it chuckles over a three-foot waterfall. The spreading, patriarchal oak with mistletoe in the upper branches looks familiar too. But it's bassackwards.

"Am I still dizzy or is everything fuzzy around the edges, like it's not fully formed yet?" Tess asks.

"Fuzzy. That's what's wrong!"

"You sound happy, is that a good thing?"

"I have a theory. Close your eyes and think about what that tree should be like."

She does. *"You mean like the oak in the front yard at home—in Cape Cod home, not Portland."*

"The one with the swing," I remind her.

Sure enough, as her mind re-creates the beloved image of happy summer days lazing on the simple board swing dangling from a stout branch ten feet up, the tree firms up. The vague smudges of green resolve into sprays of broad leaves. Clumps of acorns tip the ends. The bark ripples and mottles into the appropriate shades of brown.

When the swing drops down from the upper branches, complete with the thick splice in the rope about five feet above the board, I nearly fall off Tess' shoulder.

While I flail for balance I notice the creek. The water takes on definition. It loses the artificial feel and smell of a computer generated painting where only a few things move.

A breeze springs up, completing the picture.

But it's still upside down or twisted right to left.

Left to right.

I hang upside down on Tess' shoulder and view it all from a different perspective.

"Um, babe?"

"Yes?" Tess is gazing around in wonder. As her eyes light upon a too-bright blue jay in the tree, it begins to move as if released from a spell that froze it in place. It scolds us angrily, then flies off.

Sounds begin to form, insects, birdsong in the distance, wind in the tree canopy.

"Tess, dahling, I think we need to go home. Like now. Right now, before we do any more damage."

"Damage? It's like we are creating the place just by being here."

"That's what I mean. We shouldn't be here. This dimension isn't ready for us yet."

"You mean it's a brand-new dimension?"

"Still forming."

"How?"

"Don't know yet. But I got a theory."

"Care to share it?"

"Not yet. I need to do a little research."

"You aren't going back to the chat room by yourself! Remember what happened last time."

"All too well, babe. There are other methods of research closer to home." Like Gollum. I owe him an email. Good thing I figured out how to invade the innards of a computer.

"As long as you don't endanger yourself and therefore us." She sighs in resignation.

"Hang on tight, babe. We're going to ride the crystal ball home, the same way we came in."

I close my eyes, grab hold of an imaginary trail of swirling minerals, and slide down a sunbeam right into the driver's seat of Tess' car.

"Whew, what a ride." I wipe imaginary sweat off my brow."

"Yeah. Quite a ride. I'm exhausted. Let's go home." She turns the key in the ignition and engages the clutch.

"Remember, you promised a stop at the mall," I whine.

"One stop. And only one stop. You may buy one feather boa and nothing else."

"You're no fun."

"I work at it."

Chapter 20

M ills End Park in Portland is two feet square and was created for leprechauns to hold snail races on St. Patrick's Day. Keep Portland Weird!

"Forgive me, Tess, but I have to cut our date short tonight," Dr. Sean Connolly says as he escorts my babe to his car in the guest slot of our building's lot.

He wears a nice gray suit with a subdued silvery tie and a shirt a shade lighter than the suit. This man knows how to dress to impress. I couldn't have selected better myself. With his dark hair, fair skin, and ice blue eyes, he looks good enough to eat.

Too bad he's straight and mundane. I can't approve of him for my dahling Tess no matter how delicious.

He's not Gollum.

I'm glad I dug out Tess' little black dress that goes with everything, add Mom's pearls and it fits any occasion. Only it isn't black—Tess hates black and it drains the color from her face—it's midnight blue. I picked it out of course. I wish she'd worn the glittery sandals with two-inch heels. They fit the dress perfectly. But no, she says. She can't afford to limp in front of the good doctor. She wears the comfortable navy flats.

"Oh?" Tess replies to Dr. Sean.

I hope she at least gets dinner after all my hard work dressing her properly. If you only knew how much trouble I have talking her out of red undies. She always wears red 'cause the Sisterhood of the Celestial Blade wear only red to remind them of the blood their Sisters shed in the good fight against demons."

But red under the midnight blue? Honestly, she'd look like an American Flag. We celebrated the Fourth of July over four months ago. This is October, approaching Halloween. If she's going seasonal we'll go for gold and green.

"I'm on call at the ER from ten o'clock on." Dr. Sean looks a bit sheepish but proud too. "It's the weekend and coming up on a full moon near Halloween, even if we can't see it with this cloud cover. I'm expecting a full night."

Tess shivers a bit in the chill wind off the river laden with drizzle. Typical of the season. Great weather for growing mold.

"That's okay." Tess flashes a brief smile. "My leg is tired, and I'll want to get it elevated in a comfy chair sooner rather than later."

"Not doing too much are you?" He looks concerned as he hands her into his dark blue BMW. A really nice car but not as flashy as Donovan's Mercedes.

I prefer Gollum's rattletrap van. Mold hides in the rusting nooks and crannies.

"I drove my stick shift out to Gresham to visit my former sister-in-law." The truth, just not the whole truth. "Working the clutch was a bit much for me."

"Former sister-in-law?" Now he looks afraid.

"My husband, her brother, died about four years ago." *Four years, eight months, and three days ago. I remember 'cause that's when my Tess caught the imp flu.*

Only when she'd stumbled into the Citadel with raging fever and delirium and had the interdimensional infection lanced—leaving that beautiful scar on her face only imps and our companions can see—could she and I bond to become Warriors of the Celestial Blade.

"Sorry to hear that."

"I'm getting over it. Grief never totally goes away, but we do learn to cope." *We'd learned that the hard way.*

"Nice to see you are moving on, dating again." His grin brightened his entire posture. He must have used a professional whitener on those dazzling teeth. And yet his left eye tooth is slightly twisted. It gives him a wonderful puckish demeanor.

"Yeah, it's good to be out and about again. I've had cabin fever really bad with that cast."

"Let's see what we can do about that." He drove downtown to a cozy brew pub on the riverfront with a Celtic theme. Kelly's, our favorite. Bright music spills out every time the door opens.

"I come here often," Tess says brightly. "For the music."

She certainly didn't come for the food; she hasn't eaten enough to keep a rabbit alive since Mom died, until recently that is. Almost as soon as she hooked up with her family again her appetite and her zest returned.

Time to clear out the mold behind the beer kegs. We haven't been here for a while; the garden of my dreams should be ripe.

When I've eaten my fill, I'll double-check our hiding place for the crystal ball. The Nörglein won't find it so easily this time.

I think I know what they want with it. Can't let them have it. Not ever. The ball came to Tess for a reason. She's the guardian of that new dimension. She and me.

I take my responsibilities seriously.

Well most of the time anyway.

"WHO'S PLAYING TONIGHT?" I asked as we made our way through the standing room only crowd to a table right by the stage. The waiter whisked off a reserved sign as Sean held my chair.

"Someone new," he replied a bit sheepishly. "I've never heard Holly Shannon play, but all the music here is good. I figured we couldn't go wrong."

I couldn't help the light laughter that trickled out of me. "You are in for a treat. Holly is the best Celtic harpist on the west coast. Not a bad soprano either."

"I'm glad you won't be disappointed." He covered my hand with his own on the tabletop. Our gazes met and locked.

This could get very interesting.

The waiter interrupted us, impatiently tapping his order pad with a leaky pen. We hadn't even looked at the menu.

"What's the special?" Sean stalled while we hastily scanned the single sheet of computer printout, Kelly green ink on heavy white paper.

"Give us a minute, Ian," I said with a smile.

"Oh, hi, Tess. Sorry I didn't notice you. As you can see, we're swamped tonight. Holly's premiering a new CD. Let me get you drinks while you decide on the menu. The corned beef platter is the special, but we also have a salmon Caesar salad with fresh bread."

"River Dance pale ale," I replied without thinking.

"Do you have a nonalcoholic beer? I'm working tonight." Sean blushed slightly. "And I'd like the corned beef platter."

"Make that two, Ian."

"Sure thing. We've got three NAs, including a version of River Dance."

"I'll try it." Sean smiled.

"Should I tell the boss you're here?" Ian asked.

"As long as he doesn't make me sing. I'm on a date."

"Gotcha." Ian tipped his finger to his forehead in a salute and backed off.

"You come here often?" Sean quirked an eyebrow.

"I guess." I shrugged.

Our smiles and gazes locked again.

"So do I, but I've never been treated with such familiarity. How come I've never seen you in here?"

"Because you work crazy shifts and I usually avoid quiet times when I have time and peace to contemplate my sins."

"They can't be many. Your sins, I mean." He took both my hands and held them across the small table.

"You'd be surprised." I closed my eyes so that he couldn't see any secrets in their depths.

"Tess!" a squeal from across the room. Three twenty-something girls sped across the room, elbowing aside anyone in their way. "When's the next book coming out?" Janni asked.

Her two clone companions, Jen and Josie, nodded in wide-eyed agreement. They dressed alike, scooped their blonde curls (only one natural) back with similar clips, and wore the same shade of lipstick. I'd learned to separate them only after a full year of association at cons and pub crawls.

"Are you singing tonight?" Jen asked breathlessly.

"No date on the next book yet." I had to finish the damn thing and turn it in to get it scheduled by the publisher. "And no, I'm not singing tonight. It's Holly's concert. You won't want to bother with me once she starts."

The girls faded away in disappointment.

"I had no idea you were so famous," Sean said, his brow crinkling in puzzlement.

"Not really. Only in the science fiction and fantasy crowd. There's a lot of spillover between the Celtic music scene and the cons." Then I had to explain cons which can't really be explained. They have to be experienced.

Ian brought our drinks and set cutlery and Kelly green napkins before us.

"To an enchanted evening." Sean lifted his glass in toast.

I mimicked him. We took our first sips together.

Our conversation drifted from the smoothness of the ale to anticipation of the real music, not just the recorded instrumental being mangled by the sound system and the crowd noise fast becoming a wall of sound that separated us from normal pub activity.

"I remembered a conversation after the bruised bone in your right forearm from an over-vigorous fencing match. You bemoaned missing a concert by a local fiddler," he said when half his ale was gone.

"You've been memorizing information about me for a long time." That trip to the emergency room had been six months ago. "Should I be flattered or are you a stalker?" Only half a joke.

"Flattered, I hope. You've intrigued me for a long time. I've wondered what your life was like that you ended up in my ER so often."

"Been curious enough to read any of my books?"

"Sorry." He looked abashed. "I don't have a lot of time for reading fiction. Or anything else other than medical journals. But I did buy one of your books after your friend Allie suggested it. It's on my nightstand. I just haven't gotten around to it yet."

"Don't flinch, but you are about to see more of my life than you want." I leaned forward conspiratorially. Then I righted myself and plastered on a smile at the next woman to approach our table.

"Tess," Squishy said as she pumped my hand with genuine warmth and enthusiasm. "I don't want to intrude." She looked embarrassed as her gaze flicked from me to my date.

"Not to worry. Any more ... um ... woodland adventures?"

She shook her head. "No full moons to bring out the craziness since we talked at the con. But I did get another short story published. On-line, but professional rates."

"Congratulations. Send me the details and I'll look it up." About time I read something of hers.

She and Sean exchanged looks again. "I know you," they said in unison.

"Mercy Hospital ER two months ago. We delivered a slash and grab baby," he said cautiously. "Patricia—Newman, isn't it? I was mighty glad psych released you long enough to help."

Uh oh. Maybe Sean did have an idea of how crazy my life could be.

"The weird one?" I mouthed my question to Squishy.

She nodded.

Then something else clicked in my brain. Patricia. Pat. Psych ward. Surely she couldn't be the nurse who helped Gollum and his wife, Julia.

I don't believe in coincidences. Too often the concentric circles in my life tilt in their orbits and collide. Like Sean delivering that woodland elf baby.

"Look, I'm here on a first date and don't want to leave her too long, she's very shy and... not really out of the closet yet, even if she had a few flirtations with... friends back east. We started getting together at High Desert Con." Squishy tilted her head toward a tall, elegant woman with shoulder length brown hair that flowed in a gentle curtain, the product of the most talented of hairdressers. My mop of dishwater blonde curls always looked the same sloppy mess even when I chanced upon a really good cut. That woman would never have to worry about how her hair looked. It always looked great.

I resented her instantly.

She tucked that perfect hair behind her ear with long tapered fingers that had been professionally manicured on a regular basis. I noticed the flash of a simple gold wedding band on her left hand.

"Um ... does her husband know?" My gut sank and soared with hope and a wild roller coaster ride. Squishy's date couldn't be Julia. Not Gollum's Julia. The Squishy I knew wouldn't be so unprofessional and unethical as to date a vulnerable patient. Too easy to manipulate emotions. Too easy to take advantage.

"I've got to go." Squishy faded into the crowd as if she'd read my doubts on my face.

"The husband is always the last to know," Sean sighed.

"You okay with alternative lifestyles?" Better to know right here and now and end our friendship before we got serious if he couldn't accept some of my friends.

"Yeah. I just feel sorry for the poor sucker who married that gorgeous woman and is now going to lose her to another woman. That's got to hurt."

It might damage him emotionally. Irreparably, I thought. My gut sank again.

I forced myself to ignore it and concentrate on Sean. After all, I had no proof that Squishy was dating Gollum's emotionally fragile wife.

Our food arrived. We reached for the spicy brown mustard together and laughed away any awkwardness.

"This is really good," I said after the third mouthful of corned beef so tender it fell apart with the touch of a fork, new potatoes dripping in butter and parsley, carrots, and cabbage.

"They really know how to cook it right. My grandmother doesn't do it any better," he replied.

"Your family is Irish?"

"Second generation. Dad was born in County Cork but the family emigrated when he was two," he worked his words around bites of food.

We talked about immigrant families. Mine had moved from Quebec to Massachusetts. His had come straight to Oregon.

Acquaintances waved to me but had the manners not to intrude.

We had just finished eating and settled in with coffee and bread pudding rich with raisins and cinnamon when Holly set up her harp on the tiny stage, two steps up from the main dining floor. Wide windows behind her looked out upon the river. Who could spare a glance for mere water and sparkling lights with Holly on stage?

She tossed her flame red hair behind her shoulders, spread her embroidered linen skirt, and sat on a stool with a lap harp, carved and painted with elaborate Celtic knots.

The strings had also been painted so a side view showed a St. Brigid cross in bright colors, to match the one on her tambourine. But it was more than decoration. The design had proved an effective protection for Holly when we had a small adventure together with a Pookah. The poor creature was lost. With no way to get home, he hung around the music and fed on other people's life energy—almost to the point of death for one of them. Holly now used a St. Brigid Cross on all her instruments as a protective ward.

I helped the lost soul find a way home. In return, he gave me a prophecy.

By the light of the moon trailing a silver path along the river you shall find an end and a beginning.

I looked beyond the low stage to the river. No visible moonlight tonight.

The room hushed in anticipation.

Without introduction, Holly began a lively jig, her fingers dancing over the strings as light and lovely as a faery drunk on pollen.

Trust me, I've seen faeries dance. Sometimes I think Holly is one of them, loaned briefly to humans to impart a little joy.

The jig morphed into a poignant ballad. Her clear soprano sent knife blades of emotion to the heart. More than one cynical eye teared up. Mine always did and I never bothered to hide it.

About the time the audience needed to sniff, the ballad gave way to a whimsical story song, and then another lively tune. We sang along on the chorus. The bolder among the listeners began free-form dancing between the dining tables.

I smiled that Sean felt comfortable enough in the raucous party atmosphere, and with me, to clap along, and even lend his shouts of enthusiasm to the revelers. He didn't sing though.

Holly brought the set to a close by the simple expedient of stilling her harp strings with the flat of her hands.

Applause filled the room along with wild stomps and hoots of approval.

The harpist ran her gaze around the room, picking out new and familiar faces. She flicked past me, then back again. I tried to look away as she nodded to me with a wicked grin. Knowing what was to come, I took a sip of water.

"How about we give my vocal chords a break, folks. Some of you know my good friend, Tess Noncoiré. Join me, Tess." She held out her hand in invitation.

"Do you mind?" I asked Sean, still rooted to my chair.

"Of course not!" He avidly joined the applause.

How could I turn down that kind of response?

Holly handed me a mike as I came abreast of her. We bent our heads in a moment of consultation. Then she threw back her head and laughed long and loud.

The audience quieted in anticipation.

I hummed the first note coming from the harp to make sure I matched it. Then I caressed the microphone with my voice in the sexy foreplay of a torch song. Only the tune was an old folk ballad, "Blowin' in the Wind."

> *Where are all the aliens,*
> *Long time missing.*
> *Where are all the aliens,*
> *Gone to Roswell every one.*
> *When will they ever learn?*
> *When will they ever learn?*

More laughter as the audience crooned along.

At least Sean got the jokes. Not a bad first date. This one might be a keeper.

After we talked about that woodland elf baby.

Have I ever said I don't believe in coincidences?

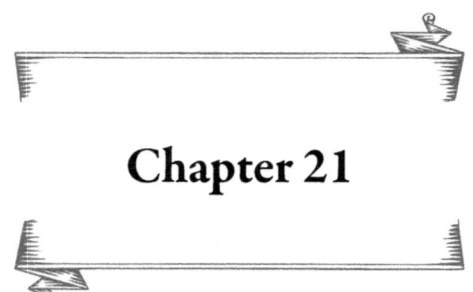

Chapter 21

In John Day, Oregon, the Kam Wah Chung State Heritage Site Museum is dedicated to a local Chinese doctor who treated local miners in the 1860s.

"Thank you for the CD," I said on my doorstep, clutching Holly's newest recording against my chest like a teenager in lust. Sean had his own autographed copy in his coat pocket.

I didn't want to burst his bubble by telling him I already had a contributor copy. This one was special.

"My pleasure. I'd have bought it even if I didn't know you sang backup on two numbers." He grinned widely while surreptitiously checking his watch.

Nine-thirty. He had plenty of time to drive the three miles to the hospital for his shift in the ER.

"We had fun tonight. I'd like to see you again, Tess," he said softly, taking one of my hands.

His warmth and sincerity spread from his touch to the coldest part of my heart.

"I'd like that." I bit my lip in indecision about something else.

"I have Wednesday off."

"Yes."

"But? You sound hesitant."

"Sean, I haven't had a lot of luck in my romantic choices. I need to go slow this time. I need to know that you will support me in the craziness and chaos I call a career, as much as I understand and support yours. If you truly want to continue dating, there's something…"

"There's someone else." His face fell from joy to crushing disappointment.

Yes, there is!

"No, there's no one else." No one available anyway.

"But? There's always a but."

"Squishy ... I mean Pat Newman confided in me a few weeks ago about a strangely deformed baby she helped you deliver."

"A trick of the light."

"Just think about it a moment. Then consider that one of the reasons I end up in your ER so often is because I'm working to keep other babies like that from being conceived."

"Are you a geneticist in secret?"

"No."

Quickly, before I lost my courage, I reached up and kissed his cheek. "I'm not insane. Read my books. Then think about it. Call me if you still want to do something on Wednesday. I'll clear the day for you."

I darted inside and closed the door. I leaned against it, waiting and listening.

He stood outside, silent for many long moments before I heard his footsteps retreat down the steps.

THE CRYSTAL BALL IS all tucked up safe and sound where it should be. I've arranged artifacts of power around it so no demon or witch or Powers That Be can sniff it out. A LARPER might stumble upon it if they went looking in the wrong place, but they have no business playing their games behind that particular locked door.

While I was playing hide and seek, I also retrieved a certain hair comb my Tess adores. I found it in Mum's front yard a couple of years ago.

Like a lot of the detritus that finds its way into Imp Haven, the comb has magic. When my babe wears the comb she can see the truth in a person's aura. We both need to know who and what this doctor is.

I don't trust him. He's not one of us.

He's not Gollum.

TUESDAY AFTERNOON I shifted impatiently around my office, pretending to work. I moved from the desk to the bookcase. I opened and closed book after book, searching for ... I don't know what.

Actually, I was hoping Sean would call.

Which felt stupid; like I was fourteen obsessing about my first crush.

Come to think on it, I hadn't had a real date with a man who didn't have an arcane agenda since back before I met Dill. Saturday night felt like my very first date.

The phone rang. I grabbed it on the first ring.

"Tess, have you seen Doreen?" Donovan asked. I heard a tenseness in his voice beneath his usual charming smoothness.

"Why would I have seen Doreen?" I tapped my foot impatiently, wanting to keep the line free for Sean. But something in his voice sent a frisson of alarm along my spine. I'd left the furniture emporium with the crystal ball just as the Nörglein and his minions invaded the back office. Violently.

"She said you'd been by the store. I thought the two of you might be becoming friends." Donovan sounded disappointed.

"I haven't heard from her since she ordered me out of the store."

"Oh."

"Anything else, Donovan? Should I be worried that you can't find your girlfriend?"

"No." He hung up abruptly.

Frustrated and a little worried, I stretched and rotated my left ankle and knee until the muscles turned to pudding, desperate to rebuild my strength and limberness. Desperate to fill the hours.

An hour later, the phone rang again.

"Found her," Donovan said. "No need to worry about us." Then he hung up just as sharply as before.

What was that all about?

A timid knock came at the front door. I slid down the hall on stockinged feet. The slick wax on the hardwood floor sped me along the way before Allie could react from her nest in the living room surrounded with bride magazines and home décor books, along with her laptop and lesson plans. She's always been better at multitasking than me. I obsess on one topic too much.

At the moment all I could think about was Sean's reaction to the finale of our first date.

As fast as I moved, Scrap appeared out of nowhere and beat me to my destination. He clung with his toes, upside down, like a bat, peering through the wood panels.

I wished he wouldn't do that. I hate bats. I hate any reminder of bats.

Donovan's tribe of Damiri demons take a bat form in their natural state.

At the door, I paused long enough to breathe, smiled brightly, opened the door, and ...

My face stiffened into a stern frown. "Do I know you?" I asked two adolescent girls shifting from foot to foot and looking about anxiously.

Of course you do, Scarp said and blew cigar smoke into their faces.

"Um ... Oak sent us," the one on the left, the older of the two, said shyly. She had dark shaggy hair that curled in odd wisps. Tall and sinewy, she towered over me and her sister.

"She's Blackberry. I'm Salal," said the younger sister. Closer to my height, she was painfully thin but not emaciated. I guessed she was very supple.

If they mimicked their namesake plants, Blackberry should be bold, thrusting her personality on one and all. Salal should be shier, hiding under things, seeking dark, damp places. But then Blackberry seemed to be in the midst of changing from little girl to woman. Her human hormones should be raging, making her extremely uncomfortable in her own body. Who knew how long puberty lasted in Kajiri demons with extended life-spans.

Lady Lucia's Damiri blood was so dilute she was unaware of it until she took thirty years to mature between eighteen and twenty-five. Even now, at the age of two hundred plus, she looked perhaps forty-five, maybe fifty.

These girls were half Nörglein. From newspaper reports of missing hikers in the local forest about fifty years ago, I suspected they were part of that batch of ill-conceived children.

"Why did your brother think I would talk to you?" I hedged, blocking the doorway.

Scrap moved to my shoulder. He stayed his normal gray-green translucence. Nothing threatening about these girls. Yet.

"Oak said you kind of understood us. That maybe you could help us... um... figure out some things," Blackberry replied. She kept her gaze on the ground.

"Things like why your body is changing?" I'd spent a few years, early in my writing career, substitute teaching to help make ends meet. Adolescent girls didn't scare me as much as they scared themselves.

Both girls blushed.

"Are you willing to part with some information too?" I asked.

"Like...?" Blackberry asked, finally looking up with the boldness that fit her namesake plant.

"Like why your family invaded the back room at Cooper's?" I wasn't about to mention the crystal ball, just in case that hadn't been the object of their quest.

Yeah, right.

"That's family," Blackberry said. She set her chin and clamped her mouth shut.

I made to close the door.

"They were looking for something to help heal Father," Salal interjected. She rammed her delicate foot in front of the door.

Try as I might, I couldn't close it, even if I was determined to crush her foot.

Demons have more strength than the average human. A lot more strength. I'd seen a Sasquatch teen, in human form, shoulder three of his fallen comrades and sprint a hundred yards without breathing hard.

Ever try to break a salal vine? The fibers will shred your hands first. Blackberries are worse, with thorns that slide under fingernails and imbed deep into tender joint tissue.

"Something special that you wouldn't know about," Blackberry added.

Oh yeah? Scrap sneered.

Both girls looked at him, then away quickly, as if remembering they weren't supposed to see him.

"Were your brothers the ones who beat up my friend, Starshine, trying to get her to part with that something special?"

"Um..." Blackberry drew an intricate design on the floor with her bare toe. It absorbed all of her attention.

"Did you have any part in that?" I asked. My feet shifted to *en garde* and I held my hand out, palm up, ready for Scrap to transform.

But he didn't. He rose up and fluttered around the girls' heads, sticking his forked tongue out at them, and lashing their hair with his tail.

"That was our brother, Cedar, and some of our father's helpers," Salal insisted. "We offered to go, but they wouldn't let us. Cedar said it was men's work. What makes one thing a man's work and the next a woman's?"

She tilted her head and stared at me in honest puzzlement.

"I think you girls should come in. I'll make tea and we'll talk," Allie said from behind me. She'd moved up silently, ready to guard my back if needed.

I opened the door and stepped out of their way. The two girls made their way to the barstools, cautiously looking over their shoulders at me with each step.

We settled around the counter that separated the kitchen from the great room. Allie and I kept to the kitchen side. I wanted the girls to feel they could leave at any time without having to go through us. Possibly violently.

Ooooh, girl talk, Scrap crooned taking a perch on the wine glass rack.

"Does he have to be here?" Blackberry asked, pointing at my imp. We all knew that the girls could see Scrap. No sense in pretending anymore.

"He's gay, no need to be embarrassed."

"We don't care if he's happy. He is male," Salal said also looking askance at Scrap's antics. But her eyes didn't truly focus on him, just tracked his general movements.

"In today's slang, gay means that he likes boys. Homosexual," Allie explained.

Our two guests stared at each other in some long unspoken communication. "Fir," they whispered.

"We'd still like this to be private," Blackberry mumbled.

"Can you take a powder, pal?" I asked. "Go find some mold to gorge on in the basement. I'll call if I need you."

Ah, you're no fun, he pouted.

Women who pout to get their own way drive me crazy. I've known too many of them—including my own mother—to put up with their practiced manipulation.

But on Scrap, the expression looked more ridiculous.

Swallowing my mirth I banished him with a gesture. I sensed he only went as far as my office and eavesdropped shamelessly.

"What do you need to know?" Allie asked, forthright and no nonsense.

"Why do I bleed?" Blackberry asked, equally forthright.

I got out a blank notebook and colored pencils. The discussion went downhill from there. I'd never had to teach sex education before, but I knew how, part of my general education degree.

"In our culture, women don't have to have babies just because the men want them to," I finished.

Blackberry opened and closed her mouth a couple of times.

"Spit it out," I said gently.

"We... we spend a lot of time in Old Town." Blackberry traced an arcane pattern on the counter with her fingertip.

"And?"

"And I've made friends with an old woman at the Asian pharmacy."

Portland has a small but thriving Chinatown and a large Asian population, Chinese, Japanese, Vietnamese, the whole range of Oriental cultures.

"And..."

"She's been giving me black cohosh once a month since I started, you know..." She tapped the drawings we'd made in the notebook.

"To keep you from getting pregnant."

"I guess." She shrugged and turned her back to us, studying the river through the broad windows.

"Okay. But a girl your age shouldn't need it. You shouldn't have to have sex unless you want it. Even then I think you are too young to fully understand a deep relationship." Gee, I sounded preachy. But I think Blackberry needed to hear that.

She shrugged again, without looking at me.

"A woman gets to choose who she has sex with and when. For the man to force her is a heinous crime," Allie expanded my statement.

"Sex is best when shared by a couple with deep affection. It is the ultimate in communication, communication that goes beyond words. Sex should be an extension of true and abiding intimacy, not just to make babies," I added.

We walked all around the issue of their father being a scumbag who needed to be wiped out, the sooner, the better.

I hoped the lingering wound I gave him from the Celestial Blade festered and caused him a great deal of hideous pain.

Salal's jaw dropped as the idea behind the words penetrated her mind first.

"How does your father feel about you having sex?"

"He has never mentioned it. He doesn't talk to us about his women and the new babies that will come to him," she whispered.

Blackberry looked off into a corner, clamping her jaw shut. I saw the muscles around her mouth twitch, as if she was grinding her teeth.

"He only talks to us about our mission to nurture the forest. Keeping out the invasive nonnative plants is a never-ending job. It's a sacred duty," Blackberry added, obviously more comfortable talking about work than life. Like most people.

Then again, a lot of people mistook their work for life. Like me.

Allie seemed to recently have made the distinction and chose the better alternative.

"What does your father do when he traps a woman and takes her home?" I asked. The girls weren't ready for the idea that their father was a nonnative invasive plant. If he didn't belong in this ecology, then they didn't either.

"Trap? He doesn't trap them. Traps are for vicious animals that go rogue," Blackberry insisted.

"He changes the paths so a woman gets lost. Then he offers her a return to safety in exchange for sex. That's a trap, coercion. And I call it rape," Allie returned equally forceful.

"What about when he traps a man, then shape-changes and spends the night with that man's wife?" I pressed on. "That's trickery of the worst kind."

"Wh ... what do you call it when he gives me to our brothers or his helpers to practice on?" Blackberry studied her tea mug as if the depths of the liquid held the answer. The whirlpool in her cup betrayed her agitation and shaking hands.

"That's abuse of the worse kind. You don't have to put up with it," I said, horror-struck.

"You don't have to go back to it," Allie added.

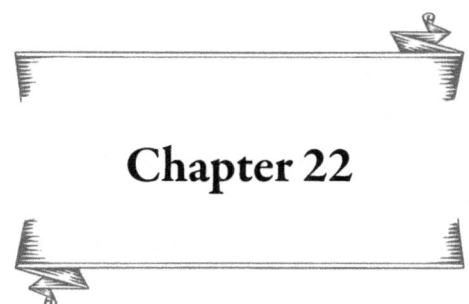

Chapter 22

1850-*1941 Portland was known as the Shanghai Capital of the world. A network of tunnels beneath the city's waterfront connected pool halls, saloons, restaurants, brothels, gambling parlors, and opium dens. Up to 1,500 men and women a year were kidnapped and sold to ship captains and brothels.*

"Father respects his women enough to put them in a trance so they enjoy the experience and do not remember him until after his child is born. He makes himself look very handsome for them. He also takes them into a back room in our home so that they have privacy." Blackberry didn't sound as convinced as she wanted to be.

She also completely ignored her own situation.

"More trickery," Allie snorted.

"Let's talk about your home. What does it look like?" If I could find the dark elf's lair, I could take him out. Once he was gone, the new forest babies could learn to let their human half dominate. Gradually, the woodland genes would fade into dormancy.

What would happen to the five teens? I had to get the girls out. Now. The boys?

Later. I'd make that decision later. Or they would. They were almost adults, ready to take responsibility for their own lives. But they couldn't be allowed to continue their father's ways.

No way. No how.

Something the girls had said wiggled and slid around the edges of my mind. Something about invasive nonnative species. Their father was out of his native environment and therefore a noxious weed.

I knew that keeping English ivy from strangling native trees was an ongoing battle with the parks department. The butterfly bush had been added to the list of pesky plants. A native of China, too many of the fragrant shrubs had escaped planned landscapes to take over creek banks, crowding out helpful natives.

The girls said that keeping those plants under control was part of their work.

Could the parks department and their volunteers manage without the additional help of a family of forest elves? Volunteer groups. They were around but how did I find them? How effective were they?

Goddess, I was digging myself deeper with every thought twist. I needed to concentrate on one thing at a time.

"What about our home?" Blackberry asked suspiciously.

If I remembered correctly, one species of blackberry, the big one with huge berries was also an invasive nonnative species too. Maybe she was named after the smaller and less aggressive local plant. The one with tiny thorns designed to hook into the delicate flesh of a bear's mouth to keep the animals from stripping the plant of greenery just to get to the berries.

"How big is your home? Forest Park is huge. There are large stretches where a small hut could blend into the background and stay hidden. But a big modern construction with lots of glass wouldn't." I needed a map.

"Not hard to hide something that's mostly underground," Salal said on a shrug. She, too, avoided her sister's horrible confession.

"Caves? I didn't know the geology of the hills was conducive to extensive cave systems." I'd absorbed bits and pieces of information about rocks and plate tectonics and such from my deceased husband. Dill had a Ph.D. in geology and spent a lot of our three-month marriage crawling around the high desert plateau of Central Oregon and Washington. I'd shipped his rock collection back to his parents, postage due, after they tried to stiff me on Dill's life insurance and inheritance of the house.

"She didn't say caves," Blackberry snorted. She didn't want to part with information her father wanted to remain secret, but as a teen she needed to let me know that her knowledge was superior to mine.

"If not natural caves..." I mused.

"Then unnatural tunnels," Allie offered.

"The Shanghai Tunnels!" I whispered. I'd seen a program on TV about what lies beneath major cities. Often whole underworlds. Portland had a sordid history of subterranean opium dens, brothels, and cells for unwilling recruits to the maritime industry. Not all of them had been fully explored. Local rumor claimed that some of them went all the way into the West Hills.

Forest Park covered a huge tract of those hills. Why couldn't some, or just one of those tunnels, lead to an elven home?

"How did you get here?" I jumped topics on the girls.

Gollum had a bad habit of expecting others to follow his rapid transitions. His mind had already made logical leaps. Unfortunately, not everyone had his intelligence and extensive knowledge of seemingly unrelated subject matter.

"We took the bus." Salal shrugged just like her sister, ducking her head into her shoulders.

Okay. They'd already admitted to ranging around Old Town and Chinatown.

"How'd you get to the bus?" I pressed them.

The girls looked at their hands folded around tea mugs.

"You don't have to tell me. I'm guessing you walked a tunnel into Old Town and came up in a back alley right near a bus stop."

Salal half nodded. "It's beside a parking lot where Father keeps his car. But Oak is the only one of us with a driver's license, other than Father, that is."

"What's his connection to the Coopers?"

"How'd you know about that?" Blackberry looked up sharply.

"Scrap smelled him there a few weeks ago. His minions and your brothers invaded the office looking for something precious."

"Oh," she said flatly. "Father works there. We all help out sometimes when they have a new shipment of antiques. The boys have learned to use the computer there."

"I want to go back to the women your father attacks," Allie insisted. "And what he makes your brothers do to you. How has he gotten away with it for so long?" Her shoulders hunched and her hands reached for the gun that no longer hung on her belt. Her new revolver was locked up in the bedroom.

"Why do you say attack? He uses no violence," Salal insisted.

Blackberry didn't look so sure.

"Does your father ask their permission? Does he court them? Does he follow up with offers of a relationship?" Allie pressed.

"N... no."

"Then he coerces them, tricks them. He doesn't get their permission. That's rape."

"Would you like it if some man did that to you?" I brought home the concept.

"Our brothers and the helpers haven't practiced on me yet, though Father wants them to," Salal defended the nasty little man.

"Um...." Blackberry hedged.

"How does your father expect you to behave when confronted with men? Do you strip off and open your legs to every man who looks at you—like a prostitute? Will you do it for your brothers when they can no longer resist his prodding?" Crude, but they didn't seem to understand subtle. "Or will you have sex with the lost travelers your father brings home just to produce more babies?"

"Yes," Blackberry whispered. "That's what he wants. That's why he insists we practice. That's why I need the black cohosh."

"He's using you like breeding cattle." Allie swallowed deeply and turned her back. She was having trouble containing her outrage.

So was I.

"Why?" I asked. "Loss of habitat and urban crowding drove him here from the Italian Alps. He doesn't belong here. Why is he so bent on rebuilding the Nörglein when there isn't enough wild land left for them all?"

"I don't know!" Blackberry shouted. She stood up, angrily pushing back her stool so that it clattered against the wood floor. Without another word she headed for the front door.

I couldn't stop her. The next decision had to be her own.

"We'd better get home," Salal said flatly. She rose more slowly, pushing her stool up next to the bar politely. She stalled by righting the fallen chair. She kept her gaze firmly on her task, never engaging me or her sister. "Thank you for the lesson on female biology. Thank you for the tea."

"You don't have to go back," I reminded them quietly.

Both girls stilled. Not even their eyelids twitched. A useful skill when hiding in the forest.

"Father will be very angry if we are late," Blackberry said after several long moments of silence.

"What will he do if you don't go back?" Allie asked. I could see ideas spinning in her head.

"He'll punish us."

"How?" I asked.

"He'll... he'll command our brothers to whip us with the vines of the other blackberry. The big ones."

I cringed in sympathy. The Himalayan variety had thorns big enough to penetrate the hide of a Yeti.

An odd thought. Bullets from an automatic weapon couldn't penetrate the hide of a Sasquatch—the North American version of the Yeti—because they were man-made. The blackberry, being natural, probably could. Something to keep in mind.

"Interesting that the coward will command your brothers to do his dirty work but can't stomach it himself."

"We'll protect you," Allie insisted.

"You are awfully generous in that 'we,'" I grumbled.

"You don't ever have to go back," Allie continued as if she hadn't heard me. "You can be like normal girls, go to school, and have friends. Learn to use a computer. Date boys and make your own decisions who you have sex with and when, preferably when you have a lot more experience of life and know what you really want in a partner, a long-term partner."

Blackberry retreated one step away from the door. Salal looked up with interest.

"You can protect us?" Blackberry asked, hopefully.

"Scrap, you on alert?"

Yeah, babe. I got your back. All clear so far. Don't think the old man has noticed the girls are missing. Yet.

"Where will you hide us?" Salal asked.

"Right here," Allie replied.

"You giving up the bed to them?" I returned.

"We'll work something out." She smiled.

"I wish I could call Donovan, he's got experience in integrating Kajiri into society." He'd reached out to me in his worry over Doreen. "I don't trust him. Gollum could help. I think I have to call him."

But first I needed a double shot of single malt Scotch. The good stuff.

OH, BOY, THIS COULD get interesting. Very interesting indeed. Too bad we can't extend this apartment into the chat room and give us more space without really adding to the building in this dimension.

Nope. That wouldn't work even if I could figure out how to do it. We don't want those girls exposed to the energies of the chat room that would bring out their elven heritage even more. We want to tamp down on those characteristics.

So who's going to sleep where? Maybe we can do it in shifts.

At least my babe is calling Gollum.

Uh oh, the phone is ringing. It's Dr. Sean. He's going to distract my babe and keep her from calling the only man she can trust to help her.

What to do? What to do?

I know, I'll send Gollum an email. Hmm, if I invade his home computer monitor I can make the screen show my message.

It's going to take some work and a whole lot of energy. Best I load up on mold first. Then I'll hit his computer just about the time he gets home from teaching.

That's the trick. Show him the message once and then make it fade like an automatic delete. He'll never know it's me and not Tess calling for help.

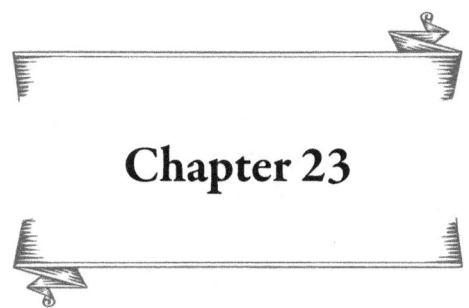

Chapter 23

*P*ortland, Oregon, is the only city in the US with a volcano within the city *limits—three of them—Mt. Tabor, Powell Butte, and Rocky Butte; all* *extinct.*

Much thought and calculation later, I decided it would be better to work with the devil I knew than the angel who could break my heart again.

"Who's the better computer hacker, Steve or Donovan?" I asked Allie.

Our two new guests had retired to the bedroom to discuss their decision to stay with me. If I was about to become their guardian, I didn't necessarily want them to know how I made it look legal.

"That's a toss-up." Allie hitched up the belt of her jeans as she would the utility belt she no longer wore. She used to do that as a subtle reminder to bullies and speed offenders that she had the firepower and the will to enforce the law. Her habits as a cop were going to be hard for her to drop. Those habits would add authenticity to her classes at the community college.

"This isn't going to be exactly legal. I don't want to involve Steve," I said as I punched number six on my speed dial.

"Halfling Gaming Systems, how may I direct your call?" A sultry female voice came on the line. Donovan's newest secretary I guessed. I wondered why Quentin wasn't the gatekeeper today. Maybe he was out planning a hit on someone. The big man who looked like he carried more Indian blood than demon had been Donovan's right hand for as long as I'd known him. He was also high on my list of suspects for the role of assistant to Donovan's foster father, Darren, on the night my husband died in an arson fire set outside our motel room.

That is if Donovan could be believed, and he didn't have a hand in that murder.

"Tell Donovan that Tess is on the line and it's urgent," I said a little less politely than my mother had taught me.

"One moment please, I'll see if Mr. Estevez is available."

Barely ten seconds passed. "Now what?" he snarled less politely than I had. "I told you not to worry about Doreen."

"I have just taken guardianship of two Kajiri girls who look twelve and fourteen. I need to make it look legal."

"What am I supposed to do about it?" He sounded interested but still cautious.

"You've done it before for others. Someone did it for you. You know what to do and how to do it."

"You'll need birth certificates."

"Can you do it?"

"Only if I put my name on them as their father."

My stomach lurched.

"If your name is on the certificate, then you'll sue for custody." And he'd raise them with constant reminders of their dark origins.

"Not if your name is listed as their mother. But then you are a firm believer in family, in two parent families. You'd have to marry me then."

I hung up on him. So much for his relationship with Doreen. It didn't stand the chance of a snowflake inside a lava flow of succeeding.

"That was short," Allie said cautiously.

"I don't even know why I bother asking him for help. He always attaches conditions that cost too much."

"He proposed again."

"Barely."

"And you refused again."

"If he'll believe hanging up on him is a refusal. But he did give me an idea."

"Such as?"

"I don't have to go through social services and getting certified as a foster parent if I'm their mother, and they've been back east growing up with my relatives. Home schooled, therefore no records. Medical records lost in an office fire."

"Tess, you're only thirty. You'd have been sixteen when Blackberry was born."

"Not all that unusual these days. So, do you think Steve can forge the birth certificates?"

"I hate to ask him. I hate that we are doing something so illegal."

"You got a better idea?"

"Gollum."

Right on cue the phone rang. The landline, not my cell phone. Gollum would call the cell.

GOLLUM JUST SITS THERE staring at my message. I blink and flash.

Ouch that hurts my head. My babe had better appreciate what I go through for her. This is going to require a big dose of beer and OJ to cure the headache.

And still Gollum sits there.

"Hey! Professor Van der Hoyden-Smythe, wake up. The love of your life needs you."

At last I think I'm getting through those thick glasses. He lets them slide down his long nose until they almost fall off. Then he caresses the words on the screen with a delicate fingertip, tracing the shape of the italic capitals as if they were the scar on my dahling Tess' face. The interdimensional scar that should be invisible to him, but isn't.

That's how I know he is the only man for Tess. He can see the scar. Donovan can feel it, but he can't see it.

Pansy Sean can't see it or feel it.

At last Gollum blinks rapidly and shakes his head as if clearing it.

Then he pushes his glasses back firmly onto the bridge of his nose and deletes my message!

Stupid idiot.

He starts scrolling through the rest of his email, replying here, saving there.

As tired as I am, I force a few phosphors to rearrange themselves.

THIS IS IMPORTANT YOU DUMB ASS. CALL TESS BEFORE SHE MAKES A HUGE MISTAKE. SHE NEEDS YOUR HELP.

Then I push myself halfway through the screen so he can see me.

Of course to his semi mundane brain I look like a rough squiggle of a cartoon, but he should get the message.

ON THE FOURTH RING I answered the phone, just before it went to voice mail. The caller ID said private name and number.

I don't usually answer calls I can't identify. Something in my gut said I needed to talk to this person. Too much was happening. Too many coincidences had fallen into place.

"Tess, don't hang up on me," Sean said hurriedly.

"Do I have a reason to hang up on you, Sean?"

Allie made an "Oh" with her mouth and withdrew, closing the office door on her way out.

"I hope not."

Should I tell him right away that tomorrow looked impossible to see him?

No. Better to play it safe and find out if he wanted to continue seeing me before I sent the message that I was having second thoughts, when I wasn't.

"Have you thought about our last conversation?" I asked instead.

"Yes." He sounded cautious. "I did some research too."

"Oh?" What could he find about me and the Warriors of the Celestial Blade? Not much. We were pledged to secrecy. But as more and more rogue portals opened between worlds, and more and more demons infiltrated our society, we had to move out of the Citadels and into everyday life, thus exposing ourselves to possible discovery every time we invoked the Celestial Blade.

"Actually, I talked to Nurse Newman."

I breathed a sigh of relief. "What did Squishy tell you?"

"Odd nickname for a woman so solidly built and strong ... But that's another topic for another day. She too told me to read your books, that the protagonist is you even if the setting is different."

Gulp.

"And..."

"And it's a little hard to swallow."

"Okay. You're skeptical. What does that mean for us?"

"I think we need to talk. I delivered another strange baby Saturday night, Sunday morning actually, right at moonset. I called in Nurse Newman to consult. The mother is fine and has the number to call for the support group you set up. I really think I need to talk to you about this. Can I see you tomorrow?"

"Actually, are you working tonight?"

"Until nine. I'm on a coffee break right now. What did you have in mind?"

I looked at the clock, almost five.

"I'd like to introduce you to two of those woodland babies grown up a bit."

He whistled long and low.

"How about I bring Chinese for four."

"Sounds wonderful. Um...."

"Um what?"

"There'll be five of us. My brother's fiancée is staying with me for a while—she's my best friend actually; we've known each other since kindergarten. It's a little crowded here. I don't suppose you have a spare camp cot or air mattress hanging around?"

"As a matter of fact I do. I have a full camping set up for when my dad and I go fishing every spring," he said on a chuckle.

I heard a page in the background.

"I've got to go. I'll see you about nine-thirty."

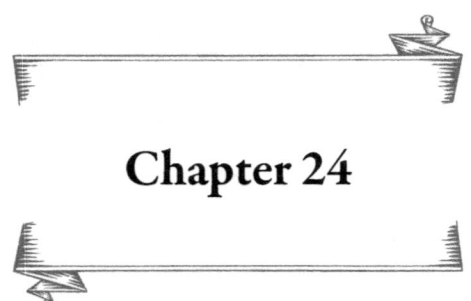

Chapter 24

Portland's Classical Chinese Garden is the largest urban Suzhou-style garden outside China.

I wasted a lot of time pacing my office. I schemed and plotted, discarded all my thoughts and started over again.

Allie finally knocked on the door with two mugs of coffee in her hands. "I threw together a vegetarian pot pie. It's hot. I wasn't sure what the girls would eat."

"Besides greasy pizza?" I drank deeply of the coffee, grateful for the caffeine hit, hoping it would clear the increasing number of cobwebs in my brain.

"Yeah. I figured we should start introducing them to normal food and clothes. Oh, Tess, they have nothing. Not even toothbrushes."

"I guess we need to raid the nearest discount store. As soon as we've eaten." I stepped toward the doorway.

Can we go to the mall? Scrap popped in right in front of me. *After beer and OJ.*

"You do look a little peckish. What have you been up to?" I eyed him suspiciously. His transparent green had faded to fairly ugly khaki and he had none of the glow he usually carried after a visit to Gingko.

You'll find out soon. Can we eat now?

We settled at the kitchen bar. I didn't want the girls to get in the habit of carrying their plates into the far corners of the condo. I was bad enough about that.

"Card table and chairs are on the list," Allie hissed at me as we dug into the casserole. Allie knew how to cook hearty for New England winters. Rich in turnip and barley, along with tomatoes and cauliflower, she'd topped the dish with two inches of mashed potatoes and a garnish of sharp cheddar cheese.

Salal and Blackberry practically inhaled it—after some basic instruction on how to use a fork and a napkin instead of fingers and tongues.

"I cooked, you clean up, share the chores," Allie insisted as the girls pushed their plates aside.

"Of course. Father always insisted on chores before fun. May we watch TV?" They looked too eager.

I eyed the last portion of pot pie. I didn't really need it, no matter how good it tasted. It would make a nice lunch for one person.

"We need to take you shopping," I said instead. "Clothes and toiletries before TV. We should get going if we're going to be back before Dr. Connolly gets here."

"Doctor?" Blackberry reared back, suddenly suspicious.

"Yes. My friend is a physician."

"We don't need a physician." Blackberry backed up, hands in front of her as if warding off something unpleasant.

"He's a friend. This is not a professional visit." I glared back at both girls. "Why do you fear doctors?"

"Nothing." They shrugged and took the dirty plates and cutlery to the sink.

Another sticky topic to be approached carefully. Slowly. After we'd built some emotional trust.

"Father says that physicians are money sucking leeches who don't know anything," Salal whispered on her way past me.

I arched my back and scanned the room, assessing what we needed to make the place habitable for two extra people. Bed, eating table and chairs, more seating in the living room. Everything!

A tentative knock on the door sent my heart into my throat. It couldn't be Sean. Not three hours early!

If anything, I'd expect a doctor to be late.

Go ahead and answer it, dahling, Scrap commanded. His dinner of beer and OJ had revived him enough to send him bouncing from wine rack to

TV to coatrack to top of the fridge and back again. *This is a good one. It really, really is. I promise. You'll thank me later.*

That made me stop short with my hand almost on the doorknob. "Why don't I believe you, Scrap?"

Ah, come on, babe. When have I ever steered you wrong?

"There was the time you forgot to tell me about Donovan being a gargoyle. There was the time you spent so much time painting iodine on your cat scratches that you forgot to follow WindScribe..."

Okay, okay, I've slipped up in the past. But this one is really, really good.

"If you say so." For the first time in a year and a half I regretted not moving the spy hole from six feet up to my eye level. With Scrap around I didn't need it. Until now.

"You'd better be right, Scrap, or you are toast. Remember who buys your beer and OJ." With that I yanked the door open and moved into a defensive stance.

All the blood rushed from my head and feet to my heart. Blackness crowded my vision.

Gollum stood there holding a single red rose and looking extremely sheepish.

"Don't pass out on me, Tess," he said, grabbing me around the waist, while managing to keep the rose undamaged.

"Um..." Not the most intelligent thing to say. It was all I could manage.

"Okay, girls, you and I are going shopping," Allie sang out.

"But the dishes ..." Salal protested.

"... Will still be there when we get back." Allie herded them out the door.

"Is that her boyfriend?" Salal whispered as she passed us.

"Will they have sex?" Blackberry continued in the same tone of voice.

I didn't hear Allie's reply over the rushing of blood in my ears that accompanied my blush.

"What was that about?" Gollum finally asked as he set me firmly on my own two feet, balanced and semi-coherent. "Did your email refer to those girls?"

"What email?" I moved back, putting distance and safety between us. The strength of his arm holding me up had felt so good, so right, like the other half of me had come home. I couldn't allow that.

"Ah, I suspect Scrap had a hand in that communication."

See ya, babe. I'm off to the mall with the girls. Think I can get a new boa, or maybe a hat with a veil out of this? He popped out with an audible displacement of air.

I stepped into the kitchen and tackled the few dirty dishes left. The girls had done a good job of cleaning up, unlike most teenagers I'd known.

Gollum, being Gollum, picked up the dish towel and began drying the clean pieces.

"So, why did I get a rather imperative summons from your imp?" he finally asked when the silence between us ceased to be companionable and grew uncomfortable.

"I'm adopting the two Nörglein girls."

"Have you thought through the consequences?"

"Not entirely. But I have to get them away from their father. He's abusive, both physically and emotionally, and ... and sexually exploiting them, turning them into little more than prostitutes just to get more Kajiri babies," I blurted out.

"Okay. What do we need to do?"

"Too much. Everything. I need to make it look legal. Probably forge some birth certificates to begin with. I presume Allie will help them select a few clothes and toiletries."

"What else? Schools? Money?"

"A bigger house real soon. And the housing market has gone belly up. I can't afford to buy something new until I sell this place, probably for a lot less than I bought it for. I can't afford to move!"

"Slow down and breathe. We'll make lists, prioritize. What else?"

"I need to assess their schooling so I know how much intensive tutoring they need before I can put them in public school."

"Home schooling is a viable option. I can get you curriculums and study aids."

"I can't seem to get the damn book written so I can have the money to do all this."

Suddenly, the enormity of it all overwhelmed me. I just stood there at the sink with my hands in rapidly cooling soapy water. More than a few tears fell.

"You aren't alone, Tess. Allie is helping. I'll do what I can. You don't have to do it alone. You never did, but you are so stubborn you can't see that."

"What can you do?" Suddenly I wanted to shove all of my problems onto his shoulders. I didn't want to live my life without him or his help.

But I had to.

"I'll call Donovan if you like. Surely he has experience in integrating barely civilized Kajiri into the system."

"I already tried. His price is too high." Memory of his demands sent my blood boiling. Anger gave me strength to wipe my tears and dump the dishwater.

"Okay. What's the first chore?"

"Birth certificates. Forged. With me listed as birth mother, father unknown."

He cocked an eyebrow at me.

"It's the only way, Gollum. Otherwise, I'd have to involve social services and formal adoption procedures. It could take years just to get me certified as a foster parent before actually beginning legal paperwork." I yanked the towel away from him to dry my hands. Then I avoided more words—and looking at him—by folding it neatly and draping it over the oven handle.

"Okay. Where's your computer and printer? Got a fax machine?"

"In there." I pointed toward the office. "Why the fax?"

"To make it look like the real birth certificates, which will be my creation, were faxed to you while the originals are still on file somewhere else." He grinned oddly. "Do you want to be a part of this, or would you rather not know how I manage?"

"I think I'll leave it to you. Can you do it and be out of here by nine?" I checked the clock on the microwave with a little trepidation. Six-thirty.

His glasses slid down and he peered at me over the tops.

"I have a date," I said firmly.

Even though Sean looked pale and ordinary in comparison.

"That's fair. I should get home in an hour or so anyway. Pat will be going to work about then."

Without another word, or argument, or condemnation, or hint of jealousy, he set about doing what he had to do.

"Oh, and can I access your bank account from here?"

"What!"

"I need to transfer some money from the trust fund to you. I think taking two children away from an abusive dark elf counts as Warrior business. I'll set it up as a monthly allowance. If the IRS asks, it's child support from the unnamed father who really doesn't want the world to know he got a sixteen-year-old girl pregnant." Again, that quirky grin.

"Thank you. Don't make it too extravagant. I intend to take care of my girls on my own as soon as I finish the book and get back on my feet financially."

"Understood." He bent his head over my computer and logged on to the Internet.

I scooped up my laptop and retired to the living room with my flash drive, oddly content and ready to work.

Chapter 25

T abitha Moffat Brown is called the "Mother of Oregon" for the orphanage she founded in 1846.

Allie's wisdom prevails. She drives the girls to the nearest all-in-one-discount store. Of course, in Portland that requires crossing a bridge over the Willamette River and driving east quite a way to 82nd Avenue and then north to the blaring lights of the parking lots and the thumping ear buster stereo systems in the cars parked there. A lot of teens who can't afford to shop the mall hang out here.

Blackberry spends the half hour drive fiddling with the radio, examining the clutch pedal, prowling through the glove box, whatever piques her curiosity.

I follow her every movement, equally eager to explore new things, but also cautious of my babe's privacy. Tess knows better than to leave anything totally personal in the car, other than necessary registration and insurance stuff. Boring.

But then there's the hairbrush in the door pocket, receipts for gas, dirty tissues, fast food wrappers, mostly empty coffee cups.

Ooooh, stale coffee with mold growing in the bottom. I slurp those up in a hurry, before the two forest girls can steal them.

"Did anyone ever tell Tess that she's as big a slob as Blackberry?" Salal snorts with disgust. She picks up some of the debris in the backseat between her fingernails and stuffs it in a makeshift litter bag that once held a hamburger and fries.

"I am not a slob. I need to sprawl. I need space to thrive," Blackberry retorts.

"Here's a notebook and paper. Start making a list of things you need," Allie jumps in, digging said notebook and paper out of her neat little purse. The purse isn't big enough to hold her gun, so she has it holstered on her left hip, hidden beneath her baggy sweatshirt. She's so organized she's no fun at all. I didn't think to remind her to bring THE gun. If Tess were here, we wouldn't need it. Evah.

If I had to live with Allie I'd die of boredom inside a week, nothing to clean up after, nothing to color coordinate. Sheesh, how come she and Tess are such BFFs? They are complete opposites.

But I digress. The issue at hand is how the two girls react to life outside a cave in the forest.

"Um . . . " Blackberry hides her hands in her armpits.

Salal looks out the window and points to a big Halloween display in front of a donut shop. There's inflatable ghosts and pumpkins, a scarecrow with crows on its outstretched arms, an ugly witch flying off the roof on a broomstick, the whole shebang.

"What is that?" she asks, seemingly quite innocent.

"Tomorrow night is Halloween," Allie says. She sounds puzzled, by the lack of awareness of the funnest holiday on the calendar, or by the avoidance of making a list?

"What's Halloween?" Blackberry asks. She relaxes her hands and returns to fiddling with the window handle—Tess' car is a bit old and stripped down. She has rolling handles for the windows rather than electronic buttons. She also has manual locks.

She says it's for safety, in case she gets into a mess and doesn't have her keys or the engine dies and she can't get out of the car. Or into it. Or something. I'm not exactly sure.

"Halloween is a contraction of All Hallows Eve. Sort of a day of the dead celebration, but it's now about parties and candy and spooky things that go bump in the night," Allie explains.

"Oh." Blackberry shrugs.

"Sounds like fun," Salal says. "I think that's the day the boys get to explore other dimensions, 'cause the portals get real weird and easier to find."

"It can be fun," Allie hedges. She bites her lip, clearly thinking multiple trains of thought. "It's also a night when some people think they have a license to play mean tricks on others and tear up property."

"You ... you mean ... rip out grass and break shrubs and strip a ring of tree bark so the tree will die?" Blackberry asks. She sounds truly appalled and frightened.

"Been known to happen, yeah," Allie replies. "Worse than that, children, and even adults can get hurt by poisons and sharp objects hidden in treats. Or by fires that start small but get out of hand."

"But they actually kill green things!" Salal is as upset as Blackberry.

"You sound like you've had to clean up after a few pranks," Allie says.

"Yes," the girls say in unison. They don't sound happy at all.

"Father is going to need help the morning after," Blackberry says.

"He's going to be very upset if we aren't there to do the heavy work for him," Salal continues. "The boys are always useless after a night prowling other lands. They get to do all the neat things while we get stuck with the work."

"It doesn't matter if your father is upset, girls. Tess and I will protect you from him. You don't ever have to go back to him."

"But who will replant the grass and stomp out the fires and properly prune the broken shrubs?"

"Why can't your father do it? Or your brothers?" Allie is starting to get mad. She doesn't believe there is any difference between men's work and women's work. It's all work and should be done by the person most qualified. "The parks department has trained arborists and a lot of volunteers to help too."

"Father says they're useless. And he can't do the work because he's sick. Tess hurt him bad," Blackberry protests.

"Did she truly hurt him or is he using the wound as an excuse to get out of his responsibilities?" Allie asks. "Lazy, manipulative bastard," she adds sotto voce.

Both girls have to stop and think about that.

Allie pulls into the parking lot. I see her scan the clumps of teenage boys gathering around tricked-out pickups and low-slung ancient sedans. She circles until she finds a spot beneath a streetlight with a direct path to the store that doesn't intersect any of the potential gangs.

"Who are they?" Blackberry asks with extreme interest. She begins pumping out pheromones.

I'm not sure if she's just being a young teen or if she's reacting to her father's training. Either way, I see trouble looming.

The tips of my wings start to turn pink. I smell a great deal of predatory anger on one group of boys. They want to hurt people. They think that's the only way to prove to the world that they control everything within their circle.

I got news for those guys. Allie's still a cop in her heart. She's also nearly six feet tall, fit, and solidly built. She'll take them down in a heartbeat without breaking a sweat.

A lady after my own heart. She'd make a great Warrior of the Celestial Blade.

Then I spot the tattoos on the inside wrists of the boys. The black ink of a skull within a pentagram glows through multiple dimensions. They have otherworldly protection.

If they are still hanging out when Allie and my girls exit, I'll fetch Tess.

AFTER FIFTEEN PAGES and eight points of needed research noted, I roused from my self-imposed stupor to find Gollum standing in front of me holding two official looking documents.

"Are you finished already?" I asked, holding out my hand for the papers.

"It's been a full hour plus," he said. His glasses slid down his nose, revealing his pale blue eyes. Tired lines made them look heavy.

And sexy as hell.

I think I gazed longingly into his soul a little too deeply. He sat next to me and drew me close.

My head automatically drifted to rest upon his shoulder.

My eyes were just about to close in guilty contentment when something on the papers caught my gaze.

"What in the hell ...?" I jerked upright. "You listed yourself as the girl's father! I told you to put unknown." I was on my feet shaking the papers at him.

Actually, I was shaking all over, my tummy doing somersaults. My deepest desire was to live my life with this man and bear his children. And now... now...

"Calm down, Tess. It makes sense. If you look at the dates it makes sense. Blackberry's birthday is the day before Julia's first suicide attempt. Salal would have been conceived the night before I left for Africa as a mercenary. It explains the blind trust fund set up by my mother to avoid scandal, to avoid hurting Julia's mother who is her best friend."

"But ... but how does it explain why no one knows about the girls, or how we met, or why you, the most honorable man I've ever met, seduced a teenager?"

Dammit, it did make sense. And it made the idea of seeing him more often plausible.

"So where have the girls been while I was in college and becoming a writer?"

"With MoonFeather. She's had numerous foster children, as well as her own two, and stray students in and out of her house for years. Why not your two?" He cocked his head and gave me one of his endearing smiles, the kind that made me want to throw my arms around him and hold him so close we merged our souls and our lives.

Okay, just about anything made me want to do that. But that smile drove a stake of enduring love and guilt and loneliness deep into my heart.

"You'd better give your aunt a heads-up in case there are official questions. I showed her as the midwife in attendance at both births."

"Gollum, is this really going to work?" Butterflies erupted into flight in my gut. Thousands of them. All at once. I wanted to shake with chilled nerves. I didn't dare.

"I think so. If we're careful. I'm anxious to get to know our daughters. They should be back by now ..."

Trouble! Scrap screamed. He burst into view bright red and flapping his wings double time.

The doorbell rang.

"Who, Scrap?"

Not him. That's just Sean. Allie and the girls need you. Now.

"Where are they?" I grabbed a pair of shoes from under the sofa, grateful they were sturdy walking shoes with good traction. I've had to fight in bad shoes before and gotten hurt.

Too far away. Too far to get you there in time. I've messed up the timing as it is. I should have come when I first noticed the bad guys. But no, I waited until Allie and the girls had finished shopping, hoping the gang bangers with demon protection tattoos had gotten bored and went away. But they didn't. They recognized the girls. Allie can't handle them alone. Hell, the police can't handle them alone.

Apparently, Gollum answered the door, keeping one eye on me, the other on my date.

"What's going on, Tess?" Sean asked. He offered me an arm for balance as I hopped around trying to put on the shoes and get out the door at the same time.

"You wanted to know about my life, Sean? You just got dumped into the middle of it. Scrap, can we go through the chat room?" Without me knowing quite how, Gollum had herded me and Sean out the door and down the steps. He had the keys to his car out and the lock button working remotely as I hit the pavement running.

Um, this could be tricky.

"Scrap, you've got to take me to Allie and the girls, now." I had one foot inside Gollum's new hybrid SUV. A red one, I noted. Sean's BMW was parked right beside it.

My heart plummeted into my stomach. "We'll never get there in one piece if you drive," I sighed to Gollum.

"What do you mean? I'm a good driver. I've never had an accident."

"Luck. Sheer luck."

"We can take my car," Sean offered.

Gotcha, hang onto your hats.

The world tilted slightly right. Light shifted slightly left. A swirl of mind numbing brightness, endless unbroken light and ...

I stumbled out of the SUV into a different parking lot. Sean fell out behind me. Light and reality snapped back into normal alignment. I held my right hand out for Scrap. Brilliant vermilion spread from his wing tips to his core. He stretched into impossible lengths and thinness.

I clamped both hands around the center of the shaft he'd become and twirled. He used the centrifugal force to curve his ears into a quarter moon sickle. At the same time his legs and tail arched into a mirror twin blade.

While he did his thing, sharpening on the inside curve, extruding tines on the outside, I scouted the battle zone.

Allie planted her left foot in the throat of a dark-skinned youth nearly as tall as she. At the same time her right fist connected with the jaw of a shorter blond boy.

What did she need me for?

The six others who ringed her. As I watched they all shook switchblades, chains, and guns out of their sleeves.

She pulled her gun from its holster.

Chapter 26

Oregon is the only state where the term "Civil War" refers to a game involving Beavers (Oregon State University), Ducks (University of Oregon), four quarters, and a football.

One shot reverberated around the parking lot. Allie shot into the air, a deliberate miss and a warning.

"That the best you can do, lady?" one of the gang bangers sneered. He swung his barbed chain insolently.

"Go, Tess. Go! I've got the girls," Gollum shouted behind me.

"How'd he get here?"

The magic of the chat room. Your boyfriends got caught up in the swirl, Scrap replied. He sounded tired already and he hadn't even tasted blood.

Without thinking further than taking down the guy with the lethal chain, I launched forward in a flying leap.

I landed less than gracefully in the middle of a gang of three. We all went down like I'd bowled a strike.

But I was on top.

I came up swinging the blade, right, left, low, high. Twist and spin, catch a swinging chain on the tines. Wind them tight and pull. The dark-haired boy didn't want to let go.

I twisted out of reach as I spun him past me, face first into the blacktop. Another raised his gun, a stubby little thing with a huge magazine of bullets.

Oops.

Allie chopped his wrist with the grip of her weapon. He dropped it. Then she grabbed and twisted his arm up behind him.

She was fully occupied holding his writhing body, keeping him out of the action. Why had she even bothered with her gun?

Another boy with a knife slid up behind her. He caught my blade between the shoulders. He slumped to the ground in a pool of his own blood.

The tattoo on his wrist pulsed red with black undertones.

"That important?" I asked as I removed the tines of the Celestial Blade from his rib cage.

Demon protection, Scrap gasped. Or was that a slurp as he tasted the blood. He'd earn a wart or two from this encounter.

The boy writhed. His wound closed. The bleeding stopped. He dragged himself to his knees sluggishly. He stalled there waiting to regain enough strength to heave himself upward. He waited a long time.

"But they aren't demons themselves. Therefore, they are vulnerable!" I whacked another gang member behind the knees and kicked the butt of the crouching boy. He hit the pavement nose first.

Blood spurted.

He screamed.

The boys paused.

We were no longer easy prey.

As I watched them watch me, a blackberry vine full of nasty little thorns snaked out of nowhere and wound around the ankles of the boy farthest back in the pack. Then it tightened.

His yowl as he tumbled to the ground sent the rest of them scurrying for cover. Any cover.

But there wasn't any in the nearly deserted parking lot. Flashing blue and red lights followed by wailing sirens caught them at the corner.

Six officers bailed out, weapons drawn, menace filling their posture.

"I think there's Chinese food in Sean's car. Full of MSG," I whispered to Scrap. "Disappear and gorge yourself."

He left the bags inside your front door.

In an eye blink, my weapon collapsed in on itself and faded to invisibility, leaving me to answer a lot of questions from authorities who didn't understand the true meaning of demons on the loose.

Goddess, how my leg hurt from the ill-planned leap into the fray. No more adrenaline. No more strength.

I sank to the curb, head propped on my hands, and waited.

"TESS," GOLLUM GENTLY prodded me with his voice.

"Hm?" I looked up through a fog of weariness. The activity around me didn't keep my attention. For such a short fight, I shouldn't be this tired.

My leg ached terribly. I didn't think I could stand up if I tried.

Gollum came down to my level, sitting beside me, stretching his long legs straight out in front of him. "I've got to take the girls home. They've talked to the police, all innocence, and told them, 'These guys just attacked us out of nowhere, tried to grab our packages.' That's all they know and they are sticking to it. I think they've done this before."

"Oh."

"I'm taking our daughters back to your place. I'll show them how to lock the door and dead bolt it, how to call you in an emergency. Then I have to get back to Julia. Sean and Allie are still here. They'll see you get home."

"Okay." I roused a little. The reminder of his *wife* felt like a slap in the face. "Thank you, Gollum. Thanks for everything." I dismissed him. I had to or I'd begin the self-destructive grief all over again.

"You too." He kissed the top of my head, squeezed my shoulders, and stood up.

I wrapped my arms around myself, instantly chilled by his absence. "Slow down and drive careful," I called after him.

"Of course. I have precious cargo."

He passed beyond my focus distance.

Allie replaced him on the curb beside me. "How do you want to explain the knife wounds?" she asked very quietly.

"They had knives. I took one away from them and used it to defend my daughters and their godmother?" I flashed her a grin, a little energy and enthusiasm banishing the fog.

"Is that how we're playing this?"

"Got the birth certificates to prove it."

"Okay." She sounded skeptical.

And then a policeman with a notebook in hand was in front of us, looming and trying to intimidate us both.

Allie flashed him her ID—her resignation from the force wasn't official for another two weeks—and stood up. Cop to cop. Cut us some slack as a professional courtesy.

"Those gang tattoos are new. You seen them back east?" the officer asked her when he'd finished taking our statements.

"They consider themselves demon protected," I piped up. "I don't know an official name for them."

"Multiracial and multi-ethnic. Unusual." The cop shook his head. "They got enough marijuana on them and in their vehicle, triple the legal limit, to charge them with intent to sell. Hopefully we can put them away for a long time without the added charges of assault and battery, attempted robbery, and possession of illegal weapons." He shook his head and made a few more notes.

"I've never seen any of these guys before. I thought I knew all the gangs in the area. You hurt them bad. Maybe they'll think twice about staking out territory in this town." He wandered off to supervise the loading of two lightly injured and one nearly dead into appropriate vehicles. The uninjured had been bundled off to jail some time ago.

I noticed Sean handling IVs for the guy who fell to a blackberry vine and broke his nose.

Once the ambulance doors closed, he joined Allie and me on the curb. "Is this why you end up in my ER so often?" he asked casually.

I had to think a moment.

"Unlikely," Allie snorted.

"Oh?" Sean cocked an eyebrow.

"You saw how she tackled those guys with a weak leg. She's graceful and self-assured. She only gets hurt by mundane things."

"Oh?" This time I questioned the statement. "I didn't feel graceful when I landed on top of the pig pile." My hand massaged my aching calf absently. Sean stripped off his bloody surgical gloves and took over the job. He did a better job.

"The point is, you landed on top and knocked three guys out of the action in one blow," Allie insisted.

"Actually, she's only mostly right," I sighed. "I've been almost self-destructive in the last year, trying to kill my grief with action, getting overtired and careless. But the last time was in pursuit of a demon."

"From what I read in your book, the Celestial Blade only manifests in the presence of a demon or tremendous evil. Which were these gang bangers?" Sean asked. He wadded up the soiled gloves and tossed them into a nearby trash can basketball style. Then he resumed his massage.

"Both. The tats on their wrists didn't originate in this world," I said cautiously.

"That explains some things," he mused.

"Like?"

"Like some victims I've seen in the ER screaming about black tattoos on their attackers that glowed red with the fires of hell."

"The otherworlds are bleeding into this one, more and more. I'm surprised everyone hasn't figured out that demons walk among us on a daily basis," Allie said. "God, I want to go home and have this day be over." She lay back on the sidewalk.

The store had closed and only security lights cast baleful shadows on her face.

"The populace at large is very good at denying the obvious," Sean said. He stood up and offered me a hand. "I think I've still got Chinese food back at your condo. You up for a mundane drive home?"

I laughed. "What? You didn't enjoy a trip through purgatory?" I let him pull me to my feet, bringing me very close to him. Allie got up on her own, dusting off her jeans.

"Is that what you call it?" Sean let his hand linger on my back as he escorted us toward my little hybrid car, the only civilian vehicle left in the parking lot. I leaned into him, just a little. Time to move on. Time to give up on my fantasies of a life with Gollum. He'd always have to go home to take care of his wife.

"Scrap calls it the chat room," Allie added fishing for her set of keys. "Hey, what happened to all the stuff we bought?" She looked around for signs of plastic bags, full or empty.

"Gollum took them with the girls," I said.

"So, how often do you have to do this?" Sean asked on a smile.

"Not as often as you might think," I hedged. "Depends on who's in town and how aggressive they are." I eyed him cautiously. This could be the beginning of something special or the end before we got started.

"I can see life with you wouldn't be boring."

"Most of the time it is. I hole up in my office for days writing and thinking and researching and thinking."

"Well, I have to say, that after the initial disorientation I had fun. When do we go after the bad guys again? And I really should do a full work-up on the girls so I have a base line if they ever get sick or hurt. And has anyone done an MRI on your brain since you had the imp flu? And..."

I shut him up by pulling his face down to my level and planting my mouth firmly on his.

He stilled in surprise, then drew me tight within the circle of his arms. A little thrill curled my toes. His mouth softened on mine, became more mobile.

We deepened the kiss, relishing the tingles and pressure and the joy of beginning something new and wonderful.

Even if I was settling for second best, I'd never let him know that.

Chapter 27

First name of Portland: *The Clearing. It was a convenient stopping place on the river route from Ft. Vancouver (now in Washington State to Oregon City, Oregon).*

I should hang out with Blackberry and Salal. They hardly know how to brush their teeth or use the microwave, or anything.

At least their time at High Desert Con taught them the necessity of toilets. Otherwise, I think they'd just go squat behind a bush outside.

It's getting kind of cold and damp for that to be comfortable. I've sworn off cold ever since Mum kicked me out of the freeze-dried garbage dump of the Universe.

I left the Chinese food for Tess when she gets home. MSG works wonders to counter my lactose intolerance, but when I've had a fight and tasted blood, I need mold, mold, mold, and more mold. A little beer and OJ doesn't hurt either.

So, now that I've restored myself with the mold in the air-conditioning unit on the roof of the café down the street, (there is never a lack of mold in the Pacific North Wet) I grab my black and silver boa—evening wear don't ya know—and insert myself on the dash of Gollum's new car. I suppose his rattletrap van had to die sometime, or he needed something classier and more reliable now that he has the infamous Julia to drive around, but it was a glorious source of mold and mildew.

For the first time in like evah, dahling, Gollum drives slowly. He's lost in thought, looking deep inside himself.

What is this? He observes stop signs even when there isn't another car in sight. He stays below the speed limit and uses his turn signals. Not once does he drift out of his lane.

I hope he's not sick.

Just after he crosses the Sellwood Bridge, he pulls off into the parking lot of a convenience store and calls home on his cell phone.

"Sorry I'm late, hon. Hope everything is okay and you're just asleep. You probably took a pill, right? Call me if you get this message before I get home. See you in about fifteen minutes."

Isn't voice mail wonderful?

Now he's worried. He speeds up a bit, but he still drives carefully.

How boring. Maybe my babe is right in moving on. I never thought I'd say that suddenly Sean looks like a better partner for her. At least he can patch her up after she tumbles.

But can he heal her heart?

BLACKBERRY AND SALAL seemed strangely subdued compared to Sean's manic euphoria. I guessed he'd never witnessed a fight before. Certainly he'd patched up the wounded afterward, but never been close to the chaos and mayhem. He reminded me of a first grader who'd just had the light bulb turn on inside his head when patterns of letters became words became sentences and paragraphs and suddenly made sense.

I let him carry the conversation while keeping an eye on *my* girls.

My daughters. I still couldn't believe I'd pulled off adopting them and getting them out of their father's violent environment. My heart swelled with dozens of emotions every time I contemplated them.

The girls succumbed first to full tummies and the listlessness of adrenaline depletion.

At around midnight, I guided them through showers and teeth brushing and the necessity of wearing pajamas or nightgowns. They got the queen-sized bed in the bedroom.

Then I pulled out the single malt.

We sat on the sofa, Allie and Sean on the ends, me in the middle pressed up close to Sean with his arm around my shoulders.

I watched Sean as he gently sniffed the heady brew. With eyes closed he took a small sip, rolling it around his mouth. His Adam's apple bobbed as he swallowed and let out a contented sigh. "*Uisge beatha,* whiskey, the water of life. The only English word acknowledged to have come from the Gaelic."

"I could learn to love a man who knows how to appreciate the good stuff," I said and repeated the ritual. Sweet flowers and bitter heat burst upon my tongue and warmed me all the way down to my stomach. Well-being spread outward. Muscles I didn't know had tensed unknotted and relaxed. The fist of God wrapped in velvet. "And I know about the origin of *uisge beatha* and whiskey and English. But I'm holding out for quaff as a derivative of the Gaelic as well."

Allie stared at her glass of amber whiskey. "Never learned to appreciate the hard stuff. And I don't want to argue word origins with you two. You can share this, I'll settle for wine. Did you leave any of the Riesling?" She set her tumbler on the coffee table and ambled back toward the kitchen.

"I've been thinking it might be a good idea to look for ways to totally separate the girls from their origins," Sean said, keeping his eyes on the magic elixir in his glass.

"I'd just as soon they forget their upbringing," I agreed.

"We could start with changing their names," Allie said plunking down beside me. She gulped half a glass of white wine and laid her head on the sofa back. "I see it in kids adopted out of abusive situations all the time. First thing they ask for is a new name."

"Blackberry and Salal do sound rather like they've been living in a hippie commune," Sean said on a half laugh as he took a bigger sip of scotch.

"My Aunt MoonFeather would give them names like that until they grew into their personalities, and they selected something that fit them better." I couldn't remember the rather mundane name my father's sister had rejected when she joined Wicca and took a craft name. I'd seen her dance nude, as light as a feather graced by moonlight on the night of the summer solstice. She had selected her new name appropriately.

Allie giggled as she downed the rest of her drink. "When I think Blackberry, all I can see is a fancy cell phone."

We all laughed at that.

"Blackberry. Cell phone ..." I played with the sounds of the words. "Phonetia!"

"Good one." Allie and I high-fived.

I took another swallow of scotch. The top of my head felt a little separate from the rest of me. A gale of giggles erupted from my toes, running upward in waves of good feelings. "Kids today seem to have their phones surgically implanted. Texting their friends is like breathing."

"Remove a teen from her phone and she feels like her arm's been cut off. But they rarely phone home," Allie added.

Sean nearly doubled over with laughter. "Phone home. *Phone home!*"

"Huh?"

"Didn't you see the movie *E.T.?*" he asked incredulously.

"E.T. phone home," I replied, my mouth threatening to gape. "Of course, Phonetia and E.T.! That's what we call my girls."

"What does E.T. stand for?" Allie asked, a little more sober than either Sean or I.

"Anything she wants."

SHORTLY THEREAFTER, I kissed Sean good night and sent him on his way in a cab. We'd all had too much to drink to trust him driving. We'd worry about his car in the morning.

Allie took the sofa, and I stretched out on the cot in the office.

I promised myself this overcrowding would only last a short time. Allie was due to fly back to Cape Cod next week to wind up her duties with the police force and finalize plans for her wedding. Maybe I should just set up a real bed in the office and consolidate the computer desk and bookcases to make room for a dresser. The file cabinet in the closet could go into the dining area.

Or I should make the living and dining area one big office and schoolroom and give the office over to the girls so I could take back my bedroom.

"This could work, Scrap."

Buy you some time until the financial markets improve.

"My, aren't you erudite and succinct. What's the matter?" I looked up from massaging moisturizer into my feet.

I don't like the tattoos on the gang bangers. We don't know who authorized the protection. Takes some big bucks, some sneaky runarounds, or clout with the Powers That Be to put those tats on mundanes. He sat on the desk fading in and out of the monitor.

I shuddered. "Don't remind me of the Powers That Be. I can't imagine anyone voluntarily asking them for favors."

You did.

"Out of desperation." Unconsciously I rubbed my scar. "I needed protection for Dad and Bill. No one else could guarantee it." My scar burned and pulsed, almost as if there was a demon in the room.

There wasn't. It was just nerve memory of the deal I'd made and signed in my own blood. The onyx pen stained with my blood lay buried in the back of the side drawer on the desk.

"Could Donovan have done it?" I asked.

Why would he?

"I don't know. But then I don't truly know why he wants to create a home world for Kajiri demons. I don't understand his obsession with me. I don't understand..."

A tentative knock on the closed door almost slid beneath my awareness.

"Come in," I said, almost as hesitant as the knock.

The door crept open a few inches. I saw a single green-brown eye peek in.

"Come in, Blackberry."

"How'd you know it was me?" She pushed open the door another few inches and slid in, closing it behind her.

"You're taller than your sister and Allie's eyes are brown. "What do you need? You should be asleep."

"I... Are we really supposed to call you 'Mom' now?"

I gulped. Mom. I'd begun to think I'd never have the privilege of hearing another person call me that.

"I'd like that if you are comfortable with it."

"Gollum ... I mean Dad said we should. It shows respect. What's respect?"

Oh, boy, was I in trouble. I had to start at square one with a teenager. The dictionary definition would probably go over her head.

Tomorrow. Or rather later today. I'd deal with their education in the morning.

"Respect is an attitude of careful listening and going along with their suggestions because you've learned they are usually right. It's treating that person as if you value them."

"Oh." She looked puzzled. Then her eyes brightened. "Oh!"

I patted the place beside me on the cot, urging her to sit, get comfortable; put her in a sharing mood.

She sat slowly, careful not to touch me directly.

"And because I respect you, I'm going to ask your approval for changing your name." Part of me wanted to drape my arm around her shoulders. I needed to respect her need to avoid physical contact. "I'd like to call you Phonetia." I explained about the mobile phone that carried her real name.

"That sounds good. I like that. Can I have one of those phones?" She flashed me a huge smile that nearly melted my heart.

"We'll talk about that when you've earned the responsibility of an expensive phone."

"Oh. What about Salal?"

"We thought E.T. would be a good name. But that's more a joke than a name." I explained the line in the movie.

"I like that. I think she will too. We can think up new words to fit the initials for each occasion."

That sounded like mischief in the making. At least these two troubled girls could find something to laugh about.

"So, what can I do for you this late at night?"

"I... uh... Salal—We should have said something earlier. We know the guys with the tattoos." She hung her head.

"You do?" Did I ever say that I don't believe in coincidences?

"We don't really know them. I mean we've never talked to them. And I don't know if they recognized us, they only ever saw me in the dark when

Father sent them to my bed. But they do business with Father... with that man... with..."

Cold invaded my bones.

Phonetia shuddered too. I put my arm around her shoulder and drew her close. A morsel of warm steadiness grew between us.

"I know who you mean. And he is your father, biologically. Let's just call him the dark elf for now. What kind of business?"

"They grow something strange. Fa—the dark elf lets them use certain clearings in our forest, and he blurs the paths so the... the law won't find the plants and destroy them."

"Marijuana?"

"I think that's what they call it. It's not native to us. It doesn't belong in our forest. Our duty is to keep the forests healthy. Nonnative invasive plants need to be cut out and burned, not carefully cultivated and protected."

"You are right. Marijuana can be a blessing when used properly as a medication. But it is a very dangerous plant if misused. So is the dark elf. He hails from a different land, a different environment. He's as invasive as the marijuana. But you and E.T. and your brothers are all native. You belong here."

She mulled over the new and frightening idea. But one that might save her sanity.

Pot had become legal in many states, but with serious restrictions and taxes in the growing and selling.

Last month three hikers on Mt. Jefferson had been shot at and chased mercilessly for days until they found their car and raced away, all for stumbling off the trail into a ten-acre marijuana patch. A SWAT team went in and cleared out the patch. They lost two members to the growers' booby traps—hidden pits filled with poisoned stakes. Tactics straight out of the Vietnam War.

Big money came from those illegal marijuana farms.

"What does the dark elf get from the growers in return for land and protection?" I asked.

"I... I don't know for sure what Fa... the dark elf gains." She looked at her hands.

"Did he demonize the tattoos?

"Is that what you call it?"

"I guess. I've never run into it before. Scrap gave me hints. I watched them glow. Not just anyone can do it. He'd have to have help, or permission, or something."

"He never talked to Salal—E.T. and me about his business. He talked to the boys. We only know what we overheard."

"Your brothers got the names of majestic trees. He named you two for lowly vines that need to be curbed and heavily pruned to control them."

"He doesn't respect us."

"No, he doesn't. I think you both have a lot of reasons to respect yourselves though. It's my job to help you do that."

"I don't know that anyone can do that." She stood up and made as if to go—reluctantly.

"I have to try."

"I respect you for the trying."

I knew she wasn't telling me everything. She might respect me, but she didn't trust me yet.

I reached for the phone on the desk. I knew someone who might fill in some of the blank spots. It wasn't too late to call Las Vegas. Lady Lucia kept vampire hours. I owed her a bunch of favors.

She owed me some explanations.

A clap of thunder made us both jump. Lightning right on top of it lit the entire room as bright as noon.

"It's Father!" Phonetia screamed as she dived under the cot. "He's really pissed."

Chapter 28

S tumptown became the nickname for Portland when stumps cleared for dirt roads were painted white after cutting, then smoothed level to the ground to show obstacles to wheeled traffic.

Kaboom. Lightning hit a transformer. The building shook. Lights flickered and died. The ever-present hum of the refrigerator silenced.

E.T. scooted into the room without knocking. As if sensing her sister's position, she joined her under the cot, covering her head with her hands.

A thunderstorm in the middle of the night? In *Portland*? We rarely get more than distant rumbles over the mountains.

A tree cracked. The splintering sounded long and angry, worse than fingernails on a blackboard. Then the thud of a tree branch crashed against the ground.

"Don't hurt me," Phonetia pleaded.

I lay down beside the girls on the floor but not under the cot. I pulled them close. "It's okay," I whispered over and over.

We clung together. Their fingers tightened on my arms like vines twining and clinging to a cliffside, desperate to survive in the harsh environment.

Then the wind came up, howling overhead like a frustrated banshee. It competed for dominance with the near continuous thunder and the hail against the roof.

This must be akin to what drove Raquel and JJ to accept shelter from the Nörglein. If the dark elf caused the storm, why didn't he bother putting JJ into a trance and transforming himself to look like Raquel's husband?

Because he'd put all his energy into the storm. He had nothing left for his usual chicanery.

Allie crept in and joined us on the floor all huddled together.

"He can't keep it up for long," I reassured the girls as well as myself. "He's hurt and sick. This has to pass soon."

The next hour felt like an eternity. We trembled as fiercely as the building. More trees fell. Wind and rain lashed the windows as if trying to break them for easy entrance to my home.

And then as quickly as it came, the storm abated. Just like a two-year-old packing up his toys and hiding in his room after a temper tantrum. Of course he had to slam the door on his way out.

One last boom, crash, and flash, followed by a torrent of hail that lasted thirty endless seconds.

"What was that all about?" Allie asked with shaking chin and darting glances. "That one was worthy of Dorothy's trip to Oz."

"I think the dark elf found out where we are," Phonetia said.

"That is one mean bastard," Allie grunted. "Glad we got you away from his clutches when we did."

"Did one of the gang bangers with a demon tat get away to inform him?" I asked. I crawled to my knees and dusted off my jeans. I really needed to clean in here.

Allie stared through the window, looking backward through her memory. Her fingers flexed as she counted bodies. "Tall, blond guy, maybe twenty-four, gold chains on his neck, one with a pendant to match his tattoo." She looked up again almost as if emerging from a trance.

"He... he's the leader of Father's minions," E.T. said quietly.

"And I bet he reported everything to the dark elf. He might have followed us home," I sighed. "You girls okay to go back to bed by yourselves? I need to make some phone calls and do some serious thinking."

"I... I guess," Phonetia mumbled.

"I'll tuck you in and stay with you till you fall asleep," Allie offered. "Has Tess talked to you about your new names?"

She herded them out of the office like an overprotective border collie.

I reached for my cell phone. The power surge had wiped out the landline.

✕

I'D JUST DRIFTED OFF to sleep when the phone rang.

I flopped awake, not sure where I was, what was happening, why my ears hurt.

The phone, babe. Answer the phone, Scrap reminded me.

His voice inside my head rattled the right synapses. I plucked the phone off the cradle, dropped it, fumbled it up again, and mumbled something into it upside down.

Lights blazed around me. The digital clock on the desk blinked red numerals showing a few minutes after twelve. The power had come back on and the phone lines had been restored only moments ago.

Then I fully opened my eyes and glimpsed the time on my cell phone beside the landline. Four in the damn morning. Who in the hell had the audacity to call now?

My heart went into overdrive. *Dad!* Something was wrong with my father.

"I was thinking about calling you. Then I returned from a party and found your voice mail," Lady Lucia chuckled. "Is this a bad time, *cara mia?*"

I flipped the phone around, the better to hear her phony Italian accent.

"I have to be up in two hours and I just got to sleep."

"Sleep is overrated. We can sleep when we are dead."

"Does that mean I get to kill you and all the Kajiri demons who cross my path?" I wasn't feeling friendly at the moment.

Lucia laughed loudly. I could just picture her throwing back her head, tossing her long blonde—artificial—tresses into the desert wind, and exposing her vulnerable neck.

A challenge.

Then I had to remind myself, she never allowed herself to become vulnerable, even if she let you think she was.

"So what were you going to call me about?" I asked on a yawn.

"I will be in Portland at the end of next month, *cara*. We must talk."

"Fine. We can meet for coffee at high noon at Waterfront Park." Lady Lucia could tolerate sunlight as well as any human, even though it didn't suit the persona she projected to intimidate friends and enemies alike.

She laughed again. This time when she spoke, she ditched the thick Italian accent. Only a hint of her native southern French Alpine origins leaked through now. "Why did you call, Tess? You usually avoid me unless you are in dire trouble."

"Thank you once again for helping clean up the mess of my mother's murder," I said graciously.

"And...?"

"And I've just adopted two daughters of a Nörglein elf. I thought you might have some pointers..."

"Nörglein? Did you say Nörglein? Impossible. They are extinct. I killed the last of them myself." She sounded affronted. "The nasty elf tried to coerce me into exchanging sex for safe passage through my own forest."

"One got away." Now I wanted to laugh.

"Impossible."

"Explain that to the nasty bugger, hiding in *my* forest, who preys on women hikers or binds males while he seduces their wives in their forms."

"Don't worry about him. They breed in cycles. One child, maybe two. Then none again for a hundred years. That way people forget about him and don't hunt him down." She suppressed a yawn.

"Not this guy. We're up to six, maybe seven rapes in the last year. I've got the two girls from his previous rampage about fifty years ago. They look to be twelve and fourteen."

"Impossible." She didn't sound so sure. "Nörglein only sire sons. And if these girls look like teenagers then they are teenagers. The longevity gene doesn't kick in for half-breeds until after puberty."

"But ... but there are no reports at all of lost hikers in Forest Park ten to fifteen years ago. If five hikers got lost in the same area in a three year period, someone would have noted it."

"They might have noted it but did they report it? Hm? Listen, *cara*, this news troubles me greatly. Your elf's genes are breaking down. He should have one son in his care. No daughters. Only one son. You say he is raising five teens and siring half a dozen more? Something is terribly wrong. I will take the next available flight. I'll call from the airport when I get in. *Ciao*."

She hung up without further explanation.

I had a feeling I should alert someone of her coming. Like Donovan. But I wasn't speaking to him at the moment. Maybe Gollum. No. Not yet. I needed time away from him. Time to forget how much I loved him so that I could move on with Sean.

A wicked chuckle erupted from deep inside. Sean would love to meet a vampire. Even if she was a fake.

Better dig out the hair comb, Scrap said. He sat on the edge of the desk, idly swinging his bandy legs and fluttering his wings. *You want to watch Lucy's aura when she arrives.*

"I hate wearing the thing. It turns my hair brittle and gives me a headache."

Necessary, dahling. Hey, did you notice my new warts? Two of them on my chestie. Makes me look real macho, don't ya think?

The phone rang again.

"Tess, one more thing," Lady Lucia said without preamble. "I've heard rumors of a crystal ball of pure beryllium surfacing. A special crystal ball with power. If you find it, do not under any circumstances let the elf get his hands on it."

"Why?" I asked suspiciously. I looked to Scrap to see if he could enlighten me.

The ball is safe, dahling. Believe me. Short-gnarled-and-mossy can't get it.

"Later. *Ciao.*" She hung up on me again.

"I guess if you're the vampire crime boss of Las Vegas you don't have to exercise manners."

I MISSED MY DAWN APPOINTMENT with the sun on my balcony. But then so did Allie and the girls. I saluted the morning light, fresh and clean after the storm, halfheartedly with a wave of my coffee cup as I went about finding breakfast stuff.

Allie rolled over on the sofa and grumbled something about too much noise.

Would the girls eat cereal? Or did they prefer eggs and hash browns? What about pancakes and waffles? If they didn't get up soon and give me some ideas we were all going to get toasted peanut butter and jelly.

My alarm over my dad made me wonder if I should call him. No, he'd be worried about me if I called outside my Monday morning routine.

A squeak from the bedroom roused my curiosity.

"Would you girls shut up and go to sleep!" Allie yelled. "All night they've been grunting and moaning. All night long." She pulled her pillow over her head.

The squeak came again. It sounded like tree limbs sawing against each other in a high wind.

"That's not teenage girls being brats!" I dashed down the hall to the bedroom. Why hadn't I heard this earlier?

"What?" Allie asked. She came up behind me, both hands wrapped around the grip of her revolver. Weapon carefully at her side.

"Phonetia? E.T?" I asked as I tapped on the door.

The muffled squeak came again, this time I caught a hint of desperation behind it.

"Scrap, what's happening?"

Heck if I know. The other side of the door, it doesn't like ... exist, he slurred. Then he hiccupped.

The fine hairs along my spine stood on end and my scar pulsed. Something was definitely wrong.

"If I go charging in there will I step into another dimension?" Like the Nörglein home world?

Unknown. If this is elf guy's work, he shouldn't be able to hide from me. Not unless ... not unless ... Back in a moment, babe, I'm gonna check on the crystal ball. He flew off in a drunken swoop.

"What did he say?" Allie's question masked the pop of displaced air as Scrap went elsewhere.

"Proceed with extreme caution. And put that thing down before you shoot someone with it. I don't think the gun will help against a forest elf. Otherworldly hide is impervious to bullets."

Allie responded by raising the gun and aiming it over my shoulder. "Open the door very slowly," she whispered. "If I need to shoot, you hit the floor."

"Okay." I drew out the word into about five uneasy syllables.

I turned the doorknob slowly. It moved easily, unlatched. A push from one finger opened it. The hinges creaked like the sound effects of a haunted house.

Different from the weak sounds coming from within the room.

Okay. Now I knew something strange was going down. My faucets didn't drip, my drawers didn't stick, and my hinges definitely didn't squeak. I made sure of that during the long hours of writer's block, insomnia, and depression over the last year.

Thick, Stygian blackness greeted me. The air felt so gelatinous and damp I could almost push it aside. It smelled of damp earth, fecund with growing things. A sharp chill redolent of fir needles and holly berries caressed my face.

Let's explore. Scrap dove back into this reality. *Whee! This is better than Disneyland!* he chortled as he thrust the magical comb into my hair. *Come on, Tessie, nothing to fear in here. It's all just a big blank nothingness filled with worms and bats. Oops, not supposed to talk about bats around you. Sorry, dahling, but one of them is just so cute and he's playing coy with his wings. What a flirt.*

"Scrap, have you been drinking?" I planted my feet firm and solid, like a deep-rooted oak.

Drunk on life, babe.

"Imp bane," I snarled. We'd run into that nasty trick before. Seems that when mistletoe, ivy, and holly are knotted together in an arcane but very specific pattern, it blocks imps' senses and prevents them from transforming into Celestial Blades.

No wonder I hadn't known what went on in this room. With Scrap blocked, so was I.

But now that I wore the comb, I caught three separate heat signatures. One was shifting about restlessly; the other two were still and recumbent.

Gathering my courage, I thrust my hand into the inky blackness and found the light switch in the usual place to the right of the door. One flip and the room sprang to light with too vivid colors and too sharp definition to each object. I saw auras everywhere; but none so vivid as around my daughters.

My girls lay on the bed, stripped to their bark and bound hand and foot with their own pajamas.

Standing over them, wearing his traditional ensemble of green coat, buff breeches, and a green tricorn hat, a thorned whip in his hand, eyes glowing demon embers, stood their father, the last of the Nörglein elves.

He must have crept in through the French doors during the storm and hidden until we all slept.

"About time you showed up, girlie. I thought you were dead the way you clung to sleep. Now you'll learn what happens to those who steal my property."

He turned and flicked the whip into my face.

Chapter 29

T he James G Blaine Society favors blocking Oregon roads at the border and setting up immigration and customs patrols.

Fizzy, fuzzy, whizzy. *My brain is too big for my head-zee and doesn't want to do anything but curl up and pluck slub-zees off of sweaters.*

No, that doesn't scan. Only half rhymes.

Something strange going down. Down, down, down I plunge.

Oops, didn't mean to kiss the floor. What's this? Pretty knots of lacy vines. Holly, mistletoe, and ivy. What a lovely song they make. I could sing of them all night. Sing to them too.

But they don't belong in my world. Something tugs at me. Hard. Pulling me back from my delightful, lazy musings.

Don't wanna go back.

Gotta go back.

A slice of pain to my brain.

Acid boils in my stomach, followed by burning anger.

The shroud of fog lightens around my mind.

Holly, Mistletoe, and Ivy.

Mistletoe, Ivy, Holly.

Knots and knots. Twists of lacey woven green. A decidedly Italian flavor to the design.

A jolt of knowledge. The Nörglein invented that spell to make imps impotent. He and his kind have been using it for centuries to keep us at bane. Oops, at bay. Bay. Bay.

Well into the bay goes the Imp bane. Gain, main, disdain, mundane.

Not exactly the bay, but the river. Sliver, quiver, dither, Indian giver.

I grab the tendrils and pop out. Almost lose them in the chat room. Can't do that. Might trap the unwary imp....

A torrent of giggles bubble out of me. There are more than a few uppity imps I'd like to trap. Starting with fifty of my siblings, a few old guys at the Citadel, and Mum.

Much as I'd like to do that, I need clear passage through the chat room whenever I want.

So blip. Pop back into reality flapping my wings like mad and drop the noxious bundles into the muddy, surging water. The currents grab them, dunk them, and whisk them away over the horizon. All that rain the dark elf spat at us last night strengthened the currents and gave them speed. Speed to separate me from my nemesis.

Now back to my babe and her elf of a dilemma.

THE GUN EXPLODED IN my ear. Echoing, stabbing. Hurting.

I dropped face first to the floor.

I heard the shots again and again. One shot? Or had my brain replayed it?

The thorn whip lashed my back.

I curled into a fetal ball, protecting my vulnerable neck with my hands. With a second lash I yelled in pain and outrage. I couldn't hear my own screams.

But I heard Scrap howling like a coyote under a full moon.

Crazy as a loon with all that imp bane around. I was on my own.

Another lash. I inhaled sharply.

"Stand up, lowly woman. Take your punishment as you deserve," the elf sneered. He sounded like a bad actor playing a mob boss.

Another shot.

Allie landed beside me. "Ricocheted right off him," she gasped, bewildered.

"Punishment!" I screamed at the Nörglein as I rolled closer to the bed. "Punishment? I'll show you punishment."

I grabbed a rapier from its hiding place in the bed skirt, unsheathed it in one long motion as I stood and lunged.

"Missed," he chortled. "What I would expect from a woman. You shouldn't be allowed to play with weapons you don't understand. There used to be laws that kept women in their place."

Another lunge. My aim followed true. I pushed the point deeper into his arm. The same arm I'd slashed with the Celestial Blade. The same arm that seeped black sap through the green sleeve of his short coat.

The blade quivered in my hand. A tiny jolt of electricity jumped from the wound to my arm. I pulled back and struck again, slapping the dull side of the blade across his head, taking his cap off.

"My hat!" he screamed like I'd run him through. "You can't take my hat!"

Scrap swooped in and snatched the green wool felt with his hind claws as he circled the room.

Not a tilt or waver in his flight.

"King Scazzy of the Orculli trolls had a hat too. All his honor and power came from the hat. Is that true for you too?"

This guy was about six times the size of the garden gnome with teeth. Still, they hailed from a similar region and were classed together in the reference book.

Scrap burped acid. A few drops dribbled onto the bright green fabric. They sizzled and burned. Acrid smoke rose from the half dozen holes, each the size of a dime.

"My hat!" the dark elf screamed again.

Then Scrap popped out again. Hat in hand. Or paws. Claws anyway.

"That's what you get for underestimating modern women. You and your kind need to be made extinct," I yelled at him, lunging for another thrust into his wound.

"Scrap, blade now!"

He popped back in, without the hat, and landed on my hand, bright red and stretching. He bared his teeth—six rows of thirty-six razor sharp points—and hissed maliciously even as he curved.

The troll shielded his face with his hands, howling in pain. He turned and dove out through the French doors, spreading shattered glass and splintered framing behind him.

I dashed to follow. He tucked and rolled, hitting the one small patch of green between me and the river. He disappeared into a cluster of juniper tams.

Imp spit. An antibiotic against demon tags for my babe, deadly poison for trolls, elves, gnomes, and demons, Scrap grinned and paled, as he shrank back to normal translucence.

"If you'd kept your mouth shut, I could have killed him right here and now," I complained.

"Do you truly want the girls to have to watch you execute their father?" Allie returned.

I turned my attention back to Phonetia and E.T. They stared at me, eyes wide with horror, mouths and limbs still bound with magic.

"IF I KILL THE LITTLE bastard, will his magic dissolve?" I asked Gollum on the phone around noon. He'd been in class and faculty meetings with his phone turned off until then.

I'd called him five times just to hear him on the voice mail.

"Unknown," Gollum replied.

I could almost see him pinching the bridge of his nose beneath his glasses.

While I waited for him to call me back, we'd untied the girls and covered them with a sheet and a blanket. I'd already filed police and insurance reports about a break in and potential burglar/rapist. We made the noon news. If short, gnarly, and green showed his face in the neighborhood without shape-changing, he was dog meat.

A glazier and carpenter had come to replace the shattered French doors.

"Well, do you know a spell that will undo it enough to let the girls talk? They may know something. I'm betting they watched the beast work the spell on many of his victims."

"I'll call MoonFeather. We'll come up with something."

My cell phone rang beside me. I checked the caller ID.

"Call me when you know something. I've got to go. Lacy Lucia may have a few tricks up her sleeve."

"Tess, wait," Gollum said anxiously. "Are you sure you want to involve her?"

"Too late. She's already in town and involved." I hung up on him, more than just a little satisfied that for once I ended the communication.

At the same time, I missed him so much my gut ached.

"*Pronto*," I answered the cell half a ring before it went to voice mail.

"Ah, *cara mia*, you learn a little Italian," Lucia's rich tones filled the airwaves. The silence in the background did not indicate airport busyness.

"That about exhausts my vocabulary," I admitted grudgingly. "Have you left Vegas yet?"

"I am in Portland, *cara*. I have checked in at the Freemont." She mentioned the exclusive private hotel downtown.

"Good. How fast can you get here?"

"What has happened?" she asked. I heard soft rustling in the background indicating she moved around the room, possibly collecting coat and purse.

I told her this morning's adventures.

"Have the children eaten anything?" she asked most anxiously.

"They sipped a little chicken bullion from a spoon. Not much." I started to pace, my own anxiety increasing as I talked.

"Continue trying. They need the salt and liquid. Give me directions. I do not trust Internet maps. I shall hire a vehicle and driver. Servants do not always know the best shortcuts if they can earn more by delays."

My favorite vampire might be over two hundred years old and enamored of Goth trappings and spooky candle holders made to look like skulls, but she embraced modern technology.

About twenty minutes later, as I was dribbling more salty broth into E.T., Allie ushered Lady Lucia into the room.

Much to my amazement Lucia carried a tiny girl, less than a year old, sucking her thumb. The little one looked up at me with wide chocolate-colored eyes. Her dark hair curled nicely around her shapely face.

She grinned at me around the precious thumb, revealing her new front teeth.

"Um..."

"Tess, this is Sophia," Lucia said, smiling fondly at her child. She looked tired and a bit... frazzled. Her usually immaculate blonde hair needed a touch-up around the roots—should have been done a month ago—her tidy business suit had developed creases and lost its crispness.

"Nice to meet you, Sophia." I held out my fingers for her to grasp. She did so with her damp hand. Then shyly hid her face in her mother's shoulder.

Half a heartbeat later, she turned back toward me, holding out her arms, begging for me to hold her.

I did so, cradling her weight against my chest, letting her fill a bit of the emptiness from knowing I'd never have a baby of my own.

Sophia touched my lips and nose with exploratory fingers. Then she tucked her thumb back into her mouth and settled her head against my shoulder.

"She is tired and in need of a nap. Travel does not agree with the very young," Lucia said, caressing the child's curls.

"I'll put her on the cot in my office," I said, moving toward the door.

"I usually put her to bed myself," Lucia sighed. "The one task I do not trust to a nanny. When I can keep a nanny more than a few days."

"You work too hard at scaring the wits out of them."

"Perhaps."

Moments later we returned to the big bedroom. Sophia had slept instantly on my shoulder and not whimpered when we transferred her to a new bed. I wondered if Lucia had used some kind of demon magic on her to gain such easy compliance.

Lucia stared maliciously at the glazier. She bared her teeth like he would make a tasty meal. He ignored her as he caulked and sealed each piece of glass. "See weirder on the streets downtown every day," he muttered.

"I suppose he must stay until he finishes." Again, with the heavy sigh, as if she wearied of the world. Or had being a mother drained her of her usual vitality? "Perhaps you and I should retire to the kitchen. I must gather supplies."

"I'll stay with the girls," Allie sat in the chair I had just vacated. She took up the task of spoon-feeding E.T.

Phonetia had spat out the last tablespoonful of life-giving liquid I'd tried giving her.

"If she doesn't take something soon, I'm calling Sean."

Lucia raised her left eyebrow in query.

"My boyfriend. He's a doctor and he figured out our ... business without me telling him."

"Useful." Without another word, Lucia led me through my own apartment, down the hall past the guest bath and office, to my galley kitchen that overlooked the dining area and sunken living room. She directed me to the tall stool at the counter while she rummaged through my cupboards and fridge.

One by one, she placed her treasures on the counter before me. A bottle of mixed herbs, a tiny canister of expensive saffron, red wine, cups, bowls, matches, votive candles.

"You didn't tell me about the baby," I tossed out a conversational gambit.

"I told no one. Especially not the father." She continued her search without looking at me.

"Who is?"

"Need you ask?" She finally gave me a direct and searing look. The arrogant and ruthless vampire returned to her posture.

"Donovan?" I coughed. Another black mark against him on my mental chalkboard.

"Yes. I should have known better than to trust someone raised by the Damiri not to use a condom. In that, I believe, you were smarter than I am."

"Yes." What else could I say? Except "I think he's in town. If he finds out about Sophia, I would not put it past him to kidnap her."

"Which is why I listed *my* assistant as the father on the birth certificate. Which brings us back to your two girls. I presume you have taken care of the legalities?"

"Yes. I have copies of the birth certificates. Duplicates of the ones on file in my home township on Cape Cod."

"Good. Get them listed on your health insurance today. You may need it."

"You don't sound hopeful for their recovery."

"They will recover. Eventually. But the longer they remain under the influence of the spell, the harder they will find it to reclaim their humanity. I noticed the older girl begins to show signs of animosity."

"Her name was Blackberry. She is ... um ... prickly in the best of circumstances. But she does try. We call her Phonetia now."

"Hm. Well, I'll try." She surveyed her array of ingredients. "Send your friend out for sweet onions, pine nuts—Italian if possible—and extra virgin olive oil, first pressing."

"That's going to be expensive." The primary reason I didn't stock the last two gourmet items.

"I will pay. But then, you will pay me back as well."

"I already owe you more favors than I can count."

"When this business is finished, you will do me one last favor and then I will be in your debt forever."

Which meant I was in big trouble if I had to do a favor that huge.

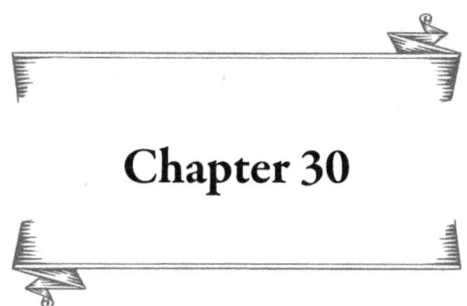

Chapter 30

51 *.3% of Oregon, 32 million acres, is forest land. One tenth of all US forests.*

"Maybe Gollum had the right idea and we should consult MoonFeather," I stalled.

"We don't have time," Lucia said, lighting a candle beneath the newly installed but not cleaned French doors. That was east.

The normal little votive in an art glass cup gave off a heady aroma reminiscent of hot dry air, salty seas, and olive trees. I followed behind Lucia sprinkling the mixed herbs in her wake. She stepped carefully, making her arc to south perfect.

Allie sat on the foot of the bed, her hands on the crossed ankles of my girls. Phonetia began to struggle at the first whiff of burning herbs mixed to provoke a cleansing of magic.

At the south end of the room, Lucia lit another candle. This one smelled of ordinary bayberry, but there was something more beneath it. She'd done something weird to my dollar store finds.

I spread more herbs around the votive. So far she set up a pretty standard ceremonial magic milieu. "MoonFeather would have done much the same," I commented.

"Your aunt would not allow me to delve into the darker side of the magic," Lucia said as she lit west. I caught snow on the wind and musky animal scents from that one.

She really had done something strange to my candles.

"I don't see a pentagram. We should draw one inside the circle before we close it." The five-pointed star inscribed inside a circle was the basis of all ceremonial magic I'd ever read about or participated in.

"Trust me, there is a pentagram." Lucia continued her ritual.

"But don't we need white magic to counter the black of the original spell?" Allie asked. She'd read all the available vampire fiction and had a passing knowledge of magical theory.

Having grown up with a witch for an aunt, and having researched magic for my writing, I too knew a lot about it. That didn't mean I believed it.

Well, sometimes I did.

"For long-term effects, you may repeat the spell with white parameters. But we don't have time. We must break the elf's hold on his daughters now, before the sun sets, or they will never take human form again."

Startled, I looked more closely at my girls. Sure enough, their skin had taken on a green tinge; their hair had begun to clump into the shape of overlapping leaves.

E.T.'s fingertips and toes sprouted poisonous berries. The digits themselves flattened and spread, taking on a green tinge.

Blackberry, Phonetia, no longer had thorns growing from her pores. Her eyes nearly shot venom at me.

"White magic works by undermining the core of evil, worming itself into every crack and crevice. That takes time. It is more long lasting. But it takes time. Years sometimes. My spell will be quick. And dirty. But it will salvage their souls and give your MoonFeather something to work with."

Lucia hovered over the last candle on the bookcase headboard.

I knew she waited for me to give her permission to complete the circle that would bind all of our energies inside.

"We have Earth in the herbs. We have Air in the incense. We have Fire in the candles. I presume you will need blood for the Water to complete this."

She nodded.

"We'll use mine," I said with more determination than I'd felt a few moments ago. "I will bind myself to them as if I were their own mother. I will become a part of them and they of me."

You sure you want to do this, babe? Scrap asked. He'd been strangely silent through the entire process. *No backing out or changing your mind once you start. If they were your biological children, you could give them up to foster care if things got too hairy. With this you can't. Not even if you wanted to. Not even if your life depended upon it.*

I had to think about that a moment. One look at my girls reverting to plants, with only a tiny bit of humanity still pulsing through them, reminded me of the face of the Green Man in folklore and in dozens of pagan artifacts. Not truly human, nor truly a creature of the forest. Lost and alone... I knew I could not condemn my girls to that kind of wild, half-existence.

"Yes, Scrap, I'm sure. Do it, Lady Lucia. Light the candle and open my vein with the knife I know you have in your pocket."

"Very well. You are wearing our ancestral pearls?"

I touched the strand around my neck beneath my sweater as a talisman. "Of course."

"Good. You will need them." She touched her lighter to the wick. The flame flared as it caught. Then it settled to burn cheerily. The scent of fresh cut pine overwhelmed my senses. Not just any pine but an Italian Stone Pine from the Southern Alps.

The natural form of our nasty Nörglein.

Instantly, a frisson of energy coursed through my veins, burning into my heart. New awareness opened in my brain.

For a moment I was back in the audience chamber of the Powers That Be, signing my name in blood upon the contract that would ensure no demon ever again tried to wrongly manipulate the sacred, neutral space where my father's bed and breakfast sat.

I jerked back into my own body and time with a new piece of knowledge. The crystal ball Scrap had hidden in the armory closet in the basement of Dad's house ate away at the fabric of reality to open a new portal. It would be permanent and independent of the ball.

"Scrap, get the crystal ball out of its hiding place now!" I screamed before the heady aromas of the magic building within the circle made me too dizzy and incoherent to think straight.

A stream of arcane syllables spilled from Lucia's mouth. She made the harsh, glottal sounds flow like a mountain stream struggling to get past sharp cascades. She grabbed my hand in a grip that brooked no defiance or escape.

She slashed her little knife across my palm. Blood welled up before I felt the sting.

Then she produced the missing pentagram. A silver medallion the size of my open palm, a five-pointed star within a circle of entwined leafy vines—perfect for the symbolism in the spell. She smeared my blood on the amulet, then slashed each girl's palm and added her blood to the pentagram.

Sharply, fiercely, she thrust it first onto Phonetia's forehead, then onto E.T.'s.

More ritual words invoked chills and searing heat that coursed through my veins as she smeared our commingled blood on the tops of their heads, brows, mouths, throats, heart, belly, and pubis.

The seven chakra points. When all were opened, they gave a doorway into the soul. Afterimages of the pentagram glowed red where it touched each of the girls.

Then she repeated the ritual on me. The pentagram left a searing impression. Seven times it branded me.

My limbs spasmed, convulsed, and cramped. I felt myself curling in on myself and falling, falling.

My back opened with wounds reminiscent of those inflicted by the blackberry vine whip. Again and again it lashed me through time as it had lashed my girls.

My mind tore open to admit seedlings of alien thoughts. The Nörglein sent barbed hooks into my mind, gleaning information and asserting control. Through him I accessed all the fear and humiliation he heaped upon Phonetia and E.T.

My soul ripped out of my body and fled from him in terror.

VERTIGO SENT MY SENSES flying in six directions at once. I lost my orientation to up and down, north and south. I fell down, down, down. Twisting around and around in a spiral of doom. Leaking magic behind in a blazing trail so bright anyone could follow me.

All Hallows Eve, the night when the barriers between worlds thinned and became vulnerable. I punched through a whole series of them, desperate to stay ahead of the dark elf. His all-consuming avarice followed me easily.

Down I passed through the shadowy illusion of the condominium complex. Past the basement, into the dirt. Rootlets reached for me, trying to snag in my hair and penetrate my skin, make me a part of the green ecosystem. Worms and burrowing beetles peered at me in curiosity, thought about feasting on what was left of me, changed their minds, and went about their business.

I became the being I feared most for my daughters, a wild thing, so much a part of the forest that I could never be human again. And yet I yearned for human contact. Any trace of language, or the touch of a hand, or shared experiences.

Isolated. Alone.

The water table flowed around me, threatening to drown what breath I had left.

And still I drilled deep, deep, deeper into the Earth, fleeing the elf mind that sought to consume me.

Darkness crowded all my senses. I had nothing to anchor myself to, if I even knew who I was anymore. Then I became aware of the pearls blazing around my neck, lighting a path of sorts for me to follow.

"I can't fight both you, evil Nörglein, and the Earth at the same time," I whispered in my mind. Exhausted, I covered the pearls with my hand and melded with the darkness. I drifted.

Which way was up? Where was home? Who was I?

"I can't do it anymore. I give up."

"Not yet, babe." Scrap reached out a pudgy four-fingered hand and grabbed hold of me. "I'm not ready to give up yet, so you can't. If you die, I die. If I die, you die."

He manifested as tall as me, solid, and reassuring. He spread his wings to enfold me in a protective blanket.

I halted the downward spiral.

"Was this what it was like for you when you were imprisoned inside the Goblin Rock by the Guardians of the Valley of Fire?" I asked him.

"Yeah. But I was alone. You do not have to be."

"What saved you?"

"I thought about what your life would be like without me. Not alive but not dead either, powerless to fight the evil that would target you the moment you became vulnerable. So I found the right answers to save us both."

"Is that what you are doing now?"

"Sorta. Come." He took my hand and led me on a new journey. Like Peter Pan leading Wendy to Neverland.

I felt like we flew sideways. But the Earth gave way to air. Tangled roots became a tapestry of branches. Leaves flowed out of me to bind themselves to barren limbs. Shadowy trees flitted past us. Insubstantial deer and rabbits peered at us curiously then returned to their browsing. And still I shed the greenery, giving it back to the original owners. I caught glimpses of sunlight, heard echoes of birdsong.

None of it real.

Except the pearls lighting our path like a fragile glow stick in the hands of a toddler on Halloween night.

I grew cold. My teeth chattered but I couldn't hear them gnash together. The landscape grew barren, devoid of green things. A frozen wasteland.

"Imp Haven," Scrap whispered, as if afraid of rousing his mum if he spoke too loudly.

More imps joined us—tall ones, short ones, young and old. Rainbows flashed across their magnificent wings. They appeared less substantial than Scrap, more present than the icy lumps of the garbage dump.

They chittered and squealed in high-pitched conversation I couldn't understand. I knew they talked about me, scolded Scrap for bonding with me as an unworthy.

One word of their tirade penetrated my understanding. *Pearls.*

"Thank you for being my friend," I told Scrap. "You're a pain in the ass, but I love you as much as I do any of my family." I couldn't remember what my life had been like before I wandered into the Citadel in a lost ravine on the high desert plateau of the Columbia River Basin in a fever delirium. The fever had opened new pathways in my brain to allow me to see and hear Scrap.

He was just a scrap of an imp, the runt who shouldn't have survived. But he was my imp. My heart filled with love.

She'll do, the other imps whispered among themselves. *Her strengths outweigh her taints. And she is the only human who could control you, Scrap. You are the only imp who can curb her instincts.* They escorted us out of the wasteland, through the shadow forest, and back into...

Chapter 31

Indian legend: Crater Lake was formed in a battle between Llao of Below World and Skell of Above World. It is inhabited by dangerous beings and access is forbidden to all by Native Shamans. Americans of European stock discovered it by accident in 1853.

My head jerked upright as if I awoke from a standing doze. I opened my eyes to find little changed in my bedroom. The candlelight nearly blinded me.

My eyesight adapted gradually, leaving afterimages of forest and candle flame superimposed upon each other.

The only evidence that time had passed was the shortness of the burning wicks and the fading of the heady incense. Twilight filled the room. The sun had set on this strange Halloween day. Trick-or-Treaters would begin their rounds soon. They rarely came here. We had no children in my building.

Except my daughters and Sophia.

My daughters. Truly my daughters now. I knew their pain and fatigue and desire to cleanse their bodies as well as their minds.

My tummy growled in sympathy with their hunger.

Phonetia and E.T. had regained their normal pink, human skin and their hair looked normal. Lank and in need of a shampoo, but normal.

"Tess? Are you okay?" Allie caught me as I swayed.

I nodded, unable to push words around a throat that felt full of dirt. I grabbed at the pearls. They'd taken on the warmth of my skin, remained clean and pure. A lifeline and an anchor to reality.

"Your eyes look funny," Allie persisted.

"Let me see!" Lucia demanded. She grabbed me by the shoulders and swung me to face her.

"Madre de Dio!"

"What?" Phonetia asked. She wrapped a blanket around her body as she left the bed to stand beside me. "Oh, my," she gasped, holding one hand in front of her mouth.

"Scrap, why are they so upset?" I figured he'd tell me the truth. He had to. I always knew when he lied. I just didn't know when he lied by omission.

Um, there's something about your ancestry I neglected to tell you.

"Like?"

Sorry, dahling, I need some mold to recover from saving your ass. And I've depleted the basement supply. See you in a bit. Unless you can follow me with your glowing red demon eyes. He popped out.

"What?" I screeched.

"I am so sorry, Tess. So very sorry. I had no idea you would be this sensitive. That All Hallows Eve would thin barriers between the worlds within you as well as between dimensions," Lucia sobbed. "That the pearls would amplify every aspect of the magic, including your ancestry."

"What are you talking about?"

"I had no idea. I am so sorry."

"Calm down and spit it out, lady," Allie commanded.

"First break the circle and let the girls clean up. I need some air." I sagged against Allie's strong body.

"Exit!" Lucia commanded. She cut through the invisible boundary of the magical circle with her ornate penknife. A true athame—ritual knife—if I ever saw one. She practiced magic often enough to have one at hand.

I wondered if I should be frightened. Something about the bowing of her shoulders and the less than crisp clothing eased my disquiet. She wouldn't hurt me.

For some reason she had extended her network of protection to include me.

We sorted out who got the shower first and what the girls should wear.

Their hunger gnawed at me. Even as I silently wondered what I could find in the kitchen to feed us, E.T. spoke quietly with meek solicitation. "Can we get pizza?"

I laughed and sent Allie to order in, making sure I got one without cheese. No sense in upsetting my fragile internal balance with anything resembling dairy.

Sophia awoke and fussily took a bottle from her mother while we settled in the living room with big mugs of hot tea, awaiting food.

I chose to stand on the balcony with the door open, letting the cold air and blustery rain bathe my mind and spirit. I could hear and be heard in the conversation but I had separated myself, indulging in my own spiritual cleansing ritual.

An almost full moon rose in the east. Its path was wrong to leave a trail of silver on the river.

"Spill it, Lady Lucia," I ordered, my face to the river. I watched the swift currents intensely, letting part of my inner self merge with the ever constant/ever changing flow. The constant renewal. The cleansing of the Earth.

Lucia sniffed and sobbed as she caressed her daughter's curls, damp from sleep. "When I was a child, I had a great aunt who was considered a witch. We locked her away in a tower of the family chateau."

"Donovan said something about that."

"The Damiri genes are so dilute in the family that they have become recessive. Only one person in every third or fourth generation exhibited the need to feed on blood, shape-change, and wield magic. And that was two hundred years ago. Nearly ten generations have passed since then."

"Except you, you got the long life gene and then discovered you like the taste of blood. Do you change into a bat on the night of the waxing quarter moon?" I replied with enough sarcasm to cut through her hesitance.

She dissolved into a frightening bout of tears.

"Get a hold of yourself," I commanded. "The Lady Lucia I know wheels and deals massive real estate transactions, collects protection money, threatens petty criminals who don't live up to her standards of deceit, entertains in high Goth vampire style, and never, ever, loses her cool, not even in Las Vegas in high summer."

Lucia straightened and turned her wrathful gaze upon me. "No, I do not shape-change. Unlike those with more recent demon ancestors, I have never felt the urge. I don't even know if I can." She dabbed her eyes on a black silk hankie. In silence she shook out the elegant square—it had a black lace cutout in one corner, probably Chantilly—refolded it carefully and returned it to the breast pocket of her blood-red suit. The long, tight skirt was slit up the left side to mid-thigh.

"So, what does this have to do with me? Why did Scrap say my eyes glowed demon red?"

"Well, they did. But they've faded now." Allie tried to reassure me.

"What you do not know, *cara mia*, is that the blacksmith I seduced to gain the magic ring you sent back to Faery was named Noncoiré."

"I know that. He got it from a distant ancestor who was an alchemist, named Noncoiré, unbeliever, because his science experiments made him question the existence of God." I shrugged.

"What I did not tell you or anyone, was that our tryst left me pregnant. The son I bore and pawned off as the child of Count Continelli, was your ancestor, Teresa Louise Noncoiré. You carry an even more dilute demon gene than I do. But you are still sensitive to demon magic. My spell, performed on this day of days, has awakened the Damiri within you."

I HAVE FAILED MY TESS once more. I have lied to her by not telling her everything I know. I do not regret this latest indiscretion. She did not need to know of her relationship to Lady Lucia. She needed to know only that the lady favored her.

Would telling my babe the truth have changed her decisions, tilted her choices, made her less self-destructive as she worked through her grief and loneliness? I cannot know.

Would the knowledge of her demon ancestors have kept her from seeking protection for Dad and Bill from the Powers That Be?

I don't know. Fortunately, the seven beings that sit in judgment over creatures across the Universe were more interested in removing a Warrior of the Celestial Blade *from proximity to the sacred neutral land of the house on Cape Cod, than on examining her father for traces of demon leanings.*

The windows in the chat room that allow me to trace the history of an artifact do not allow me to see the future. Only the Powers That Be can do that. And I'm not certain they can manipulate time threads. They are, after all, merely seven beings chosen from among the sentient and benign races. I do not believe their powers change when they don the cloak of the supreme arbitrators of Universal Justice.

I do not believe they take higher precedence than the deity, whichever name you give to Him/Her.

The sin of cowardice is something I must deal with. I could not bear to disappoint my dahling Tess again. I'm sure it will not be the last time, given who and what I am.

Her pain is my pain. When she hurts because of my misdeeds, my own aches and regrets multiply.

So I wait from the safety of the roof. I listen while Lucy tells Tess the truth.

I cringe as Tess vents her anger against one and all. I wait for her to throw a piece of pizza against the wall.

I watch neighborhood children decked out as fairy princesses and spacemen and skeletons run from door to door gleaning a year's worth of sweet treats. They giggle and shout "Boo." They glory in this night when all too many monsters can creep through the dimensions seeking prey.

But none of the children or the monsters come near our building. I can see an invisible bubble of energy protecting the cement and steel and wood.

My fellow imps have woven this net for Tess. They do not tell me why. I can only hope it comes from respect. She is a true and honorable Warrior of the Celestial Blade, no matter her ancestry. Any one of them would be proud to partner her.

I wait until Lucy has taken her baby back to the hotel.

I watch Tess and Allie help Phonetia and E.T. prepare for bed and watch the news. Their education into modern life outside the forest must begin sometime.

Finally, when all is quiet, I do one last check on the crystal ball in its hiding place. No time to move it yet. No place to move it to. I creep back to Tess' side. I do not wake her. Instead, I sit in silence at the top of her pillow, watching through the night, ever alert to any danger. Even if the danger is only the Nörglein trying to invade her dreams.

My fellow imps assure me he cannot penetrate their net now. I almost trust them.

I shall not fail my Warrior again with my sin of cowardice.

Chapter 32

*P*ortland, Oregon, has more bookstores per capita than any other US city.
Phonetia and E.T. stared in incomprehension at the paper in front of them. I'd put six simple arithmetic equations on the page, big numerals, bold addition and subtraction marks.

We sat at a new card table with padded folding chairs. Not ideal, but cheap and easy to move around as we renegotiated space in the condo.

I drowned my self-disgust and anxiety about being part demon in work. My own and schooling my daughters.

Allie was out doing Allie things. She was due to return to Cape Cod the next day and had lots of last minute stuff to do in setting up the purchase of a house she and Steve liked.

"It doesn't mean anything," Phonetia complained. She turned her head away and folded her arms across her chest.

I felt her confusion as a solid barrier between my mind and hers.

E.T. at least tried looking at the squiggling lines upside down.

"They do make sense if you know what to look for," I said patiently. Back to basics. First grade level math. More like kindergarten.

I looked around for inspiration. My gaze lighted upon a bowl of apples and nuts on the counter. I grabbed it and set it in front of me at the table.

"This is one apple." I held up the red and gold Jonagold before them.

"That's obvious," Phonetia snorted, arms still wrapped around her, physically separating herself from our activities.

"Still obvious if I record it on the paper." I drew a neat one on a clean sheet of paper. Then I put a plus mark beside it. "Just as obvious if I add a second apple. I put the two pieces of fruit at the center of the table and drew a second numeral one on paper. Then I put in the equals sign.

Phonetia reached over, grabbed a pencil awkwardly, and made two randomly angled scratches to the right of the equal sign.

"Right thinking, but we have a more sophisticated method of keeping track. Two apples." I replaced her hash marks with a neat two.

"Totally illogical." Phonetia turned away.

"What if you have seventy-two apples? That's a lot of marks to count. What if I sent you to the store to buy six apples, eight nuts, five oranges, and two carrots? How would you keep track?"

"I'd remember!"

E.T. continued to peer at the problem from all angles, comparing the new sheet to the first one. "There! That's the same." She pointed to the correct equation.

"Let's back up one more step." I started over listing the numerals for one through twenty. I'd just closed the zero on the last one when the doorbell rang.

"Scrap?"

No answer. Where had he taken himself off to while I worked with the girls?

Coming. Can't a guy have one minute of privacy?

"Nope," I replied. "Who's at the door?"

Curiouser and curiouser. He popped in and out. *Go ahead and open it,* he almost chattered in excitement.

"Gollum?" I asked, almost hopeful and dreading the encounter at the same time.

Better. Open it. Open, open, open.

I left the security chain on and opened the door a minimal crack.

"Delivery for Tess Non ... non ... crux ..."

"Noncoiré," I corrected the youngish man in striped overalls with Cooper's emblazoned above the breast pocket. He had curly dark hair and just a hint of a Latino accent.

"What?"

Just open the damn door and see, Scrap commanded.

I sensed the girls gathering at my back, staying close. Fear wafted off them in almost visible waves. Visible to me anyway.

"Delivery of what?" I asked, getting ready to slam the door closed.

"I need a signature before I haul it all up three flights," the man from Cooper's grumbled. He held up a clipboard for me to see a stack of carbonless receipts. He returned the clipboard under his arm before I could read it.

But I'd seen his wrists. No demon tattoos on the inside or outside of either of them.

Cautiously, I opened the door. Scrap flashed several shades of lustful green.

"Don't sign it, Tess," Donovan said, clomping up the stairs. He hefted a long narrow box under each arm.

"Why not?" I wasn't about to sign for anything I hadn't ordered. But if Donovan said no, I needed to say yes just to be perverse.

"Because any gift from Lady Lucia comes with tangled strings attached." He topped the last riser and rebalanced the boxes. The writing on them suggested they might be lamps.

"The only contract in this transaction is between me and Lucia Continelli's bank. Her credit card cleared. That's all I care about," Doreen Cooper countered as she came up behind Donovan. She carried bed pillows with comforters and sheets balanced on top of them.

"Let me see the clipboard." I reached out a hand for it.

The man in coveralls relinquished it reluctantly.

"Start bringing up the rest of it," Doreen ordered him. "I'll handle the paperwork."

"What's this about?" I asked, scanning the delivery order. Two twin beds with mattresses and linens, two nightstands with lamps, two dressers, two student desks with more lamps. One Craftsman-style, round oak table with six matching chairs.

I gasped as I flipped through the pages. No contracts, no subtext.

"Oh, and there's a note," Doreen fumbled with her awkward burden trying to fish in her pocket. Donovan reached in and retrieved an envelope of rich creamy paper, the weight and texture of a wedding invitation. A familiar crowned embossed C on a sticker closed the flap.

I reached for the note with shaking hands.

"My apologies," I read in Lucia's florid hand. "A small token to ease you through the transition." Below that, her signature took up half the page.

"Small token?" I gulped. I knew how much that table and chairs cost. The rest of the stuff on the list doubled the price. At least.

When I tried to stuff the folded note back inside the envelope it caught on something. I pulled out a second piece of paper. A check. One thousand dollars in US currency, also signed in Lucia's elegant calligraphy. On the memo line she'd neatly printed "For clothing."

"We also have orders to help you move your office into the living room, clearing that room for the new furniture," Doreen added. "That's why I brought extra muscle." She nodded toward Donovan.

There was some subtext there I was too stunned to examine closely. Not that I cared. Donovan was no longer a part of my life. And never would be again.

Still ...

He scowled. "You didn't have to come," he complained.

"Yes, I did. Lady Lucia ordered. I obey. May we come in, Tess?"

"Yes, you may." I stepped back—almost treading on Phonetia's toes—and opened the door wide.

"What's going on here, Tess," Donovan asked the moment he'd cleared the doorway. He totally ignored Phonetia and E.T., who had retreated to the balcony, barefoot and coatless in the chill November damp. Not unusual for them, I'd learned.

"That is between Lady Lucia and me," I replied. No way was I going to relate our adventures in demonland two days ago.

"You can't trust her, Tess."

"Again, that is between Lady Lucia and myself. None of your concern, Donovan."

"I want it to be my concern," he choked out in a tight whisper. He finally looked at the girls. After a quick but thorough assessment, he checked over his shoulder to see where Doreen was.

More subtext. I had an idea what was going on. After my last rejection he'd gone running to the nearest willing female. A typical pattern for him. But he wasn't banking on that relationship if he could crawl back into my good graces.

Doreen was welcome to him.

"Did you know that Lady Lucia has hired staff and rented office space in her hotel in downtown Portland?" Doreen asked.

"I know she has business in town."

"Doesn't look like she's leaving any time soon," Donovan added. "I need to know why."

"Not necessarily. Her agenda has nothing to do with you or your grand plans." I signed the receipts with page ripping determination and handed the clipboard back to Doreen as she prowled the rooms with a decorator's eye. She ripped off the bottom copy and handed it to me. "At least I don't have to worry about clashing with your décor. I can start from scratch."

"Excuse me?"

"Just planning on how to rearrange things. I suppose the television is necessary with teenagers in the house, but I'd rather not have to work around it."

"Just dump everything. I'll manage to put everything where I want it." Anger began to boil up from my gut.

"I have my orders. Lady Lucia said to set it all right before leaving. You aren't supposed to have to do any extra work."

"That must be one huge favor she owes you," Donovan said. He raised one eyebrow practically begging me to tell him all.

"Fine, do what you want. I expect the work to be complete when I return in one hour. Lock up when you leave. Come on, girls. Shoes and jackets. We have some errands to do. Then you can have a walk in the park."

"Can we pick up litter?" E.T. asked meekly.

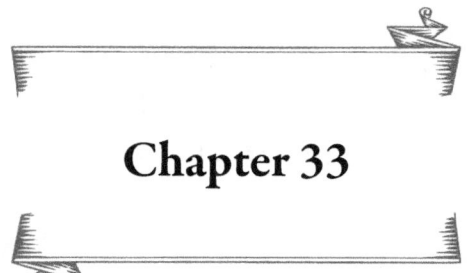

Chapter 33

1863: *Californians first referred to Oregonians as Webfoot due to nearly incessant rain from November to March.*

"Would you like to see the new SciFi movie *Space Pirates of the Outer Antares III*?" Sean asked when he called me the following morning.

"I'll have to ask Allie if she'll stay with the girls. It's her last night in town."

Go out with your boyfriend, babe. I'll keep an eye on our girls. And I promise to fetch you at the least sign of trouble, Scrap urged.

"Um, have you seen the first two movies?" I asked.

"I rented them last week." He paused to listen to a page in the background. "I admit though that I found the long sequences of special effects a bit boring on the small screen," he said calmly. The page wasn't for him. The next one might be.

"And I bet you were multitasking while they played so when there was a bit of plot and character interaction you missed them."

"There's a plot?"

"Not much of a one, but, yes, there is a plot, and a love triangle," I explained.

"Could have fooled me."

"On the big screen the special effects can be a bit overwhelming. They are indeed the stars of the show."

"So do you want to go see it?" he asked hopefully.

"Of course!"

"Good. I should be free by five. We can grab some burgers and still catch the six-thirty showing."

"Or the seven, or the seven-thirty. It's playing on three different screens at different times at the neighborhood multiplex." We laughed and hung up the phones. I hummed the love theme from the movies as I returned to the girls and the never-ending quest to help them delve into the depths of simple addition.

We skipped the burgers because Sean got delayed in an emergency surgery.

But he bought me popcorn and a giant soda to complete the movie experience and fill my empty tummy with empty calories.

"The first movie was based on a short story. Very loosely based," I whispered as we took seats dead center in the theater. Midweek we had plenty of seating options.

"Have I read the short story?"

"Wouldn't make any difference if you had. Other than the basic premise of a smuggler laying low while piloting an interstellar garbage scow, there's no similarity. In the story the smuggler is old and retired. He's recycling the Universe by moving society's throwaways to places where scraps are valuable. Making the pilot a younger man—played by the sexiest actor in Hollywood—and having him end up rescuing a gorgeous female diplomat on the run from terrorists are all new."

The lights dimmed and the usual ads and previews blasted across the screen.

"Rumor has it, Holly composed the love theme music, but I haven't seen her name in any of the official credits," I dropped my voice to a whisper.

"By changing the plot I'm guessing the producers left plenty of room for sequels and prequels," Sean returned to the topic of the movie in hushed tones.

"Hollywood loves sequels ad nauseum. In this case they don't have to worry too much about scripts and actors, though Malcolm Levi is mighty easy on the eye and really can act. These movies launched his career. I saw him in an historical drama as Attila the Hun. He did a great job."

"So, Hollywood spends most of their money on special effects. That's what people pay money for at the theater."

"Shush," the couple behind us admonished us.

We slunk down a little lower in our seats, embarrassed.

"Should we have brought the girls and Allie?" Sean asked on a whisper as the movie opened with a long shot of a boxy and beat up spaceship hauling an uglier crate four times its size that leaked bits and pieces of garbage.

"I don't think the girls are up to this yet. They're having enough trouble understanding reality. This kind of fantasy would challenge them more than I want to have to deal with."

"This isn't fantasy, it's science fiction!" the couple behind us insisted.

Sean looked as if he wanted to debate that issue. I touched his arm to quiet him. He turned his hand over to clasp mine.

We sat there like teenagers on a first date.

Sean's cell phone vibrated and buzzed before the opening credits had finished. Not an actual ring, just an audible reminder that he had to answer the damn thing.

A dozen people in widely scattered seats turned and frowned at him.

"I've got to go," Sean groaned. "Stay and watch the movie. Here's cab fare home." He reached for his wallet.

"Just drop me off at home. I've watched enough movies alone." A gaping hole threatened to open in my chest. Loneliness, rejection, depression vied for dominance.

"Okay if I call you when I'm free?" He held my hand as we exited the theater by a back route directly into the parking lot without having to wind through a crowded lobby.

"Sure. I'll be up, most likely working, after the girls go to bed."

Ten minutes later, I stood on the sidewalk outside my condo in the rain, watching his taillights reflect like blurry demon eyes in the puddles. "Is this what my life will be like if I stay with Sean?" I asked the ether.

Probably, Scrap answered. He alighted on my shoulder and tickled my ear with his boa.

"Will I ever get used to knowing his work is more important than I am?"

No.

"Something to think about anyway."

I spent the rest of my evening surrounded by the girls helping Allie pack. I made popcorn for them and let them drink soda. We giggled and made sure Allie took her bride magazines with her.

She made a point of showing me where she'd hidden the revolver in my walk-in closet since she couldn't take it on the plane and didn't trust it in her luggage.

Eventually, we settled the girls in bed, and I curled up on the sofa with the laptop, while Allie channel surfed for something more interesting on the TV than travelogues.

"That was fun," I confessed while I waited for the computer to boot up.

"More fun than dinner and a movie with your boyfriend?"

I had to think about that a moment.

"Maybe not. But I've missed girl giggle fests as much as sharing a movie with a friend."

"I think you are fully mended now, Tess. I can leave you with a clear conscience. Except I worry about you alone with the girls."

"We'll manage for the few weeks until you and Steve come back. And we'll fly east for the wedding. I'll make sure you get your full share of godparent time with them."

We laughed together.

Around midnight, my phone rang. I took it in the bedroom. Alone. "Hi, Sean," I said with only a brief glance at the caller ID.

"You're still awake, good. I was afraid I'd wake you."

"I told you I'd be working. I finished another chapter."

"Did you miss me?"

Did I? Sort of, but not nearly as much as I thought I would. "Of course," I lied.

"Tess, I looked up your professor on the Internet," he said. Was that a trace of guilt in his voice?

Every nerve ending in my body froze.

"There are a lot of holes in his profile."

"I know."

"Did you know he's married?"

"Yes. He and Julia have been together since they were children, married quite young and stayed together." Sort of.

"So there's nothing between you?"

"Not anymore."

"I'm guessing he was one of your mistakes, one of the reasons you want to go slowly in our relationship."

I gathered my courage, as if preparing to face a demon in a full fight. "I'm over him."

Liar! Scrap sneered at me from somewhere else.

WHILE TESS AND THE girls take Allie to the airport the next day, I scoot back to Cape Cod. I've postponed this trip longer than I should. Tess needed me close. Her psyche is fragile. Knowing that Damiri blood flows in her veins, no matter how dilute, preys upon her mind. It eats away at her sense of self. She doubts that she is the proper person to raise our daughters.

That's right, they are my daughters too. And I won't let Tess change her mind about raising them. Not that she could with that magic bond and all.

Tess needs to realign herself with her former life as a Celestial Blade Warrior. When I get back, we'll do a little meditation so that she can connect with her friends at the Citadel.

As I hightail it through the chat room, I note that the Sasquatch are back on duty. They've kinda been quarantined since that little kerfuffle with a rogue portal underneath Donovan's uncompleted casino at Half Moon Lake. Donovan lost a lot of money when we imploded his investment in order to close the portal.

He has recovered financially. I don't know if his agenda was truly damaged or not.

Speaking of which, I wonder if he knows that Tess is Lady Lucia's descendant. If he knows, that would explain his unrelenting pursuit of her as his ideal mate, the mother of the children he craves, the matriarch of his planned homeland for half-breed demons. The connection is another form of power. He thrives on power.

I land on the boundary of the two point five acres Tess used to own. She and her late husband, Dill—Doreen's brother—bought this place for many reasons. The special energies of the place are particularly inviting. Calm, peace, security.

Since time out of mind, this plot of land is where treaties were ritually completed, alliances negotiated. All welcome without prejudice. That invitation is stronger now that Dad and Bill run a B&B here. Actually, Bill owns it. Dad put it in his name for arcane tax reasons. And Bill has no demon blood in him, dilute or otherwise. Dad has a drop more than Tess but super recessive. He's never even heard of the Warriors of the Celestial Blade.

The land has a Neutral owner once more.

Except...

Something eats away at the neutrality. I can peel threads of power out of the air around me. They come from every direction, every dimension. They twine together. They twist into arrows seeking a way of penetrating the boundaries of this dimension. They burrow upward. They spiral downward. Little bits here and there, not so much as to draw attention, unless you are looking for it.

They seek the crystal ball. The echo of its presence is a focus that will linger long after I steal it away. It draws diverse strands of life together from this place and that.

A whiff of something elusive crosses my nose. I follow that thread as far as I can without going into the chat room.

I have smelled that particular odor before. Sort of imp. Sort of something else. Something older and rotting with insanity. There are cracks in the diamond ring we sent back to Faery. Energy leaks through those cracks.

The ball is funneling energy into the new dimension from every crack and crevice that no one thinks to shield. Like from the ring. That needs to stop. Who can control it? Who should be the one to claim that new dimension and shape it?

Not the Nörglein, that's for sure.

I creep around to the sloping cellar door against the outside foundation. Overgrown shrubs hang in shielding blankets of intertwined branches over the door. The big oak crowned in mistletoe with a swing slung from the limbs in the yard shadows it. Even if the Powers That Be have set a watchdog here I do not believe they will notice me. Watchdogs get lazy if they are not challenged.

The deal Tess signed in blood guarantees that unauthorized personnel cannot come here.

I'm not exactly authorized anymore. Just because I shouldn't come back here doesn't mean I can't. Tess and I lived here almost three years. I know secrets about this place outsiders will never find.

If I pop into the chat room and back inside the cellar, the transition will alert someone. I need to be sneakier.

I flit from shadow to shadow watching and sniffing for any trace of observers. Ah, there in the oak hangs a bat, upside down with wings only partially wrapped around him. He's awake. No self-respecting bat from Earth would show his face with the sun nearing high noon. It's too small to be a Damiri. Must be someone else. Someone to be avoided.

The presence of a bat almost guarantees that Tess will stay away from here. She hates/fears bats.

I fold the shifting light around me, circling with the wind like a fallen leaf—there are lots of those around. The bat ignores me when I land on the old slats of the door. There's a gap between two of them, just a teensy bit wider than the others.

I squeeze through into the dank and moldy cellar.

Mold! Glorious mold. It permeates the dirt walls; it hides in the corners near the floor. And it tops the discarded jars of jelly Mom put up. Clearly Bill and Dad don't clean down here like they should. They've moved the washer and dryer up to the attached apartment for convenience.

Of course the mild repulsion spell MoonFeather placed on the armory door beneath the stairs would make even the most insensitive feel prickly and uneasy.

The padlock on the door is firmly in place. As it should be. But what's a mere padlock to an imp?

I slide underneath the door into the closet that has been a priest hole, a station on the Underground Railroad, and housed Tess' collection of mundane and not so ordinary blades.

She took all the good stuff with her. Most of it's in mini storage now. But she left a few cheap replica weapons just to make it look like she doesn't have an armory elsewhere.

I stashed the crystal ball here because of the magical shielding MoonFeather added.

And there it is, sharing a shelf with a stiletto. It glows and pulses, more powerful now than before. It pulls energy into itself.

I am afraid of what I will see if I look too deeply into the swirling milky depths of the sphere.

But look I must.

First I light a cigar, one of my favorite black cherry cheroots. Three quick puffs and I feel fortified to face anything.

I expect to find spirals of malicious black sparked with red embers, something stark and barren and evil.

Much to my surprise, I find green and blue with pink and white sparkles. The entire globe is filled with The Essence of Faery. Not just the little patch Tess and I explored.

Faery lost more energy than we could account for while a smarmy producer kept twenty real faeries imprisoned in his casino in Las Vegas. Tess and I rescued the faery dancers. We thought we closed the portal that brought them to this world. Apparently, we didn't seal it tight enough. Faery is still leaking.

All that energy in the new dimension is waiting for a hand or mind to turn it to good or evil, a haven for refugees, or a hiding place for outlaws and renegades.

And the crystal ball is the only portal.

Chapter 34

1844 *Oregon law forbade slavery in Oregon. It also forbade free blacks to live in Oregon as well.*

Um, Tess, are you awake? Scrap asked.

I looked up from scrubbing my face. Scrap showed up as a dim outline of wavy lines reflected in the bathroom mirror.

Six very long weeks of sleeping on sofas and cots, I hadn't fully adjusted to having my own room and private bath back.

No word from Lady Lucia since the furniture delivery this morning. Her guilt gift. But Scrap informed me she had hired a new nanny and was running her empire from a second suite in her hotel.

I'd made a little progress assessing what the girls could and could not do academically. A mixed bag of skills. Math went no further than the girls painfully copying the numerals in order. They read the classics beautifully but could not write, not even their own names.

"You know I'm awake, Scrap. What's wrong that you felt you had to ask?"

I fetched the crystal ball, just like you told me.

"I asked you to do that days ago. But we've been a little busy since then. What did you do with it?"

I hid it at the bottom of the river. I can get it back any time you need it.

"Will I need it?"

Probably.

"Why will I need it?"

Bargaining chip with the Powers That Be.

"Huh?"

Then he told me about the power leakage from every corner of the Universe. He held something back. He always did.

"Scrap, I'm not likely to need to get out of my bargain with the Powers That Be."

What about Sean?

"We haven't gotten that far." I wasn't going to jump into a serious relationship after the last three disasters. "How come you aren't pushing me to renew my relationship with Gollum?" My heart sank. If Scrap gave up on us, then there really was no hope.

You know that he truly loves his wife.

"Yes, I know that."

I mean more than just a need to protect his childhood girlfriend.

I sighed. "Yeah, I know. If he only needed to protect her, he'd have set up a trust fund and divorced her. She probably wouldn't know the difference while she was in the asylum."

And now she's out. And he's committed to her, come hell or high water.

"It's probably going to take both of those and then some to separate him from her. If she is Squishy's new lover, I'm not sure even that will separate them. So, do you think Sean and I might make a go of it?"

See how he reacts to the con and filking before you decide.

"Good advice. If he can't survive two days at the local con, he'll miss out on a big part of my life. He won't know what makes me tick, why I need the stimulation and support of that community. He'll already miss big chunks of my life because of his job commitment."

At least he's reading your books, and some recommended classic SF. I peeked. He's gone through almost half your list in a week.

"Is he really reading and enjoying them, or just skimming to please me?"

Scrap gave an impish shrug.

"He calls me and talks about the books as if he has a passing acquaintance. And he is cute. And sexy. And intelligent. But he keeps worse hours at work than I do. It's a little difficult to base a relationship on telephone calls."

Tess, what are we going to do about the new dimension?

"I don't know yet. Do we have to do anything?"

Yeah, I think we do. Donovan would move heaven and earth to have access to a whole new dimension for his Kajiri. The Nörglein is trying to breed an entire new tribe. He'll want a homeland for himself. The Powers That Be have the ability to back up their decrees. They know how to stop the leakage. Some of it is still coming from Faery. The big shots need to make the decision of who gets the place.

"But will they ever make that decision, or just let it ride, holding it as a carrot in front of the applicants to force them into obeying their rules?"

Unknown. You may be right.

"Phonetia suggested the forest elf might need the crystal ball to heal the wound I gave him."

Possible. But think about it. If he can claim the new dimension by right of first possession, he gets to set up the parameters. He can make it so that just stepping into his new home cures him. Like Prince Mikhail needed to go back to Faery to heal after the dynamite explosion in this dimension.

"We can't allow the Nörglein to get near it. I won't let the little bastard live to rape another woman."

What about his sons?

"I'll reserve judgment to see if they are redeemable. Are you sure they can't fish the crystal ball out of the river?"

No.

"Then move it again. Keep it moving so no one with the talent to sense it can home in on it. What about the freeze-dried garbage dump of the Universe?"

The cold in Mum's front yard might make it inert. But I doubt it. I found the comb and the Celestial Goddess brooch there and they are less powerful than the crystal ball.

"I wish I knew someone I could entrust it to."

Lady Lucia could protect it.

"I said, someone I trust!"

SOMEONE I TRUST.

I slapped my forehead then pounded it into the desktop. I'm an idiot. And then some.

As Sean so aptly pointed out, part of my depression and self-destructive tendencies stemmed from my isolation. I'd grown too used to having to work on my own, without any guidance from the source of my status as a Warrior of the Celestial Blade.

I needed to reconnect with the Citadel. Deep in a lost ravine between here and there, part of the twilight world that forms a barrier between light and dark, good and evil, I'd stumbled on the place in a fever delirium.

Sister Serena, the physician, had cut the otherworldly infection from my body, leaving sickle shaped scars from my right temple to jaw, beneath each breast, and across my belly. Because the infection originated outside current reality, the scars remained partially outside normal sight as well. Only another Warrior could see them. Or Gollum—I still hadn't figured out how he could. All Warriors bore at least some of those scars.

I needed to reconnect with my origins.

With Scrap perched on the windowsill watching for danger, I propped myself up against the headboard with extra pillows and relaxed.

Meditation requires stillness within.

Not an easy task for one as restless as me. If I'm uncomfortable in an exotic yoga pose, I might as well forget even trying.

I went through a ritual of progressive muscle clenches and releases, working from brows to toes, letting the energy flow more readily. Once my body felt as if it melted into the quilted coverlet, I visualized a bright tornado of tension spiraling down from my mind to my feet and out into the world.

My subconscious took over, relaxing me to almost sleep, and brought new energy into me. I visualized it creating a bubble around me. A bubble that would transport my thoughts on a direct line north by northeast to the home of my Sisterhood.

Past midnight. The Sisters slept the sleep of the just. Their routine demanded long hours keeping the Citadel mostly self-sufficient along with harsh training in the military arts. During my year there, I had collapsed in my bed every night, too exhausted to dream.

But someone was always on watch. The Citadel sat atop a portal to a demon world. We could not allow our enemies to breach it while we slept.

"Who?" a weary mind answered my gentle probe.

I flashed an image of myself to the woman on guard. Telepathy isn't so much an actual conversation as a series of images and impressions, it's just easier to transcribe in words.

"Oh, Tess. Greetings."

"Tess, where are you?" Gayla, the senior Sister interrupted. I'd been the one to admit Gayla to an overcrowded Citadel when she burned with the imp flu. I had cut the infection from her.

She had defied the previous leadership to send me backup when I faced an entire horde of rampaging Sasquatch.

We'd been close ever since.

"Home. Why?"

"Ginkgo said that Scrap said we needed to talk. I called just a bit ago. Your line was busy."

"Huh? Scrap, who's on the phone?" I searched my tentative connection to the girls. Both slept soundly in their room.

Line's clear now. Scrap sat a little further forward, alert.

Previously, I'd have defaulted to calling Gayla, since she was obviously awake.

Having sunk deep into meditative mode, I decided to stay there. Less chance of eavesdroppers.

"I have an artifact of power that needs to disappear for a while, but still be accessible to me," I said as I showed an image of the crystal ball as I'd last seen it, resting in my hand, inviting me to gaze deeply into the swirls of milky minerals, losing myself in the power and the other worlds it tapped.

"Wow! You aren't kidding, that's an artifact of power. I'd give up my claim on the Goddess Brooch for that."

"I claim both as gifts of fate!"

Me, territorial? Just look at how long it took me to come to the practical solution of giving up my office.

"Acknowledged," Gayla said formally. "Where should I put it?"

"At the bottom of the midden. I don't care, just so long as it doesn't get near the portal. It might totally dissolve the barriers."

"Agreed. Have Scrap drop it off to me and me only. There are a few malcontents—overachievers actually—we've recruited recently. They want to storm the portal and slay anything they can find on the other side."

"Are they candidates to go rogue?" Technically, I was rogue since I fought the forces of evil on the outside. We used to be rare. With shifting portals, changing power dynamics, and Donovan's half-breeds agitating for a home world, we needed more people on the outside than in the past six centuries.

I wondered if the crystal ball had something to do with these changing times.

It needed to go to someone powerful enough to control it. Not yet.

"Not yet," Gayla echoed my thoughts. "I don't trust these new Warriors on their own. They'd go looking for trouble without backup."

"Been there, done that." We both chuckled.

"You, I trust to have common sense eventually. These gals, I don't. So what have you been up to?"

"Too much." I uploaded the rescue of my daughters from their abusive father in a series of tableaus, carefully editing the aftermath of Lady Lucia's spell.

I hadn't come to terms with my demon ancestry enough to entrust that knowledge to even a dear friend.

Gayla whistled through her teeth. "I'd offer to train the girls and keep them isolated but they'd meet opposition right, left, and sideways."

"Which is why I didn't ask."

"Ginkgo just dumped the crystal ball in my lap. I'd better do something with it quick, while the boys are off for some quick cuddling."

We signed off with proper telepathic protocols, an image of a good-bye wave, then a gray wall that faded to black. I slowly withdrew from the meditation.

When I opened my eyes, both Phonetia and E.T. stood in my doorway staring at me with eyes wide in awe.

"We thought only Father could communicate that deeply," Phonetia whispered. "Did Lady Lucia's spell give you that power?"

"I've always been able to contact my Sisterhood this way." But never so easily or completely.

I didn't want to think about how or why.

"Practice. It just takes practice."

"We can't do it and we've practiced," Phonetia insisted. "Same with our brothers. We just have this general awareness of where you are and what your mood is. Like we used to have with Father and the boys."

"Why are your eyes glowing red?" E.T. asked.

My heart sank.

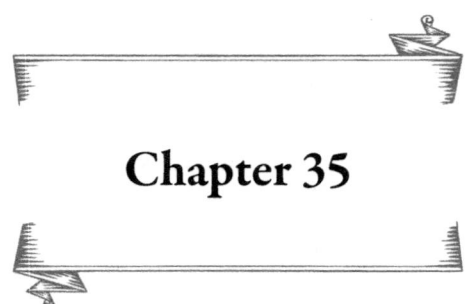

Chapter 35

In 2006, the American Podiatric Medical Association listed Portland as the #1 US city for walking.

"Phonetia, what did I tell you about wandering around the house naked?" I demanded the next morning.

"Ah, Mom," she whined. No excuses or explanations.

"You don't live in a cave in the woods anymore. There are rules of civilization. Wearing clothes is one of them."

"Clothes are dumb." She tried walking past me from her bedroom to the bath.

"You didn't think so when you and E.T. spent an entire afternoon trying on the new outfits Lady Lucia's money bought you."

"E.T. snores. Why can't I move into the big room and *you* share with her?"

"Because then I wouldn't sleep either. You really don't want to deal with me when I'm sleep deprived." Like today. After last night's easy communication with Gayla and E.T. proclaiming that my eyes glowed demon red, I hadn't slept much. When I did, my dreams were filled with strange aches in my joints and a need to fly.

No way in hell would I transform into a bat.

I couldn't suppress my atavistic shiver of fear. Bats! Anything but a bat.

Phonetia rolled her eyes like any teenager with the weight of the world on her shoulders. Hey, it's part of the job of being a teenager.

"Get your shower and put on some clothes. Breakfast will be ready in twenty minutes."

"If you say so."

"I don't snore. You do! I don't want to share with you either," E.T. yelled from deep within the tangle of a typical teen's room. All those beautiful, expensive, new clothes and they couldn't figure out how to hang them in the closet or pick up dirty underwear. They'd shared that room only a few days and already it looked like ground zero of a force ten hurricane.

"Scrap tells me that I'm the one who snores, so you're both wrong," I proclaimed. "We've got a full day of lessons and cleaning your room today so get moving while I fix waffles."

"With strawberries?" E.T. asked. She stuck her head out the door. She at least held her nightgown in front of her, protecting my modesty if not hers.

"Strawberries are out of season, and I don't like frozen. How about blueberries? They survive the freezer better. And I've got whipped cream." Girls who loved the same food I did, what more could a mom ask?

"Waffles aren't any good without bacon," Phonetia sniffed superiorly.

"Bacon I can do. Better hurry or your sister and I will eat it all."

Finally she made tracks for the bathroom, presenting her long slender back to me.

I gasped at the snaking scars showing white against her youthful skin.

"Did the dark elf do that to you?" I stopped her with a gentle hand on her shoulder. I remembered the agony of the blackberry whip hitting me repeatedly as my blood worked to share the lives of my girls during Lady Lucia's spell. I'd barely endured. How had this child survived such abuse?

"Yeah, what of it. He said I deserved it."

"No child deserves that kind of punishment no matter what their problem."

"If you say so." She shrugged out from under my touch.

"I say so." My words got lost in the slamming of the bathroom door.

"Mom," E.T. asked hesitantly, still hiding behind her nightgown.

"What, sweetie?" I rearranged my face from stern disapproval to careful concern.

"She called Oak last night, after midnight. We thought you were already asleep. Maybe you'd just gone quiet in your meditation."

That explained the busy phone line.

Everything inside me stilled. "Why would Phonetia call your brother?"

"She's worried. The spell, the one Lady Lucia performed . . . it severed our link to our brothers as well as our fa... the dark elf. We can't tell if he's taking out his anger on the boys."

"Is he?"

"We don't know. Oak didn't answer the pay phone on Second and Ankeny at the prearranged time."

I should have known. These kids were close. They roamed the city, knew the bus routes, spied for their father. Of course, they'd have communications backup.

"Get ready for breakfast. If your lessons go well, we'll walk the river path after lunch." I squeezed her shoulder reassuringly.

"Can we go south this time? We haven't been that way and we need to pick up litter."

"I think that can be arranged."

The doorbell rang as I forked the last piece of bacon from the frying pan onto paper towels to drain.

"I'll get it!" Phonetia called, sliding down the hardwood floor on stockinged feet. Her dark hair flew out behind her in a silken wave. A whiff of fresh evergreen and mown grass followed her. She curved and braked with uncanny precision right in front of the spy hole.

She'd donned new green jeans, mint polo, and a sweatshirt that splashed bright autumn leaves across the front in puffy rubber paint. No visible scars. She looked pretty, fresh, and eager, like a typical fourteen year old.

"It's just Dad." She flung open the door and stalked to the table.

"Who were you expecting that I'm such a disappointment?" Gollum asked from the doorway.

"Your brother, Oak?" I asked quietly.

"How'd you know?"

"That bond we have, the one forged of blood and magic. I try not to pry, Phonetia, but it's dangerous to maintain contact with your brothers."

Gollum wandered by, snagging a piece of bacon.

"Do you have a reason for dropping in for breakfast unannounced?" I scraped more batter into the waffle iron.

He found his own plate and cutlery to put on the table along with the three primary settings.

"Do I need a reason to drop by to see my daughters?" His glasses slid to the end of his nose and he peered over them at me. A gentle smile lit his face.

"Yes." I turned my attention to coffee for me, milk and juice for the girls. Let him get his own damn coffee.

"Actually, Julia wanted to go to her psychiatric appointment by herself after I arranged for TAs to take my classes all day. I dropped her off. Pat will pick her up. Then they plan to hit some of the Veterans Day sales."

The girls each gave him a hug before they took their places at the table. More affection than they gave me.

"How would you like to help the girls with their lessons? I could really use some time alone with my laptop to get some work done."

"Oh, Mom, do we have to?" the girls chorused.

"Yes, you have to do schoolwork. With me or with your dad, take your pick."

They chose Gollum, thinking he'd be a gentler taskmaster. I had news for them.

Three hours later, with three chapters edited and a new one written, I peeked out of my bedroom, amazed at the happy giggles and soft murmur of voices.

"May we please go pick up litter in the park, Dad?" E.T. asked.

"If you've finished your spelling practice."

I eased into the hallway. "You know the drill, girls," I said authoritatively. "Shoes, coats, and hats. Gloves and trash bags, one for garbage, one for recycling and one for returnable bottles and cans." They'd picked up the idea of recycling faster than they did writing and math.

"Yes, Mom." They both rolled their eyes as if my rules were the most outrageous ideas of all time. To them shoes, hats, and coats in a cold November drizzle were unnecessary.

I listened as they thumped down the concrete and steel stairs. When they jumped off the last two steps to the ground, I moved to the French door to watch them amble along the river path.

"You don't need to watch them every moment. They've been roaming the city on their own for years," Gollum said, coming up behind me. He stood too close, the warmth of his body filled me with yearning.

One and a half dates with Sean plus a lot of phone calls when he canceled on me, and I still longed for the man I couldn't have.

"I know. But I'm still new to this mothering business."

"Do you trust Scrap to keep an eye on them and alert you to any danger?"

"Of course. He's the best baby-sitter ever invented. Sometimes I think he thinks he's their mother."

We both laughed.

"Have you told Julia about your illegitimate children?" I had to ask. I had to put the psychic distance between us.

"Not yet."

"Will you?" I moved away from him, into the kitchen. I stirred a hearty beef stew that simmered in the slow cooker. (I'd discovered that the girls ate just about anything. They preferred vegetarian more from habit than choice.) Something to do. Anything to keep me from throwing myself at him.

That was dinner. What would I do for lunch, especially if Gollum hung around?

"I don't know if I'll tell Julia or not. I don't trust this new stability and happiness. She's been like this before, usually just before a major crash that sets her back years in her recovery." He bent his head as he polished his glasses with a pristine handkerchief he'd fished out of his pocket.

"Veterans Day is this Monday. That means the local convention happens this weekend, day after tomorrow." I checked the wall calendar to be sure. I'd gotten so caught up in the girls that I'd forgotten one of the most important weekends of the year for my career.

"I'm obligated to go." I didn't tell him that I'd given my guest membership to Sean. He was really looking forward to the costumes and nonsense, the music, the fight demonstrations, and the literary discussions.

If he didn't get called in to work.

"Maybe we should take the girls," Gollum said happily. "I'm sure they'll enjoy it."

"I know they will. They'll disappear into the gaming rooms, and I won't see them for seventy-two hours. They still bug me to call someone and find out who won the interrupted game at High Desert Con last month."

"Pat thinks she should move out. Maybe this would be a good test to see if Julia can be left alone."

"Um." An image of a pale woman with exquisitely cut hair sitting in a corner of Kelly's Brew Pub while Squishy spoke to Sean and me flashed before my mind. Was that Julia?

For my sake I almost wished it were. For Gollum's, I wasn't so sure. How would he handle the news that his wife loved another woman more than him?

But if it was Julia on her first lesbian date, at least Squishy was moving toward an ethical separation from her patient.

I almost chuckled at how Sean had made a point of dismissing me as his patient before he asked me out.

"I'm close enough to commute to the con, so I won't stay at the hotel," I mused, making plans and lists in my head, half thinking out loud. "That means a little closer supervision of the girls when I bring them home at night."

"You'll miss out on some of the best filk," Gollum reminded me. "They usually don't get started until after ten. And Holly Shannon will be there."

"There is life outside of filk." As if the music on the stereo in the background was anything else but the folk music of Science Fiction-Fantasy conventions.

"There may be life after filk, but is it a con without it?"

"Barely," I acknowledged. Gollum and I had found common bonds at the filk sessions of our first con together.

Would I feel like I had to sing "Heart's Path" again?

I had to remind myself that I had moved on. I had Sean. We liked each other. We shared a lot of common interests.

Trouble, babe. Scrap popped in and out again.

"Scrap?"

"What?" Gollum asked. He'd already scooped up his jacket and headed for the door.

"Where are the girls and what is wrong, Scrap?"

Path, two blocks south. Oak, Cedar, and Fir are waiting for them.

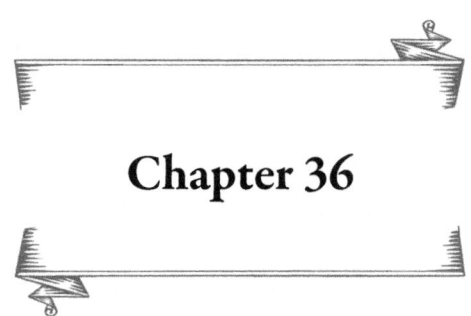

Chapter 36

Teasel thistle seeds were brought to Oregon by Methodist missionaries to card wool in their mission mills. They escaped and became an obnoxious ditch weed.

"Hold back, Tess." Gollum grabbed both my shoulders as I passed him on the paved path.

I tried to wiggle out of his grasp. "The hell I will. Those are my girls." I pointed to the two figures ahead of us, rapidly disappearing around a curve.

They bent their heads together in close sisterly discussion.

"Their brothers are waiting for them. Family. Blood kin. They need to see them," Gollum said.

"No. You don't know half of what their father has done to all of them." I slipped my jacket, leaving him standing there, holding the damp garment while I ran forward, full tilt. My left leg ached. I ignored the protest of atrophied muscles just coming to life again. Good thing I'd doubled up on my PT exercises. My therapist was nearly ready to dismiss me because I'd recovered strength and maneuverability so rapidly.

"Scrap, what's happening?" Between the mist rising from the river and the drizzle sliding into my eyes, I could barely see the two blocks to where the girls had passed beyond my sight. A fat raindrop plopped from my tangled hair into my left eye, further blurring my perception.

I cursed and shook my head like a dog shedding bathwater.

"What has the elf done?" Gollum demanded. He kept up an easy loping stride; his long legs matched my running pace.

"He's training the boys to continue his work of begetting an entire tribe of Nörglein. He wants them to practice on Phonetia and E.T. and strengthen the DNA in their children. I think he may have given Phonetia to his marijuana growing minions as a reward."

"Shit!" He increased his pace, quickly outdistancing me.

I couldn't remember ever hearing him curse. I wondered if outrage of this magnitude would push him to break his vow of nonviolence.

Better hurry, babe. I'm getting hot and thin, Scrap snarled.

A burst of adrenaline gave my feet near levitation. Blood flowed strongly through my legs, eliminating lingering traces of my injury.

"Scrap, report," I barked as the girls came into view again.

They ambled forward, oblivious to our pursuit or the danger that awaited them in the little hollow where the trail dipped and blackberries crowded close.

Demon tats in the shrubs behind the boys.

Damn.

I held out my hand as I ran, willing Scrap to land there and transform.

He obeyed.

A deadly calm replaced my panic. My stride evened out and stretched. Scrap elongated, thinned, curved. Faster than I'd ever seen him, he sharpened the inner curve of the twin blades and extruded tines from the outside.

The quarter staff balanced precisely in my hand.

I bounced around the girls and skidded to a halt, blade at the ready, feet *en garde* just as Oak, Cedar, and Fir stepped onto the path.

"Oak!" Phonetia called. "You didn't answer the phone."

I brought the Celestial Blade horizontal, blocking him.

Both Phonetia and Oak took one step forward, looked at the blade, then at me, and back again to my weapon.

"I will protect the girls with my life," I announced.

Six men, late teens and early twenties, who sorely needed showers and shaves, stepped from the concealing shrubbery. They twirled long chains with barbed links and unsheathed long knives. Their demon tats on their inside wrists pulsed red beneath the black ink.

"We can take her," the leader, a stocky, bleached blond with swarthy skin, said. He wore a silver pendant on a black thong that replicated his tattoo. He extended the length of chain, coming dangerously close to Phonetia.

E.T. wisely retreated behind Gollum.

Easy pickings, Scrap snarled to me.

None of the forest elf children or the demon-protected seemed to hear him.

Gollum came up beside me. He held his hands up, closed his eyes, and relaxed into an easy, martial arts pose.

"What are you, some kind of blind Ninja?" the blond delinquent asked. He started swinging his chain.

"Something like that," I replied, not wanting to break Gollum's concentration.

Before I finished speaking, I swished the blade, tangling the chain in the tines. I yanked.

This guy wisely released his weapon. I stumbled backward with the unexpected change in balance. E.T. yelped and retreated as I stepped on her toes.

Blondie's comrades flanked him, trying to ease around our backs.

Gollum pushed his hands out in front of him.

I heard air displacement. I felt the recoil as the leader flew backward and landed on his butt in a tangle of blackberry vines and jutting teasel thistle, a nasty place. He had to hurt almost as if the Nörglein thrashed him with his wicked whip.

Gollum hadn't laid a hand on him.

The five remaining men flowed into the space left vacant, advancing with weapons drawn.

The tree boys faded out of my periphery.

Duck, parry, turn, jab. I flew into action. Scrap took a long strip of skin off of one arm. Blood flowed freely. At the moment crimson drops touched the tattoo the elven minion yowled as if he'd been burned. The enchanted ink dissolved. His entire arm flushed with a serious inflammation. He rolled into the wet grass trying to extinguish the magical fire raging within him.

The men gave ground until we came abreast of where the leader pulled himself upright. He brandished a gun at me.

A little gun easily concealed inside his pant leg. A big magazine, almost as big as the gun itself hung below the barrel. He pushed the muzzle forward until his reach ended mere inches from my chest.

I froze in place. The sweat on my brow and back turned to ice.

My mind whirled, trying to figure a way to get the gun away from him. Could I block a bullet with the blade?

"We want the girl," Blondie sneered.

"You can't have her."

"Her father said we could," he laughed, an evil sound that had no humor in it.

"The Nörglein isn't her dad. I am," Gollum insisted. He shifted his feet and hands, gathering energy again.

"Please, Miss Tess, don't fight us," Oak pleaded.

"Did he hurt you?" Phonetia called from behind me.

Oak stood stalwart, off the path but still part of the action.

"He whipped you, didn't he!" Phonetia cried. She sidled toward her brother.

Before I could stop her, or protest, her broad-shouldered middle brother grabbed her arm with one hand and wrapped his other arm around her throat.

"Try to stop us and I kill her," he said.

"Cedar, no!" Oak took one step closer.

Cedar tightened his pressure on my daughter's throat.

She gargled something, struggling for air.

Cedar backed up, dragging his sister with him. "Father whipped me, too, for letting the girls get away. I won't let that happen again." Anger and pain warred for dominance in his voice.

The demon tats moved between the retreating boy and me. The leader kept his gun leveled on me as I tried to follow.

I slashed at his gun hand.

The weapon exploded, near deafening me. I dove for the ground.

Ducks and geese squawked mightily, rising from the water with much awkward fluttering.

Boaters paused and reached for communications.

"Follow her!" I commanded Scrap and dropped my blade. He dissolved into the barest outline of an imp. Then he was gone.

I returned to my knees, checking to see who was hurt.

Gollum held E.T. tightly against his chest, her mouth working in protest.

"You want to fight dirty?" I asked Blondie. Nothing left to lose. Before the last syllable escaped I hit the gun with a roundhouse kick and smashed the flat of my hand against Blondie's nose.

The gun skittered across the ground until it plopped into the water.

Blondie grabbed his bleeding nose with both hands and fled.

His minions followed close on his heels.

"Scrap? Where are they taking my girl?"

A car. Shiny new Hummer, black. Peeling out of the parking lot. I'm on the roof.

"License plate?" I asked, noting Gollum had his cell phone out.

Mud encrusted. Only dirt on the vehicle. Oregon custom BAD2BNE.

I repeated the number. Gollum spat it into the phone. "Police are on the way. Amber alert in progress."

"I'm going after them."

"Without Scrap?"

"He'll be there when I catch up. Take care of E.T."

"I must help," Oak said. Fir slunk behind him. "They will hurt my sister a lot before they turn her over to my father," he added quietly. "I can't allow that."

"Your father hurt her a lot every day she lived with him," I told him, fists clenched and aching to slam them into his face.

"I know. That is why I sent the girls to you."

"Then why did you agree to bring them back?" This time I yelled loud enough to startle the geese again.

Mutely, he turned around and lifted his T-shirt.

I gasped at the bloody mess of his skin.

"The only way I could get him to stop was to promise to bring Blackberry back to him."

"We'll *all* go after them. Two cars. You take E.T., I'll take the brothers," Gollum decided for us.

Cruising up Pill Hill, back road, Scrap informed me.

The Medical School and VA Hospital connected by a sky bridge crowned a couple of hills southwest of downtown—a lot of trees, ravines, and places to get lost around and behind. The forest there melded into Forest Park, the home of the Nörglein.

"On our way!"

PHONETIA STRUGGLES against the duct tape binding her. Something about the unnatural fibers keeps her from morphing into her native plant. Otherwise, she could sprout fat thorns sharp enough to slice through the tape.

The Hummer careens around a twist in the narrow road. I'm nearly flung off the car. Only my talons latched around the roof rack keep me in my observation post. The wind tries to catch beneath my wings and lift me wide and free.

We come to an abrupt halt on a gravel shoulder that overlooks the city spread out far below. A pretty city. I don't have time to admire the view. No guard rail between us and the steep cliff. The Hummer barely fits. Half of two wheels rest on the pavement. A couple of cars pass, honking at the intrusion of the wide vehicle into their space.

When the traffic passes, leaving the road open and free for a bit, the back door flies open. Blondie and Cedar jump out, dragging my Phonetia with them. They cross the road and head into the woods. The Hummer speeds away.

Cedar leads along a creek and up a narrow ravine.

I flash images of the spot to Tess. Then I fly after our fleeing quarry. Fatigue drags at my wings. Adrenaline pushes me forward.

If only I could rest a bit by perching on Phonetia's head.

Can't risk it. Cedar will be aware of me if I get too close.

Phonetia drops to her knees, dragging Blondie with her. He yanks and yanks at her arms trying to get her to stand up and follow them.

She goes limp and slides through his grasp. Good girl.

Then she thrashes around breaking sword fern fronds and snagging alder branches. A blind man could follow the path she leaves. Cedar closes his eyes and concentrates hard. I can feel the plant life flowing over the break in its growth where deer, coyote, and raccoons have beaten the ground hard. Their roots resist pushing through the narrow game trail. He's too young and inexperienced to make them obey. He's close to panic and loses his concentration before the plants complete their task. Then he has to start over.

Blondie grows impatient and drags Phonetia deeper into the woods, oblivious to signs she leaves in their wake.

Gollum will know what to look for.

If they get here in time, before we meet up with the Nörglein and he truly obscures the path.

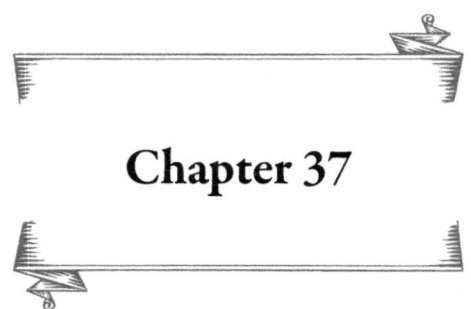

Chapter 37

The joint Occupancy Treaty of 1815 between the US and Great Britain forbade a military presence from either nation in the Oregon Country, but settlement was open to citizens of both from California to Alaska, the Rockies to the Pacific.

"Where is it, where is it, where is it?" I murmured as I yanked the steering wheel right and left, taking the curves uphill way too fast.

Behind me, Gollum, driving his new SUV, trailed at a moderate speed. He braked and accelerated smoothly. When did he learn to drive!

"There, there, there," E.T. pointed excitedly to a widening of the shoulder on our left.

I stomped on the brake and clutch so abruptly Gollum's vehicle came within inches of rear-ending me. Thankfully, he has amazing reactions. All that Aikido and other martial arts training. We squeezed both cars into the miniscule gravel area.

"This way," E.T. called over her shoulder as she flung open the door and scooted across the road without looking for traffic.

My heart nearly stopped as a car coming downhill way too fast skidded and screeched to avoid hitting her. The middle-aged woman driving leaned out her window and yelled obscenities. But she didn't slow down much or stop to make sure E.T. was okay.

I ran after my daughter just as recklessly. Gollum and the two boys jogged along hard on my heels.

"They came through here just minutes ago," Oak said, glancing at a swath of wreckage through the underbrush.

"Scrap?"

Under log bridge. Left uphill away from the creek. He sounded breathless and anxious.

I spotted the huge Douglas fir that had uprooted and fallen across the ravine, its top branches bent and broken against the opposite hillside. We all ducked and squeezed beneath it then stopped.

If anyone had gone this way within the last century, I couldn't spot it.

Fir did. He loped upward, pulling himself along by grabbing branches, ferns, and protruding roots that formed steps across the path. Oak paralleled him, using his greater strength to kick footholds into the steep incline.

E.T. climbed as nimbly as her brothers, inserting her wiry body between branches and trunks.

Gollum and I looked to each other in puzzlement, shrugged, and followed more slowly.

We crested the slope. Nothing around us but underbrush, fallen trees, and impenetrable blackberry thickets.

The boys had disappeared. E.T. looked as confused as Gollum and I.

"Scrap, now where?"

I don't know, he wailed landing heavily on my head. *I can't do it anymore. I'm too tired. Couldn't go sharp if I had to.* He curled up and started snoring.

"I'm sorry, buddy. I shouldn't have asked so much of you, transforming, fighting, barely tasting blood, then chasing the bad guys without a break or food." I reached up and petted him.

A lump formed in my throat. Tears of frustration and despair pricked my eyes. I checked the link between me and Phonetia. A faint tendril of life glowed in my heart. Unharmed, but frightened.

"I hear something. This way." Gollum blinked rapidly behind his glasses as he held back crossing fir branches. Sure enough, another narrow pathway opened before us.

Shouts ahead drew us onward. Gollum led, breaking the way through and beneath the overgrown bush.

"Bushwhacking in Africa," he explained briefly. He didn't have his backpack filled with essential tools. But he had experience. I trusted him to get me to my daughter.

The link between Phonetia and me suddenly flared.

I surged forward, passing Gollum.

"Put the gun down, little boy, before you hurt yourself," Blondie sneered.

"Let my sister go or I'll shoot," Fir announced firmly, not a bit of a quaver in his voice.

Hope flared within me, fueled by Phonetia as much as the conversation.

"Fir, they wear Father's protection. The gun won't kill them," Oak explained calmly. Anxiety tinged his voice.

"Maybe I can't kill him. But I can hurt him."

We burst through the last thicket of alder saplings just as Fir lowered his aim from Blondie's chest to his groin.

Phonetia threw herself sideways and down. She rolled until she fetched up at Gollum's feet. He pulled her upright as he produced a pocketknife and began sawing away at the multiple layers of duct tape around her wrists. More strips covered her mouth.

He seemed absorbed with his task, but I saw his eyes flicker, keeping the boys and the marijuana farmers under close observation. "At the first opportunity you and your sister need to run. Get back to the cars and lock yourselves in," he whispered.

I nodded firmly, seconding his order. My connection to the girls surged with agreement. They were both scared enough not to fight me.

A quick scan of the miniature clearing, and Blondie was the only demon tat I could see. I closed my eyes for half a second, concentrating on the tiny sounds of the forest.

Where had the others gone?

Waiting with elf daddy at the home base, Scrap murmured, half awake.

"Give me the gun, Fir," Blondie ordered, holding out his hand.

The weapon exploded. Blondie flew backward from the impact. I cringed.

"Run!" Oak commanded.

Gollum grabbed both girls and headed back the way we'd come. Downhill. He only needed to keep going downhill and he'd hit the road sooner or later.

I stayed put. My feet took a defensive stance.

Oak and Fir closed ranks between me and Blondie. Cedar crouched over the fallen man, oblivious to the poison oak that brushed at his legs and hands.

I looked for blood. None. The bullet hadn't penetrated. I wondered if the demon tattoo protected Blondie from the toxic oils of the plant too.

"Take care of my sisters," Oak said to me. "Get out now, before Father comes to investigate."

"Come with me."

"We have to stay here to blur your path."

"He'll kill you."

"No, he won't. He'll hurt us. But he won't kill his sons."

"He values you more than his daughters," I sighed.

"Girls are only good for sex and bearing children," Cedar said. He came up from his crouch and leaped at me, hands folding into tight fists.

Oak caught him, then cast him aside as if he weighed no more than thistle down.

"Run, Miss Tess. Run quickly. You haven't much time to get free of the forest before Father finds you."

I ran. I'd never run from a fight before, but I ran from this one.

For the sake of my daughters, I ran, skidded, and slid downhill. I had to stop thinking like a Warrior and start acting like a mother.

Lady Lucia had warned me about this. She'd told me never to get involved, never let my emotions get between me and my job.

I had to. I had to protect my daughters.

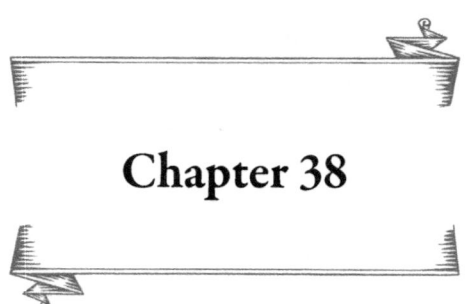

Chapter 38

*P*ortland native Matt Groening is the creator of "The Simpsons" TV show, proving to audiences, one and all, that life really is just a cartoon.

Thursday afternoon, the girls huddled over registration forms I'd downloaded from the local con. Their lesson after lunch consisted of figuring out how to write the correct information in the appropriate boxes.

I'd learned to read and write at the same time. They'd only learned to read. Writing came hard.

I sat at my desk in front of the computer, adjacent to the dining table. My concentration wandered from the view out the windows, to the half-written page in front of me, to blatantly eavesdropping on their whispers. Much as I wanted to jump up and prompt them through the procedure, I knew they needed to figure out as much as possible on their own with the help of a few writing samples I'd left for them.

They seemed to have recovered from their confrontation with their brothers and the dark elf's minions the day before. I hadn't. My hands still shook when I thought about how close we'd come to losing Phonetia.

Scrap sat on the balcony railing smoking a big fat cigar. He could see all of us, the river path, and if he craned his neck, around the side of the building, the parking lot.

Interesting, he said as he flew off.

"Scrap, what's up?"

Oh, this is a good one, babe. Forget about pretending to work and answer the door. He popped back into the room and hung upside down from the wine glass rack. *E.T. needs some help here.*

"Scrap, what is going on?"

Just answer the door. Your guest has her arms full.

Her. That eliminated the Nörglein and his sons and minions.

I heard clumping on the metal stairs. A bit of anger and frustration was in those footsteps.

Then I heard a baby cry. Not the basic needs kind of cry of a tiny infant. This was the full-blown temper tantrum of a toddler. I flung open the door.

A roundly built young woman, barely out of her teens wearing loose jeans and a purple sweatshirt, trudged up to the last landing, a squirming Sophia in her arms. Lady Lucia's daughter protested as loudly as possible to the entire world that nothing was right in her Universe. Nothing. And no one could ever make it right. Ever.

The young woman looked up. A deep frown and extreme anger turned her pink and white complexion into a parody of Little Orphan Annie. Her short blonde curls no longer bounced. All her energy went into confining Sophia and lugging her diaper bag.

"Are you Tess Noncoiré?" she demanded.

"Yes." I stepped toward her and held my arms out to Sophia.

She half turned in the woman's grasp and held out her chubby little arms to me. Her chin quivered and her cries turned from angry to forlorn. Pleading with me to tilt her world back on its axis.

"Ms. Continelli said I was to come to you in an emergency." The woman practically shoved Sophia at me.

"Where is Lady Lucia?" I cradled Sophia's head against my shoulder. She sobbed and beat her fists but did not squirm.

"How the hell am I supposed to know? And she isn't any lady. At least not by my definition."

"You must be the newest nanny."

"Ex-nanny. I quit." She unslung the diaper bag and dropped it at my feet.

Phonetia scooted out of the doorway and grabbed the bag. She and her sister stayed at my side, blatantly observing.

"What happened?" I asked. "Look, why don't you come in and have a cup of tea. We'll talk. I'll call Lucia. I have her emergency cell phone number."

"I've already called it three times. She's not answering."

"What's your name?"

"Anita Madison. I'm a licensed nanny. I graduated top of my class from the Northwest Nanny Institute. I love kids. Kids love me. But not that one." She pointed accusingly at Sophia. "I've tried everything. And she won't settle. And Ms. Continelli gives me the creeps. She keeps blood in the fridge. She decorates in skulls and swaths of black around pictures of graveyards. And those teeth! She bares her fangs all the time."

"Anita, it's all stage dressing."

"I don't care. She gives her own baby nightmares. Sophia wakes up so frightened, her muscles clenched so tight she spasms. That's not right. I'm out of here. Even without a reference. Just keep the kid safe until that... that vampire comes and gets her." Anita turned abruptly and stomped down three flights of stairs. "And tell her that I'm keeping the car she gave me. I'll leave the baby seat and stroller at the foot of the stairs along with that hideous black uniform she insisted I wear. Straight out of Jane Austen!"

Having exhausted herself, Sophia laid her head on my shoulder and stuffed her thumb in her mouth. Then she spat it out and began whimpering again.

"Hmm," I mused. Something about the way she worked her jaw reminded me of my sister Cecilia's youngest.

"Back to work, girls. I think I know the baby's problem."

"What?" E.T. asked, fascinated by the tiny child.

"Teeth. She's got new teeth coming in. Probably crooked. A tiny bit of scotch rubbed on her gums ought to help."

"You'd get better results putting the scotch in her bottle." Phonetia turned and stalked back into the condo. But she took the diaper bag with her. She rummaged around in it until she found a soft pink flannel blanket with a worn satin binding. She wrapped it around Sophia, making certain the little girl could clutch the edges.

The baby immediately rubbed the satin against her cheek and settled. But her mouth still hurt.

An hour later, as the sun neared setting, Lady Lucia blew in. Her pencil slim, black suit skirt that teased her ankles was slit to the top of her thigh. The short-waisted matching jacket strained to close beneath her breasts with a single jet button the size of Sophia's hand. I'd seen that red blouse before, or its twin, with silk ruffles on the deep v-neck and French cuffs.

She'd had her hair touched up since I'd last seen her. The glossy blonde length was twisted into an elegant chignon complete with antique mantilla comb scintillating with jet and rubies.

"What now?" She tapped her foot impatiently just inside my door. She rocked back and forth on her black four-inch stiletto heels. "I was in a very important meeting."

"Your latest nanny quit and left Sophia with me." I caressed the baby's dark head where she slept on my lap. "Too bad, Anita might have been a good one. She might even have figured out that your daughter hurt when she cut a new tooth if she hadn't been so spooked by your décor."

I took a good-sized sip of single malt. Sophia had only needed a few drops to numb her gums enough to get some relief from the troublesome tooth that had poked through red and swollen tissue about ten minutes before. It looked twisted. If the adult tooth followed the same path, she'd need braces in about ten years.

"What is wrong with the servant class these days?" Lady Lucia flung herself into the armchair that I'd set at an angle to the sofa. She didn't reach for her child. "Phonetia, I need a drink. Bring me some of that." She pointed toward my scotch.

Phonetia looked to me for instructions.

I shook my head slightly. My daughter went back to the problem of figuring out how to write her birth date.

"That's part of the problem," I said curtly. "Nannies aren't servants to be exploited. They are highly trained professionals to be respected. You owe her a good reference. She could have just left Sophia with a hotel maid or someone totally unsuitable."

"I paid her twice the going rate and gave her a car so that she could take Sophia with her on errands and such." She threw up her hands, completely forgetting her order for Scotch.

"You still treated Anita like she should cower before you and obey your whims without question. Society has changed since you had a nanny of your own, Lucia."

"Unfortunately, you are right."

"Anita said Sophia has nightmares. Bad ones. The kind a baby shouldn't have."

"Anita? Is that her name?"

I grunted my disgust.

"Will you please keep Sophia a little longer? I must get back to my meeting or I will lose a great deal of money and much respect from my associates."

I looked at the clock. Five-thirty. "Sophia may stay for a short time. I hate to disturb her now that she's fallen asleep. I'll feed her when she wakes. But I need you to fetch her by eight. *My* daughters and I have things to do before we go to the con tomorrow."

Lucia opened her mouth to protest my restrictions. Then closed it, thought a moment, and heaved a sigh of resignation. "Very well. I shall return at eight. I should be able to conclude my business by then." She left without so much as looking at her daughter.

And she didn't come back until nine.

"WE NEED TO TALK," LADY Lucia said before Phonetia had finished opening the door for her.

"You bet we do." I entrusted a wide awake Sophia to my daughters. They seemed delighted to entertain her by stacking brightly numbered and lettered blocks together. Sophia was more interested in knocking down the teetering towers, clapping her hands as she made new patterns of the colored squares.

I heard more than a few whispers over the similarity between the numbers on the toys and on their daily math sheets.

"Five and three equal eight!" E.T. whispered excitedly. "They equal eight!" she chortled louder.

"I don't see it," Phonetia murmured.

Her embarrassment that her younger sister figured it out before she did burned on my nape.

Hmmmm . . . building blocks; back to kindergarten again. Whatever worked to get the girls thinking in twenty-first century terms. Or even nineteenth century terms.

Lucia perched on the comfy armchair like she would a board of director's chair or a throne. "I have been thinking for some weeks now that I am not a fit mother for Sophia," she said.

I could almost see the clipboard in front of her as she mentally ticked off items on the agenda.

"You think?" I still steamed at her offhand treatment of the child earlier. And her deliberate intimidation of her nannies.

"Therefore, I have decided that since you are my closest blood relative, you should adopt my daughter," Lucia announced. Her eyes tracked Sophia's every move. A drop of bright moisture glistened in the inside corners of her eyes.

Oh, yes. Yes, we have to do it, babe, Scrap said. He flitted about the room three times before taking up a perch on the wine glass rack where he could oversee everything.

"What about her father?" I asked, not daring to hope, not daring to breathe.

A baby! Lucia offered me this charming baby as my own. I'd never have one of my own, but, oh, how I longed for one.

Our baby, Scrap reminded me.

"Donovan is an adolescent. I do not trust him."

"Adolescent?" I choked. "He fell over fifty years ago. He was a teenager then. That's a very long adolescence."

"When Donovan fell, he was a teenager because he was barely into adolescence in gargoyle terms when he took form inside a statue. He has barely had time to mature by Damiri standards." Lucia dismissed my objection with a wave of her hand.

"I wonder if all of his *faux pas* are just teenage posturing?" I mused.

"Besides," she continued as if I had not spoken, "if Donovan ever obtains a home world for the Kajiri, he will take his children there, and he won't allow them to know their humanity. I want my child here, in this dimension, learning her full potential."

"Lucia, you are asking a lot. As you noticed, this place is barely big enough for me and my daughters. To add a baby would complicate things beyond measure." My middle began to ache with longing.

A baby to call my own!

"Details. We can figure out the details later. Will you adopt Sophia?"

Do it, do it, do it, Scrap pleaded from his perch on the wine glass rack. He flew down beside Sophia and rubbed his cheek against her arm.

She patted him idly and went back to destroying more block towers.

"I need time to think about it. It is an honor but a huge responsibility." I twisted my hands inside my sweatshirt to keep from reaching for Sophia and holding her close, never letting her go.

"A responsibility you are equal to."

"You are the one who told me never to take on emotional entanglements that will interfere with my work as a Warrior of the Celestial Blade."

"Perhaps I spoke prematurely. Perhaps I merely said the words you needed to hear in your moment of great loss." She shrugged.

"Of course," Phonetia whooped. "Three plus five equals eight." I almost heard the click in her brain as numbers began to make sense.

"Sophia will help Phonetia and E.T. learn more about their own humanity," Lucia reminded me. Her voice—devoid of the Italian accent she affected with strangers—sounded desperate.

"Let me get through the convention this weekend. I'll be very busy with my own schedule as well as monitoring two teenage girls. We'll talk again on Monday."

A baby! Lucia was giving me a baby. I had no doubt I'd agree to almost any terms to bring Sophia into my family.

A baby of my own. And not my firstborn, so the Powers That Be could not take her away from me.

Chapter 39

P ortland is often called the City of Roses. Founded in 1907, the Grand Floral Parade during the Rose Festival in early June is the largest floral parade in the U.S.

"What do you do if you see one of the men with a demon protection tattoo?" I stopped E.T. and Phonetia from entering the front door of the downtown hotel where the local Science Fiction-Fantasy convention was being held.

"We call you," E.T. said brightly, holding up her new disposable phone.

"And if I don't answer?"

"Then we call Dad, after him we call Dr. Sean, and Lady Lucia as a last resort." E.T. beamed at me proudly. "I programmed all their numbers into my phone."

"I'm named after a super phone, why can't I have one?" Phonetia demanded. She placed her hands on her hips, not acknowledging her own disposable cell in a green fabric holster on her jeans' waistband. She'd shown E.T. how to program numbers.

"Because I think you should have to earn that phone by showing a great deal of responsibility." I glared back at her, more stubborn than she.

"Whatever." She shrugged. "Can we go and start gaming now?" She peered longingly over her shoulder at the lines of people in front of the con registration desk. A half smile brightened her face as she recognized someone, probably from High Desert Con.

I wasn't sure at all that we should have come. My instincts told me to sandbag the door, cover the walls in St. Brigid crosses and other wards, lay in enough food for a siege, and never emerge from the condo again.

If I did that, I'd admit that the dark elf had won, and I wasn't a worthy Warrior of the Celestial Blade.

"Let's go buy your memberships, then I'll introduce you to the people in the Green Room where I'll pick up my badge and schedule. The volunteers in the Green Room are a last resort backup. There is always an adult there who can summon help. You just have to tell them you think you picked up a stalker."

"Do Oak, Cedar, and Fir count?" E.T. looked a little scared.

"The tree boys count. So does the Nörglein."

"There's Dr. Sean!" E.T. jumped up and waved both arms at the man who scurried across the parking lot.

I waited for my heart to do that silly little flip of joy. Nothing happened. I hadn't seen him since our abortive movie date.

Phone conversations on the run are okay, but they aren't a solid basis for a lasting relationship.

My mind kept darting toward Lady Lucia and her proposal. A baby to call my own. My heart was more excited about that than about Sean.

He leaped over a puddle that had collected at the curb, landing neatly at my side, a wide smile on his face. His mouth met mine in a quick kiss of greeting.

I pulled back first, fully aware that my heart wasn't engaged.

I'd seen Gollum only a few days ago, talked to him twice since then. Sean was certainly more handsome, less enigmatic and frustrating, a good solid partner in the making. A possible father for my growing family?

He wasn't Gollum.

He seemed oblivious to my coolness and just draped an arm over my shoulders as he escorted me and the girls into the hotel lobby.

He doesn't smell right, Scrap grumbled.

He changed his aftershave, I replied on a tight telepathic link. *He smells like a bright crisp winter morning when the snow has snapped the pine trees. I loved that smell as a kid back home. The fir trees out here are great but not the same. We don't get the cold and snow nearly as often.*

Yeah, right. I need some mold. He flew off in a wide circle, looking decidedly jealous green.

But I knew he scouted the terrain for possible enemies.

We got in line to purchase memberships for the girls. Not too bad a crowd yet. Noon on Friday before a long weekend. Most of the young people were still in school and their parents at work.

"E.T., come back here," I called as she dashed ahead of us. Three groups of people stood between me and my girl.

She skidded to a halt in front of a short boy about her own age. His ears and throat apple were too big for his narrow frame and matched the thickness in his glasses.

"That's just Adam. She met him at High Desert," Phonetia explained, clearly bored. But she openly searched the growing crowd.

Suddenly, her eyes brightened, and she waved at a stout girl a year or two older than her. "Mom, may I go talk to Barbara?" she asked politely.

Ah, some of my lessons in civilized living had penetrated. She must want something more than permission to talk to a friend. Like an expensive phone.

"Yes, you may. But come right back when we get near the front of the line."

She hastened toward her acquaintance with a little more dignity than her sister.

"Friends are important at that age," I muttered, as much to reassure myself as Sean. "Friends are a sign that they grow into normal young women."

Sean just chuckled and pulled me closer, as if the absence of the girls gave him permission to show more intimacy.

I had an idea where this was going. I should lean in to him, give him a quick kiss for reassurance.

But I couldn't. I just couldn't.

So there I stood, my heart a heavy lump in my gut as we inched forward. I had to keep my concentration on my girls, not think about my boyfriend who was absent more than present, or a new baby.

At last we were close enough to call the girls back.

"They're reviving an old version of *Dungeons and Dragons*," E.T. gushed.

"Some of the older kids are getting together to go for pizza later," Phonetia added. "May I go with them? I'll need some money." Aha. That's what dragged the politeness out of her.

"Find me just before you leave. I may want you to go for dinner with me and my friends. If not, I'll give you some extra money then. You both have your allowance for snacks and gaming pieces?" We'd eaten lunch before leaving home.

They nodded enthusiastically.

"I'll get the memberships," Sean said, easing forward, arm still draped possessively around me.

"Have you filled out the forms I downloaded for you?" I asked the girls.

E.T. bit her lip before nodding.

I held out my hand for the much folded and slightly soiled paper. Phonetia handed hers over more readily.

I scanned their block printing carefully, in case I'd missed something this morning when they weren't looking. Then I fished a pen out of my belt pack and signed on the line marked parent or guardian.

Pride filled me. These were *my* daughters. They shared my name, right down to the correct accent mark on the last e of Noncoiré.

"Your birth date, E.T.," I reminded her softly.

"I . . . don't remember . . ."

"September twenty-first," I prodded.

"Okay." She wrote that down, using the registration table to hold the paper. "But the year?"

"Can you subtract twelve from this year?"

A tear gathered at the corner of her eye.

I wrote the numbers on a corner of scrap paper and showed her. Dutifully, she copied them into the proper box and handed the paper back to me.

Then I handed it to the volunteer behind the table.

"Oh, hi, Tess," she said brightly. "Glad to see you back this year. But you're a pro, isn't your badge over in the Green Room?"

"Hi, Maggs. Yes, my badge is. But my daughters need to register. We didn't know until the last minute they'd be coming." I placed one hand on each girl's shoulder, thus shrugging off Sean's clinging attention.

Sean plopped his platinum credit card on the table for the volunteer. Maggs swiped it and recorded the information on her official forms while the mini printer spat out the double receipt for his signature. Then she half turned to a computer keyboard and began entering information faster than I could type. She paused a moment, peering at both the registration forms and her terminal.

"E.T.? Are you really an alien?"

"No. It stands for Eternally Tenebrous," E.T. said proudly.

"I don't even know what that means," Maggs muttered, shaking her head. "No doubt about it, they are your daughters, Tess."

"It means obscure. You could try Extra Troublesome," I laughed. "What did you two do? Stay up all night reading the dictionary?"

"Of course," Phonetia returned. "It's our favorite book."

"Definitely your daughters, Tess."

SOMETHING IS WRONG. I want to fly off and scout out the entire con, check out who's here and who's missing. I need to find stashes of mold ahead of time.

I need to mark hidey holes for both my babe and me and the girls in case of multiple attacks.

My range has decreased to a line of sight with Tess. If I turn my back on her or try to go around a corner I find myself thrown backward in a straight line toward my Warrior.

I can fly up to the top of the dome over the central courtyard and play hide and seek among the prisms arcing down when the sun peeks through the cloud cover and strikes those lovely panes of glass.

I can tweak the hair of the girls at the hotel registration and make faces at the parrot on the shoulder of one of the con members. I flick my hot pink feather boa in the face of a black pug in a harness that matches my accessory. The ugly mutt sneezes and snorts like a steam engine. No demon hiding in that body. Pugs are weird but they aren't evil.

A couple, way back at the end of the prepaid registration line, have a fat tabby cat in a canvas-and-mesh shoulder bag. Cats are evil. I don't know which dimension spawned them, but they don't belong in this one any more than the full-blooded Windago Tess and I fought a couple of years ago. But cats are everywhere. This overweight antique shouldn't hinder my movements though.

I can do all these normal things. But I cannot pop into the chat room or get out of Tess' line of sight.

So I find a perch in a ficus tree that's trying to pretty up an overflowing trash can—some great mold in the can—and watch.

I'm good at watching and noticing things that don't fit patterns. Demons can mask themselves, but they can't hide forever. Sooner or later they will do something outside the pattern and I'll see it.

This means I can't keep an eye on E.T. and Phonetia in the gaming rooms. I can't monitor the con as a whole.

Maybe I need some help. That parrot has potential. The pug, too, she's crazy enough to chew through her leash and run around yapping at everything outside her limited experience, including demons. But I'll never enlist that damned cat to our cause.

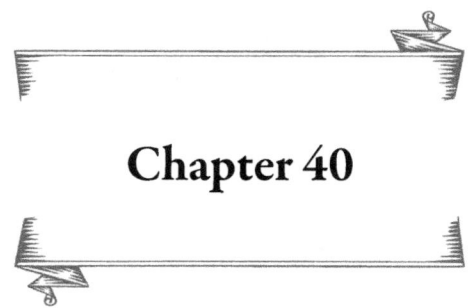

Chapter 40

A.L. Lovejoy and Francis W. Pettygrove flipped a coin to name their land claim, known only as The Clearing, after their hometowns: Portland, Maine and Boston, Massachusetts. Pettygrove won and the city of Portland began building.

I led my troupe around the domed courtyard at the center of the hotel. A paved path encircled the area, lighted by the multiple triangles of lightly tinted glass four stories above. Graveled paths wandered through small landscaped mounds with fanciful fountains and park benches. Tasteful groupings of roses dotted the gardens. Portland was known for its plentiful and award winning roses. At the very center of the lobby a bevy of volunteers set up the weapons demonstrations on a raised cement slab that could serve double duty for small concerts and filking. An array of boffer weapons, specially designed with cushy balls on the ends of arrows or padded PVC tubing in place of swords, lay stacked untidily all around.

I explained to Sean about the arena. "No one gets inside the circle without a helmet and padded gloves. The only people allowed to wield real weapons—and only if they've been foiled—are armored historical re-creationists."

"Good idea. If I wanted to spend my weekend patching up people I'd have stayed at work."

We took a side corridor to a ground floor suite with sliding glass doors that opened onto the indoor pool. Guests of the con, professional writers, costumers, and other panelists or presenters gathered in the Green Room for snacks, networking, consulting with the con volunteers on scheduling, and just a resting place away from the nonsense of the rest of the events.

We went through the drill of introductions once more. Volunteers gave me my badge and printed schedule and then had to hunt for Sean's. I'd listed him as my guest when I filled out the forms on-line. As usual, someone's badge always got lost in the melee.

While they searched, I turned away and showed the girls how to find the schedule in their pocket program, making sure they read the modern words correctly—they excelled at convoluted classical sentence structure but still struggled with modern abbreviations. And glory be, the program actually matched the duplicates on the back of my badge and on my table tent, the folded piece of card stock with my name printed in two-inch high letters. With all that duplication, you'd think that authors tended to get spacey and forget.

Well, duh. I've had idea attacks that completely removed me from reality for days on end until the story or chapter was committed to words.

The girls scampered away, eager to begin gaming again. Thank goodness I hadn't had time to show them computer games and on-line groups. They'd never surface again.

I checked my telepathic link with them and knew precisely where they'd stopped in the courtyard to study the hotel map and find the gaming room they wanted.

"Oh, Tess, I need to tell you there's a last minute addition to your three o'clock on folklore. An anthropology professor from McLoughlin College agreed to join us," the volunteer called to me. "He's going to be quite an asset on a number of panels, and he's going to do a slide show on Saturday afternoon on the anthropology of dragons."

"I've met Dr. Van der Hoyden-Smythe. He puts on quite a show." I grew hot all over. At the same time a chill began eating at my fingertips and toes.

"Let's go get a cup of coffee." Sean steered me toward the door.

"We have coffee and hot water for tea, and a few snacks," the volunteer added hopefully.

I glanced toward the buffet table at the far end of the suite. Already half a dozen authors crowded around the free food. During the early years of my con life I'd lived exclusively on the free food. The only way I could afford the con was to crash on the floor of someone else's room and stuff myself on the free snacks.

"Oh, and your daughters might like to know that the owner of Halfling Games has joined our guest list too," the volunteer added.

Now I really did need to sit down. Rather than an opportunity to reconnect with the writing and fan community, this was turning into a convention of my exes.

"Now all I need is for Lady Lucia to show up."

Don't look now, babe, but her pearl gray limo just pulled into the porte cochere. Scrap nearly chortled with glee. *And she brought the kidlet, complete with stroller and diaper bag!*

"I guess she couldn't find a new nanny. Let's go to the coffee shop, Sean. I think I'm going to need more fortification than just snacks." Then sotto voce I said, "Scrap, start loading up on mold now. You're going to need it."

Can't I play with Sophia first?

LUCY AND SOPHIA HAVE taken over a banquette in the back corner of the garden café. She has a name badge discreetly clipped to the waistband of her ankle-length, pencil slim, slit to the thigh, hot pink skirt. Only a long strand of black pearls adorns her tight black blouse with ruffles at neck and cuff. Her badge has a KIT sticker on it. That's Kid-In-Tow, so people know that the kidlet with a matching sticker belongs to her. Sophia's badge hangs from the hem of her frilly black skirt. Her hot pink tights and knit top are wrinkled and just a bit saggy, as if she's rearranged her clothing trying to get out of Mom's clutches.

Dr. Sean and Tess have taken a table across the café. The buffet and some more dusty ficus trees block the path between Lady Lucia and them. They don't seem to notice each other. But I can see both.

So I alight on the lady's table and waggle my boa in her face until she notices me. She pretends not to. But she has just enough demon blood in her to make me almost visible to her.

"Hey, crime boss lady, I can keep an eye on Sophia. Let her run a bit."

Lady Lucia sighs, almost in relief. "I've hired and fired three nannies in as many weeks. I don't know what I'm going to do until Tess agrees to our little arrangement."

"Let me baby-sit a bit. I'm good at it. Really, really good at it. Just ask Tess how good I keep an eye on E.T. and Phonetia."

"Okay. But just for a minute to let Sophia stretch her legs." She lifts the toddler out of her high chair and sets her on her feet.

The little girl squeals in delight, balances briefly—I can actually see her thinking about taking a step—then plops to her bottom. She rolls to her knees and hits the floor crawling. I have my work cut out for me, herding her in circles that don't intersect Tess' line of sight. Tess needs to concentrate on whatever is hanging around the con that keeps me within her line of sight, not longing over the baby coming our way.

Sophia and I have fun!

And Lady Lucia smiles fondly at our antics.

"ALL THAT CHOLESTEROL is going to clog your arteries," Sean said with distaste as I polished off the last of my hot turkey sandwich with gravy and mashed potatoes, cranberry sauce, and steamed mixed vegetables. I'd also had a salad with Italian dressing. Now I was eyeing the desert menu.

Out of the corner of my eye I caught a glimpse of Scrap playing hide and seek with a laughing toddler. He was doing a good job of staying between me and the little girl. But he is transparent. Sophia was probably the most beautiful child I'd ever seen.

And if I played my cards right, in a few days she'd be *mine*. I think I paid more attention to Scrap and the baby than to Sean.

As soon as I recognized Sophia, I spotted her mother in the back corner. Okay. The vampire crime boss of Las Vegas wanted to watch from the shadows, observe my lifestyle to see if she still approved of me. I'd let her. For a while. Until I figured out why all the remnants of my Scooby gang gathered here this weekend.

Did I ever say that I don't believe in coincidences?

"I'll worry about too much fat, salt, and sugar later. The imp flu supercharged my metabolism. Let's get to the dealers' room before the big crowds show up." I pushed back from the table, my appetite barely satisfied.

"Will they all be set up?" Sean took the bill to the cash register and once more presented his credit card. On our few and too brief dates he'd paid cash. Must be close to the end of the pay period for him. I'd have thought he made enough money not to run low on cash.

"The dealers set up last night or early this morning," I replied, seeking the proper escalator to the ballrooms on the mezzanine. The one rising behind the cash register should dump us right in front of the section designated for dealers. It also passed right above Lady Lucia. I'd be able to scout her unobtrusively.

"You only have an hour and a half before your first panel," Sean said, consulting his pocket program. "*Thinking outside the Celtic Box: folklore of other lands in SF/F literature*. Sounds a bit boring."

"Just wait and see. Fans get a bit passionate about their favorites. Even the most boring topic can turn into a verbal brawl. Depends on the people on the panel." I took his arm and nearly pulled him onto the first riser on the escalator.

"You and this professor person seem to agree a lot."

"But we don't have to on a panel. He'll probably quote some obscure African myth and I'll counter with American Indian. The young adult writer will throw in something Japanese; the audience will say something about validating the cultural heritage of the majority of Americans—usually of British descent. Or Irish," I chided him. "Then we're off and running. But in the end we'll all agree that a story should hold a universal truth. That's what folklore and myth do. Sometimes I think modern SF/F writers are creating the new myths and folklore for our multicultural world that no longer anchors itself in a single past or ethnic bond."

New energy and enthusiasm countered the heaviness of my meal. I really loved a good con. Next year I could bring Sophia with me.

Three dozen dealers had opened for business. A few still arranged stock on their tables, but they were all ready and willing to take our money.

I left Sean in front of an array of used classic SF books and movies. Starshine's crystals and minerals brightened the back corner. She'd turned on mini black lights to make some of her specimens glow.

On close inspection I could see fading bruises beneath her heavy makeup. I'd never seen her wear makeup before. Not that I knew her well.

Her eyes darted about, warily searching every shadow.

"Oh, hi, Tess," she greeted me in a lackluster whisper.

"Starshine, I need you to know that a certain object is safe," I replied cryptically. "And the men who tried to take it from you are also taken care of."

Her face brightened a bit. "You're the first to know that everything on the table is half price after noon tomorrow. I could give you the discount a little early."

I raised my eyebrows in mute question.

"This is my last show. I've sold the business. Retiring."

"I'm sorry. I know you love working with the minerals. Who bought it?"

"Her." Starshine pointed to a tall woman, dressed in flowing red draperies that disguised her broad hips, striding gracefully toward us. A white streak ran from each temple the full length of her long black hair flowing down her back. No neat chignons or twists today. No business attire either.

She looked more natural, happier, and . . . beautiful.

"Doreen Cooper."

"You know each other?" Starshine asked. She slithered back behind her tables and off to one side, leaving the gap between them open for Doreen.

"Her brother was my deceased husband," I said.

"So that's why she entrusted the artifact to you," Starshine said.

"Yes. How do you two know each other?"

"We met at a flea market where we both tried to buy that artifact," Doreen said. "Starshine got to it first." Doreen swept past me, her gaze taking inventory. I was sure she knew to the penny the exact value of each item and the total."

"Semiprecious stones and minerals are a bit out of your usual merchandise, Doreen. Dill would have loved them though."

"I got bored with furniture." She turned defiant and angry eyes upon me. "I got tired of working for the parents rather than managing the business so they could retire. I got tired of working with the rather questionable employees they took in from . . . from homeless shelters in the forest. And their sons and friends."

I didn't flinch, much as I wanted to.

"This won't be nearly as lucrative," I hedged.

"I won't need the money. Donovan Estevez and I are getting married on Thanksgiving Day." She flashed a large but ordinary solitaire. Easily two carats in a simple setting that demanded one look at the stone and only the stone.

The antique ring Donovan had offered me, the one I'd sent back to Faery where it belonged, had a stone just as large, square cut, surrounded by an elegant filigree. That ring demanded one look at the whole and gape in awe at the beauty and power contained within. The stone and setting belonged together, were incomplete alone.

So that's why he hasn't been sniffing around lately, Scrap giggled.

Did you know about this? I asked him.

I know she's already preggers. I can smell it on her. Not far along, maybe only a week, possibly two.

A week. The night I asked him to forge birth certificates for the girls. True to form, Donovan hopped into bed with someone else the moment I rejected him.

Or he was already in bed with her.

"Get a good pre-nup from him," I warned Doreen.

"Done. I drew it up. No loopholes. He stays faithful to me or he loses half of everything. And if I die in unusual circumstances half of everything he owns goes to our children in an unbreakable trust with my surviving brother as executor. If he predeceases me, you are executor. Neither of us wants to tangle with you."

"Sounds like you don't trust him any more than I do."

"I trust him to be who he is and loyal to his own best interests. He'll grow out of his teenaged self-absorption sooner or later. He's still a good man at heart."

I saluted her. Not a bit of jealousy ate at my bones. In fact, I felt enormously relieved. Maybe now Donovan and I could be friends without the sexual tension that had brought us together in the first place. I trusted him with my life, just not my heart and soul.

"I hope Donovan is here at the con to support her and not for his own agenda," I whispered to Scrap. Donovan's agenda always revolved around finding a home world for half-breed demons, like Doreen.

Mr. Toxic's agenda includes DBC and her new business. Otherwise, she wouldn't be here.

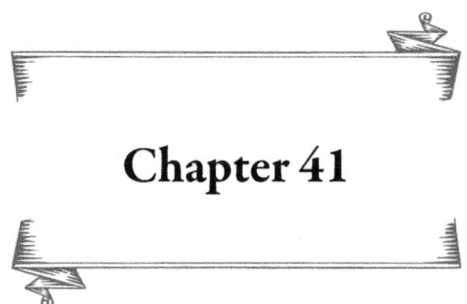

Chapter 41

1962 *Columbus Day storm, a late season Pacific hurricane, felled fifteen times more trees than the 1980 Mt. St. Helens eruption.*

At the book dealer, I succumbed to a signed first edition of Marion Zimmer Bradley's *Mists of Avalon*. I'd read it, of course, had a trade-sized paperback of it around somewhere. But a signed first edition hardcover of this classic couldn't be left behind for someone else. It made a dent in my revived checking account, but nothing too serious.

Strangely, Sean passed up a number of out of print classics I suggested for him. I hoped his passionate reading hadn't waned.

"Do you need time to prepare for your panel?" he asked as we wound our way out of the dealers' room.

"Not really. I've presented workshops on the topic before. I have good co-panelists. We'll wing it."

"But isn't that unprofessional?"

"That's the physician in you talking. This isn't a major research presentation. Though Gollum will come prepared with reference books, illustrations, and possibly a power point presentation. A con is casual and unrehearsed. It's more about spontaneous fun than serious education. Lighten up, Sean." *And let me think about Sophia.*

"Okay," he said reluctantly. "Let's peek in on the girls. We want to make sure they are safe."

"The girls are safe. And having fun." A little bubble of mirth behind my heart told me that. "But I'd like to make sure I know where the gaming rooms are and who they are with."

Teenagers faced human predators as well as demons.

My link led me unerringly to the three connected rooms at the end of the conference wing. E.T., her new friend, Adam, and another girl slightly younger occupied stools in front of a computer terminal. Each of the kids had a game keyboard in front of them. Gone were the simple joysticks of my youth. Now they needed a full array of high-tech remotes.

Phonetia was a little more difficult to locate in the midst of an intense board game filled with multi-sided dice and arcane figures. With her head bent in concentration, she blended in with all the others.

How could she figure out complex dice combinations in moments but still be puzzled over simple numerals and addition problems?

Funny, I'd never noticed the green streaks in her hair brought out by the fluorescent lights. Or maybe her intense concentration thinned the boundaries between her human body and her native guise.

Something to remember. E.T seemed to have embraced her humanity a lot more readily than her older sister.

I wondered if Phonetia needed to maintain a bit of dark elf in her makeup to justify to herself the sexual abuse she'd endured. Elves didn't consider it wrong. Humans did. E.T. hadn't been sexually abused by the Nörglein or his tattooed minions. Yet. She approached puberty rapidly. I'd gotten her out just in time.

"Okay, time to check in to the Green Room to see if my other two panelists are there before going to the programming rooms." I dragged Sean away from a fascinated study of the gaming process.

Should I leave him there?

"I find this counterculture amazing," he said, holding my hand as we trekked back the way we had come. "To think I never knew it existed right under my nose."

"A lot like the Kajiri demon culture. It's out there in the least expected places, alive and thriving, though very few even believe it could exist and turn a blank eye when they do see it."

As we passed the garden café I noticed a familiar figure engaging Lady Lucia in conversation. Squishy, or Pat, the psych nurse. And beside them, her elegantly frail companion played peek-a-boo with Sophia.

"Um, maybe we should just go straight to the programming room. The other panelists will find us."

"What's wrong, Tess?"

Sean looked suddenly alert, scanning the knots of people for signs of trouble.

"Someone I don't want to talk to just yet."

"You sure?" He looked at me with concern and affection.

"It's okay. A personal difference of opinion that has nothing to do with my problems with the tree boys or their father."

AS LONG AS MY BABE takes her time wandering through the courtyard I can run interference and check in with my spies.

"Report," I demand of the parrot.

"Awk, all quiet. All quiet. Only humans. Two, tall enough to perch on. Smell like humans."

"Gotcha." I spot the pair wearing stilts. "Keep your beak looking for anyone that smells like a plant."

"Awk, lady left got roses on her skin."

I fly over to the wide female swathed in about ten yards of Gypsy red and purple with bells and beads and bangles all over her hips and head. Nothing weird in a demon way about her. Just con member normal weird. She's got a perfume that fills the air with the scent of roses in a ten-meter aura.

More than one sensitive nose explodes in cascades of sneezes as she passes.

Mine too. I'm surprised the parrot hasn't developed sinusitis.

Time to check in with the black pug wearing the lovely harness accessory. She wiggles her entire body in ripples of skin from tail to squashed nose. I wonder if she can smell the artificial roses through her wheezes and snorts.

"Report!" I bark at her.

She yips and wiggles some more.

"No one I want to widdle on," she sighs. "But I could use a walk on that nice patch of grass around the arena. My leash won't stretch that far and my person is too interested in flirting with the Klingon showing too much cleavage to notice my needs."

"No problem, friend." While her person, a slender man wearing a shapeless and sagging stretch shirt that's supposed to look like a TV spaceman's uniform,

has his eyes superglued to the alien's boobs, I untangle the hot pink leash from his belt clip. It's barely looped in a slip knot. The stupid dog stops tugging at the first point of resistance. She doesn't realize that a bit of a yank would release it.

It takes me a bit of manipulation to come into this dimension enough to wiggle the knot. Then I slap the dog's wrinkled butt. She dashes toward the grass and shrubs in their redwood tubs.

With an audible sigh of relief she squats right beside a spindly tree in a redwood tub. It's trying to imitate a Norfolk Pine but looks a lot like a grand fir sapling.

A distinctly human foot extrudes from the trunk and kicks the dog away. She yips and scoots back to her person, tail between her legs, as much as a pug with a cropped tail can drop her appendage. Her person greets her with an admonition for obedience.

The dumb dog cowers against his leg, accepting his reprimand gladly.

I flit up to Tess' shoulder and whisper in her ear.

She whirls to return to the gaming rooms.

"Not yet, babe, let them call you."

"That may be too late!"

"Let them learn to trust you a bit. Hey, where's the boyfriend?"

"Sean went back to look at books. The folklore panel doesn't really interest him."

Huh? I understand his fascination with books, the way he read through Tess' list so quickly. But not interested in folklore? Half of what SF/F is about is folklore.

"Let me circle about and see what's up." *I hadn't told her that for a while I had to keep her in sight.*

Now it seems I can fly into dark rooms and down halls. I peek in on the girls. They are still obsessed with their games. Not a plant in sight.

Back in the dealers' room I find the book dealer wrapping up a stack of books for Squishy and her lady. No sign of the good doctor.

I sniff for his Winter Pine aftershave and find him in the hospitality suite checking out the box of donuts with a large can of cola in his hand.

Double huh. I did not expect this.

I SHOULD HAVE EXPECTED Gollum to arrive at the panel early with a stack of reference texts and a power point multimedia projector.

"Why should I even bother sitting on the panel?" I slumped against the doorjamb, arms crossed. I had to bite my cheeks to suppress the wave of joy that swamped me.

I kept trying to tell myself I had moved on with Sean. I wanted a real life, not the depressed pining I'd endured for a year and a half.

Just thinking about Gollum made my heart flip. The sight of him and his inevitable laptop took my breath away.

He pushed his glasses up to the bridge of his nose and peered at me across the room, a gentle smile softened the worry lines radiating out from his eyes and mouth.

I needed to smooth those lines away.

Before I could act on my impulse a half dozen people pressed behind me, eager to weigh in with their own opinions on the discussion.

I flowed forward with the surge, letting their momentum carry me toward the long table at the front of the room. To mask my emotions, I fussed with pouring myself a glass of ice water from the carafe, setting up my table tent and a small display of book covers and bookmarks.

We started a little late. The sparse audience remained sparse—it was early on the first day of the con.

"*Star Wars* is a retelling of the Arthurian legends in a milieu that speaks to modern audiences," I said about twenty minutes later in the midst of a discussion on the value of ancient legends to a diverse and multicultural society.

"No way!" Gollum protested. "Light Sabers are Samurai Swords. Look at the two-handed fighting stance..."

"The story is about more than your fascination with swords," I returned. "We have to look at the story and the moral lessons imparted."

A fluster of movement in the back of the room captured my attention. A bigger audience maybe?

Squishy and her lady took seats in the back row. They held hands and leaned their heads close. A sense of intimacy isolated them from the rest of the room.

Gollum froze, mouth half open, his retort swallowed.

I had no more reason to wonder if Squishy's lady was Julia. I knew.

I opened the discussion to the audience, letting Gollum retreat into unnatural silence, power point presentation forgotten.

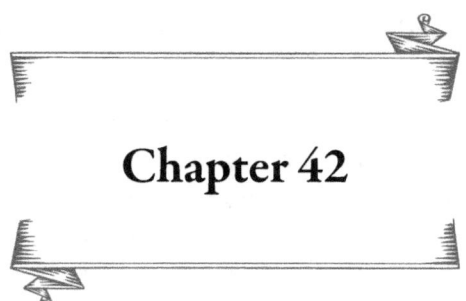

Chapter 42

O regon has twenty-one active volcanoes, the most in the U.S: Among them, Mt. Hood, Mt. Bachelor, Mt. Jefferson, Mt. Mazama (Crater Lake), South Sister (Charity), and Newberry Crater.

"Sorry I flaked out on you, Tess," Gollum said quietly as I dismissed the audience five minutes before the hour. I'd have gladly let them go half an hour before.

"No problem." The other author on the panel flashed me a grin. Somewhat shy about butting into a discussion, she'd managed to insert more of her opinions than usual with only me sharing time with her.

"Tess, I owe you an explanation." Gollum stopped me with a hand on my arm from clearing my nice display.

A couple from the audience dashed forward and snatched some bookmarks before I could put them away.

"No, you don't, Gollum. She owes you an explanation. I think the three of you need to go find someplace private and talk. Don't let either of them dance around the issues."

"You knew?"

"I suspected when I saw them at Holly's concert a few weeks ago. And I don't know that Pat is Julia's first flirtation. Now go talk to them and let me continue with the con. I'll cover your next panel with the power point if you want."

"Thanks. But the panel on dragon evolution isn't until tomorrow afternoon. If you could stash this stuff in the Green Room I'd appreciate it. And I'll let you know if I can't get back." Awkwardly, he moved behind me and used his long legs to eat the distance between him and his wife and her lover where they lingered in the back corner. They left with a minimum of discourse. All three walked as if treading on dragon scales, not wanting to awaken the beast.

I occupied my curious mind and imagination with packing up the power point stuff rather than speculating on the conversation taking place elsewhere. Then I could always think about Sophia and my girls. There was plenty to occupy my thoughts without speculation about Gollum and the ladies.

"Scrap, how are the girls?" I whispered.

Still okay and still no sign of plants. He darted out of the room and back again in an eye blink. *Heads up, babe. New crop of demon tats filling the doorway.*

"Shit. Where's the Nörglein getting them?" Five young men in their late teens blocked the entrance. They all wore expensive leather jackets and ragged jeans. Their grimy T-shirts smelled of compost, heavy on the manure.

No sign of Blondie with his pendant to match his tattoo.

What grabbed my attention about the new group were new tattoos of a pentagram around a skull. The placement on the insides of their wrists had to hurt more than inserting the ink on the back of their arms. To my eye, the ink pulsed red around the black lines. That was raw infection from the recent and inexpert application. I couldn't see any sign of other dimensional origins to the ink.

Druggies looking for easy money growing a secure crop of weed.

"Payback time, lady," the first one through the door growled. His buddies made an impenetrable phalanx behind him, crowding out the surge of con members trying to get in for the next panel.

"Scrap, get to the girls. Don't let Tree Daddy near them while I'm distracted."

Um, dahling, I'm turning a lovely shade of red. You are in danger. I can't leave you."

"Just a little pink around the edges. Get your ass over to my daughters. I can handle these guys." To prove it, I took an *en garde* stance and looked for a mundane weapon.

"Hey, Tess." A semi-familiar voice piped up from the doorway. "Use this!" A fan I recognized from last year's con tossed me an unsharpened broadsword from his Conan costume. It had a plastic band around the grip indicating his "Peace Bond" or promise not to draw the weapon while at the con.

I plucked the sword out of the air by the grip, flipped it expertly, and readied to fight my way out of this mess.

"Call security!" I called to anyone listening.

"On their way. These guys have fake badges."

"Ghosts as well as bad ass and ugly," I sneered.

"We ain't dead yet." The leader advanced one step.

I whopped him upside the head with the flat of the blade. "Ghosts are scumbags who don't bother to pay for their memberships," I explained whirling to catch the next two with a side kick to the groin and an elbow to the nose.

"The attitude and the smell I could cope with. Forging a con badge? That's unforgivable."

My combatants staggered into the audience and got shoved back and forth for their trouble. Off-balance and confused, the leader dropped to his knees right in front of the chain mail clad giant who wore a bright red ribbon on his badge that proclaimed to the world "Security."

He hauled that one up by the collar of his pricey leather jacket, caught another by his belt, and marched them out. My friend, Conan, grabbed another one and followed.

The other two, the ones I hadn't engaged in combat, fled.

"Incompetent newbies," I muttered. "You'd think Tree Daddy would give them a bit of training before turning them loose. Demon tats don't protect minions like they used to."

Or maybe Tree Daddy had run out of goodwill with the higher ups and had to use his own dwindling magic to demonize the tattoos. The bespelled ink wasn't as strong or as effective as the real thing.

Scrap had destroyed his hat, taking with it a power reserve.

If that were the case, he'd be getting desperate to get his girls back and begin inbreeding to strengthen the elf DNA.

I dashed to catch up to Conan and return the sword. "No one saw me draw this, right?" I called back to the room at large.

"What sword?" someone yelled.

"Could someone get the power point stuff back to the Green Room for me?"

"Sure thing, Tess."

"Anything for our Tess!"

Goddess, I love a con. Where else could I trust strangers to provide me with a weapon, and return expensive audio visual equipment to a secure location? Strangers in wild costumes. But then the costumed ones are loyal, come back every year, and thrive on the con culture. At a con everyone is your new best friend, especially when crowding into an elevator drives us to more intimate than casual contact.

And I had to get down to the gaming rooms to make sure nothing terrible happened to my daughters that would close down the con prematurely. I didn't want two thousand fans angry at me.

"Scrap, report!"

"ABOUT TIME YOU SHOWED up," I *squawk to Tess as she dashes down the winding steps to the garden café, makes a screeching turn past Lady Lucia, scanning briefly to make sure Sophia was still there, and into the suddenly murky corridor.*

"Fuck!" she screams as she barks her shin against an abandoned redwood tub. Rich soil spills out of it. I smell dirt filling the air, clouding the lights, making the place inhospitable to all but the most determined.

In short, it smells of Nörglein.

I can see traces of a masculine footprint tracking dirt on the vinyl flooring. A bare foot, no shoes.

"Had to have been Fir," I tell Tess. "He was masquerading as a Norfolk Pine but he looked more like a grand fir to me." My voice comes out an octave higher as my body stretches.

Hot blood quickens in my veins. My wing tips are near scorching. My tail gives off a pulsing red glow.

I fly just ahead of Tess, guiding her to the gaming rooms.

"Oh, hi, Cedar," Phonetia says blithely, as if we didn't know that the tree boys have become her enemies. "Pull up a chair. I think we can roll you into the scene in about three moves."

The stocky—or is that stalky—boy bites his lips, eyeing the game board avariciously.

Fir stretches tall and peeks over his brother's shoulders. "Can I play too? I think I can pick up where I left off at High Desert Con."

An addiction in action. Is it stronger than the compulsion their father laid upon them?

Some of the heat bleeds off my extremities. I'm still ready to taste blood, if only my babe will command me.

But we are in a public place. Not good to reveal ourselves just yet.

This is a con. Who'd notice anything out of the ordinary? I've already seen three Celestial Blade replicas in honor of characters in Tess' books.

"Scrap, stay close and ready. I'm going to see if I can get the boys away from Phonetia," Tess whispers as she edges up behind the two boys.

"No need, Lady Tess," Oak says, skidding to a halt beside her. "I will contain my brothers."

Huh? both Tess and I grunt.

"I want my sisters to be safe from all harm. Even that inflicted by the family."

"Believe him, babe. He smells human. I can't find a trace of elf, dark or light, or otherworld on him, except that he brings in a breath or two of fresh air hinting at rain-washed forest."

"Are you sure, Oak?" Tess asks him, almost as concerned for him as the girls.

That's my Tess. She does love kids. Too bad she's not likely to ever have any of her own, even if Gollum does work out his problem with the elegant and fragile Julia so he can return to Tess.

We'll have to settle for Sophia. Though she's pure joy, not settling for less.

"I am sure." Oak looks grim and sad. He knows what's coming.

"You know what I have to do, Oak?" Tess clasps his shoulder and squeezes reassurance.

"I know. And though I cannot bring myself to do the deed, I trust another to do what they must to keep my sisters safe. Now I will remove Cedar from *the premises. He is still confused about his loyalties. Fir is young enough and innocent enough to learn new ways. I entrust him to you, my lady."*

With that, the boy verging on manhood gives Tess a little bow of respect. Then he grabs Cedar by the collar and retreats out the fire exit onto the rain-slick streets of the city. No longer part of the con.

"Scrap, check Fir's badge, see if it's real or a forgery," Tess says quietly.

"It looks real and smells of the people at the registration desk."

"Then we'll leave him to the game. Now let's make sure E.T. is okay."

"HI, SEAN," I GREETED my date.

He jerked his head back as if startled. "Oh, um, hi, Tess." He paused in his inching progress through the computer room. "Do you see what's on those computer screens? This is all very strange."

"Agreed," I chuckled, taking in realistic action figures jumping and shooting and diving through some arcane adventure. "I'm free until Opening Ceremonies at seven, then we have our choice of filk or Pictionary at eight."

"Are the girls okay here by themselves for so long?"

"I believe they are." I checked my link. As far as E.T. and Phonetia were concerned nothing existed beyond their games. Nothing alarmed them, except Fir's next unorthodox move in the tabletop game.

"What about... you know, the forest folk?"

"I can account for the boys. They'll be no trouble for a while. Scrap will tell me if Tree Daddy enters the premises." I took Sean's arm, companionably. "Come on, let's do the art show before it gets crowded, or I get too busy. Or if you'd rather, I think we can just sit and talk to my friend Lucia where she has set up camp in the garden café." *And I can hold the baby.*

Sean looked around him nervously. "The art show sounds fun. I'd like to see some of the paintings that became book covers."

We nearly skipped back down the newly bright corridor. The redwood tub still rolled on its side, spilling dirt, but the air had cleared. I smelled a new freshness instead of the usual hotel cleansers and recycled air.

Sean chose the path that took us around the central garden—on the opposite side to the café—and upstairs to the ballroom adjacent to the dealers' room.

My heart didn't even twinge when I spotted Donovan and Doreen, arm in arm, heads bent together entering the gallery ahead of us.

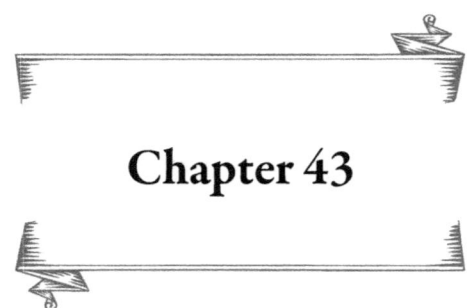

Chapter 43

Douglas Firs reach an average of 200 feet and grow up to 325 feet. The wood is claimed to be stronger than concrete.

"As of this moment, your name is Doug," I told Fir as I led him and the girls out to my car at eleven o'clock that night.

I'd sung my lungs out in filk, with Sean sitting quietly off to the side. And I had sung "Heart's Path." I was still working out what I would do if Gollum and Julia resolved their differences and stayed together.

I didn't dare hope. So I buried my emotions in the problems of my growing household.

And then there was Sophia. Lady Lucia continued to hold court in the café with the tired and cranky baby. I needed to take that child home, give her a bath and a good supper, and put her to bed for about twelve hours.

Sean barely brushed the surface of my consciousness.

"Cool," Doug said, scouting the parking lot. "Oak said I need to stay with you now. I'm not really a fir anyway. I'm more of a filbert." He shrugged.

We call hazelnuts filberts in Oregon. And we grow a goodly portion of the world's supply in the Willamette Valley.

Then he spotted my little hybrid car. "Can I drive?"

"No."

"But I drive Father's car. It's a real tank, a 1974 Buick Riviera, forest green, V-8, automatic." He proceeded to give me statistics on the engine and gear ratio that meant nothing to me.

"That car probably only gets fourteen miles to the gallon. It's hypocritical for him to drive a gas hog like that when he claims to be the guardian of the forest trying to correct pollution and global warming."

"That describes the old man perfectly," Phonetia snorted as she claimed the shotgun position, relegating the backseat to Doug and E.T. He grumbled a bit about male superiority.

"But you're gay, so you aren't truly male," E.T. objected.

"Just try convincing Father of that." His buoyancy evaporated.

"The Nörglein and his opinions don't matter anymore as far as you three are concerned. He no longer has authority over you," I replied. "My imp is gay. So I have no problem with you preferring boys, Doug. I have no expectations from any of you on that front."

Silence reigned during the short drive back to the condo. We were suddenly overcrowded again, lacking bed space, and three teens sharing one small bathroom guaranteed squabbles. Where would I put a crib? In my room. The only place left that wasn't occupied.

I might have to sell at a loss to get into a bigger place sooner rather than later.

I'd worry about that next week, after the con. In the meantime, I had to come up with another cover story to explain the sudden addition of Doug into the family. No way could I pass the tall gangly youth as my own. I'd already stretched that lie to near the breaking point.

Time to consult Gollum, Scrap suggested.

"I don't dare call him tonight. We'll talk tomorrow." I had no idea how he fared with his own family issues.

Tomorrow. I'd deal with that tomorrow.

"Scrap, can you keep watch tonight? I really need some sleep."

Can do, babe. Doug wants to watch TV since he's sleeping on the sofa. I'll make sure he doesn't find the porn stations.

"I don't subscribe to any porn stations. They're boring."

Hee hee hee, that's what you think. Doug needs an education. And I'm just the imp to give it to him. But not tonight.

"But he can't see you. Can he?"

Nope. The girls can't either, but they can sense my presence. That's enough for now. Your family is my family.

"Does that mean your family is my family?" I'd really like to meet his harridan of a mum.

No way, babe. No freakin' way would I wish any of my family on you. Be content with what you can get since there won't be any of your own, even if Gollum frees himself from Julia. I bet you won't even mind changing diapers for a baby as cute as Sophia.

"You're right," I sighed in regret. I had always wanted children of my own, lots of them.

"WHAT AM I GOING TO do, Allie?" I wailed into the telephone at six the next morning.

I could hear the children stirring. They'd want breakfast and an early start at the con. Soon I'd have to settle squabbles over who got the shower first and fix them something to eat. Maybe they'd settle for cold cereal.

"About the dark elf?" Allie asked. She sounded bright and chipper, but then she was three hours ahead of me and had probably slept the night through.

"That and Gollum. What if he and Julia make up their differences and stay together?"

"You'll go on as you have been. How are things with Dr. Sean?"

"Okay." I couldn't drag any enthusiasm out of my tired mind.

"Concentrate on him until you know any different," she advised solemnly.

"I know. But I don't love Sean. Gollum's the only man I truly want."

"What did Lady Lucia tell you about family and relationships? They don't fit with the life of a Warrior."

I laughed at that. I hadn't told her about the baby. Not until I knew for sure. "But now I've got the girls and Doug. I have children," I hedged.

"Teens. You have teens, not infants. Teens can be left alone occasionally. Teens can actually help you, act as spies and such. Teach them to be your allies." The last sentence faded and veered off, as if she got distracted.

"Did I call at a bad time?" Dammit, she was my friend. She should be there when I wanted to talk about my problems.

"Steve's in town for the weekend. We're getting ready to go talk to the priest about the wedding," she replied. "Look, I know you need a friend right now. But I've got to go. Call me tonight and we'll hash it all out. There's nothing you can do about Gollum until you actually talk to him."

"What about the Nörglein and the kids?"

"Take that one step at a time. That's what motherhood is all about. Live from one minute to the next. Deal with each crisis as it comes."

"When did you get so smart?"

"Since your brother and I decided to get married and I started thinking about having children of my own. Wasn't sure I could handle them while I was a cop. Now I'm not a cop and I really, really want babies. Lots of them."

"So do I." But I'd never get my own children. Just the strays that fell into my lap.

The Powers That Be had made sure of that. Unless . . .

What had Scrap called the crystal ball? A bargaining chip?

"Bye, Tess. I've really got to go. Call me tonight. Even if it's the middle of the night." She rang off, leaving me alone with my problems.

As alone as I'd ever been.

"You got first shower yesterday. It's my turn!" E.T. yelled.

"What about me? I haven't had a real shower in ages," Doug chimed in.

Except now, I had to deal with three teens on my own.

"ANDIAMO, CARA MIA TESS," Lady Lucia gushed a few hours later as I passed her in the garden café. If she hadn't changed clothes to black slacks, red silk blouse, and simple gold necklace and hoop earrings, I'd think she'd spent the night in the corner with Sophia.

I held out my arms to the little girl and she toddled two steps to hug me about the knees.

"Oh, my, her first steps!" Lucia looked as if she might cry.

"I'm honored, Sophia, that you chose to walk to me for those first steps." I picked her up and hugged her close.

She tugged on my dangling dragon earrings with her right hand while sucking the middle two fingers of her left.

Gently I extricated her sticky fingers from the pewter jewelry. "Maybe she just wanted to investigate rather than honor me," I laughed, taking a seat beside Lucia, the baby still in my arms.

This is what it would be like if I accepted Lucia's offer. Sophia in my lap by right and preference.

"I believe you should have this," Lucia said, pasting a KIT sticker on my con badge that matched hers and Sophia's. "I ordered an extra just in case you needed it."

"I'm not..."

She held up a hand, blocking my protest. "In case of emergency, you may stay with my daughter without questions." Then she signaled the waitress for a new carafe of coffee and an extra cup for me.

"I never needed coffee until Sophia was born. Now I cannot live without it," she said, almost apologetically. "More refreshing than blood."

I almost gagged but smiled squeamishly instead. I knew she had killed a man by draining his blood. Gary Gregbaum was a scumbag of a white slaver who had upset forever the balance of Faery to the other dimensions. He needed to be taken out. But that way? I honestly didn't know if Lucia had served justice or not.

"I will host a party in my suite next week. I'd invite you to share my volunteers, but I need you to keep Sophia. She should not be exposed to my life... style." She added the last word almost as an afterthought.

"Nothing is fully decided yet. I have to check my calendar. I have *three* teens to consider now."

"If you must. I trust you with my daughter more than any of the nannies I have hired. They all quit after only a few days."

"You scared them away."

I covered my unease with a sip of very good coffee. "Bless you. I barely had time for a single cup with breakfast before my girls and their brother dragged me out this morning. They couldn't wait to get back to their games. I hope they aren't disappointed that their friends might not be here yet."

"Very interesting, this convention of yours. In some ways it reminds me of the market fairs in my youth."

"Not terribly different from Renaissance Faires and Highland Games. A gathering of people who want to celebrate a certain aspect of their hobby or culture," I replied.

"I do not fully understand the source of this con culture."

"Then you haven't read much science fiction or fantasy."

"No. But I have seen this 'Star Trek' as part of the exhibit and rides in Las Vegas."

"There are Trekkers here too."

"I saw the costumes. Some are very good. Some not so."

"People do what they can within their budgets and sewing talents. The idea is that they help re-create their favorite part of the genre."

"Ah. And the vampires?"

"That's part of the genre too. Though I don't think many of them will take it as far as you have."

She grinned, baring her fangs. Very good implants to complete her persona. "Perhaps I can find new recruits . . ."

"Leave it alone, Lucia. These people are mostly innocent. The hard-core Camarilla followers hang out in different venues. You've found them already if you're hosting a party next week."

"Ah, wishful thinking. I need a dose of my reality." She sighed and shrugged her shoulders. "Since Sophia came to me I have not the taste for innocent blood that I used to. Most of my party guests are flying in as... um... escorts to business people I need to entertain in high Goth style."

"You mean intimidate them into signing one-sided contracts."

"Of course."

Sophia climbed over me to return to her mother. Then she slid down beneath the table and crawled out to the opposite side where she pulled herself up by the chair. Carefully she eyed each potential handhold and how many exciting steps she'd need to take to get there.

"No holding her back now!" I said. Since I was closest to her, I stood and hovered over the little girl to make sure she didn't get into trouble.

Lucia looked relieved that she didn't have to move.

"Can I leave Sophia with you for a brief time? I need to... um..."

"Sure. The ladies room is in the corridor to our left." Idly I followed Sophia a whole three steps before she wobbled and plunked onto her bottom with a wail. I picked her up, comforting her. She cried from disappointment more than any hurt. Her bottom was very well padded with diaper and frilly panties.

I put her back into her highchair and offered her some breakfast. She nibbled a triangle of toast, getting more grape jelly on her face than in her mouth while I savored the very good coffee. Fortunately, her frilly dress was royal purple. The jelly stains wouldn't show, much. If... when... the child was mine, I'd have her in sturdy, washable rompers.

Lucia returned. She'd freshened her makeup and brushed her lustrous hair. She looked less weary and worried. I wondered if she had a flask of blood secreted in her bag.

Sophia ignored her. Finding more interest in my dragon earrings than her mother.

"You two look well together, *cara mia* Tess. Like you belong together," she said, resuming her place on the corner of the banquette as if sinking onto a throne. Her regal bearing invited lesser folk to approach but not to get too close. "Fitting, that you are my only living relative. Of sorts."

"I have a brother and sister, nieces and nephews. My father is a Noncoiré too. He has brothers and sisters. One of them, MoonFeather, is a witch."

"But they have not your special talents. Nor do they have an imp companion to bridge the gaps between this world and the next." She gestured vaguely to where Scrap dangled from a tree in the garden area, seemingly conversing with a pet parrot and a pug wheezing on the ground.

"Can you see him?" I asked, remembering Scrap's comments from the night before.

"Not really. Just an awareness that he is somewhere close, in that direction. If we both concentrate, we can communicate."

That was a relief. Lady Lucia wasn't really as spooky as I first thought. Most of her violence and bloodlust was an act to intimidate enemies, business associates, and district attorneys.

"I have decided. Tomorrow morning we will go to early Mass together. You will stand as godmother to my baby." An order, not a request. "A prelude to your adoption of my child."

"I'm honored... Are you sure? Can you step onto sacred ground?" Vampires couldn't, if you believed the literature. Fiction and legend weren't so detailed about very dilute demon blood. I had no trouble in churches. But Lucia was almost two hundred years closer to the source than I.

"I would not ask if I were indecisive. And I have been baptized. I attended Mass most every day of my life until I escaped from Count Continelli. Since then?" She shrugged as if not interested. "You are the only one I trust with my daughter's soul, and her upbringing. I have already changed my will, regardless of your decision to adopt my baby or not."

"Then I'll see you at St. Mary's at six." Before dawn, in keeping with her persona. I felt honored by her trust. But I was also a little afraid of the heavy portent in her words. Life wasn't going to be easy anytime soon.

"You are wearing the pearls?"

"Almost always." I fingered the strand hanging beneath my bulky Aran Isle sweater.

"Good. You never know when you'll need them."

What did that mean?

She turned her focus onto Sophia, pulling a wet wipe out of the diaper bag and cleaning jelly off her face, hands, knees, dress front...

"Thank you for the coffee, Lady Lucia." Somehow her manner indicated she required the title now rather than the more familiar form. "I need to talk to some people in the Green Room before my ten o'clock panel."

"I can spare you. But first, tell me where is the charming physician who escorted you yesterday?"

"Sean should be here anytime. Unless he got called to work on an emergency. He's supposed to have two full days off, but that doesn't always happen."

"I understand. And was that Donovan Estevez I saw with Doreen Cooper yesterday?"

"Sure was. They're engaged."

"Ah, that is good. He will have less need to take interest in me and my child. The Cooper woman will be a steadying influence on him. He will be an impressive man when he matures into his responsibilities."

"Still might be a good idea to stay out of his way."

"Agreed. Now off with you to your appointment. I have things to prepare for the baptism. White lace gowns in the appropriate size are very difficult to find."

"Harder to keep clean."

Chapter 44

The World Forestry Center next to the Oregon Zoo has 20,000 square feet of exhibits and two working forests to teach about world trees and their importance to all life on the planet.

Doreen waits for my dahling Tess in the Green Room. She cradles a cup of very fragrant coffee between her lush breasts. Her eyes are half-closed and her thoughts turn inward. I think she knows that new life has begun inside her. She marvels at the idea. And yet I smell a touch of sadness in her.

"Tess." She nods succinctly.

"Doreen. I got your email. What's up?" Tess fills a plain black ceramic mug of generic coffee from the carafe on the side table. Only a brief wince betrays the staleness of the brew. It's not the good stuff Doreen sips.

"Not here." Doreen looks around warily. A dozen or more pro writers, artists, and other guests of the con mingle, fixing bowls of cereal, nibbling on toasted bagels, and chatting amiably about everything from politics to the business of writing, to their next panel topic.

"This sounds ominous, babe. Let's decamp to the back of the dealers' room. They don't open for another hour and it's nearly deserted," I suggest to Tess.

She and Doreen come to an agreement. I flit off to check on the kids. They need me more than the ladies do.

DOREEN WAITED UNTIL we were tucked behind her sales table in the back of the dealers' room. Then she turned on me with impossible quickness. "Is the crystal ball safe?"

"Yes." I sent a quick query to Scrap.

Of course, dahling.

"Do you know how to use it?"

"Not really."

"Will it... will it help you find someone?"

"Possibly."

Donovan would kill me or anyone else who stood between him and that crystal ball if he knew what it could do.

Doreen was engaged to Donovan.

The Nörglein wanted it too. For his own purposes.

He worked for Doreen's parents.

Too many connections. Best say as little as possible.

"Can we make a date to try it?"

"Later. After the con."

She nodded in mute understanding. "I saw you with two girls yesterday. I recognized them."

"They are my daughters now. I have the paperwork to prove it and... and a magic link to them stronger than any birth mother's..."

"Are you sure it's a stronger link than a true mother to her baby?"

"I don't know that for sure since I've never had a child of my own."

"But you believe in that link."

I thought of my own mother and how often she'd sensed my moods and problems before I did. I still missed her terribly. "Yes, I believe in a mother's link to her children."

"Will you use the crystal ball to help me find my son?"

I paused a moment in puzzlement. "I didn't know..."

"The Nörglein used me—at my parents' prompting but without me agreeing—"

"He raped you."

She nodded silently. "Sixteen years ago. Then when I wouldn't turn over my baby to him, my parents gave my son to the monster."

"That's awful. I'm surprised you waited so long to go out on your own."

"I tried. Desperately. Fourteen times I packed a suitcase and went looking for my son. My parents always found me and dragged me back home. They've bound me with magic so many times I know the ritual backward and forward. But not how to break it. Only how to let it wear off over time. This time I have Donovan to protect me. They approve of Donovan."

"Of course they do. Do they know he's fully human now, even though his sympathies lie with the Kajiri?"

"Yes. They have blinders on when it comes to the grand scheme of a Kajiri home world. They hate their human connections. They hate the restrictions of living in secret among humans."

"They certainly had no use for me as a daughter-in-law."

"I cannot know for certain, but they may have agreed to Dill's murder. Since he embraced his humanity and a human wife, they had no more use for him."

My breath caught in my throat. My heart froze and threatened to shatter. Again. "I have evidence that Dill planned to betray the 'great plan' to a human. To my archivist."

"I helped him find Professor Van der Hoyden-Smythe. Neither my parents, nor Darren Estevez could allow Dill to live after that. I've thought about who Darren might have used as an accomplice. Quentin is loyal to Donovan, despite his love of money and lack of concern how he gets it. I think the Nörglein may have been a little too eager to help."

We mourned together a moment for the man we'd both loved.

"Is your son Oak, Cedar, or Doug . . . I mean Fir?"

"I don't know." A long moment of silence as she mastered her breathing and blinked back tears. "I named my child Dillwyn, after my brother. I loved my brother very much. I wanted him to be happy. I loved my baby too."

"Does Donovan know about the boy?"

"Yes. He promised to help me find him. We started talking at Dill's funeral, reminiscing about Dill and the time Donovan stayed with us before he was sent to Estevez. Then one thing led to another and another. Now we're in love. Or at least compatible with a similar agenda."

"How will he know which boy is yours if you can't tell?"

"I don't know. All three boys are very close in age. All three have medium brown hair and hazel eyes. I can't find a Damiri trait among them and I have studied them carefully. The Nörglein—we call him Pete by the way—brings them to work sometimes to help with moving merchandise and such. I've talked to all of them. Searched their faces. Nothing. The magic my parents bind me with is Pete's spell. It keeps me from asking the boys if they want to come to me."

"Pete? I suppose that could be a shortening of *Purzinigele*, his real name," I said quietly. "Professor Van der Hoyden-Smythe gave me a file full of information. The name was in there. If I speak his real name out loud, in his hearing, he'll be forced to leave the region. But he'd just set up shop elsewhere. Become someone else's problem. I need him dead, or permanently exiled to another dimension under lock and key."

"Unfortunately, King Scazzamurieddu of the Orculli can't lock him up in the pandimensional prison for rape. Only for endangering the balance among the Universes," Doreen agreed. The foreign words tripped from her tongue as if part of her native language.

"If he stole the crystal ball, I could turn him in. But he'd have to steal it. I can't arrange for him to 'find' it."

"Damn."

"Fir is the youngest," I mused. "He came into my family last night. We call him Doug. He looks like he'll be the tallest, slender too."

"Is he truly the youngest, or the least mature? The men in my family are slow to go through puberty."

I shrugged. "Cedar appears to be the middle child, he'll be broader in the shoulder than Doug, maybe not as tall. Oak is the oldest. Not as tall, but he has heavier bones and muscles. He acts the oldest, taking responsibility for the younger ones, doing what he can to protect the girls and Doug, who has decided to be gay."

"I doubt that Doug is mine. Damiri are never gay."

"Okay." I thought a moment. "Scrap, get your ass back here. Now."

But E.T. is about to make a power play.

"E.T. will tell you all about it later. I need you now."

What's so fraggin' urgent? he snarled, landing on my shoulder, blowing cigar smoke in my face.

I grabbed the noxious weed away from him and stubbed it out in my coffee cup. The coffee wasn't worth drinking anyway. "No smoking inside. That's the law."

Stupid law, he sulked.

"Scrap, I need you to concentrate. Is there a way to tell if Doreen is the mother of any of the tree boys?"

Oooh, now that's a piece of gossip. Do tell all!

"Later, brat. We need to know now. Is there a way to tell, short of a blood test?" Which would take two weeks once it cleared the backup and paperwork. Possibly a year or two.

Maybe. I'd have to take them both into the chat room to be sure.

"What about the crystal ball?"

Scrap's eyes turned red with an inner glow of excitement. *That's a good idea. Want me to go get it?*

"Not yet. I think we should wait until after the con. I have this nagging feeling that I'm missing something. Before we do anything, I want the Nörglein out of the way, permanently."

"Good luck," Doreen said skeptically. "I've tried killing him at least a dozen times. He's always one step ahead of me. Smarter and faster. He lies and cheats. Anything to get his way."

"He is truly evil," I agreed.

"But without him the forest will die. Are you willing to take on that responsibility?" Doreen reminded me. "I will take the responsibility, but I don't know how to cut out invasive plants, balance destructive and helpful insects, deter people from damaging it beyond repair."

"Let me think about that." My aunt MoonFeather came immediately to mind. And so did the World Forestry Center and their army of volunteers and educational programs.

No one person should have to protect the forest on his own, like I had tried fighting demons on my own. And failed.

I had backup now. I had family and friends.

LUNCH CAME AND WENT with no sign of Sean or Gollum. I checked my cell phone for about the sixth time to see if I'd missed a call from either of them. I had a lot to think about between times.

I wondered if Donovan and Doreen would take both Cedar and Oak. A good resolution as long as I got "Pete" out of the way. Deprived of all three of his sons, he just might go berserk, raping even more women.

"Have you seen Squishy?" a Green Room volunteer asked while I checked out the power point equipment and slides. Evolution of Dragons. I could do this. Mostly Gollum had assembled pictures of early artwork depicting dragons. The Egyptian stuff was new to me but flowed naturally into the classical Greek. Then a gap. The Middle Ages and modern fantasy book covers grew out of odd connections and shifted from good to evil and back to good. The section on Oriental dragons felt strange and wonderful and awesome. I could probably wing it.

"Um, no I haven't seen Squishy," I replied. "She was here yesterday."

"And she left in a hurry, blowing off her five o'clock panel on field treatment of sword wounds. Then she missed her eleven o'clock this morning on small press scams," the volunteer grumbled.

"I heard that she might be moving soon. Maybe something came up and she had to move out sooner than expected," I hedged. I hoped she had a new roommate moving in with her too.

"Maybe so. But it's not like her to not say something, or apologize, or *something*."

"Yeah, you're right." Maybe bad news for me. I didn't dare hope for good news.

Sean hurried into the suite. He paused for only half a breath until he spotted me on the sofa beneath a window at the far end. Then he zeroed in on me with a big smile and flattering haste.

"I am so sorry I'm late," he said on a gush. "I got tied up at... work." He plunked down beside me and took my hand in both of his—the one I was using to fiddle with a setting on Gollum's laptop. Gently he kissed the back of my hand, then turned it over and flicked his tongue along the pulse point of my wrist.

Tingles flashed up my arm, robbing me of balance for a heartbeat. Oh, boy, this could get interesting.

At least I had someone to turn to if Gollum and Julia got back together.

"I don't suppose you have a few hours free this evening. We could slip away to my place for some privacy. Blackberry and Salal are so engrossed in their game they won't notice." He continued pushing up the sleeve of my sweater to kiss the inside of my elbow.

My bones began melting.

Not a good idea, dahling. Scrap swooped in and landed on my head. His talons tangled in my hair. Just enough pressure to jerk me back to reality.

"Um . . . Sean, don't you remember, we changed the girls' names? You came up with E.T. 'Phone home.'"

"Of course. I'm just flushed from my hurry to get here. Phonetia and E.T."

The children are getting restless, Donovan is zeroing in on Lucia, and Gollum has entered the building.

My breath caught in my throat.

"The imp will leave us alone, won't he?" Sean continued, taking responsibility for my breathlessness.

I had to remind myself he couldn't see or hear Scrap.

"Can I have a rain check, Sean?" I asked. I had to breathe to speak. I had to breathe for my heart to continue beating.

My skin twitched with uneasiness.

Gollum was in the building. I'd know soon if we had a chance of a future together.

Awkwardly, I rose from the deep sofa cushions and extricated my hand from Sean's grasp. "Later. I have an appointment," I lied.

It took all of my willpower not to run out the door in search of Gollum.

I'd no sooner cleared the doorway and veered right when someone caught my elbow and steered me left.

Two sharp breaths later Gollum pressed me into the alcove by the service elevator. I opened my mouth to ask the most important question of the moment.

But he stopped me with his mouth planted firmly atop mine. My arms crept about his neck. He deepened the kiss and pulled me tight against his chest.

The world fell away. We had only each other, this moment, the glorious blending of two people into one.

Satisfaction, well-being, a sense of belonging right here and nowhere else settled all of my nerves.

Our tongues found each other in a questing dance filled with life and love. My body molded to his along with my soul.

When we finally came up for air, he lifted me off the ground and swung me around in joy.

"Don't suppose you could put me up for a few days while Julia and Pat move elsewhere?" he asked softly, still holding me aloft, pressed against his long length, held in place by his incredibly strong arms. "I talked to my lawyer last night. The divorce is in the works, papers to be filed at eight 8 am Monday."

I gulped air praying for strength and common sense. "You can move in the day your divorce is final."

"I plan on walking you and our daughters down the aisle the day after the divorce is final. If you'll still have me."

"All you have to do is ask. And give me details," I laughed. "What happened last night?"

"Julia has done what a lot of victims of abuse do. She found a sense of safety in a homosexual relationship with a woman her own age. She started with other patients in the asylum who were hungry for any kind of peer relationships. Then she latched onto a health care professional. Typical pattern. She'll never truly feel safe with me because I'm the one who abandoned her to the asylum where her mother could come and go at will. Nurses and aides were the only ones who ever put a buffer between Julia and Bridget. The fact that she interprets that sense of safety as love is not necessarily correct, but she took a risk, made a decision on her own. *She* approached Pat. She made a choice that wasn't me. I'm free! Free to marry you."

"I will."

"You know what the funnest part of last night was?"

I shook my head, too happy to speak coherently.

"I got to tell Bridget! She sputtered and snarled and threatened to cut off Julia's trust fund, but I reminded her I'm a professional researcher. I know things about her and her family tree she doesn't want known."

"Then I don't have to send Lady Lucia to have a talk with her?"

He laughed long and loud. "One bloodsucker to another. I love it. Later, when things are a bit more settled, I'll get down on bended knee with the biggest diamond I can find and propose properly." He kissed me again and set me on the ground. We clung together, neither of us certain we could stand upright on our own. "Consider this a promise. But right now, I'm obligated to lead a discussion about the evolution of dragons."

"And I should go see about slaying one."

He quirked an eyebrow.

In short and choppy sentences I related the latest developments. "Pete's desperate, Gollum. He's lost three of his children, his ability to demand demon protection on his pot-growing minions, and his hat. That's a lot of power gone in a short period of time. I have a feeling he's up to something. I just don't know what yet. I've got to stay close to the kids today. Even if it means dragging them out of their game to sit with me on panels."

"Meet me back in the Green Room at five. We'll take them out for pizza and see if they can come up with some ideas. No one knows the Nörglein better than they do."

"Pete might have confided in, or bragged to Doug," I continued his thought. "What are we going to do about legitimatizing him?"

"Don't you have any ideas?" he asked.

"Fresh out. Do you have any relatives who might have orphaned him? He says he's gay by the way." I let my fingers brush the fine hair on the back of his head, cherishing the silky texture.

"Hmmm. Let me think a moment."

"None of my family knows your family. Could he be your nephew sent to us because his parents can't deal with him?" I speculated.

"Yeah." He paused in thought. "First cousin and his wife on Dad's side—Mom doesn't speak to them, and I haven't seen them since Dad's funeral—are frothing at the mouth conservatives and really hate gays. They'd throw a kid out very quickly at the first hint of alternative sexuality. I'll do the paperwork tonight. And take him home with me. He can have Pat's old room since she's sleeping with Julia these days."

One more quick kiss and we parted to our mutual con obligations. I couldn't help smiling and barely noticed Sean's frown when he joined me.

Chapter 45

*B*oring, Oregon was named for W.H. Boring, not a comment on the social climate.

My nose twitches. Something is wrong. Very, very wrong. Time to check on the kidlets. I fly ahead of Tess.

And slam into a force field. It's as thick and as hard as anything Donovan used to emit. Maybe he still has enough gargoyle left in him to set up the same kind of barrier. But I've overcome the darkness in my soul so he doesn't repel me anymore.

My nose hurts. I wiggle it to make sure it's all in one piece.

Hey! I've got a new wart there. All this protecting our girls from their blood relations has its rewards. Gingko is going to think me more beautiful than evah.

Flapping my wings rapidly and awkwardly to regain my balance, I return to Tess' shoulder, my tail around her neck and my talons clutching her really drab, cream colored cable-knit sweater. At least it doesn't clash with her brown slacks and gold blouse. She even put on amber beads and earrings. The pearls, as always, are next to her skin, covered with clothing. We were so busy this morning I didn't have time to choose her outfit. How did she manage to color coordinate anything without me? Maybe some of my good taste is rubbing off on her.

Good. That will give me more time to work with our girls on their hair and wardrobe.

Anyway, we pass the spot that stopped me. Not something ahead of us keeping me out.

I fly behind us. This time I'm more cautious and see a faint shimmer in the air moving forward.

Something dangerous is keeping me close to my babe.

So I park my cute behind on top of her head, tuning my ears to every sound, tasting the air with my tongue as well as my newly adorned nose.

Sean's musky pine aftershave gets in the way of smelling anything untoward.

I know something is wrong I just can't figure out what it is yet.

"Tessie, babe, swing by the gaming room," I advise. "Something isn't right."

AS SCRAP TANGLED MY hair in his talons and yanked, I pulled out of my euphoria long enough to notice Sean scowling and Lady Lucia approaching with a fussy Sophia sucking her fingers while strapped into her stroller.

I crouched down in front of Sophia noting her tear-streaked face. "What's the problem, little one?"

She held out her arms to me and bounced in the stroller, clearly not happy confined.

"It is time for her nap, but there is too much activity in the garden. She will not go to sleep and she will not stop crying," Lucia complained. She sounded like any other frustrated mother. "She needs your special touch."

"I'll run a quick check on the girls in the gaming room," Sean said. He didn't look too happy at my delay. "Meet me there."

Without asking, I removed the straps from around Sophia and picked her up, blankie and all. She instantly returned her fingers to her mouth, dropped her head on my shoulder, and fell asleep.

Her warmth and absolute trust filled me with longing. I cherished these few moments with my godchild.

Relief warred with jealousy on Lucia's face. "You will be a wonderful godmother and mother," she finally said. "Tomorrow morning, six o'clock Mass." She turned and started to leave, without the stroller, diaper bag, or her daughter.

"Aren't you forgetting something?"

"She will awaken if you remove her from your shoulder."

"Not now." Carefully, I shifted Sophia back into the stroller, tucking her blankie beneath her head when it lolled sideways. She whimpered briefly but fell back to sleep. "See? Now she just needs quiet for a few moments more. Then she'll be out cold for at least an hour."

I pushed the stroller beside Lucia as we returned to the central garden area. Holly was on the stage testing sound equipment and tuning her harp. She wore a full long skirt made of patchwork velvet and a white velour peasant blouse embroidered with Celtic knots and St. Brigid crosses at neck and cuff. The costume was new, her absorption in her task typical.

"I heard you sing last night." Lucia paused at the edge of the open area.

Late afternoon, more and more people congregated here, getting the parties started. Many wore costumes in preparation for the masquerade competition scheduled right after Holly's concert.

A man and a woman, both in chain mail, helmets and surcoats, bashed each other with broadswords made of PVC pipe and foam rubber. They wove around the arena below the stage in the intricate dance of dueling.

Utter chaos. And I loved it all.

"I enjoy singing filk," I replied to Lucia.

"You inherited your talent from your mother."

I swallowed a moment of sadness that Mom had just found a new life as a chanteuse in Vegas when she was murdered.

"I'm not nearly as good a singer as my mother," I replied around the lump in my throat.

"Do not be so sure of that. You have the pearls to amplify your talent. They are special pearls. The seed they are cultured around is a fragment of a goddess' bones. No one remembers which one, something Greek I believe."

"What!" I stopped dead in my tracks.

"Didn't I tell you that already?" A quirk of mischief entered her eyes. Her posture flowed from frustrated and exhausted mother to Goth manipulator, dribbling secrets on her own schedule.

"No. You told me nothing about the pearls other than that I should wear them always because I'd never know when I'd need them." I narrowed my gaze to concentrate on her. "Doreen has a similar set."

"Yes."

Scrap mumbled something anxious in the back of my mind. But the girls were quiet and content. I had a few moments to explore this new bit of information.

"I had forgotten how much I miss music in my everyday life," Lucia's voice drifted off into nostalgia.

"Tell me more about the pearls," I demanded, before she could veer off topic in her maddening way.

"They were mine once. Given to me by my great-grandmother on my wedding day. She was one of the ones we thought were witches but really just displayed her demon origins. She said the pearls always go to the one who needs them. I left them with my son in France with his Noncoiré grandparents. They passed from generation to generation in a not very straight line until your mother received them on her wedding day from your grandmother. Strangely, she didn't really need them. She was just a conduit to get them to you."

"My mother's ability to hold an audience captive with a song..."

"Her own talent. She didn't know how to invoke the pearls. She didn't need to."

"But what about the seed being a bone fragment from a goddess?"

She shrugged and started walking away. "I know nothing more about them. Have you, by chance, recorded music? I should like to take your voice back to Las Vegas."

"I did some back up for Holly's latest CD. Along with some other people. That's the best I can offer. I'm not a pro and don't pretend to be."

"Then you will join Miss Holly in her concert tonight?"

"Maybe. If she asks."

On the stage, Holly whipped her cell phone out of her skirt pocket. She spoke quietly for a moment and smiled. Then she closed the phone decisively and marched toward the front entrance.

I thrust the stroller back toward Lady Lucia. "I've got to check on my own daughters now." Before she had a chance to offload Sophia onto me, again, before I was ready to take her full time, I made my exit, wondering who Holly had comped for her concert. She was always giving away tickets—or in this case a con membership—to some special fan. Many of them celebrities.

A hush fell over the crowd.

I swiveled my attention back to Holly's mop of red curls by the revolving door. A tall man with flowing blond hair stepped free of the rotating glass panels.

Malcolm Levi, star of *Space Pirates of the Outer Antares.*

Every woman in the lobby gasped at one of the most beautiful men in the film industry. One of the finest actors of this generation and he'd come to the con as Holly's guest. I wondered if he was just a fan or something more. The hug she gave him could be interpreted as anything from deep gratitude to close friend to lasting lover.

Then I remembered a cryptic acknowledgement on the CD to the sweet tenor voice on a love ballad sandwiched between two rollicking fun cuts. The tenor was listed as M. Levinski—Malcolm Levi?

Oh ho. So there was something special between them.

Sixty-five cell phones appeared in hands as if by magic. Thumbs worked furiously, snapping photos, texting, and posting the news at the speed of sound.

People all over the hotel began streaming out of side corridors and converging on the lobby to gape in wonder at the celebrity in our midst. Lucia pushed forward to the command position three feet to the left of Holly. An aggressive teen with a cell phone camera shoved her aside. The vampire crime boss of Las Vegas bared her fake fangs. The teen bared her longer fake fangs and continued taking pictures.

The railing on the mezzanine was pressed hard to hold back the eager viewers. Front and center Doreen stood tall and Junoesque with short and dumpy Starshine right beside her. I think they both drooled a bit. Malcolm Levi was as beautiful in his own way as Donovan.

Either man could set a woman's hormones jumping.

Gollum peered over the tops of several heads at the commotion. His presentation must have ended abruptly when the room emptied upon the news.

I smiled and waved at him. He waved back.

My heart flipped with joy and my interest in Malcolm Levi faded—looks and fame aren't everything.

The kids deserting the gaming rooms drew my attention back to my mission. I needed to check on my daughters. Our link told me only that they were a bit confused by the excitement.

They had no way of knowing about the famous man who smiled so endearingly at Holly.

"What's going on, Tess? A whole roomful of gamers just deserted my presentation," Donovan said emerging from a big room on my left.

"Malcolm Levi just showed up to attend Holly's concert. Even you and Halfling Games can't compete with the star of *Space Pirates of Outer Antares*." Hence Holly's new costume, reminiscent of the one worn by Malcolm Levi's love interest in the movie. I chuckled and moved on.

Donovan followed his audience.

I continued on to the gaming center. The computer room where E.T. should be was empty. And it looked as if someone had turned out the lights but left the computers running.

The corridor had grown dim as well. Moisture lay heavy in the air, almost visible. I smelled wet earth, musky rotting leaves, and heavy evergreens.

A Pacific Northwest rain forest. The Nörglein's preferred environment.

The hair on my nape stood on end.

"Scrap, we've been through this dirty air before."

Yeah, babe. I still can't smell what's wrong though. Sean's aftershave keeps blocking up my nose. And I haven't turned even a blush pink yet.

Odd memories of sentence fragments and ideas began to coalesce. I didn't like where my thoughts took me.

I stepped cautiously through the open accordion door separating the rooms, holding my right hand out for Scrap.

A bit brighter in here. E.T., Phonetia, and Doug sat hunched over a gaming board, gazes firmly fixed on their twenty-sided dice and fantasy figures. Sean faced them, anger stiffening his shoulders.

"Blackberry, Salal, Tess says you are to come with me now." A swirl of humid murk kept me from seeing fine details of his form.

"Sean, why did you just call the girls by their former names? This is the second time you've done it." Once a slip. Twice a problem. Another memory slipped into place: The Nörglein's victims complaining about his *pine* aftershave.

I took a defensive stance and held out my hand for Scrap.

Sean turned confused eyes on me, keeping his body half facing the children, so that they never got totally out of his line of sight. "Tess, sweetheart, when they didn't agree to come the first time, I had to try something more drastic."

Phonetia shook her head slightly.

He was lying.

Scrap flushed red all over.

I smell fear, babe. The kids are desperately afraid of Sean who isn't Sean. All three of them.

"You called them by the old names because you're not Sean, you slimy bastard. Show your real self, shape-changer!"

This was why he'd tried to lead me back to Sean's home to seduce me. I was to be his next victim. Some fast math in my head told me I was fertile and vulnerable.

"I got news for you, elf, my firstborn is already promised to the Powers That Be. You'll never get your hands on me or my children."

"Your bargain with the Powers That Be is less than my need. Your demon blessed DNA is a triumphant bonus."

"How did you know?"

"All Warriors of the Celestial Blade have a drop or two of demon in their genes. That's the only way the imp flu can infect you. That's the only way you can find the Citadels halfway between dimensions. But I don't truly need a child from you. I want the crystal ball."

"You can't have it."

"I'll find it eventually."

"Not bloody likely."

Scrap had stretched and curved, halfway to ready.

"You won't run away from me this time, Nörglein." I slashed at him with the still dull blade.

"This time I came prepared." The words were barely out of his mouth when he shrank and broadened. His face took on the color and texture of mellow yellow pine as his nose and chin elongated, reaching toward each other. Modern jeans and polo shirt melted into a short green coat and tricorn hat over buff breeches and shirt. The hat was brand-new and lacked the luster of power in his real one. Large, hairy feet replaced the athletic shoes.

And he drew a long, wickedly sharp sword from a fine leather sheath on his belt. This was no foiled weapon legal at the con. This was a deadly serious blade meant for a duel to the death.

Chapter 46

O*regon Shakespeare Festival in Ashland was founded in 1935. It is the largest repertory theater in the US. Supposedly, the ghost of Charles Laughton haunts the place in his* King Lear *costume, though he died before he could actually perform there.*

"I have removed these children from their mothers, I will take them from you more easily," the Nörglein snarled. His sword lashed out in a neat swipe across my middle.

I ducked and backed up. Scrap was still curving and sharpening.

The elf lunged with a circle down with his blade. He'd trained in the old, classical Italian dueling style.

No polite chitchat while I got ready to fight. No salute or referee. No confines of a fencing strip set to tournament regulations.

No rules or honor either.

I retreated to the corridor, twirling Scrap to help him finish transforming. We were alone.

Another cut and stab.

This guy was good. He handled his weapon like he'd studied with Cassanova himself.

He probably had.

"Phonetia, get your brother and sister to Gollum or Lady Lucia. Now." I didn't want them to have to watch one of us die.

"You stole us?" Phonetia screamed. "You stole us from our mothers? Then you raped me from the time I started bleeding. You freaking pervert! We could have been raised with love, gone to school, seen movies. We could be normal. Not your fucking slaves and brood mares."

"Such language, Blackberry. You never learned those words from me. A sure sign I should be the one to raise you," the elf said, almost congenially. He used his bland demeanor to cover his next vicious attack.

I blocked his thrust with the shaft, twisted and set the outer tines to scrape his torso.

Scrap tasted blood and chortled.

"Phonetia, get out. Protect Doug and E.T. That's an order," I said with more calm than I felt.

Tree Daddy slashed again. I backed up, not sure where I was going.

I heard my kids scramble toward a sliding glass door that led to the domed pool area. From there they could easily get to the Green Room.

The tip of one half moon blade scraped the corridor wall on my next slash, throwing off my timing and my aim. Not a lot of room. Better than the water slick floor of the pool deck.

I continued backing up, searching for an opening.

The dark elf only stood four feet tall but he had extraordinarily long arms that seemed to stretch and withdraw with each movement.

I shifted my grip to one end of the Celestial Blade, grabbing the shaft two-handed, like a broadsword.

Duck and lunge. Parry and riposte. My long hours in the fencing salle came back to me, thought became instinct.

The Nörglein twisted his blade in a neat circular parry and riposte. I caught the tip on my left arm. Barely a pinprick of pain as adrenaline countered the nerve reaction. Then a hot trickle of blood. My arm felt as if he'd stabbed deep and long. The muscle spasmed.

Damn, this elf knew his business.

I cut over and jabbed at his lower left. He yelped and skipped back. But not for long.

Before I recovered to *en garde* he was on me, fast and furious.

I kept backing up, chancing quick looks over my shoulder to make sure I didn't trip.

A roar of applause and the squeal of microphone feedback erupted behind me. Close. We were too close to the lobby. Innocents could get drawn in.

But then so could my backup. I couldn't count on them. A rogue Warrior of the Celestial Blade worked alone.

Not anymore. I had family and backup.

The noise invigorated the elf's smile. He showed a lot of pointed teeth, black around the edges.

"Forget to floss?" What can I say? I get sarcastic when I'm scared.

Come to think on it, his toes and fingertips looked like they were crumbling back to dirt. This guy was old and rotting.

And therefore, more desperate than I thought. Well-armed, trained, and still strong. I had to come up with a plan. I had to become more devious than he.

He forced me back. One step. Then two more. I lunged under his blade. He retreated just enough to evade. Then pressed me harder.

My breath caught in my lungs, sharp and short. My legs grew heavy with fatigue. Scrap looked a little dull. We flagged, in serious danger of getting hurt from carelessness.

Don't say his name. We can still take him. Scrap sounded breathless and far away.

My muscles grew heavy. His name rose to my lips.

I clamped them shut.

I had one chance and one only. The lights behind me grew brighter as we cleared the forest murk the Nörglein had raised. He blinked rapidly.

I skipped back into the light.

Three people hopped out of my way. "Ooh, a new demo," a large woman swathed in Gypsy red and purple silk scarves with lots of dangling jewelry crooned. She smelled strongly of roses. Artificial roses.

The Nörglein sneezed and lost his attack posture.

"Clear the way!" I shouted, dashing for the open arena around the stage.

Tree Daddy followed me, eyes and nose clearing.

"Fight, fight, fight," the crowd chanted.

I spotted Squishy physically holding people away from my path. Cameras flashed and thumbs sped over cell phone keypads.

We danced around the arena twice, blades flashing in the bright lights before I could catch my breath.

"What have you done with Sean?" I demanded as I pressed my foe closer to the stage. Gollum leaped up onto the raised platform from the other side. He grabbed a length of sound cable ready to loop into a noose.

"You will never find your boyfriend," the dark elf chortled. "I have destroyed the paths."

"He's an innocent in this. He deserves to be rescued."

"But not by you. I will set him free when I am done with you. As I have honorably done to all the men who loaned me their wives."

"That's rape. None of them were willing participants in your scheme to repopulate this world with your get."

"You know nothing. I have the right to protect my race from extinction. Now, where is the crystal ball?" He slashed again.

I parried half a heartbeat too late. Blood poured down my left arm, making my grip on the staff slick and uneven.

I could say his name.

Desperate to end this, I lunged again. Scrap sharpened enough to slice Pete's old-fashioned shirt from left shoulder to right hip. Somewhere in there we got a piece of skin. Green-black blood stained the creamy linen.

The lights, the noise, fatigue, and blood loss took their toll. My lunge skewed my balance. I tilted too far forward. My right knee gave up trying to support my weight, followed by the collapse of my left.

My left shoulder hit the floor first sending long lances of pain down my back and up into my skull.

I lost my grip on my blade.

The Nörglein didn't wait to gloat. He raised his sword in both hands, ready to plunge it into my heart.

"Purz . . ."

I rolled, expecting the fatal blow in my back. The end of his name got garbled in the tangle of plants that caught me.

Nothing.

I rolled farther away.

"Drop the weapon," Donovan said very slowly and precisely.

No sign of Gollum on the stage.

A quick glance over my shoulder showed my rescuer holding a plastic ray gun to the Nörglein's neck.

"Mundane weapons cannot hurt me." The troll raised his blade another fraction, shifting his aim.

"Who said this is an ordinary weapon?" Donovan asked. Still no emotion in his voice.

Then Gollum was at my side, wrapping his handkerchief around the slice on my arm, reaching to help me up, handing me my blade. My girls clung to his belt behind him.

The Nörglein hesitated, weighing possibilities.

Donovan eased the pressure on the Nörglein's neck.

Pete shifted his feet and his grip, engaging my blade once more.

I tangled his sword in the tines. We stared at each other, frozen in impasse.

Phonetia's arm morphed into blackberry vines, shooting out from her sweatshirt sleeve faster than Spiderman's web. Vicious thorns bit into the elf's woody hide at ankle and calf. The plant fiber looped and doubled back on itself. She tightened the vine around the elf's feet and yanked.

He fell forward onto his ugly nose, yowling in pain and outrage. "How dare you defy me!"

Gollum, the eternal Eagle Scout produced plastic zip strips from his pocket and snapped them in place around thick troll ankles and wrists.

The Nörglein fought his mundane restraints.

"Artificial. He can't manipulate the fibers," Gollum said, pushing his glasses higher on his nose. He looked ready to lecture the audience.

"You can't do this to me!" The Nörglein wiggled.

Donovan placed his heavy foot in the middle of his chest.

Phonetia withdrew her vines.

I lifted my blade for the coup de grace.

"Before you send this heap of garbage off to hell, I need to know something," Doreen demanded. She stayed my blow with a brief touch of her hand. "Which of the boys is my son?"

"How am I supposed to remember that?" the Nörglein replied. "They're all alike."

"But you stole my baby from me! Surely you remember that," Doreen cried.

"Why should I?"

Anger at the elf's total lack of care for his children sent waves of fire through my blood. I raised the blade.

Loud applause stopped me. The con populace really didn't need to see the execution of this guy. We weren't play acting. My girls didn't need to watch me murder the being who had raised them, even if he had abused them.

"We'll do this." Oak appeared at the edge of the crowd, Cedar close beside him.

"No. I will. This has been a long time coming." Donovan hauled the bound Nörglein to his feet and slung him over his shoulder.

"Allow me." Lady Lucia bared her fangs. "I thought I killed you once, you disgrace to decent timber. This time I will make sure. This time we dump the body in the river so you cannot regenerate in the soil. Tess, watch the baby."

Before they could take two steps toward the rapidly clearing corridor to the gaming rooms, the Nörglein shuddered and spasmed.

Donovan dropped him unceremoniously. He landed with only a light wisp of sound. Smoke streamed upward from where the plastic strips bound his wrists and ankles. It smelled sweet, like burning pine, but with a bitterness of old and rotten wood beneath it.

The dark elf screamed, high and piercing.

"God, I'm sorry. I had no idea the plastic would do that to him." Gollum bent to remove the lethal restraints.

Cedar beat him to it. The boy bit his lip and tears moistened his eyes.

"No." Oak stayed his brother with a firm grip on his arm. "What will be, will be. We agreed. He's no longer fit to maintain the forest. He needs to be culled."

"If my forest dies, let it be on your head, Tess Noncoiré. You are responsible for the death of all the trees and the living things that depend upon them!" The dark elf fixed an angry, defiant gaze upon me. Smoke poured from his mouth.

His eyes remained open, accusing me as his body convulsed once more and lay still.

My girls fell on me, hugging me tightly, crying and shaking.

I wasn't too steady myself. Gollum joined the family with Doug close on his heels. He pulled another handkerchief and a wet wipe from somewhere, taking care of my wounds even as he joined the family embrace.

Through the shimmering veil of my own tears of relief, I noted Doreen approaching Cedar and Oak with a tentative offer of her own embrace. As tall as she, the boys clung to her, silently burying their faces in her shoulders.

Donovan and Lucia made off with the smoldering body. "The river," Lucia said quietly. "It's the only way. Too bad he's already dead. I looked forward to a long, slow, tortuous feed."

Scrap dissolved and crept off to recover. I knew he'd find ample mold in the basement levels. But I'd make sure I provided him with beer and OJ in the café.

"Pretty good skit. The smoke was a nice touch. But the blood was too dark, not green enough," Malcolm Levi laughed over the noise of the clapping crowd.

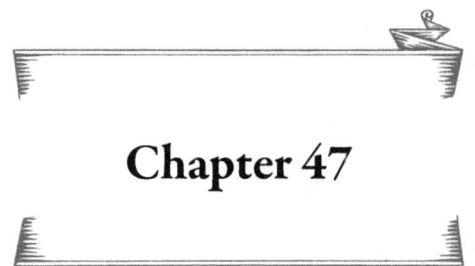

Chapter 47

Between 1870 and 1930, seventy miles of tunnels beneath Pendleton, Oregon, housed entire businesses from butcher shops to opium dens.

"We need to find Sean," E.T. whispered, still clinging to me.

"The binding will wear off . . ." I said hopefully.

"If Pete doesn't return by midnight, the minions with demon tats will kill the man," Doreen said. She and the boys joined our group. Cedar and Oak had withdrawn from her, mastering their emotions in stoic acceptance. She looked disappointed and lonely.

Gollum continued to fuss over my already healing wounds.

"A little imp spit would work faster than those wet wipes, but Scrap's not around," I whispered. My love for him grew and blossomed, threatening to choke me.

"The paths have been destroyed," Oak said. "I don't think either Cedar or I could find our way home again."

"Is there a back door?" Gollum chimed in. He accepted a gold silk scarf from a fan's costume to tie his makeshift bandage in place.

"Back door?" Oak's face went blank.

"There is always a back door. Only a fool builds a secret lair with only one entrance," Gollum replied. "First law of super villains."

"The tunnels," Phonetia said barely above a whisper.

"The what?" Cedar shot her a wicked glare.

"I don't have to keep the old man's secrets anymore," she returned haughtily.

"I know an entrance three blocks from here," E.T. said quietly. "It's nearly blocked in places between there and the main passage. Hard going.

But it's not as heavily trafficked around the entrance. And it's raining hard out. We'd get soaked before we found the trapdoor."

"A rainy Saturday night in Old Town, the parking will be difficult at best. We'll probably have to walk half a mile. Might as well take the more difficult but closer tunnel," Gollum added.

"Let's go." I stepped back and nearly tripped over Sophia's stroller. She woke up and wailed.

My heart flipped with the need to hold and comfort her. At the same time, I sank within myself, knowing I'd have to wait for Lucia to return before I could go find Sean. At this point every moment of delay endangered him from the latest batch of men with demon tattoos.

More incompetents or had Pete held back the best of his minions?

I was betting on the latter and Scrap was in no condition to help.

"I'll watch the baby for Lucia," Doreen offered.

"Can I trust you to return Sophia to her mother, and only her mother? If Donovan comes back first..." With the baby's Damiri black hair, he might assume the obvious and claim her as his own.

I looked around at the assembly. Most of the crowd drifted off or found seats in front of the stage waiting for Holly to begin her concert.

I needed my girls and their brothers with me, leading me through the tunnels. I wanted Gollum at my side.

Solemnly, I approached Squishy and Julia, hovering indecisively in the background. "Hi, I'm Tess," I introduced myself to Julia. "I saw you playing with Sophia yesterday. Could I trouble you to watch her for a little while until her mother returns?"

"You trust me with her?"

"I trusted you with Gollum's heart. Nothing is more precious to me. You gave that back to me. I trust you with my goddaughter as well."

"Thank you," she said graciously. "I never meant to hurt him."

"I know. We're all happier this way. And I know we all have to get along. So why not start now. Can you watch Sophia?"

"Yes. I'd be honored," she said enthusiastically reaching for the little girl.

Sophia willingly went into her arms and immediately began playing with her expensive golden knot earrings.

I transferred the KIT sticker from my badge to hers.

"Well done, Tess," Gollum said, kissing my temple. "I think we need to get a move on though. Phonetia says it will take us a least an hour to hike up to the hills."

"Let's get moving. Maybe Scrap will recover enough to help by then."

Don't bet on it, I heard a disgruntled mumble in the back of my head.

"Squishy, why don't you and Julia take Sophia to the café? Order a beer and an orange juice. Don't be surprised if it disappears on its own."

"Draft or bottle?" Squishy called back.

"Doesn't matter." A new thought wiggled forward in my mind. I fished my cell phone out of my fanny pack and tossed it to Squishy. "Call Raquel and JJ Jones. Tell them they can keep their baby! Spread the word to the entire support group."

SQUISHY IS A GOOD BABY-sitter for me. Julia is an attentive baby-sitter for Sophia. The two women make an interesting couple. Physical opposites. Emotional opposites. They're kinda cute together. Maybe they really are in love.

They coo and fuss over Sophia with poignant joy, knowing they will never have a child together but delighting in this little bundle of energy.

Sophia has decided a bottle is too tame. She wants a cup. And she wants it now. She makes a mess of the peanut butter and jelly sandwich Julia orders for her. But amazingly most of it ends up in her tummy.

Squishy takes a few moments to make the requested phone call. She's smiling by the end of it. I can hear Raquel's joyful tears through the tiny speaker.

I watch from the safety of the bank of ferns in a raised bed behind their table. The moment the beer and OJ arrive I creep out from my safe observatory and take a few sips. Then I creep back and wait a few minutes for the waters of life to work their magic. Another few sips and I'm up to making faces at Sophia.

She blinks at me, not certain she sees me. Then she sticks out her tongue, aping me. She's so cute. I waggle my wart enhanced bum at her.

She stands in her highchair and flashes her ruffled panties at me.

Squishy coaxes her back to sitting with more PB&J.

Doreen joins us, gazing at Sophia with intense longing. Movement in her peripheral vision draws her attention to the side passage. She's impatient for Donovan to return. At the same time, she wants to enjoy the baby as long as possible.

A couple more sips of beer and I can almost work up the energy to go find some mold.

You okay, Scrap? Tess asks from someplace dark and dank. Oh, I bet she's got good mold all around her.

Working on it, I flash back to her. Where are you? I could find out if I just thought about her for a moment. But I don't have the energy yet.

Deep in the tunnels. E.T. says we're about a hundred yards from the main passage.

Careful. I think there's a rockfall just ahead of you.

I see it. Gollum has the most amazing flashlight.

Of course he does. He's Gollum.

And his backpack, of course.

He's always prepared.

Lucia returned from her errand yet?

Nope.

Scrap, hurry and get your strength back. This place is really, really creepy. I feel like I'm being watched by a thousand ghosts and none of them want me here.

Working on it. Stay close to Gollum. Keep the girls from straying. I'll be there as soon as I can.

She fades from my consciousness and I finish my beer and OJ. My skin glows a bit orange and my tummy bulges. Time for dessert.

Sophia reaches for my tail as I prepare to fly off. Oops, can't allow that. There's this special grip that only Tess is supposed to know about. When she tangles her fingers just above the barb, I can't get away, even though I'm only partly in this dimension and should be able to slip through anything. This little lady is looking to learn the grip quite by accident. And she's not yet a year old.

I sense a Warrior in the making. I'll keep a look out for a likely imp to bond with her. Can't let just anybody infect my Sophia with the imp flu.

Chapter 48

The largest gold nugget found in Oregon weighed seventeen pounds.

"What was that about you having demon blood in you?" Gollum asked quietly as he helped me negotiate a pile of cave debris that nearly blocked the passage.

I didn't really need the help, but it felt good to let his strength and height aid me.

I took comfort that I wasn't alone in these tunnels. There was a malevolent presence here. Resentment. Fear. Greed.

"Um..."

"We didn't tell anyone," Phonetia said. "The Nörglein figured that out on his own."

So I told my Gollum how Pete had bound the girls and how Lucia and I had broken the spell. Then I slowly and carefully told him about Lucia and my Noncoiré ancestor, sounding out my own emotions as I spoke. He had a right to know.

"In a weird way that makes sense," Gollum said. Then he grew silent.

"What? No lecture? No dissertation?"

I sensed his shrug more than saw it. I had to watch where I put my feet on the uneven ground in the limited light.

"I can see the safety lights in the main tunnel," E.T. announced.

"Thank God," I muttered.

Help me! A faint cry in the distance froze me to the bone.

"Did you hear that?" I started shaking. My feet refused to take the next three steps, even though the way was clear.

"Hear what?" Phonetia asked. She stopped too, turning her head right and left.

Get out! a different voice said, closer this time.

"I don't hear anything," Gollum said. He pushed his glasses higher on his nose, as if that enhanced his hearing.

Despair threatened to overwhelm me. Tears burned in my eyes. No hope. No way out. Nothing but this endless darkness, pain, thirst, hunger. Fear. Alone.

I was going to die alone in this god-awful place.

My legs turned to jelly. I sank to my knees weeping. My shoulders felt too heavy to remain upright. I curled in on myself, resting my forehead on the cold earth, not caring that a sharp rock pressed against sensitive flesh.

Gollum knelt beside me, cradling my body against his.

No help. No use.

"Maybe it's the ghosts," E.T. whispered.

"They don't bother with us much," Phonetia added.

"Father never cleared them out," Oak added. "He said they kept mundanes from penetrating the tunnels far enough to know just how deep they go."

"Greed from the gold rush eras intensifies all the emotion of the spirits that refuse to leave," Doug added. He spun in place, arms extended, palms up, absorbing the psychic emotions.

"Is it true that Doreen is the mother of one of us?" Cedar spoke for the first time.

"Yes," I said, clinging to the ordinary world of words, questions, and answers.

The heavy ache of despair lifted a little. I was able to pull myself up a bit.

"You're more sensitive than most to otherworldly creatures," Gollum said. "We already know you're a projecting empath. Probably a receiver too. You've got to blank your mind to the echoes of the past. They are long dead. They cannot hurt you. There is nothing you can do to help them."

"I can get a priest down here tomorrow morning and exorcise them," I replied firmly. Determination returned. I stumbled to my feet. Gollum rose up with me, taking my hand in his.

That little bit of connection to a living human helped banish the weight of the dead. I wasn't alone.

We moved on, clambering over the last obstacles to the clear passage that rose gradually. Brick archways led to side tunnels, each one the subbasement of a different building. Wooden walls closed off holding cells for the Shanghai shipmasters and the white slavers.

I guessed we turned west, uphill and away from the river.

I heard footsteps, loud and clear from the northeast. I started shaking again.

Gollum thumbed off his light.

"They're real this time," Phonetia whispered. She and her sister melted against a smoothly carved dirt wall, blending with the earth, becoming invisible. I followed their example, finding worn bricks and crumbling mortar behind me. At times I can become a chameleon. A shift of posture, rearrangement of hair and costume and I blend in, sending questing eyes everywhere but at me.

All three boys did their own disappearing act in a shadowed alcove fitted out with stacks of bunk bed frames, four up on each of three walls with barely three feet walking space in the center. An opium den.

"Probably just a caretaker," Gollum whispered, drawing me closer with an arm around my shoulders.

"Tess? I know you're down here somewhere," Donovan called.

Gollum turned on his light again, aiming it directly into the newcomer's eyes.

Donovan shaded his brow with one hand as he walked hesitantly out of a side corridor.

"Where'd you come from?" I asked, pushing Gollum's hand down so Donovan wasn't blinded by the flashlight.

"I own the building that used to house a saloon with a Shanghai trapdoor. The trapdoor is still there if you know how to find it. But it's easier to come down the cellar stairs into the basement." He flashed a grin.

"Shanghai trapdoor?" I mused. "That explains the ghosts."

Donovan blanched, then recovered his normal aplomb.

"You hear them too, don't you," I commented, stepping out from behind the light so Donovan could find me.

"The passage is clear and easy going for about a half mile, then it gets rough, narrow and steep. You up to it?" Donovan avoided the subject of ghosts. He'd probably lived with them every day during the eight hundred years he inhabited a gargoyle statue.

"Did you complete... your... errand?" Gollum asked. He kept a wary eye on all five of the children.

Donovan nodded mutely. "The old bastard won't rape any more women or bind any more men. Lady Lucia made sure of that before we weighted the body with plastic bottles filled with stones and dumped it into the river." He turned his head away and swallowed heavily.

"I bet that Lucia's handling of the body wasn't pretty."

We all nodded in mute agreement. I swallowed my gag reflex. Motherhood had mellowed Lady Lucia but only when it suited her. I briefly worried about Sophia's upbringing with a bloodthirsty demon mother. Lucia was right to give her to me.

Suddenly, I didn't want that sweet and innocent child growing up like her mother. I'd made my decision and wouldn't postpone our discussion any longer. We'd figure out the details tomorrow. My feet really wanted to retreat and protect the child.

But I owed Sean a rescue first.

Determinedly, I set a brisk pace through the tunnel. I didn't look right or left. I didn't want to know the horrors that had taken place down here when Portland was an ungoverned seaport. Gold in California, gold in eastern Oregon, gold in the Black Hills. All that greed had prompted men and women to behave as badly as any demon.

"Is it true, Mr. Donovan?" Oak asked quietly as we trudged along.

"Is what true?"

"That the Cooper woman is mother to one of us." Like the boys didn't believe me.

"Yes."

"Which one?"

"We don't know. But when I marry Doreen in two weeks, I will adopt both of you. Doug too if he wants to stay with you rather than your sisters."

Good for him.

"Unless Tess agrees to marry me first. Then I'll adopt all five of you." Donovan flashed me a bright grin. His teeth nearly glowed in the beam of the flashlight. "I'll give you the saloon as a wedding present and you can turn the tunnels into an amusement park."

I groaned. "Not a chance, Donovan. I'm spoken for." I slipped my hand into Gollum's.

"Isn't he taken?" Donovan protested.

"Not anymore," Gollum replied. Then he stopped abruptly, playing the light over a seemingly blank brick wall with a pile of dirt and building debris at its base. "End of the road. We'll have to turn back. Maybe one of the side tunnels," he said.

The ones filled with ghosts.

"No, it's not the end of the road," E.T. said. She surged from behind and grabbed the light from Gollum. "See this crack between dirt and brick?"

Before we could reply she twisted sideways and slithered through. She shone the light backward, illuminating the impassible path.

"It's easy," Phonetia echoed. She too slid inward.

"Maybe for you two. You're vine skinny," I complained.

"So are you, love." Gollum pushed me forward. Sure enough the crack was wider than it looked. Rough rock and dirt scraped my sweater, reopening the mostly forgotten sword wound as I inched my way through. Then I popped out into a wider room. I could just barely see steps cut into the rocky slope that formed the back wall.

"Not far now," Oak said as he too came through the barrier.

"I don't want to be adopted. Not by you. Not by anyone even if the Cooper woman gave birth to me," Cedar said defiantly. He blocked Donovan and Gollum from entering the crack.

"Cedar, we talked about this," Oak said. He sounded worried.

"Who will guard the forest if we give in to these people? Who will tend it with the love and care it needs to protect it from casual bits of harm and major influxes of danger?"

We all stopped and thought about that.

"Cedar, you don't have to do it all alone. It's time to let humans help you," I reassured him. That was a lesson I'd found hard to learn.

"Father says... said that humans are incompetent and more dangerous than fire during a drought." He stood solid and strong in the wind of my argument.

"The Nörglein never grew with the times. He knew humans with the medieval belief that the forest was a dark and dangerous place to be destroyed or avoided. Because he kept it that way."

I let that sink in a moment before continuing. "Because of the Nörglein and creatures who didn't really belong there, the forest *was* a place to be exploited and eliminated for the protection of people and their families. Humanity has learned a lot about the value of the forest. We're working hard to preserve what we have and restore some of what we've lost."

"You've lost too much! The forest we have is barely enough!" Cedar cried. Moisture gathered in his eyes. He truly loved his patch of wilderness.

"I know someone who has trained volunteers to help a forest grow and thrive," I said quietly. "My aunt, MoonFeather, is a special person. She has an affinity with the natural world. She'll know how to keep you involved with the volunteers while you lead a more human life in a family. In case you haven't noticed, Portland . . . the entire state has spearheaded conservation. With your help we can do even more."

Cedar bit the insides of his cheeks. "I'll help you tonight because I do not like the minions with tattoos growing marijuana in *my* forest." He pushed himself through the crack with some difficulty, his barrel chest scraping the dirt hard. "But I will not leave with any of you when you remove the Sean person from my home."

Donovan reached an arm through and grabbed the boy's shirt.

"Easy. Don't force the issue," Gollum said.

"He only knows threats and violence. He won't respond to anything else," Donovan protested.

"All the more reason to break the cycle of threats and violence," Gollum insisted. "Give him a chance to get used to the idea of regular meals, a comfortable home, and family to keep loneliness at bay. There will also be friends, books, TV, movies, more cons, and gaming for him to adjust to. Let him think."

My Gollum knew what he was doing. He planted the seeds of ideas. Only time would tell if they fell on fertile ground.

"We'll talk later," Donovan promised.

We pushed upward in silence.

My calves burned from the steep climb. Too often I felt Gollum push my back upward and welcomed the boost.

E.T. and her sister bounced up the steps as if they danced on the flat. I thought I was fit. They put me to shame.

A whiny tenor voice drifted downward:
We wuz made to pump all night an' day.
Leave her, Johnny, leave her!
An' we half-dead and bugger-all to say
An it's time for us to leave her!

I recognized the old Irish drinking song about a ship. Taken out of context, as it usually was, it could mean a whole lot of bawdy things.

The girls rolled their eyes and pressed on.

"What?" I mouthed more than whispered.

"Shush. We're close. They'll hear us," Phonetia admonished. "Sound carries strangely here."

We'll leave her tight an' we'll leave her trim,
Leave her, Johnny, Leave her!
We'll heave the hungry bastard in.
An' it's time for us to leave her!

I finally recognized Sean as the off-key vocalist. He wandered around several high notes before finding one he could settle on. Not the one meant for the song.

I can sing better than that, Scrap said on a yawn as he popped out of nothing and onto my shoulder with precision I hadn't seen in him before.

Oh, sing that we boys will never be
Leave her, Johnny, leave her!
In a hungry bitch the like o' she.
An' it's time for us to leave her!

"Pinpoint landing, Scrap. Good one." I relaxed a bit knowing my friend and ally had come back.

Tight quarters, babe. Tight time line.

Uh, oh. Scrap had lingered in his recovery too long and had to use a bit of time travel to get back to me before disaster struck.

He wouldn't have risked slipping up on the tricky maneuver if disaster weren't about to close in on us.

A dozen demon tats armed with Uzis and ropes of ammo. Straight out of a Mexican Bandito movie.

Chapter 49

Hells Canyon, between Oregon and Idaho along the Snake River, is the deepest river cut gorge in North America. At one point, it's 8043 feet deep, 1/3 mile deeper than the Grand Canyon.

"We're marching into hell. Again," Tess says.

I feel her wilt beneath my talons.

"I'm tired of killing," she whispers. Her hands go to her mother's pearls. She ratchets them around and around her neck. She's favoring her left arm, the one the Nörglein stabbed.

"Wrong answer, babe," I reply. "These guys are mean. They're territorial, and you've just taken out their protector and mentor."

"But the Nörglein was old and rotten to the core, a being from another dimension that didn't belong here. These are men. Humans, no matter how warped and murderous. They need to go to the law."

The pearls increase their speed around her neck, then stop suddenly as she stares at them.

I can see ideas forming behind her eyes. She quirks a half smile.

"Not enough, dahling. You can't be sure this plan will—like—work."

"I calmed a plane full of panicking passengers on the verge of a riot," she says. "I kept them from opening the hatch of a pressurized cabin at twenty thousand feet. And I didn't have the pearls to help."

"These guys aren't panicking."

"No, but they are nervous and vulnerable. Sean's off-key singing has set their nerves on edge. All I have to do is tip them over the edge to hopelessness and despair. Like the ghosts down below did to me."

She turns to her crew with bright eyes and a jaunty set to her shoulders.

I really don't like this plan. I don't trust it. But I'm tired enough, I hope it works. At best it will give me a few extra moments of rest before transforming again.

"DONOVAN, FOLLOW ME in with your famous smile," I ordered as I fingered the latch on the back door to the Nörglein's lair.

"And which smile would that be?" he asked, flashing me the one that used to seduce me.

"The one you use to lull a crowd into agreeing with you no matter how outrageous your words." If that wasn't seduction, I'd eat Scrap's boa.

"Oh, that smile." Donovan showed his teeth. They shone nearly as brightly as Gollum's flashlight.

We didn't need to worry about being heard. Sean had ramped up the volume of his drinking song more than a notch. His wavering tenor kept sliding just far enough out of tune that he made my teeth hurt.

I don't think I could ever be truly happy with a man who couldn't filk with me. Good thing Gollum had come back. I liked the way he fit his light baritone in a neat harmony with my soprano.

But I had to remember acutely the eighteen months of loneliness while my one true love lived with another woman.

"Gollum, got any more of those zip strips?"

"Of course." He drew a whole wad of them out of his backpack.

"Boys, stay behind Gollum and help him restrain the bad guys the best you can. Girls, collect weapons and ammo and stash it out of reach. But don't leave any fingerprints. We want the law to find them in the marijuana patch. We'll get them on illegal weapons charges as well as unlicensed drug production."

I took a deep breath and touched the pearls one more time for luck and for insight. I needed to channel my mother's talent and invoke the goddess within.

You have your own talent, dear, I heard her sultry voice in the back of my mind.

I opened the door and peeked into the candlelit bedroom. A massive four-poster bed sat dead center, with rich green-on-green damask coverlet, curtains, and canopy. A matching wardrobe stood against the far wall with padded damask insets in the doors. They belonged in a seventeenth century Italian villa.

Very modern wing back chairs in the same upholstery and stark end tables sat in a grouping in the far corner. I'd seen almost identical chairs and tables at Cooper's. Four bored banditos slumped in the chairs, weapons across their laps, deceptively small guns that could hide inside a jacket or down the leg of baggy pants. The young men supported their heads in their hands, rubbing temples as if to relieve a headache.

A headache caused by Sean. He stood stark naked—and a very nice body he had—at the foot of the bed, singing at the top of his lungs, swilling something dark and thick from a glass mug.

Leave her, Johnny, leave her.
An' we half-dead and bugger-all to say.

The air reeked of burning marijuana and other herbs.

The Nörglein didn't need magic to bind a victim with that heady mixture. His magic had grown dim and he didn't waste it when he had drugs that did the same thing.

I opened my mouth and let the first notes of "Heart's Path" slide under and around Sean's bawdy ditty.

He paused and stared at me through bloodshot eyes that didn't focus or track well.

I raised my voice and poured all of my loneliness and pain into the words. With eyes closed and chin trembling I let all of my pent-up emotions, the sense of betrayal and desertion, the grief, the aching emptiness that had built into a year and a half of depression, bleed through the music.

I have watched you go; I have seen the change
Though my pledge to your side I will keep
It is not enough to be who I am

And to savor your smiles in my sleep

I opened the ache of all the nights I'd tossed restlessly, reaching out to the emptiness beside me in the bed. I relived the horrible heaviness in my heart as I watched Gollum walk away. I cried all the tears I had bottled up for eighteen months.

He will tell you now that three is a crowd
And you know that I leave with my heart
It is not enough to just take what is left
So I'll love you and serve you apart
Follow your heart's path, in Valen's name
Now it leads me away to defend.
I will fight, I will die, I will be what you wish
And my love for you will never end.

I repeated the last two lines with emphasis on "I will die."

I heard a sniffle behind me. Phonetia dashed tears away with the back of her hand. E.T. cried openly.

The guys in the corner stared at me dumbly, not moving, not raising their weapons.

So I stepped closer, aiming my voice at them and sang the song again. This time I held the pearls, twisting them around and around my neck, as I'd needed to twist the faery ring to activate it.

"Ah, Tessie, 'tis a mournful day the Irish left the Emerald Isle behind," Sean slurred. He took one step toward me and tumbled onto the bed, snoring.

One of the bad guys looked up, blinking rapidly. "Who . . . who are you?" he asked, swallowing several times.

I felt the lump in his throat and the trembling in his chin.

"I am the avenging angel who is going to end your tyranny over the forest," I sang, keeping the song, and the agony alive in conversation. I projected as much fear as I had ever felt into the statement.

All four of them fell to their knees, holding their heads. Three of them bent double, sobbing uncontrollably.

Then I sang an Irish lullaby. *Tura lura, lura.* Those three men fell asleep, sniffling and sobbing in their twisted dreams. Still, the one who spoke resisted me.

So I found in my memory the tune of a Scottish dirge, usually played on the bagpipes, and gave him all of the anguish I felt when I'd held my mother in my arms as she died, the last words on her lips, "I love you."

By the time I breathed before the third phrase, all four men had zip strips on wrists and ankles. The girls stashed the weapons and ammunition in the wardrobe.

Then E.T. shoved tiny toxic berries from her fingertips into their mouths. "Just enough to make them sick," she said on a grimace. "Not enough poison to really hurt them."

Four down, eight to go in the outer rooms, Scrap reminded me.

He turned bright pink as the door crashed to the floor and those eight men flooded in. I heard eight safeties click off as I stared down the muzzles of eight very nasty guns.

Chapter 50

The largest meteorite found in the US, 16th largest in the world, was dug up in West Linn, Oregon, in 1902. 32,000 lbs, 10' tall, 6'6" wide and 4'3" deep. It is now in the American Museum of Natural History in New York. Negotiations to return it to Oregon continue.

Donovan stepped in front of me, putting a solid barrier between the bad guys and the rest of us.

"You don't really want to do that," he said calmly.

"Wanna make a bet?" Blondie sneered in reply. Then he spoiled his menacing attitude by scratching his ass. Poison oak had breached his protections. Or was that *breeched?*

I caught my giggle in mid-throat, nearly choking.

"The demon tattoos are protecting them from your smile, Donovan," I whispered.

"Shouldn't make a difference," Donovan replied, clearly puzzled, though he kept the smile in place.

In my peripheral vision I saw all five children sidling along the walls, converging on the crowded doorway.

"Tura lura lura," Sean sang into the damask bed covering, still mostly unconscious in his drunken stupor.

"Huh?" Blondie said.

Donovan backed up a bit, pushing me deeper into the room.

I planted my feet, ready to resist, when I saw Phonetia lighting a smudge pot. The sweet aroma of burning marijuana filled my senses. My vision reeled.

Careful, babe. Breathe short and shallow.

On the other side of the room, Doug carried another smudge pot. This one reeked of something else.

Blondie raised his weapon.

Scrap flashed bright red and stretched. From one eye blink to the next he changed from cute little imp to lethal weapon.

Even before he finished sharpening, I lashed out from behind Donovan, whacking three weapons out of slack hands.

Phonetia loosed her sharp blackberry arms, grabbing another rifle.

Oak and Cedar launched into a flying tackle that tumbled the entire bunch of startled men into a tangled heap.

I reversed my blade, scraping each demon tat with the tines, drawing blood. They writhed with inner fire of magic foiled. Or was that fouled?

Somehow Scrap managed to emerge from the blade just enough to spit into each of the wounds.

Imp spit.

A powerful antibiotic against a demon tag. Poison to all else. *Borrowed the idea from E.T.*

Wild screeches and howls pierced the drug haze swirling around the room.

The demon tats no longer protected them.

Gollum whipped out plastic zip strips. The boys snapped them in place.

And it was over before I had time to breathe.

I didn't have to kill anyone and I didn't have to bring down a band of criminals alone.

MY TESS SORT OF WILTS. Working magic takes a lot of energy and she just loosed some pretty powerful juju.

I'm tired for her, but in better shape for all the ambrosia I ate. The food, not that awful ink tainted blood on the wrists of the bad guys. Humans don't taste all that great at the best of times. Lightly spiced with demon makes it worse.

I'm still spitting out the acrid bile of it while Oak, Cedar, and Doug haul the bad guys off in the wooden wheel barrel to their little drug farm. Donovan helps with the heavy lifting—keeping an eye on the boys, watching for signs of Doreen in any of them.

Teams of bad guys have beaten a pretty heavy and careless path to their marijuana patch. Seems that now the dark elf is dead and his magic negated, the natural paths in the forest have opened on their own. The stupid minions trusted the Nörglein's magic too much.

Don't they know that super villains always either get killed at the end of the movie, or they betray and sacrifice their employees? If the minions had half an ounce of the wits they were born with, they'd have a backup plan.

Donovan pauses in the work long enough to call in a report to the police about the marijuana patch and how to find it.

The girls find Sean's clothes in the wardrobe and pour him into them. He's still singing, but quieter now, more maudlin and keeping closer to in tune.

I said closer, not all the way there yet.

Then the girls open both the front and back doors wide and prop them open. The air starts to clear of the heady mixture of drugs.

They've done this before.

Meanwhile, Tess wraps an arm around one of the tree-trunk-sized bedposts and concentrates on staying upright. She pretends she's supervising. Mostly she's just watching the others do what has to be done. They don't need her direction anymore.

Feeling useless is preying on her energy as much as the huge expenditure of magic.

Then Gollum creeps up to her and falls to his knees. "Oh, God, Tess, I had no idea I hurt you so badly. I am so very sorry. How can you forgive me?" He hangs his head.

Tess tangles her fingers in his fine, silver gilt hair and whispers, "Because I love you."

WE RETURNED TO THE con en masse. I wasn't much interested in the crowds and party atmosphere, but Gollum convinced me I should stop in for a few moments on the way to my car, at least to catch the last of Holly's concert. I revived a little while we trekked back through the tunnels toward civilization. The farther away I got from the drugs and the Nörglein's lair the better I felt.

Even Sean stumbled along with us, growing more sober with each step, but still strung out.

Someone had to drive him home. Not me. Maybe Squishy and Julia could do that.

The rain had stopped by the time we emerged from the tunnels through the basement of an old department store that filled an entire block. Fitful clouds allowed a waning sliver of a moon to peek through. I glanced toward the river. A slender trail of silver snaked along the black water.

"An end and a beginning," I whispered, reaching for Gollum's hand. "The prophecy fulfilled."

As we all trooped into the hotel by one of the back doors, I heard Cedar speak behind me. "I'll go with you tonight, Oak. I'll stay a short while only. You promised that if I helped you remove Father, the forest would be mine."

"I'll abide by my promise," Oak replied. He sounded very adult and honorable. "Explore the possibilities of help before you cut all ties to humans."

Donovan stopped short and turned toward the boys. One side of his mouth tugged upward. "That's Doreen's boy. Oak. I know it," he whispered to me.

"Don't bet on it. Mr. Surly and Selfish better fits the definition of a Damiri, if you ask me," I replied.

Donovan acted as if he didn't hear me.

"I don't see why we can't all continue living in the cave as a family. Our own family," Cedar continued to whine. "The girls are safe from Father now."

"But are they safe from you?" Doug asked so quietly I had to strain to hear him.

Cedar shut up.

"You know I just pretended to be gay to make the dark elf mad," Doug said on a laugh. Then he sobered. "And so I wouldn't have to fulfill his expectations of me." His glance lingered lovingly on his sisters. "I'd never hurt them. Ever. You should have shown more courage and creativity to defy the old bastard, Cedar."

Lights and noise and crowds assailed my eyes and ears the moment we stepped from the quiet corridor into the lobby.

"I thought it was later," I said, suddenly tired again. "I expected all the excitement to have died down."

"It's only seven-thirty. We've been gone about two hours," Gollum replied. He'd kept his arm about my waist most of the trip, letting me lean on him until I had enough strength to manage on my own. He's good about that sort of thing.

The noise that had blindsided me turned out to be applause for Holly. Seven-thirty. She'd only been singing for half an hour.

As I watched, she signaled for Malcolm Levi to join her on stage. He bounded up the three steps and took her hand in both of his. The audience went wild. I winced at the noise.

Then Holly crooned a low note filled with longing and promise. I recognized the chords she plucked from her lap harp. She sang sweetly of new love, innocent love. Malcolm picked up the chorus. Together they sang the ballad from the CD.

Haunting chords echoed but did not match the love theme from his movie. I knew Holly had composed that song. For him.

The entire audience sighed with content.

Holly had my mother's talent. Her voice became more than a memory. She made the music a fully shared experience.

Donovan led us all toward the garden café, ordering coffee and sandwiches all around. The girls amended that to herbal tea for them.

I sank gratefully into the chair Gollum held out for me. With the special emotions of the song filling the high domed area, I found myself leaning into him, cherishing his warmth and treasuring the affection that surged between us.

Squishy and Julia with Sophia and then Doreen joined us, adding a second table to our crowded group. Sophia raised her arms to me from the confines of her highchair. She looked tired, verging on cranky, upset that her mother had left her for so long with strangers.

I brought her into my lap and let her suck her fingers while clinging to her blankie as I stroked her dark hair.

The ballad came to an end and our coffee arrived. I drank greedily. Squishy plied cup after cup into Sean. But he fell asleep with his head on crossed arms on the table halfway through the third cup. Scrap made another beer and orange juice disappear in short order.

Julia shook her head in amazement. "Pat says I have to read your book to understand this," she said.

We all laughed a little nervously. At this rate, Scrap wouldn't remain a secret much longer. I needed to do something about that, but my brain was too tired to know what.

"Um, Pat, where did the nickname Squishy come from?" I asked, just to have something else to think about.

"My brothers," she replied. "Patricia became Pasquisha when they wanted to make me mad. That morphed into Squishy. It's a useful on-line and con handle." She shrugged and added sugar to Julia's coffee.

"Mr. Levi and I will be available for autographs here on stage at the conclusion of the masquerade, coming up next," Holly said into her microphone. Before the audience could react she launched into a rousing piece that nearly required rhythmic clapping and stomping feet from everyone within earshot.

"You have a way with my daughter," Lucia said, coming up behind me.

I started, then forced my nerves back into calm order.

"She misses you," I replied. I knew I should relinquish her to her mother one last time, but the precious weight of her against my arms felt more natural than I wanted to admit. I needed to hold on to each moment like this as long as possible. I'd never have a baby of my own. Not if I had to give it up to the Powers That Be, much as the Nörglein's victims had their babies stolen from them.

Sophia whimpered and I stuck a bottle into her mouth. Instantly she settled.

"I have decided. You need to sign these papers now. Not tomorrow after the baptism as I planned. Now." Lucia threw a fat manila envelope on the table in front of me.

"What is that?"

"Sign it. You may read it later."

"No way. I know how you put traps and clauses subject to misinterpretation into legal shenanigans." I tried to reach for the envelope but found my hands full of Sophia.

Gollum, bless him, withdrew a stack of legal size documents, several stapled together.

"This first one is the formal adoption of Sophia Maria Teresa Continelli by Teresa Louise Noncoiré," he read, peering over his glasses at the fine print.

"Agreed," I sighed. Tonight. In a few moments, as soon as I put my signature on that paper, she'd be mine.

Sophia popped the bottle out of her mouth and fussed.

I jammed the nipple back between her teeth before her protests became a wail louder than the crowd.

"It is for the best, Tess," Lucia said, pulling another chair up to our table. "I like my life in Las Vegas. I like midnight hours and Goth parties. I like the taste of blood. That is no way to raise a child. She has never tasted blood. She has never tasted meat. I want a real family for her. You are the closest I have to a relative. I want you to raise my daughter and never tell her about who and what I am until I deem fit." She produced an onyx fountain pen, unscrewed the top and handed it to me. It looked an awful lot like the pens used by the Powers That Be when they needed a signature in blood. "Sign and the child is safe with you."

I inspected the pen for traces of blood on the nib. Sure enough, a bit of rusty brown clung to the point. If I signed, with or without my own blood, Lucia was bound to keep the agreement. If she backed out or broke it in any way, her blood would boil and she'd end up facing the Powers That Be.

"Lucia, you were the one who told me, practically ordered me, to remain alone, focused and angry enough to complete the jobs the Universe hands me."

"Si," she sighed. "But now the Universe hands you a new task. You proved tonight that you can quell demons without violence. You can protect your children and still care for them. A new path opens for you, Warrior of the Celestial Blade."

"We'll see." I nodded for Gollum to read the next clump of documents.

"This establishes a rather substantial trust fund for Sophia naming you as trustee." He read the pages rapidly. "Fairly standard setup. Interest to be used for normal household expenses and education—including extra artistic endeavors like ballet and horseback riding. Fairly liberal wording. This one is safe to sign. If you choose."

"If *we* choose to adopt Sophia." Though how I could give her up at this point, I didn't know. "What's the last set of pages?"

"That's the deed to a house!" Donovan proclaimed, reading upside down. "I don't have to read the particulars to recognize the format."

"Donovan is correct," Lucia said, still holding the pen out. "I had to foreclose on the dwelling and repair large sections of it. That is what brought me to Portland originally."

"Foreclose?" I asked hesitantly, wondering what the family who had lived there was doing for shelter without it.

"I took the house as collateral on a *legitimate* business loan. A trusted employee franchised certain aspects of my, um, enterprises. Unfortunately, the economic climate in Portland is different from Las Vegas. He did not succeed. I gave him a year longer than I should. Do not worry that I have evicted children. The man is single, and I suspect guilty of embezzlement. No one steals from me and goes unscathed. I have sent his accounts—both sets of them—to the DA and the IRS."

"I know that address, Tess," Gollum said under his breath. He swallowed heavily. "The president of my college lives on that cul de sac. The house is huge, mock Tudor brick with a three-car garage. Two acres is the standard lot in that neighborhood. This one is bigger."

"And a guest house you can use as an office to get away from the children while you work, Tess," Lucia prompted.

"I can't . . . it's too generous."

Sophia yawned and snuggled down for a much needed nap. I held her close.

"The house is in trust for Sophia," Lucia said. "I'm not abandoning my child."

"Let me see those. I'll tell you if it's safe to sign." Donovan grabbed the entire stack. He and Doreen bent their heads over them.

"She's really smart about papers and stuff," Doug said around a mouthful of a veggie and cheese sandwich. He'd taken out the ham and packed half his salad between slices of bread. The girls had done the same. No problem getting them to eat their vegetables.

I bet Doreen knew her way around legal documents if she drew up the prenuptial agreement she'd forced on Donovan. A vague memory of my husband, Dill, came to mind, of him explaining to me that while he'd pursued his doctorate in geology, his sister had gone to law school. But she hadn't bothered to take the Bar.

Her parents probably put a stop to that just to keep her close.

"The documents are amazingly straightforward, without hidden provisions or sleeper clauses. Not one vague word subject to misinterpretation in them," Doreen pronounced. "I'd say it's safe to sign, if you want to adopt the child." She touched her own belly possessively.

"Gollum, if *we* do this, we'll start our life together with four children. They've been seriously abused. They'll need counseling, special schooling, and all the unconditional love we can pour into them. Do you truly want that? Can you do that?" I would. Gladly. Oh, yes, I wanted them all with every molecule in my being.

"Yes, Tess. That is what I want." Gollum rested his hand over mine and fixed his gaze on me, glasses halfway down his nose so I could see his eyes clearly and know his sincerity. "And I look forward to adding a couple of our own children to the family. I want all our children to be close to Cedar and Oak too. I don't mind if Pat and Julia wander in and out at odd hours. I want our lives overflowing with children, with family, and laughter and love."

I took a deep breath and shot a silent query to Scrap.

The more the merrier. Remember that empty kitchen table in Cape Cod? Remember how often you regretted you hadn't a chance to fill it with children? Now's your chance, babe. Grab it!

"We'll baby-sit during your honeymoon, if you'll watch the boys during ours," Doreen offered. "Both Cedar and Oak are coming home with us tonight."

"Okay. We'll do it."

The entire table loosed a collective sigh of relief.

I grabbed the pen from Lucia and affixed my name (ink only, I didn't need blood to bind me to this) in a dozen places, then passed each paper to Gollum so that he could add his name and signature and become part of the legal process. Then Donovan witnessed each page. So did Pat.

"Now there is one chore left," I sighed.

No, Tess. No way. You can't do that. This is the worst plan ever. Worse than... worse than... you know what it's worse than.

I ignored Scrap. He'd go along with me. Because it was the only way I could find the happily ever after Holly promised in her love ballad.

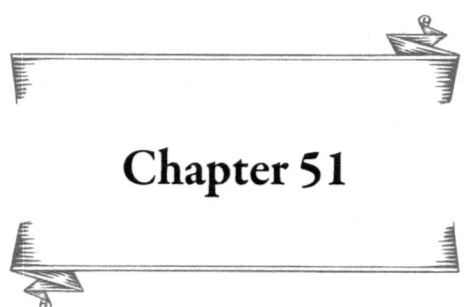

Chapter 51

*O*regon was the first state to levy a gas tax to take advantage of tourist
dollars.

"I can't believe you talked me into this," Donovan whispered as he
surveyed the vast emptiness of the chat room.

"I can't believe you finally convinced me the Kajiri demons need a
home world," I replied, barely breathing. As often as Scrap had dragged me
through here, I never quite got used to the lack of sensory input. All white,
no direction, no dimension, no sound other than my heartbeat and our
quiet words that seemed to bounce and magnify.

The lump of beryllium in my pocket weighed three times as much here
as it did back home.

"That's just it, I didn't convince you. The kids did. You see in them the
need for an occasional time out, away from the pressures of humanity."

"I hope the kids are safe while we're here." I chewed my lower lip,
wondering how Gollum and Doreen were managing with six children in
my tiny condo.

"Don't worry. Gollum and Doreen are sensible and smart. They'll be
okay, even if you and I don't make it back alive."

And if we didn't make it back? I couldn't, wouldn't believe such a thing
was possible.

But I'd made contingency plans and updated my will at the last
moment.

"Will you guys shut up!" Scrap ground out.

Another thing I never got used to, Scrap bigger than me, and solid,
with a deep voice. A new array of warts adorned his wing joints. I spotted a

special one on his pug nose and another on the tip of his tail—highly prized locations for Imps.

I'd worked him hard these last few weeks.

"There's a Cthulu demon on guard today," Scrap added. "You really don't want to get on his bad side."

"Don't the demon guards always work in pairs?" I asked.

"Cthulus don't need a partner. They're mean enough on their own."

We tiptoed past the sort-of-squid shape with more head and arms than the ocean-bound critters I'd seen on TV. It kept its eyes closed, supposedly sleeping on duty.

I didn't trust it. It probably had six or more layers of eyelids and could look asleep while still having four more steps to go to blot out the flat light.

He, or his kind, had let me pass before. I bowed politely to it. "We're going to the Powers That Be. That's allowed," I said.

An extra eyelid winked at me. *Allowed. Not recommended.*

"You know, of course, that very few people who get called before the Powers That Be survive the encounter," Donovan reminded.

"You did."

"Barely."

"I did, once before. But then I sought them out, they didn't drag me in to face justice."

"They don't like their privacy disturbed."

"Maybe. Maybe not. Ever think they might get lonely trapped in their courtroom for eons at a time?"

"Impossible."

I shrugged.

Scrap planted himself in front of the ornate door with the huge brass knocker. "You can still back out, babe. I'll cover your ass."

I centered myself to find my courage. "I have to do this." Then I lifted the ring above the lion's head and let it fall.

The brass bonged loudly, bouncing back for a second clang and then a third. The noise echoed through the vast white space, reverberating down all the hidden corridors and through all the closed doors to other dimensions.

"No privacy when you call on the Powers That Be," Donovan quipped.

The door swung inward slowly, silently, revealing a dim room, lit by unseen fixtures with a reddish hue. Spooky. Alarming to the uninitiated.

Stage dressing.

I gathered my determination, firmed my chin, and marched forward until I stood before the long judicial bench that looked like a solid ten-foot mahogany wall.

Scrap cowered beside the door. Today, he was only my escort, not willing to be a part of these proceedings.

"Anybody home?" I called up to the seven empty seats.

"Not so loud!" Donovan admonished. "They might hear you."

"That's the idea. I think they're more afraid of us than we of them."

"Not very likely."

I raised my eyebrows at him in a parody of his sardonic cocking of one brow.

"Who dares approach these hallowed halls?" a deep voice boomed from above us.

"If you don't know then you aren't very observant or don't have a good memory."

"Tess, careful. You need to be respectful."

"No, I don't. I have something they want very badly. And they are going to have to bargain hard for it." I fingered the cool ball of beryllium in my pocket.

I heard a group gasp above my head.

The judicial bench sank back to normal size, about level with my shoulder. All seven of the Powers That Be arranged themselves behind it, including a larger version of the Cthulu on guard in the chat room. This guy looked as big as the glacier on top of Mt. Rainier, the first place I'd spotted him.

Maybe he was a god and not a demon. What's the difference if he's from a different dimension preying on innocents in mine?

"Why have you come?" asked a heavily cloaked figure from deep within its cowl.

I just made out burning embers where the eyes should be.

"The last time I was here, you made me sign in blood that I would give up my firstborn child to you in return for the safety of my father, and end the ownership dispute over the piece of neutral ground where his home now sits." The home that had once been mine.

"Yes," intoned another voice. This one almost feminine.

A piece of parchment fluttered out of the air to land on the desk. I recognized my signature in rusty brown dried blood.

Beside me, Donovan shuddered. He tried to slink behind me. He'd signed one of those documents too, promising never to reveal his origins. He hadn't told me he'd fallen from being a gargoyle. I figured that out on my own.

"You signed in blood. You cannot reverse the agreement," a third voice said. This one was high and reedy. Impossible to discern gender or species.

"I don't want to reverse it. I still need protection for my father from rogue demons who will seek to use the neutral energies of that land to open a new portal that bypasses the chat room. I want to exchange the price of that protection."

"Impossible," a group denial.

"You have nothing we want more than your firstborn," that was the first deep voice.

"Oh?" I held up the crystal ball. The milky swirls deep inside the mineral matrix caught the red hues of the lights, swished them around and turned them into sparkling faery dust.

The scintillating pinpricks of light shifted and formed the image of a gateway arch framed in bright flowers.

"What is that?" asked the feminine voice. She pushed back her hood and leaned over the bench for a better look. Her head remained in shadow. Impossible to tell her true form, but I thought she might have been a faery originally.

"A portal," I replied.

"We have many portals available to us," said the reedy voice.

I caught a whiff of fish from his breath. Did he eat fish, or did he have fins?

"Not like this one. The crystal ball opens a doorway that doesn't exist anywhere else."

"Impossible."

"Ever wonder what happened to all the energy that drained out of Faery until I returned the kidnapped dancers where they belonged and sealed that portal?" I stared longingly into the crystal ball a moment longer, then reluctantly made to return it to my pocket, taking it off the bargaining table. Or at least threatening to.

"Wait, please," the former faery pleaded. She reached a long-fingered, elegant hand out for the treasure.

I kept the ball firmly in my own hand.

"A new dimension?" asked the androgynous voice.

"Yes," I replied. "A new dimension that only the possessor of this crystal ball can gain access to. A new dimension ready to be shaped by a single mind."

Donovan shifted from foot to foot. I touched his arm, trying to convey the need for a solid, confident front. We had to let these pettifogging bureaucrats know that we could walk away from this deal without changing a thing.

"The crystal ball belongs to us," the deep voice announced.

The squid reached a long tentacle across the bench, ready to pluck the thing from my hand.

I closed my fingers around it and pocketed it for real this time. They'd only get it by stealing it. Wouldn't put that past them.

"Not yet it doesn't." I turned on my heel and headed toward the door, dragging Donovan with me.

"What do you want for the ball?" the faery asked.

"I want the dimension opened to the Kajiri as a home world. A place where they can retreat when the demands of their half-breed status grow too heavy. A place where they can be either human or demon, they can succumb to their instincts and not hurt innocents."

"We agree," a new voice interjected. This one sounded old and wavery, like the oldest person in the Universe weighed in.

I fingered the ball in my pocket, thinking.

"What else?" asked the old one. He (she?) sounded almost human in tonal quality.

"If I entrust this ball into your keeping, I want to exchange possession of it for my firstborn child."

Donovan gasped at my audacity. "It's true?" he whispered.

"Of course, it's true."

"How could you make such a bargain?"

"I had nothing to lose. At the time I knew I'd never marry you, and Gollum had gone back to his wife. I didn't think I'd have the opportunity to bear a child, except by artificial insemination and I'm a bit too Catholic to do that."

"Oh." He sounded deflated. "I never had a prayer of winning you, did I?"

"Nope."

He heaved a sigh of resignation. Then he turned back to the Powers That Be, squared his shoulders, and approached the bench with pride and dignity. This was the man I'd longed for him to grow into. But he didn't value *me* enough for him to become honorable for me. He remained a manipulative, lying cheat.

Or was that a teenager in an adult body?

I remembered a band of Sasquatch with unlimited and unsupervised access to pizza, pot, and beer. They thought they were terrorists and big bad kidnappers. In actuality their worse crime was being teenagers.

"Your honors, I have worked long and hard to find a home world for Kajiri, half-human, half-demon, belonging in neither world. I respectfully request the duty of administering this new dimension."

"Granted," the faery agreed hastily, before the others had a chance to argue for the sake of arguing.

"Possession of the ball must come to us first," Fish Breath demanded.

"How will I access this new dimension if you possess the ball?" Donovan asked. Back to Mr. Manipulation.

Seven heads bent in hooded consultation.

"We will send a representative there who will open a new portal and give you the key. That key may be revoked and the portal closed at any time for any reason," deep voice pronounced. "We keep the ball."

"You'll need to close the energy leaks from all over the Universe," I reminded them. "One of those leaks is from the cracks in the faery ring that took Prince Mikhail home."

"The ring that entombs a live imp inside a diamond?" the former faery asked.

"Yes. Seems that every time it changes ownership, the diamond cracks a tiny bit, allowing the black imp to foully manipulate the wearer of the ring."

"Done!" the old one announced.

"What about my father's safety?" I demanded, ignoring the squid's twitching tentacle tip.

Another longer consultation among the shadowy hoods.

"In return for the ball, we grant your request. New agreements must be signed, one for each of you."

"I don't suppose we can use regular ink?"

"No."

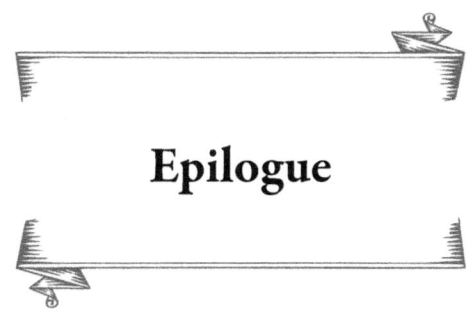

Epilogue

The town of Bridal Veil is now home only to the waterfall that once powered a lumber mill and gave the town its name, a community church, a cemetery, and a post office. The number of wedding invitations sent there for postmarking each year more than pay the postmaster's salary and support the post office.

"Can we get a dog, Mom?" E.T. asked. She bounded out of Gollum's old van—the only vehicle between us with enough room for two adults, three teens, and a baby in an unwieldy car seat—without waiting for an answer. She carried Gandalf, Gollum's ancient long-haired, white cat, over her shoulder.

Better a dog than that evil cat. I won't share digs with a cat! Scrap insisted from his perch on the dashboard. He sneezed for emphasis, reminding me of his allergies.

Since I'd inherited his lactose intolerance, I too might become allergic to the white lump of fur Gollum held so dear to his heart.

I ignored Scrap's complaints, just sitting and staring out the window at the house. Three stories and a basement, interesting windows, protrusions and nooks at every turn, gables, crosshatched brickwork, everything I wanted in a home.

And big. Six bedrooms, three and a half baths, formal dining room and parlor, family room upstairs and in the finished basement. Plenty of room for three teens, a toddler, and however many children Gollum and I wanted to have together.

Phonetia followed her sister out of the car and headed right for the rose garden on the far side of the driveway. She started deadheading the soggy and spent blossoms, piling the debris neatly at the edge of the circular garden space. She swept the stone bench clear of leaf litter, then leaned over the edge of a small fountain, peering into the dirty water.

"At least we won't have to hire a gardener to tame two point eight seven acres," Gollum muttered.

Doug piled out next, but he took the time to release Sophia from her car seat and carry her along the brick pathway toward the front door. When she fussed to get down, he let her wrap her tiny fists around his fingers for support so she could "walk."

Scrap hovered nearby, anxious that the toddler might fall and scrape her knees—less likely in her pink corduroy rompers than the frilly dresses Lucia had insisted upon.

At moments like this, I thought Scrap loved the children as much as I did. But he hated Gollum's cat.

"Have you noticed how much the kids enjoyed the music at the con?" Gollum asked.

"How could I avoid noticing? They sang Holly's music all day yesterday, adding their own harmonies and bizarre rhythms." I groaned.

"Maybe we should help them form a garage band. All five of them. It will give them focus, and a creative outlet for the anger and frustration they are bound to feel over and above normal teenage angst."

"Good idea. Later. I'm too tired to deal with it today."

"You have the keys?" Gollum asked. He didn't seem in a hurry to leave the quiet car.

I held up the key ring shaped like a faery in flight with four shiny new keys. I knew they'd all fit into the pristine locks. A huge yawn escaped my mouth rather than words.

After six hours of sleep Saturday night, I'd shuffled through Sunday's baptism ritual and the wind down of the con, barely aware of what I was doing. Another twelve hours of sleep last night and I thought I might begin functioning again.

I could use another thermos of coffee.

"We've only got an hour to explore before we leave to meet Steve and Allie at the title company. Their flight is on time," Gollum said consulting his phone.

"It's just . . . just surreal, everything falling into place like it did." I stared at the huge house, wonder making my jaw gape. Gables and brick facing, bay windows and lots of angles creating nooks and crannies inside. My dream of a proper home.

"I know. My divorce papers got filed this morning and my lawyer said that since there's no contest, the house where Julia and I have been living belongs to the college, we each have our own money, nothing to split, it should only take a couple of weeks to get an appointment with a judge. Then you and I can get married and live here with *our* children."

"Valentine's Day?" Three months away, plenty of time for inevitable legal delays. Hope brightened my mind and banished the last of the cobwebs. "April Fools Day might be more appropriate considering how we live our lives."

"Whatever you want. Put together the wedding you've always dreamed of. Invite everyone you've ever met. I don't care. I just want to be with you. Forever." He kissed me long and lingering.

I didn't want to let go of him long enough to breathe. Sophia's squeals of delight dragged my attention away from how he nibbled my lower lip.

"Let's go see what kind of kitchen I'm going to have. MoonFeather and Josh are bringing Lilly for Thanksgiving. Donnovan and Doreen are coming too. We might as well invite Julia and Pat, they will always be family. I want to put on the biggest and best holiday feast for the whole west coast clan. Then the following week we all fly east for Allie and Steve's wedding."

Holding hands, we ambled up the path toward the front door. Morning sunshine broke through the scattering clouds, turning the last of the raindrops trapped on the grass and in the cups of dying flowers to crystal prisms.

"Faery dust," I gasped.

"Not quite," a strangely accented male voice said from the region of my elbow.

I whirled, ready to fight. I hadn't done much else for the last three months. "Mickey!" Tension and anxiety fell away as I threw my arms around the crown prince of Faery.

The silver circlet around his brow had turned into three gold strands twisted and knotted intricately.

"Mom, who's he? I thought the con was over?" E.T. asked, returning to my side. No cat on her shoulder. A lump of long white hair on the flagstone porch must be the geriatric beast. "People aren't supposed to wear costumes out in public."

I'd drilled that one into the girls yesterday when they fell in love with space pirate uniforms.

"Costume?" Mickey's eyes twinkled. He gazed in mock puzzlement at his gold tights and white on gold brocade tunic. Even his blue butterfly wings had shifted to gold with just a hint of blue and white sparkles on the edges. "This is no costume. This is what I wear to work." He laughed.

"Huh?" Phonetia chimed in. She left her work with the roses to join us.

Doug returned from the covered porch with Sophia in his arms. "He wasn't at the con. I'd remember those wings. They're cool. How do they attach? And those ears. Those aren't gelatin attachments."

"No, they're the real thing," I told the children. "Prince Mikhail of Faery, meet the children."

Mickey bowed formally. The kids mimicked him. Sort of.

Hey, Mickey, what's with all the gold tarting up your outfit? Scrap flitted from the top of my head to Mickey's shoulder and back again.

"I'm afraid I have been promoted to King of Faery," Mickey sighed as if shouldering a great burden. "After rescuing the kidnapped dancers—with your help of course, Lady Tess and Professor Gollum—my people decided I was better suited for the job than my stepmother who allowed the kidnapping to take place."

"I think your people chose wisely," I said. "Thank you for telling us the news in person. But that is not why you came, I think." I nodded my head in respect.

"May we have a moment of privacy? You and Professor Gollum, Lady Tess?" Mickey asked.

"Certainly. Phonetia, take the keys, you and the others can go choose your own bedrooms. But wipe your feet on the mat. There's new carpet and tile so take your shoes off before you go beyond the entrance."

"Shoes should always be left outside," E.T. replied. She grabbed the keys out of my hand and ran to the door with them.

Doug and Sophia followed.

"I'd rather finish grooming the roses," Phonetia said, looking back to her project.

"A fine idea, Miss Phonetia. I will walk with Lady Tess and the Professor to the gazebo in the back. This should not take long." Mickey bowed again and gestured for Gollum and me to lead the way around the house on a different brick path.

"We have a gazebo?" Would wonders never cease? I'd always wanted a gazebo. With roses climbing the arched entrance.

What's the latest gossip out of Faery? Scrap demanded to fill an awkward silence as we progressed past French doors and a wide side patio to a scraggly herb garden and then merged into an expanse of overgrown lawn extending beyond another flagstone patio, complete with gas grill and sagging and saturated lawn furniture.

I could just see the roofline of the guest cottage and greenhouse beyond a blackberry thicket.

Gollum's eyes lit with excitement as he tried to veer toward the grill.

But it was the gazebo that captured my attention. It sat off to the side next to a deep goldfish pond. White paint flaked from the slats, but it looked sound, cozy, and inviting.

"Faery heals," Mickey said at last. He seemed weighed down with sadness. Worry added lines around his eyes and dimmed their sparkle. "Slowly. But we heal. The loss of energy from the previous crises caused much more damage than I thought possible."

"I'm sorry. Is there anything we can do to help?" I touched his hand in sympathy.

"You have done more than could be expected of any human, Lady Tess." He mounted the three steps to the gazebo and sank onto a bench to the left of the entrance. Two-person benches circled a gas fueled fire pit made of more flagstones. I fell in love with the place. Dreams of sitting out here with my laptop on hot summer afternoons, or sharing a glass of scotch with Gollum on brisk autumn evenings with the fire going, almost took me away from dowdy reality.

"How long will the healing take?" I knew we couldn't replace the energy that had built a new dimension.

"Longer than I want to admit. I need to close Faery," Mickey said.

"I'm sorry," Gollum added. "Faery has always loaned brightness and joy to the other dimensions. Your loss is a huge loss to the Universe."

"The Powers That Be have removed the three demon ghettos from my dimension and housed them elsewhere. I don't know where. That has stopped a huge drain on our resources. They have healed the cracks in the imp diamond as well. But it isn't enough."

"What more can you do?" I asked. "I can give a few faeries space in my garden if they need it."

"That is not the problem, Lady Tess," Mickey flashed me a grin, reminding me of the lighthearted taxi driver who befriended me in Las Vegas. "I thank you for the offer but the solution is the opposite. We need to keep all of the faeries in Faery."

"That might be hard, since they are used to popping in and out at will," Gollum mused.

"Yes. And so I have closed the portals into and out of Faery. All except one." He twisted a ring around his finger idly, as if a long habit.

Everything in me stilled. He didn't twist the ring in agitation.

He can use the ring to open a portal! Scrap chortled. *I knew I smelled imp. The black imp is still imprisoned in the diamond.*

"An imp can go anywhere, anywhen," I said.

"This ring is a great temptation to my people. And to me," Mickey removed his fingers from the diamond that glittered more brightly than sunshine on raindrops. "I would enjoy visiting with you more often and longer, but I owe the entire realm of Faery my duty to remain there as long as it takes to heal the damage."

"What do you have in mind, King Mikhail?" Gollum asked solemnly. "That ring is an artifact of power. It requires protection. It also needs to be kept secret from the Universe at large, or many who would not use it wisely will covet it."

"I know. That is why I offer the ring to you, Lady Tess and Professor Gollum. I know of no one else who could protect it as it must be. You can hide it where no one will expect to find it."

Hey, with the ring we can whisk any bad guys off to Donovan's new dimension for a time out before they have a chance to threaten the kids. You can almost retire and I can baby-sit.

"And where would I hide this ring?" I asked almost fearfully. Power pulsed from the intricate gold work and large diamond like a huge magnetic field.

"In plain sight."

"Huh? I was thinking along the lines of Scrap's mum and the freeze-dried garbage dump of the Universe. The cold and the other powerful artifacts will mask it."

Nope, nothing can mask that kind of power. And a black imp in Imp Haven is just asking for trouble. He'll get more powerful in his home dimension. The ring needs subtle magic to make it look like it belongs where it is, Scrap lectured. He sounded like Gollum when he got wound up on a favorite topic.

"The most powerful of the subtle magics Scrap speaks of is love." Mickey looked from Gollum to me, the twinkle back in his eyes. "I freely gift this ring to both of you as an engagement token. Anyone looking for the ring will sense the power and assume it is you, Lady Tess, and the love you share with the professor, not an artifact."

Before I could object he ripped the ring from his finger and placed it in Gollum's hand, gently closing his fingers around it.

"Now if Scrap will return me to my home, we will give you two a moment alone." Mickey rose to his majestic height.

Scrap landed on his shoulder. *Much as I'd like to stick around and eavesdrop, I think Mickey has the right idea. You ready, Mr. King?*

"Yes, Mr. Imp."

They disappeared in a showy blanket of scintillating mist. I thought I caught a glimpse of Scrap's face lingering in the swirling lights.

"Tess." Gollum got down on one knee in front of me and took my left hand in both of his. "I promised to do this. The time seems most appropriate. Tess, beloved, will you marry me?"

I had to swallow twice to get rid of the lump in my throat. "Yes," I whispered. "Yes!" I said louder. "Yes," I shouted loudly enough to draw children's faces to the windows above us and from around the corner to the rose garden.

"Yes!" I shouted with glee.

Then *my* Gollum gently slipped the ring on my finger. It snuggled behind the knuckle as if made for me.

About the Author

Irene Radford is a founding member of Book View Café[1]. You can find many of her books, both reprints and original titles, at the café, including her earliest books being released throughout 2023 and 2024. She has been writing stories ever since she figured out what a pencil was for. Editing, as Phyllis Irene Radford, grew out of her love of the craft of writing. History has been a part of her life from earliest childhood and led to her BA from Lewis and Clark College.

Mostly she writes fantasy and historical fantasy including the best-selling Dragon Nimbus Series and the masterwork Merlin's Descendants series. Look for her writing new historical fantasy tales as Rachel Atwood, a different take on the Robin Hood mythology in *Walk the Wild with Me*, from DAW/Astra Books and the sequel *Outcasts of the Wildwood*. In other lifetimes she writes urban fantasy as P.R. Frost or Phyllis Ames, and space opera as C.F. Bentley. Lately she ventured into Steampunk as Julia Verne St. John.

If you wish information on the latest releases from Ms Radford, under any of her pen names, you can follow her on Facebook as Phyllis Irene Radford.

---

1.   https://bookviewcafe.com/bookstore/v

About Book View Cafe

Book View Café LLC (BVC) is an author-owned cooperative of over twenty professional writers, publishing in a variety of genres including fantasy, romance, mystery, and science fiction. Since its debut in 2008, BVC has gained a reputation for producing high-quality ebooks. BVC's ebooks are DRM-free and are distributed around the world. The publishing company is now bringing that same quality to its print editions.

BVC authors include New York Times and USA Today bestsellers as well as winners and nominees of many prestigious awards, including:

Agatha Award
Campbell Award
Hugo Award
Lambda Award
Locus Award
Nebula Award
Nicholl Fellowship
PEN/Malamud Award
Philip K. Dick Award
RITA Award
World Fantasy Award
Writers of the Future Award

BVC

Book View Café
304 S. Jones Blvd. Ste 2906
Las Vegas, Nevada 89107
www.bookviewcafe.com[2]

---

2.   http://www.bookviewcafe.com